M. P. Caldwell

Caldwell's Practical Land Surveying

The art of surveying made easy

M. P. Caldwell

Caldwell's Practical Land Surveying
The art of surveying made easy

ISBN/EAN: 9783337392918

Printed in Europe, USA, Canada, Australia, Japan

Cover: Foto ©Andreas Hilbeck / pixelio.de

More available books at **www.hansebooks.com**

ESTABLISHED 1884.

BEST, FOX & CO.,

BRASS FOUNDERS, IRON PIPE FITTERS

AND

MACHINISTS

SOLE MANUFACTURERS

OF

CLIMAX BRONZE TUYERES, COOLERS, NOTCHES,

BOSH PLATES AND BOXES,

VALVES AND SEATS.

ROLLING MILL, ENGINE, LOCOMOTIVE AND CAR BEARINGS,

ALSO

MANUFACTURERS OF AND DEALERS IN

PIPE, VALVES, FITTINGS & SUPPLIES

FOR STEAM, WATER AND GAS.

OFFICE AND WORKS.

TWENTY-FIFTH, RAILROAD STS. & ALLEGHENY RIVER,

PITTSBURGH, PA., U. S. A.

CATALOGUE F.   1894.

TRADE MARK

LONG - - -  *TELEPHONE*
DISTANCE *PITTSBURGH.*

Nº 989

DIRECT COMMUNICATION TO ALL POINTS.

TELEPHONE AND TELEGRAPH MESSAGES

RECEIVE PROMPT ATTENTION AT

ALL HOURS, DAY AND NIGHT.

CATALOGUE F.

INDEX.

100

300

500

700

900

INDEX.—CONTINUED.

INDEX.—CONTINUED.

TEL.
CYPHER

100

300

—

500

700

BEST, FOX & CO.

TELEGRAPH CYPHER.

FOR INQUIRY AFTER, AND PURCHASING, BRONZE TUYERES, COOLERS, NOTCHES, BOSH PLATES, ETC.

QUERIES AND ORDERS.

Addie......................Ship immediately by express.
Alice....................Ship immediately by rail (freight).
Carrie.... ....Suspend shipment of order of ...... inst.
Clara....................Suspend work on order of ...... inst., until further instructions.
Ella......................Letter received, make as you specify therein.
Emma ....Letter received, cannot use with alterations mentioned.
Jane......................How soon can you furnish ....?
Lizzie ....Have you in stock, and can you furnish ....?
Maggie..................At what price can you furnish ....?
Mary....................At what price and how soon can you furnish ....?
Maud ....When can you ship ....?
Nellie....................Have you shipped order of ...... inst.?
Frank....................Please reply immediately by telegraph.
Sarah....................Will send particulars by mail.
Stella ....

ANSWERS TO QUERIES AND ORDERS.

Adam...................Your order was shipped by express ...... inst.
Albert ....Your order was shipped by rail (freight) ...... inst.
Charles................Have suspended shipment of order of ...... inst.
Daniel.................Have suspended work on order of ...... inst.
Edward...............Order received, shipped same to-day by express.
George................Order received, shipped same to-day by freight.
Harvey ....Order received, will ship ...... inst.
Henry..................Order received, see letter for specifications.
Howard ....We can ship in .... days from receipt of order.
James..................We have in stock and can furnish at once.
John.... ....We can furnish at ...... cents per lb.
Paul ....We have none in stock, but will make and ship by ...... inst.
Frank..................Please reply immediately by telegraph.
Ralph..................Have sent particulars by mail.
Robert.................

LONG DISTANCE TELEPHONE.

Telegraph and Telephone MESSAGES receive PROMPT ATTENTION at *all hours*, day and **NIGHT**.

Cable address, "BESTFOX," PITTSBURG.

SPECIAL NOTICE.

Please DESTROY *on Receipt of this Catalogue,
any TELEGRAPH CYPHERS sent by us
that you may have.*

INDEX

For Bronze Tuyeres, Coolers, Notches, Bosh Plates and Boxes, Valve Seats, Etc.

100

300

500

700

90C

INDEX—Continued.

For Bronze Tuyeres, Coolers, Notches, Bosh Plates and Boxes, Valve Seats, Etc.

INDEX—Continued.

For Bronze Tuyeres, Coolers, Notches, Bosh Plates and Boxes, Valve Seats, Etc.

300

500

700

900

INDEX—Continued.

For Bronze Tuyeres, Coolers, Notches, Bosh Plates and Boxes, Valve Seats, Etc.

INDEX—Continued.

For Bronze Tuyeres, Coolers, Notches, Bosh Plates and Boxes, Valve Seats, Etc.

500

700

900

INDEX—Continued.

For Bronze Tuyeres, Coolers, Notches, Bosh Plates and Boxes, Valve Seats, Etc.

INDEX—Continued.

For Bronze Tuyeres, Coolers, Notches, Bosh Plates and Boxes, Valve Seats, Etc.

700

90

INDEX—Continued.

For Bronze Tuyeres, Coolers, Notches, Bosh Plates and Boxes, Valve Seats, Etc.

INDEX—Continued.

For Bronze Tuyeres, Coolers, Notches, Bosh Plates and Boxes, Valve Seats, Etc.

BEST, FOX & CO.

INDEX—Continued.

For Bronze Tuyeres, Coolers, Notches, Bosh Plates and Boxes, Valve Seats, Etc.

INDEX—TUYERES.

SHORT—Less than 12 in. long.   *MEDIUM*—Between 12 and 16 in. long.   *LONG*—Over 16 in. long

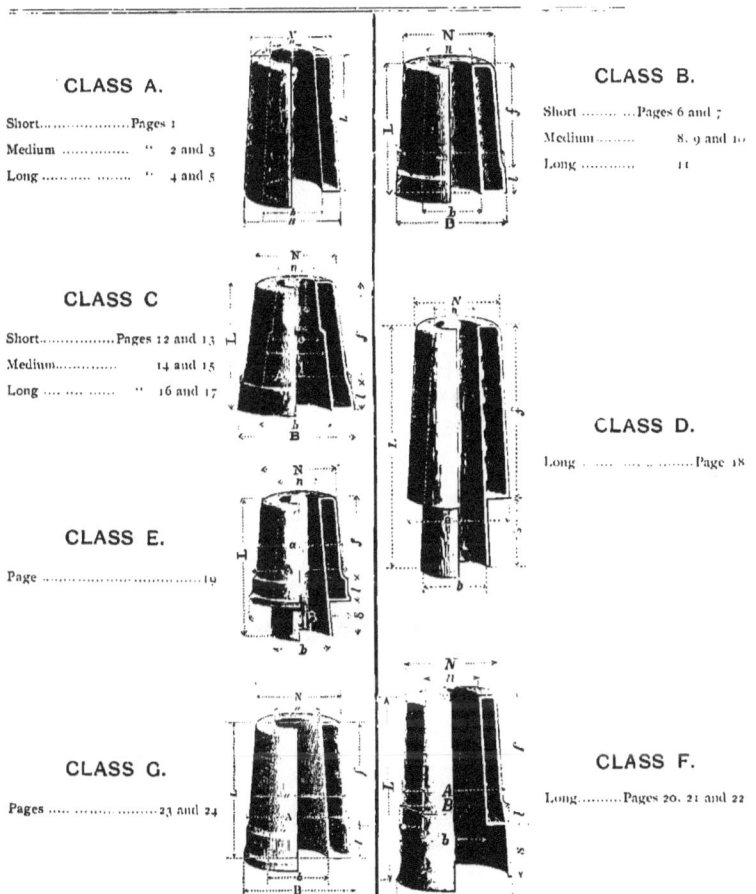

CLASS A.

Short......................	Pages 1
Medium	" 2 and 3
Long	" 4 and 5

CLASS B.

Short	Pages 6 and 7
Medium........	8, 9 and 10
Long	11

CLASS C

Short.................	Pages 12 and 13
Medium..............	14 and 15
Long	" 16 and 17

CLASS D.

Long	Page 18

CLASS E.

Page	19

CLASS G.

Pages	23 and 24

CLASS F.

Long...........	Pages 20, 21 and 22

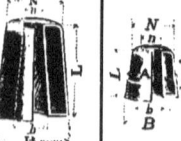
CINDER NOTCHES.

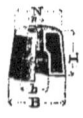

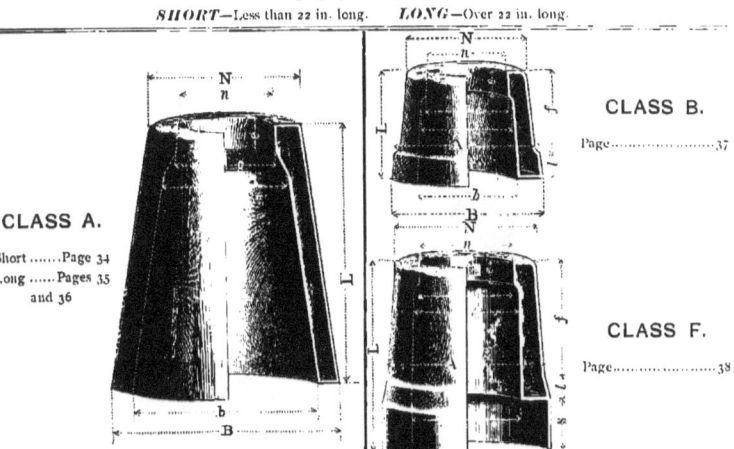
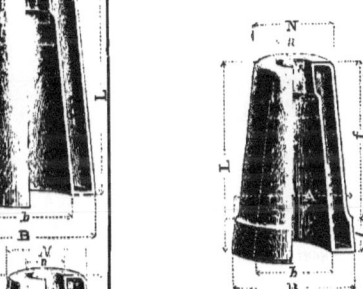

BOSH BOXES.

FRONHEISER'S PATENT.

CLASS A.

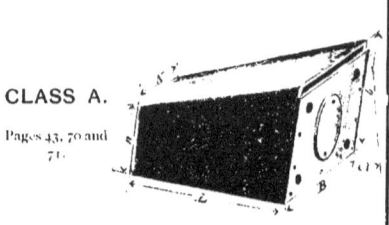

CLASS B.

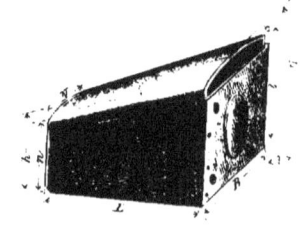

CLASS C.

HEARTH AND BOSH JACKET.

HUNT'S PATENT.

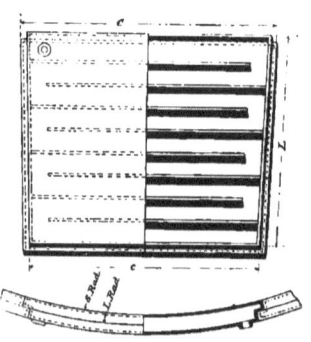

BOSH PLATES.

CLASS A.

(KENNEDY'S PATENT.)

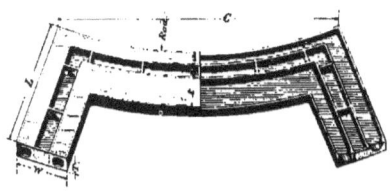

CLASS B.

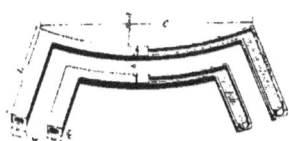

CLASS C.

(POLLOCK'S PATENT.)

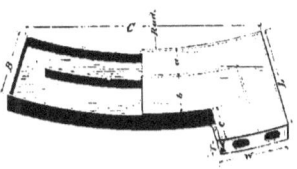

CLASS D.

(SCOTT'S PATENT.)

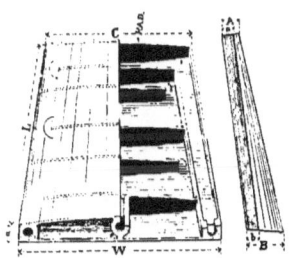

BOSH PLATES.—CONTINUED.

CLASS E.

CLASS F.

CLASS G.

(GAYLEY'S PATENT.)

CLASS H.

(GAYLEY'S PATENT.)

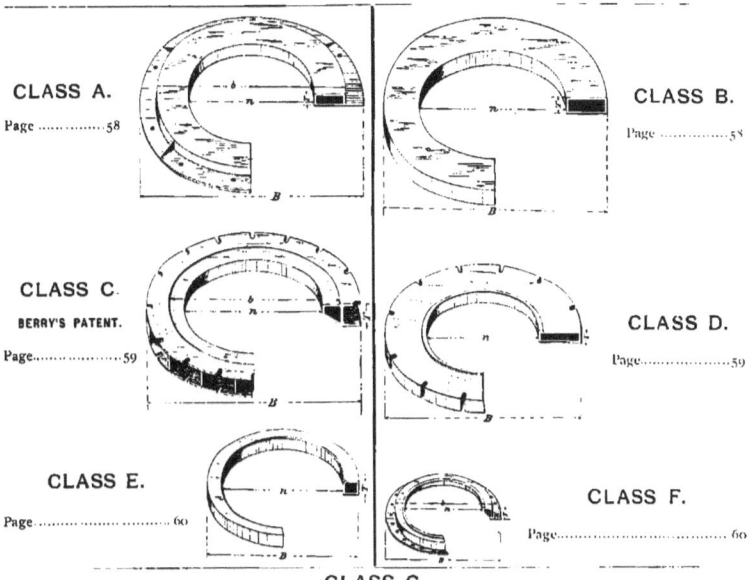
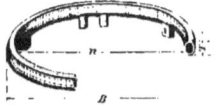
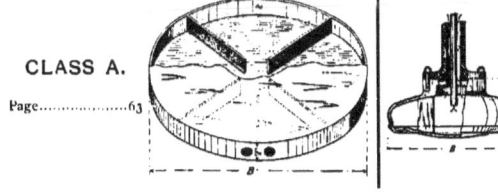

BEST, FOX & CO.

BEST, FOX & CO.

TUYERES.

CLASS A.

SHORT.

All Weights given are Approximate.

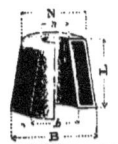

DESCRIPTION.

n—Inside diameter at nose.
b "   "   " butt.
L—Length over all.
B—Outside diameter at butt.
N "   "   " nose.

2½ INCH TUYERES.

Number.	n	b	L	B	N	Wt.	Cypher.

3 INCH TUYERES.

Number.	n	b	L	B	N	Wt.	Cypher.

3½ INCH TUYERES.

Number.	n	b	L	B	N	Wt	Cypher.
176	3½	5½	8	10¼	9¼	47	Baritzau.

4 INCH TUYERES.

Number.	n	b	L	B	N	Wt.	Cypher.
121	4	5½	8	10¼	9¼	47	Ballister.
143	4	6½	6	12	10	45	Banisher.
195	4	7½	9	12	9¾	59	Batch.

4½ INCH TUYERES.

Number.	n	b	L	B	N	Wt.	Cypher.
87	4½	5½	8	10¼	9¼	48	Bacchus.
182	4½	6½	6	12	10	45	Base.
207	4½	7½	9	12	9¾	60	Bavaroy.
637	4½	5¼	6	12	10⅛	48	Calico.

5 INCH TUYERES.

Number.	n	b	L	B	N	Wt.	Cypher.
99	5	6½	6	12	10	46	Bag.
209	5	7½	9	12	9¾	60	Bawd.

5½ INCH TUYERES.

Number.	n	b	L	B	N	Wt.	Cypher.
262	5½	7½	9	12	9¾	60	Bergmote.

6 INCH TUYERES.

Number.	n	b	L	B	N	Wt.	Cypher.
465	6	7	10	11½	10⅜	70	Brooklime.
695	6	6½	6	12	10	46	Canine.

6½ INCH TUYERES.

Number.	n	b	L	B	N	Wt.	Cypher.
376	6½	7½	9	12	9¾	58	Boudoir.

7 INCH TUYERES.

Number.	n	b	L	B	N	Wt.	Cypher.

BEST, FOX & CO.

TUYERES.

CLASS A

MEDIUM.

All Weights given are Approximate.

DESCRIPTION.

n—Inside diameter at nose.
b "   "   " butt.
L—Length over all.
B—Outside diameter at butt.
N "   "   " nose.

2½ INCH TUYERES.

No.	n	b	L	B	N	Wt.	Cypher.
108	2½	6¼	15½	10⅛	8	90	Bailiff.

3 INCH TUYERES.

No.	n	b	L	B	N	Wt.	Cypher.
13	3	6	15½	10⅛	8	76	Acacia.
446	3¼	6	15½	10⅛	8	80	Briton.
519	3¼	7	16	11	8	79	Bulwark.

3½ INCH TUYERES.

No.	n	b	L	B	N	Wt.	Cypher.
63	3½	6	15½	10⅛	8	75	Arsenal.
127	3½	7	16	11	8	90	Banana

4 INCH TUYERES.

No.	n	b	L	B	N	Wt.	Cypher.
14	4	6	15½	10⅛	8	80	Access.
98	4	7	16	11	8	78	Baffle.

4½ INCH TUYERES.

No.	n	b	L	B	N	Wt.	Cypher.
15	4½	6	15½	10⅛	8	79	Account.
129	4½	6⅜	15½	10¾	9	88	Band.

5 INCH TUYERES.

No.	n	b	L	B	N	Wt.	Cypher.
16	5	6⅜	15½	10¾	9	81	Acid.
189	5	7	15½	11	9½	83	Basque.
248	5	7	15½	11⅜	9¼	98	Believer.
321	5	6½	13	10⅜	9	71	Blunder.
332	5	7⅞	12	13⅜	10½	92	Bobbinet.
341	5	6	12	11¼	9½	76	Bohea.
507	5	7	16	11	9¼	98	Bulblet.

TUYERES.

Class A

MEDIUM.

All Weights given are Approximate.

DESCRIPTION.

n—Inside diameter at nose.

b " " " butt.

L—Length over all.

B—Outside diameter at butt.

N " " " nose.

5½ INCH TUYERES.

No.	*n*	*b*	*L*	*B*	*N*	*Wt.*	*Cypher.*
12	5½	7½	12	12	9	78	Abyss.
61	5½	7	15½	11	9½	84	Armor.
697	5½	7⅞	16	13⅜	9½	104	Cannabis.
510	5½	6	12	12	9	80	Bulker.

6 INCH TUYERES.

No.	*n*	*b*	*L*	*B*	*N*	*Wt.*	*Cypher.*
60	6	9	14	13⅜	10½	112	Armada.
230	6	8	15	13¼	11	115	Beckon.
311	6	8¼	12	13	11½	101	Block.
677	6	7⅞	12	13⅜	10½	87	Camomile.

6½ INCH TUYERES.

No.	*n*	*b*	*L*	*B*	*N*	*Wt.*	*Cypher.*

7 INCH TUYERES.

No.	*n*	*b*	*L*	*B*	*N*	*Wt.*	*Cypher.*
231	7	8	15	13¼	11	116	Bedder.
353	7	8¼	12	13⅜	10½	98	Bondue.

TUYERES.

CLASS A

LONG.

All Weights given are Approximate.

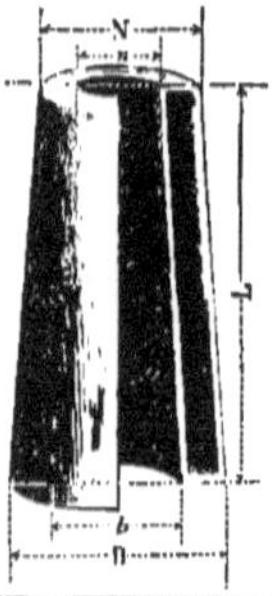

DESCRIPTION.

n—Inside diameter at nose.

b " " " butt.

L—Length over all.

B—Outside diameter at butt.

N— " " " nose.

2½ INCH TUYERES.

No.	*n*	*b*	*L*	*B*	*N*	*Wt.*	*Cypher.*
18	2½	5	20	9	7	69	Acre.
147	2½	5½	20	10¼	7¾	95	Bankrupt.

3 INCH TUYERES.

No.	*n*	*b*	*L*	*B*	*N*	*Wt.*	*Cypher.*
21	3	6½	20	10⅞	8	105	Adamite.
162	3	5½	20	10¼	7¾	92	Bargain.
270	3	4¾	18	8¾	7	70	Bias.
317	3	7½	20	12	9¼	123	Blotter.
654	3	6	[illegible]	11	8	146	Calumba.
675	3	5	24	9	[illegible]	[illegible]	Cammas.

3½ INCH TUYERES.

No.	*n*	*b*	*L*	*B*	*N*	*Wt.*	*Cypher.*
19	3½	5½	20	10¼	7¾	94	Actor.
75	3½	8	18	12¼	8¼	105	Awl.
110	3½	6½	20	10⅝	8	97	Bait.
639	3½	7½	22	12	9	138	Calin.

4 INCH TUYERES.

No.	*n*	*b*	*L*	*B*	*N*	*Wt.*	*Cypher.*
20	4	6½	20	10⅝	8	104	Actress.
76	4	8	18	12¼	8¼	105	Awning.
106	4	7⅜	20	11¼	9	103	Bail.
117	4	7½	20	12	9¼	125	Balk.
161	4	7½	22	12	9	130	Barfee.
308	3¾	6	30	11	8	150	Blinker.
313	4	6	24	10	7	110	Blomary.
386	4	6	24	10¼	7¼	80	Boxer.
549	4	7½	24	12	8¾	150	Burlesque.

TUYERES.

Class A

LONG.

All Weights given are Approximate.

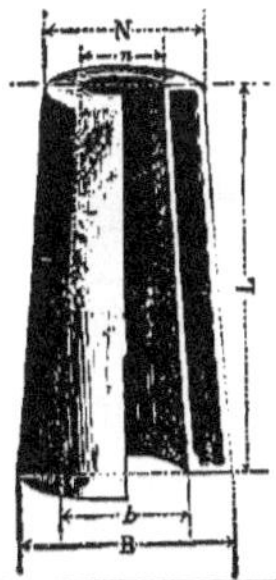

DESCRIPTION.

n—Inside diameter at nose.

b " butt.

L—Length over all.

B—Outside diameter at butt.

N " " nose.

4½ inch TUYERES.

No.	n	b	L	B	N	Wt.	Cypher.
88	4½	7½	22	12	9	133	Bachelor.
91	4½	8	28	12⅛	9	170	Backset.
168	4½	7½	20	12	9¼	121	Baronet.
183	4½	7⅛	20	11¼	9	104	Basement.
305	4½	8½	18	13¾	10⅜	138	Blenny.
358	4½	7	18	11	9	100	Booley.
364	4½	7½	24	12	8¾	136	Borate.
429	4½	6	30	11	8	137	Bridge.

5 inch TUYERES.

No.	n	b	L	B	N	Wt.	Cypher.
1	5	7½	20	12	9¼	120	Abacus.
17	5	7⅛	20	11¼	9	105	Acorn.
235	5	8	28	12⅛	9	166	Bedstead.
263	5	8	24	12½	9½	150	Berlin.
282	5¼	7⅛	18	11¼	9¼	102	Binnacle.
283	5	8½	18	13¾	10⅜	135	Binot.
307	5	7	18	11	9	100	Bleyme.

5½ inch TUYERES.

No.	n	b	L	B	N	Wt.	Cypher.

6 inch TUYERES.

No.	n	b	L	B	N	Wt.	Cypher.
257	6	8½	18	13¾	10⅝	136	Benefit.
271	6	7	22	11½	10¼	139	Biceps.

6½ inch TUYERES.

No.	n	b	L	B	N	Wt.	Cypher.

7 inch TUYERES.

No.	n	b	L	B	N	Wt.	Cypher.
255	7	9	26½	13¾	11½	210	Bender.

TUYERES.

CLASS B

SHORT.

All Weights given are Approximate.

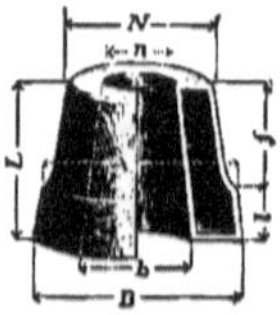

DESCRIPTION.

n—Inside diameter at nose.
b " " " butt.
L—Length over all.
B—Outside diameter at butt.
A " " " cooler bearing.
N " " " nose.
l—Length of cooler bearing.
f " projecting beyond cooler.

3 INCH TUYERES.

No.	n	b	L	B	A	N	l	f	Wt.	Cypher.
206	3	6⅞	9	11⅜	11	9¼	3	6	57	Bavarian

3½ INCH TUYERES.

No.	n	b	L	B	A	N	l	f	Wt.	Cypher.
506	3½	6	6	11	10½	8½	3	3	40	Bulbel

4 INCH TUYERES.

No.	n	b	L	B	A	N	l	f	Wt.	Cypher.
152	4	6⅞	9	11⅜	11	9¼	3	6	55	Bantam
246	4	6	9	11⅝	10⅞	9⅝	2½	6½	67	Belial
469	4	6⅞	9	11	10½	9¼	3	6	57	Brother
715	4	7	10	13¼	12½	10½	3	7	83	Capitalist

4½ INCH TUYERES.

No.	n	b	L	B	A	N	l	f	Wt.	Cypher.
185	4½	6⅞	9	11¼	10½	9¼	3	6	54	Basil
676	4½	8¼	8	12⅞	11⅞	11	3½	4½	69	Cammock

5 INCH TUYERES.

No.	n	b	L	B	A	N	l	f	Wt.	Cypher.
82	5	6⅞	9	11¼	10½	9¼	3	6	56	Babel
104	5	6½	6½	11⅝	10⅞	10⅛	2½	4	53	Bagpipe
135	5	6⅞	6½	12⅝	11¼	10¾	2½	4	50	Bandle
234	5	5½	11	10⅝	9¾	8⅝	3¼	7¼	65	Bedroom
306	5	6⅞	9	11⅞	11 3/16	9¼	3	6	56	Bletonist
518	5	5⅝	9	11½	10½	9¼	3	6	59	Burler
557	5	7⅞	8	13½	12¾	10¼	3	5	68	Burton
583	5	7½	9	12	11 1/16	9¼	3	6	60	Cabiai
607	5	7	10	13¼	12½	10½	3	7	76	Cage
728	5	8	10	12⅝	11 1/16	9⅞	3	7	78	Capuchin

5 INCH TUYERES.

No.	n	b	L	B	A	N	l	f	Wt.	Cypher.

TUYERES.

Class B

SHORT.

All Weights given are Approximate.

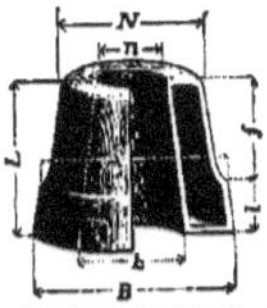

DESCRIPTION.

n—Inside diameter at nose.
b " " " butt.
L—Length over all.
B - Outside diameter at butt.
A " " " cooler bearing.
N " " " nose.
l—Length of cooler bearing.
f " projecting beyond cooler.

5½ INCH TUYERES.

No	*n*	*b*	*L*	*B*	*A*	*N*	*l*	*f*	*Wt.*	*Cypher.*
89	5½	6½	6½	11⅝	10⅞	10⅛	2½	4	54	Backbone
179	5½	6⅞	6½	12⅛	11¼	10¾	2½	4	45	Barytone
398	5½	5⅝	9	11½	10½	9¾	3	6	59	Brand
514	5½	8¼	9	13	11 13/16	10½	4	5	75	Bullfice
517	5½	6½	10	12	11¼	10	3	7	67	Bultel
584	5½	6	9	12¾	11⅞	10⅜	3	6	69	Cabin
622	5½	6	11	12¾	11⅞	10	3	8	80	Calamish
636	5½	6½	10	12	10 7/16	9½	3	7	65	Caliber

6 INCH TUYERES.

No.	*n*	*b*	*L*	*B*	*A*	*N*	*l*	*f*	*Wt.*	*Cypher.*
90	6	6⅞	6½	12⅛	11¼	10¾	2½	4	44	Backer
303	6	8¼	9	13	11⅝	10¾	3	6	73	Bleacher
343	6	7½	9	12	11¼	10¼	3	6	62	Boiler
360	6	7½	10	12 7/16	11½	10⅜	3	7	72	Booser
409	6	6¼	9	12½	11½	9¾	3	6	67	Breaker
445	6	7	8½	13⅛	12½	11¼	2½	6	72	Britannia
466	6	7⅛	10	12	11¼	11	3	7	67	Brookmint
474	6	8⅛	8½	13¼	12½	11½	3	5½	75	Bruise
513	6	8¼	9	13	11 13/16	10½	4	5	76	Bulletin
576	6	7¼	10	13¼	12½	10½	3	7	80	Cabal
581	6	8⅛	7	13½	12½	10¼	3	4	70	Cabason
606	6	7	10	13¼	12½	10½	3	7	81	Cafenet
647	6	6½	10	12	11¼	10	3	7	70	Caller
700	6	8¼	8	12⅞	11⅞	11	3½	4½	50	Cannonade
701	6	7	8	12⅛	11½	10⅝	2½	5½	64	Canoe
717	6	7½	10	12	11¼	11	3	7	71	Capoch
723	6	8	10	12⅝	11 1/16	9⅞	3	7	77	Capsule

6½ INCH TUYERES.

No.	*n*	*b*	*L*	*B*	*A*	*N*	*l*	*f*	*Wt.*	*Cypher.*
642	6½	8¼	8	12⅞	11⅞	11	3½	4½	67	Calipers

7 INCH TUYERES.

No.	*n*	*b*	*L*	*B*	*A*	*N*	*l*	*f*	*Wt.*	*Cypher.*
296	7	7⅛	10	12	11¼	11	3	7	64	Blackcap
439	7	8¼	9	13	11⅝	10¾	3	6	50	Brimstone

TUYERES.

Class B

MEDIUM.

All Weights given are Approximate.

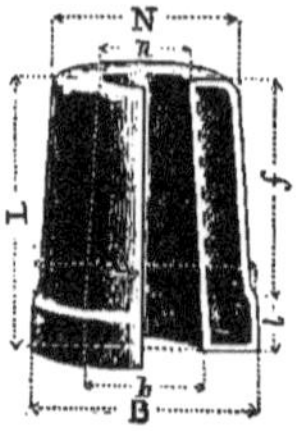

DESCRIPTION.

n—Inside diameter at nose.
b— " " " butt.
L—Length over all.
B—Outside diameter at butt.
A " " " cooler bearing.
N " " " nose.
l—Length of cooler bearing.
f— " projecting beyond cooler.

3 INCH TUYERES.

No.	n	b	L	B	A	N	l	f	Wt	Cypher.
105	3	6	12	11⅛	10¼	9¼	2½	9½	72	Bahar
139	3	5	12	10⅛	9¼	8	2½	9½	88	Bane
297	3	7	12	12⅛	11 7/16	9⅜	2½	9½	80	Backleg
560	3	7½	12	12	11¼	9¼	3	9	80	Basket

3½ INCH TUYERES.

No.	n	b	L	B	A	N	l	f	Wt	Cypher.
144	3½	6	15½	11½	11	7¾	3½	12	79	Banjo
166	3½	6	12	11⅛	10¼	9¼	2½	9½	73	Barometer
184	3½	5	12	10⅛	9¼	8	2½	9½	69	Bashaw

4 INCH TUYERES.

No.	n	b	L	B	A	N	l	f	Wt	Cypher.
62	4	6	15½	11½	11	7¾	3½	12	79	Arrow
120	4	7½	12	12	11¼	9¼	3	9	75	Ballet
130	4	6⅜	12	12	10¾	9½	2¼	9¾	78	Bandage
134	4	7	12	12⅛	11 7/16	9⅜	2½	9½	87	Bandit
169	4	6	12	11⅛	10¼	9¼	2½	9½	74	Baroscope
181	4	5	12	10⅛	9¼	8	2½	9½	70	Basanite
573	4	8½	15	14½	12½	9⅞	6	9	114	Buzzardet
596	4	8¼	12	12⅞	11⅞	10¼	3½	8½	90	Cashalong

4½ INCH TUYERES.

No.	n	b	L	B	A	N	l	f	Wt	Cypher.
5	4½	7½	12	12	11¼	9¼	3	9	72	Abbot
132	4½	7½	12	11⅞	11 1/16	9¼	3¼	8¾	76	Bandbox
133	4½	8	14	12⅛	11 1/16	9¼	3	11	90	Bander
141	4½	6⅜	12	12	10¾	9½	2¼	9¾	104	Bangle
171	4½	6	12	11⅛	10¼	9¼	2½	9½	75	Barrel
188	4½	7	12	12⅛	11 7/16	9⅜	2½	9½	80	Baslard
660	4½	8½	15	14½	12½	9⅞	6	9	119	Calycle

TUYERES.

Class B

MEDIUM.

All Weights given are Approximate.

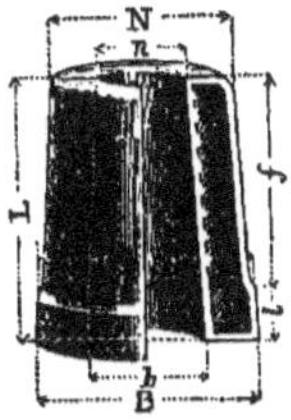

DESCRIPTION.

n—Inside diameter at nose.
b— " " " butt.
L—Length over all.
B—Outside diameter at butt.
A— " " " cooler bearing.
N— " " " nose.
l—Length of cooler bearing.
f— " projecting beyond cooler.

5 inch TUYERES.

No.	n	b	L	B	A	N	l	f	Wt.	Cypher.
6	5	7½	12	12	11¼	9¼	3	9	72	Abhal'
25	5	6⅜	12	12	10¼	9½	2¼	9¾	85	Adult
37	5	8	14	12⅛	11 1/16	9¼	3	11	90	Aloe
94	5	7½	12	11⅞	11 1/16	9¼	3¼	8¾	77	Baculite
115	5	7	12	12⅛	11 7/16	9⅜	2½	9½	79	Bale
123	5	8½	15	14½	12½	9⅞	6	9	110	Ballow
156	5	8	15	13¼	12¾	11	2½	12½	110	Barbacan
165	5	6	12	11⅛	10¼	9¼	2½	9½	76	Barnacle
264	5	7	15	12⅛	11 7/16	9	2½	12½	95	Berme
335	5	7½	14	12	11¼	9⅞	3	11	92	Bocal
377	5	7½	13	12 5/16	11½	9⅝	3	10	78	Bough
535	5	7¼	12	13¼	12½	10⅝	3	9	96	Burdener
570	5	8¼	12	12⅞	11⅞	10¼	3½	8½	88	Buxine
595	5	7¼	15½	13¼	12½	10½	3	12½	112	Cachiri
615	5	7½	12	13¼	12½	11¼	3	9	84	Caitiff
678	5¼	7½	15½	12	11¼	10¼	3	9	96	Campana

5½ inch TUYERES.

No.	n	b	L	B	A	N	l	f	Wt.	Cypher.
2	5½	8½	15	14½	12½	9⅞	6	9	110	Abandon
103	5½	8	15	13¼	12¾	11	2½	12½	108	Bagnio
201	5½	7½	15	13¼	12¾	10	3	12	110	Batton
301	5½	6½	13½	11⅛	10¼	9½	3	10½	79	Blazer
334	5½	7½	14	12	11¼	9⅞	3	11	90	Bobtail
491	5½	7	12	12⅝	11 7/16	10¼	2½	9½	82	Buddhist
536	5½	7¼	12	13¼	12½	10⅞	3	9	90	Burdock
537	5½	8¼	12	12⅞	11⅞	10¼	3½	8½	90	Bureau
552	5½	6½	12	11⅝	10¼	10	2½	9½	80	Burnoose
609	5½	8¼	14½	12⅞	11⅞	9¾	3½	11	98	Cagmag
691	5½	7	12	12¼	11¼	9¾	3½	8½	80	Candle

TUYERES.

Class B

MEDIUM.

All Weights given are Approximate.

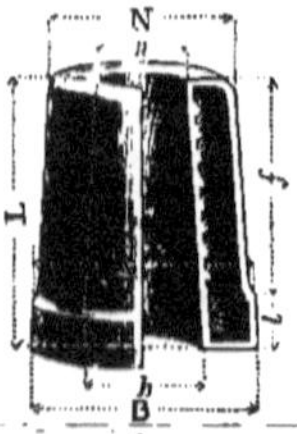

DESCRIPTION.

n—Inside diameter at nose.
b— " " " butt.
L—Length over all.
B—Outside diameter at butt.
A— " " " cooler bearing.
N— " " " nose.
l—Length of cooler bearing.
f— " projecting beyond cooler.

6 inch TUYERES.

No.	*n*	*b*	*L*	*B*	*A*	*N*	*l*	*f*	*Wt.*	*Cypher.*
11	6	7½	12	12	11¼	10½	3	9	80	Abstract
101	6	7	12	12⅜	11 7/16	10¼	2½	9½	80	Bagman
114	6	8	15	13¼	12¾	11	2½	12½	108	Balcony
202	6	7½	15	13¼	12¾	10	3	12	126	Batz
269	6	7¼	15½	13¼	12½	10½	3	12½	110	Beverage
292	6	7¼	15½	12	11¼	10¼	3	12½	100	Biter
304	6	8¼	15	13	11⅝	9⅞	3	12	100	Blemish
325	6	7	15	12⅛	11 7/16	10⅜	2½	12½	94	Boarder
333	6	7½	14	12	11¼	9⅞	3	11	89	Bobolink
339	6	8½	15	14½	12½	9⅞	6	9	160	Bodice
357	6	7½	12	12	11¼	10½	3	9	80	Bouten
359	6	7½	13	12 3/16	11½	9⅝	3	10	82	Boomerang
430	6	7¼	12	12	11¼	10½	3	9	85	Bridler
447	6	7¼	12	13¼	12½	10⅞	3	9	92	Broach
504	6	7	12	12	11¼	10⅜	3	9	85	Builder
538	6	8¼	12	12⅞	11⅞	10¼	3½	8½	92	Burgall
547	6	8	15	13¾	12⅝	11	3	12	111	Burlace
562	6	6½	12	11⅝	10¼	10	2½	9½	80	Buss
593	6	7½	12	13¼	12½	11¼	3	9	92	Cachalot
600	6	8	12	13¼	12¾	11¼	2½	9½	85	Caddow
655	6	7	15	13	11⅝	9⅞	3	12	106	Calumbine
659	6	6½	15½	13¼	12½	10¼	3	12½	112	Culvinist
688	6	7¼	12	13¾	12½	9⅞	3	9	92	Candidate
726	6¼	7½	12	13¼	12½	11¼	3	9	91	Captor

6½ inch TUYERES.

No.	*n*	*b*	*L*	*B*	*A*	*N*	*l*	*f*	*Wt.*	*Cypher.*
10	6½	7½	12	12	11¼	10½	3	9	79	Abcess
160	6½	8	15	13¼	12¾	11	2½	12½	110	Barcon
186	6½	8	15	13⅛	12¼	11¼	2¾	12¼	119	Basinet
320	6½	7	12	12⅝	11⅞	10¼	2½	9½	85	Bluff
444	6½	8	12	13¼	12¾	11¼	2½	9½	85	Brisure

7 inch TUYERES.

No.	*n*	*b*	*L*	*B*	*A*	*N*	*l*	*f*	*Wt.*	*Cypher.*
4	7	8	15	13¼	12¾	11	2½	12½	105	Abbey
119	7	8	15	13⅛	12¼	11¼	2¾	12¼	122	Ballast
312	7	7½	12	12	11¼	10⅞	3	9	76	Blockade
345	7	8	15	13¾	12⅝	11	3	12	110	Bollard
450	7	8	12	13¼	12¾	11¼	2½	9½	80	Brocket
716	7	7½	12	13¼	12½	11¼	3	9	90	Capitule

TUYERES.

Class B

LONG.

All Weights given are Approximate.

DESCRIPTION.

n—Inside diameter at nose.
b— " " " butt.
L—Length over all.
B—Outside diameter at butt.
A— " " " cooler bearing.
N— " " nose.
l—Length of cooler bearing.
f— " projecting beyond cooler.

3 INCH TUYERES.

No.	*n*	*b*	*L*	*B*	*A*	*N*	*l*	*f*	*Wt.*	*Cypher.*
355	3	7½	18	12	10½	8¾	6	12	100	Bonito

4 INCH TUYERES.

No.	*n*	*b*	*L*	*B*	*A*	*N*	*l*	*f*	*Wt.*	*Cypher.*
85	4	7½	18	12	10½	8¾	6	12	105	Bac
561	4	7¼	18	13¼	12½	10¼	3	15	124	Buskin

4½ INCH TUYERES.

No.	*n*	*b*	*L*	*B*	*A*	*N*	*l*	*f*	*Wt.*	*Cypher.*
86	4½	7½	18	12	10½	8¾	6	12	105	Bacca

5 INCH TUYERES.

No.	*n*	*b*	*L*	*B*	*A*	*N*	*l*	*f*	*Wt.*	*Cypher.*
378	5	7½	17	12	11¼	10⅛	3	14	106	Bouncer

5½ INCH TUYERES.

No.	*n*	*b*	*L*	*B*	*A*	*N*	*l*	*f*	*Wt.*	*Cypher.*
36	5½	9	32	13¾	12½	10¼	7	25	240	Almond
481	5½	7½	17	12	11¼	10⅛	3	14	115	Bryonine

6 INCH TUYERES.

No.	*n*	*b*	*L*	*B*	*A*	*N*	*l*	*f*	*Wt.*	*Cypher.*
35	6	9	32	13¾	12½	10¼	7	25	238	Alley
159	6	8	22	15½	14¼	11½	3½	18½	190	Barber
212	6	7½	17	12	11¼	10⅛	3	14	109	Bayonet
550	6	8	15	12⅛	11½	10⅜	2½	12½	99	Burnet
554	6	8	18	13¼	12⅝	10⅛	3	15	136	Burrock
731	6	8	18	13¼	12¼	10¼	2½	15½	125	Caramel

6½ INCH TUYERES.

No.	*n*	*b*	*L*	*B*	*A*	*N*	*l*	*f*	*Wt.*	*Cypher.*
34	6½	9	24	13¾	12½	10⅞	7	17	173	Alien
180	6½	8	22	15½	14¼	11½	3½	18½	188	Basalt

7 INCH TUYERES.

No.	*n*	*b*	*L*	*B*	*A*	*N*	*l*	*f*	*Wt.*	*Cypher.*
59	7	8	22	15½	14¼	11½	3½	18½	190	Arena
611	7	9½	21	17¼	15¾	11⅜	6	15	192	Caimacan

BEST, FOX & CO.

TUYERES.

CLASS C

SHORT.

All Weights given are Approximate.

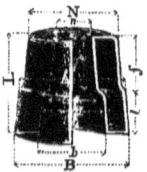

DESCRIPTION.

n —Inside diameter at nose.
b   "   "   " butt.
L—Length over all.
B—Outside diameter at butt.
A   "   "   " cooler bearing
N   "   "   " nose.
l—Length of cooler bearing.
f   " projecting beyond cooler.
c—Small diameter at nose contraction.
e—Length of   ·   "   "
d—Large diameter   "   "

3½ INCH TUYERES.

No.	n	b	L	B	A	N	l	f	c	e	d	Wt.	Cypher.

4 INCH TUYERES.

No.	n	b	L	B	A	N	l	f	c	e	d	Wt.	Cypher.

4½ INCH TUYERES.

No.	n	b	L	B	A	N	l	f	c	e	d	Wt.	Cypher.
220	4½	5¼	10½	10	9⅛	8¾	3	7½	4½	4	5⅛	56	Bear
233	4½	5½	11	10⅝	9¾	8⅝	3¼	7¾	4½	4	5¼	63	Bedouin

5 INCH TUYERES.

No.	n	b	L	B	A	N	l	f	c	e	d	Wt.	Cypher.
126	5	8½	11	12⅞	11⅝	10½	5	6	5⅛	6	7½	82	Bau
349	5	7	11	11½	...	9⅝	...	...	5⅛	6	6¼	77	Bombate

TUYERES.

Class C

SHORT.

All Weights given are Approximate.

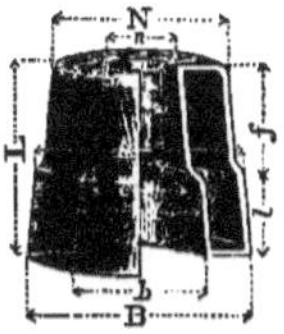

DESCRIPTION.

a—Inside diameter at nose.
b— " " " butt.
L—Length over all.
B—Outside diameter at butt.
A " " " cooler bearing.
N " " " nose.
l—Length of cooler bearing.
f " projecting beyond cooler.
c—Small diameter at nose contraction.
e—Length of " "
d—Large diameter " "

5½ INCH TUYERES.

No.	*a*	*b*	*L*	*B*	*A*	*N*	*l*	*f*	*c*	*e*	*d*	*Wt.*	*Cypher.*
109	5½	8½	11	12⅞	11⅞	10½	5	6	6	6	7½	80	Bairn

6 INCH TUYERES.

No.	*a*	*b*	*L*	*B*	*A*	*N*	*l*	*f*	*c*	*e*	*d*	*Wt.*	*Cypher.*
72	6	8½	11	12⅞	11⅞	10½	5	6	6	6	7½	84	Avenger
218	6	6⅞	11½	12⅞	12	10½	3½	8	6	2	6⅞	88	Beaker

6½ INCH TUYERES.

No.	*a*	*b*	*L*	*B*	*A*	*N*	*l*	*f*	*c*	*e*	*d*	*Wt.*	*Cypher.*

7 INCH TUYERES.

No.	*a*	*b*	*L*	*B*	*A*	*N*	*l*	*f*	*c*	*e*	*d*	*Wt.*	*Cypher.*

BEST, FOX & CO.

TUYERES.

CLASS C

MEDIUM.

All Weights given are Approximate.

DESCRIPTION.

n—Inside diameter, at nose.
b "   "   " butt.
L—Length over all.
B—Outside diameter at butt.
A "   "   " cooler bearing.
N "   "   " nose.
l—Length of cooler bearing.
f "   projecting beyond cooler.
r—Small diameter at nose contraction.
e—Length of   "   "   "
d—Large diameter   "   "   "

3½ INCH TUYERES.

No.	n	b	L	B	A	N	l	f	r	e	d	Wt.	Cypher.
128	3½	7¾	15	12½	11¾	9¾	3½	11½	5¼	8	6⅝	95	Banco
245	3½	9	15	13¼	12½	11	3½	11½	6¾	6	7⅝	109	Belgian

4 INCH TUYERES.

No.	n	b	L	B	A	N	l	f	r	e	d	Wt.	Cypher.
149	4	7¾	15	12½	11¾	9¾	3½	11½	5¼	8	6⅝	96	Bannock

4½ INCH TUYERES.

No.	n	b	L	B	A	N	l	f	r	e	d	Wt.	Cypher.
177	4½	7¾	15	12½	11¾	9¾	3½	11½	5¼	8	6⅝	97	Barton
224	4½	7	13½	13	12	9½	3	10½	6	5	6⅜	98	Beaufet

5 INCH TUYERES.

No.	n	b	L	B	A	N	l	f	r	e	d	Wt.	Cypher.
67	5	9	15	13¼	12½	11	3½	11½	6¾	6	7⅝	100	Attic
68	5	7¾	15	12½	11¾	9¾	3½	11½	5¼	8	6⅝	96	Auction
225	5	7	13½	13	12	9½	3	10½	6	5	6⅜	93	Beaufin
449	5	9	15	13¼	12½	11	3½	11½	6⅝	9¾	8⅜	112	Brocade

TUYERES.

Class C

MEDIUM.

All Weights given are Approximate.

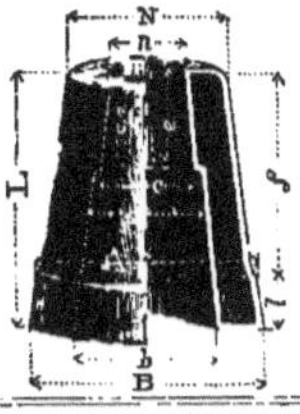

DESCRIPTION.

n—Inside diameter at nose.
b— " " " butt.
L—Length over all.
B—Outside diameter at butt.
A " " " cooler bearing.
N " " " nose.
l—Length of cooler bearing.
f " projecting beyond cooler.
c—Small diameter at nose contraction.
e—Length of " "
d—Large diameter " "

5½ INCH TUYERES.

No.	*n*	*b*	*L*	*B*	*A*	*N*	*l*	*f*	*c*	*e*	*d*	*Wt.*	*Cypher.*
138	5½	9	15	13¼	12½	11	3½	11½	6¾	6	7⅝	100	Bandoline
226	5½	7	13½	13	12	9½	3	10½	6	5	6⅜	90	Beauty

6 INCH TUYERES.

No.	*n*	*b*	*L*	*B*	*A*	*N*	*l*	*f*	*c*	*e*	*d*	*Wt.*	*Cypher.*
73	6	9	15	13¼	12½	11	3½	11½	6¾	6	7⅝	106	Avenue
350	6	9	15	13¼	12½	11	3½	11½	6⅝	9¼	8 3/16	109	Bombyx
390	6	7¾	15	12½	11¾	9¼	3½	11½	6¼	8	6⅝	100	Bracket
411	6	9	12	13¼	12½	11	3	9	7	7	8¼	93	Breather

6½ INCH TUYERES.

No.	*n*	*b*	*L*	*B*	*A*	*N*	*l*	*f*	*c*	*e*	*d*	*Wt.*	*Cypher.*
146	6½	9	15	13¼	12½	11	3½	11½	6¾	6	7⅝	100	Banker
251	6½	9	19	13¼	12½	10½	3½	15½	6¾	10	7⅝	140	Beluga

7 INCH TUYERES.

No.	*n*	*b*	*L*	*B*	*A*	*N*	*l*	*f*	*c*	*e*	*d*	*Wt.*	*Cypher.*
3	6¾	9	15	13¼	12½	11	3½	11½	6¼	6	7⅝	100	Abatis

BEST, FOX & CO.

BEST, FOX & CO.

TUYERES.

Class D

LONG.

All Weights given are Approximate.

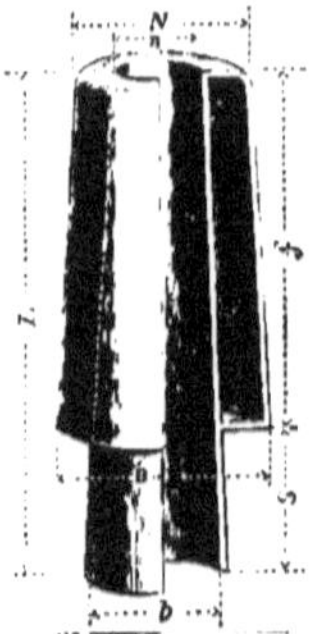

DESCRIPTION.

n—Inside diameter at nose.
b— " butt.
L—Length over all.
B—Outside diameter at butt.
N— " nose.
S—Length of sleeve.
f— " beyond sleeve.

2½ INCH TUYERES.

No.	*n*	*b*	*L*	*B*	*N*	*S*	*f*	*Wt.*	*Cypher.*
131	2½	7½	28	10⅛	8	12½	15½	104	Bandana
116	2½	7½	28	10⅛	8	12½	15½	106	Brent

3 INCH TUYERES.

No.	*n*	*b*	*L*	*B*	*N*	*S*	*f*	*Wt.*	*Cypher.*
29	3	7½	28	10⅛	8	12½	15½	104	Agent

3½ INCH TUYERES.

No.	*n*	*b*	*L*	*B*	*N*	*S*	*f*	*Wt.*	*Cypher.*
170	3½	7½	28	10⅛	8	12½	15½	108	Barrack

4 INCH TUYERES.

No.	*n*	*b*	*L*	*B*	*N*	*S*	*f*	*Wt.*	*Cypher.*
30	4	7½	28	10⅛	8	12½	15½	110	Aisle
157	4	8	28	11¼	9	8	20	125	Barbarian
196	4	8½	28	10⅛	8	12½	15½	114	Bather

4½ INCH TUYERES.

No.	*n*	*b*	*L*	*B*	*N*	*S*	*f*	*Wt.*	*Cypher.*
31	4½	7½	28	10¾	8	12½	15½	112	Album
111	4½	8	28	11¼	9	8	20	126	Baize
142	4½	8	28	10¾	9	12½	15½	115	Batrian

5 INCH TUYERES.

No.	*n*	*b*	*L*	*B*	*N*	*S*	*f*	*Wt.*	*Cypher.*
32	5	8	28	10¾	9	12½	15½	116	Alcove
33	5	8	28	11¼	9	8	20	130	Alder
208	5	7½	25	11¼	9	5	20	123	Bawble

5½ INCH TUYERES.

No.	*n*	*b*	*L*	*B*	*N*	*S*	*f*	*Wt.*	*Cypher.*

6 INCH TUYERES.

No.	*n*	*b*	*L*	*B*	*N*	*S*	*f*	*Wt.*	*Cypher.*

TUYERES.

Class E

All Weights given are Approximate

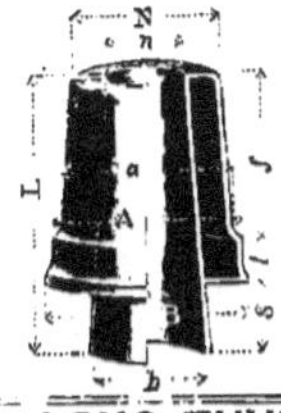

DESCRIPTION.

n—Inside diameter at nose.
b— " " " butt.
L—Length over all.
B—Outside diameter at butt.
A— " " " cooler bearing.
N— " " " nose.
S—Length of sleeve.
l— " " cooler bearing.
f— " " beyond cooler bearing.

4 INCH LONG TUYERES.

	No.	*n*	*b*	*L*	*B*	*A*	*a*	*N*	*S*	*l*	*f*	*Wt.*	*Cypher.*
4 in. Long.	**140**	4	8¾	18	12	10½		9¼	6	6	6	90	Bang

4½ INCH SHORT TUYERES.

	No.	*n*	*b*	*L*	*B*	*A*	*a*	*N*	*S*	*l*	*f*	*Wt.*	*Cypher.*
4½ in Short	**252**	4½	5⅝	9¼	9 3/16	8¾	8½	8	1¼	3	5	49	Bema

4½ INCH MEDIUM AND LONG TUYERES.

	No.	*n*	*b*	*L*	*B*	*A*	*a*	*N*	*S*	*l*	*f*	*Wt.*	*Cypher.*
4½ in. Medium ... and Long.	**163**	4½	6⅞	16	12	10 7/16	10¼	9¼	4	3	9	70	Barker
	175	4½	8¾	18	12	10½	...	9¼	6	6	6	89	Barter

5 INCH SHORT TUYERES.

	No.	*n*	*b*	*L*	*B*	*A*	*a*	*N*
5 in. Short	**314**	5	5[illegible]	9¼	9 3/16	8¾		8

5 INCH MEDIUM AND LO

	No.	*n*	*b*	*L*	*B*	*A*
5 in. Medium .... and Long.	**71**	5	6⅞	16	12	10[illegible]
	95	5	8¾	18	12	
	368	5	8¾	16½	11⅛	
	689	5	8¾	16½	12[illegible]	

6 INCH MED

	No.	*n*	*b*
6 in. Medium ..... and Long.	**356**	6	
	707	6	

TUYERES.

CLASS F

LONG.

All Weights given are Approximate.

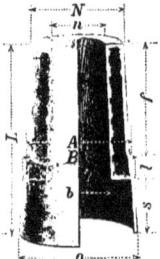

DESCRIPTION.

n—Inside diameter at nose.
b— " " " butt.
L—Length over all.
B— Outside diameter at butt.
A— " " " cooler bearing.
N— " " " nose.
O— " " " of sleeve.
S—Length of sleeve.
l— " " cooler bearing.
f— " beyond cooler bearing.

3 INCH TUYERES.

No.	n	b	L	B	A	N	O	S	l	f	Wt.	Cypher.
151	3	5	20	$10\frac{1}{8}$	$9\frac{1}{4}$	8	$10\frac{3}{8}$	8	$2\frac{1}{2}$	$9\frac{1}{2}$	87	Banshee
178	3	6	20	$11\frac{1}{8}$	$19\frac{1}{4}$	$9\frac{1}{4}$	$11\frac{3}{8}$	8	$2\frac{1}{2}$	$9\frac{1}{2}$	112	Bartram

3½ INCH TUYERES.

No.	n	b	L	B	A	N	O	S	l	f	Wt.	Cypher.
118	$3\frac{1}{2}$	6	20	$11\frac{1}{8}$	$10\frac{1}{4}$	$9\frac{1}{4}$	$11\frac{3}{8}$	8	$2\frac{1}{2}$	$9\frac{1}{2}$	100	Ballad
187	$3\frac{1}{2}$	5	20	$10\frac{1}{8}$	$9\frac{1}{4}$	8	$10\frac{3}{8}$	8	$2\frac{1}{2}$	$9\frac{1}{2}$	88	Basket

4 INCH TUYERES.

No.	n	b	L	B	A	N	O	S	l	f	Wt.	Cypher.
40	4	5	20	$10\frac{1}{8}$	$9\frac{1}{4}$	8	$10\frac{3}{8}$	8	$2\frac{1}{2}$	$9\frac{1}{2}$	89	Ament
113	4	6	20	$11\frac{1}{8}$	$10\frac{1}{4}$	$9\frac{1}{4}$	$11\frac{3}{8}$	8	$2\frac{1}{2}$	$9\frac{1}{2}$	104	Balance
172	4	7	20	$12\frac{1}{8}$	$11\frac{1}{8}$	$10\frac{1}{4}$	$12\frac{3}{8}$	8	$2\frac{1}{2}$	$9\frac{1}{2}$	105	Barrier

4½ INCH TUYERES.

No.	n	b	L	B	A	N	O	S	l	f	Wt	Cypher.
94	$4\frac{1}{2}$	6	20	$11\frac{1}{8}$	$10\frac{1}{4}$	$9\frac{1}{4}$	$11\frac{3}{8}$	8	$2\frac{1}{2}$	$9\frac{1}{2}$	101	Anchor
133	$4\frac{1}{2}$	7	20	$12\frac{1}{4}$	$11\frac{1}{8}$	$10\frac{1}{4}$	$12\frac{3}{8}$	8	$2\frac{1}{2}$	$9\frac{1}{2}$	105	Barb

TUYERES.

CLASS F

LONG.

All Weights given are Approximate.

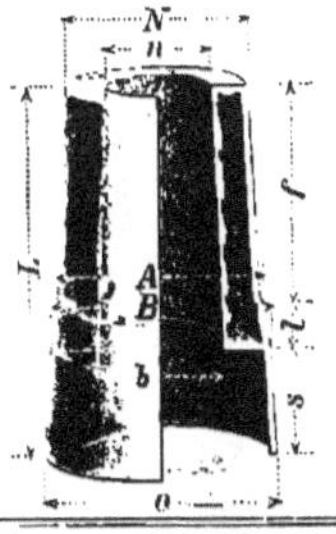

DESCRIPTION.

n—Inside diameter at nose.
b— " " " butt.
L—Length over all.
B—Outside diameter at butt.
A— " " " cooler bearing.
N— " " " nose
O— " " " of sleeve.
S—Length of sleeve.
l— " " cooler bearing.
f— " beyond cooler bearing.

5 INCH TUYERES

No.	*n*	*b*	*L*	*B*	*A*	*N*	*O*	*S*	*l*	*f*	*Wt.*	*Cypher.*
42	5	6	20	11 1/8	10 1/4	9 1/4	11 1/4	8	2 1/2	9 1/2	100	Ancient
148	5	7	20	12 3/16	11 7/16	10 1/4	12 3/8	8	2 1/2	9 1/2	111	Banner
217	5	7	19	12 1/16	11 7/16	10 1/4	12 3/8	8	2 1/2	8 1/2	103	Beadle
227	5	6	21	12 1/8	10 3/4	10	12 3/8	7 1/2	4	9 1/2	124	Beaver
260	5	6	15	11 1/8	10 1/4	9 5/8	11 1/4	8	2 1/2	4 1/2	84	Benzine
298	5	7	18	12 1/8	11 1/4	10 1/4	13	6	2 1/2	9 1/2	108	Blade
638	5	7	22	12 1/16	11 7/16	10	12 3/8	8	2 1/2	11 1/2	119	Caliduct

5½ INCH TUYERES.

No.	*n*	*b*	*L*	*B*	*A*	*N*	*O*	*S*	*l*	*f*	*Wt.*	*Cypher.*
43	5 1/2	7	20	12 1/16	11 7/16	10 1/4	12 3/8	8	2 1/2	9 1/2	109	Andiron
213	5 1/2	6 1/2	18	11 5/8	10 3/4	10	12	6	2 1/2	9 1/2	104	Bazar
471	5 1/2	9	14 3/4	14 5/8	13 1/16	9 3/4	15 1/4	7	3	4 3/4	102	Brownie
501	5 1/2	5 3/4	20	12 1/16	11 7/16	10 1/4	12 3/8	8	2 1/2	9 1/2	114	Bugle

TUYERES.

Class F

LONG.

All Weights given are Approximate.

DESCRIPTION.

n—Inside diameter at nose.
b— "   "   " but't.
L—Length over all.
B—Outside diameter at butt.
A— "   "   " cooler bearing
N— "   "   " nose.
O— "   "   " of sleeve.
S—Length of sleeve.
l— "   " cooler bearing.
f— "   beyond cooler bearing.

6 INCH TUYERES.

No.	n	b	L.	B	A	N	O	S	l	f	Wt.	Cypher.
44	6	7	20	$12\frac{1}{16}$	$11\frac{7}{8}$	$10\frac{1}{4}$	$12\frac{3}{8}$	8	$2\frac{1}{2}$	$9\frac{1}{2}$	100	Angel
47	6	$8\frac{1}{2}$	16	$13\frac{1}{2}$	...	$10\frac{1}{2}$	$14\frac{1}{2}$	4	...	12	110	Ankle
214	6	$6\frac{1}{2}$	18	$11\frac{7}{8}$	$10\frac{3}{4}$	10	12	6	$2\frac{1}{2}$	$9\frac{1}{2}$	105	Bench
216	6	7	19	$12\frac{3}{4}$	$11\frac{1}{16}$	$10\frac{3}{4}$	$12\frac{3}{8}$	8	$2\frac{1}{2}$	$8\frac{1}{4}$	105	Bend
242	6	$7\frac{1}{2}$	17	$12\frac{5}{8}$	$11\frac{3}{4}$	11	13	6	$2\frac{1}{2}$	$8\frac{1}{2}$	106	Beholder
244	6	7	16	$12\frac{1}{16}$	$11\frac{7}{8}$	$10\frac{3}{8}$	$12\frac{3}{8}$	8	$2\frac{1}{2}$	$5\frac{1}{2}$	92	Belfry
265	6	9	22	14	...	$10\frac{1}{2}$	$14\frac{3}{4}$	4	...	18	146	Berry
280	6	7	18	12	$11\frac{1}{2}$	$10\frac{1}{4}$	13	6	$2\frac{1}{2}$	$9\frac{1}{2}$	107	Billot

6¹⁄₂ INCH TUYERES.

No.	n	b	L.	B	A	N	O	S	l	f	Wt.	Cypher.
45	$6\frac{1}{2}$	8	25	$13\frac{1}{8}$	$12\frac{1}{4}$	$11\frac{1}{4}$	$13\frac{3}{8}$	10	$2\frac{3}{4}$	$12\frac{1}{4}$	138	Angler
203	$6\frac{1}{2}$	$7\frac{1}{2}$	21	$12\frac{3}{8}$	$11\frac{3}{4}$	$10\frac{3}{4}$	13	6	$2\frac{1}{2}$	$12\frac{1}{2}$	125	Banbee
223	$6\frac{1}{2}$	$7\frac{1}{2}$	17	$12\frac{3}{8}$	$11\frac{3}{4}$	11	13	6	$2\frac{1}{2}$	$8\frac{1}{2}$	106	Beater

7 INCH TUYERES.

No.	n	b	L.	B	A	N	O	S	l	f	Wt.	Cypher.
46	7	8	25	$13\frac{1}{8}$	$12\frac{1}{4}$	$11\frac{1}{4}$	$13\frac{3}{8}$	10	$2\frac{3}{4}$	$12\frac{1}{4}$	142	Animal
204	7	$7\frac{5}{8}$	21	$12\frac{3}{8}$	$11\frac{3}{4}$	$10\frac{3}{4}$	13	6	$2\frac{1}{2}$	$12\frac{1}{2}$	127	Baudkin
434	7	$7\frac{1}{2}$	17	$12\frac{3}{8}$	$11\frac{3}{4}$	11	13	6	$2\frac{1}{2}$	$8\frac{1}{2}$	110	Brigand

TUYERES.

Class G

All Weights given are Approximate.

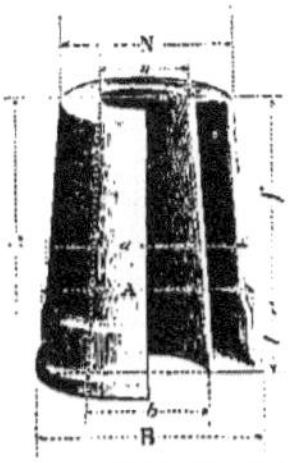

DESCRIPTION.

n—Inside diameter at nose.
b— " " " butt.
L—Length over all.
B—Outside diameter at butt.
A— " " " cooler bearing.
a—Small " beyond cooler bearing.
N—Outside " at nose.
l—Length of cooler bearing.
f— " beyond cooler bearing.

4 inch TUYERES.

No.	n	b	L	B	A	a	N	l	f	Wt.	Cypher.
136	4	6½	13	12 3/8	11 3/8	11 1/8	9	3½	9½	79	Bandog
210	4	8	13	14¾	13 1/8	12½	8½	3	10	93	Bawler
295	4	5½	10	10	9	8¾	8	3	7	49	Blackbird
369	4	7¼	15½	12 7/8	12	11¾	10½	3½	12	112	Boscage
698	4	6½	12	12 1/16	10 7/16	10¼	9¼	3	9	71	Cannibal

4½ inch TUYERES.

No.	n	b	L	B	A	a	N	l	f	Wt.	Cypher.
116	4½	6½	13	12 3/8	11 3/16	11 1/8	9	3½	9½	78	Baleen
124	4½	6½	12	12 1/16	10 7/16	10¼	9¼	3	9	65	Balm
256	4½	5½	10	10	9	8¾	8	3	7	48	Benedict
590	4½	6	9	11¾	11	10 5/8	9 3/8	3	6	65	Cabriolet
649	4½	7¼	15½	12 7/8	12	11¾	10½	3½	12	78	Callus
665	4½	7¼	9 3/8	12 7/8	11 13/16	11¾	10	3 5/8	6	77	Camber
686	4½	6	12	11¾	11	10 5/8	9 1/8	3	9	79	Cancerite

5 inch TUYERES.

No.	n	b	L	B	A	a	N	l	f	Wt.	Cypher.
100	5	6½	13	12 3/8	11 3/8	11 1/8	9	3½	9½	80	Baggage
107	5	6½	12	12 1/16	10 7/16	10¼	9¼	3	9	65	Bailer
174	5	7¼	15½	12 7/8	12	11¾	10½	3½	12	115	Barse
219	5	5¼	10½	10	9 1/8	8 7/8	8¾	3	7½	56	Beamlet
344	5	7	13	12 3/8	11 3/8	11¼	9¼	3½	9½	89	Bolis
370	5	6¼	9	11¾	11	10 5/8	9 5/8	3	6	66	Bosset
598	5	7	16	12 3/8	11 3/8	11 3/16	9¼	3½	12½	99	Cacodyle
722	5	6¼	12	11¾	11	10 5/8	9 1/8	3	9	81	Capstan

TUYERES.

Class G.

All Weights given are Approximate.

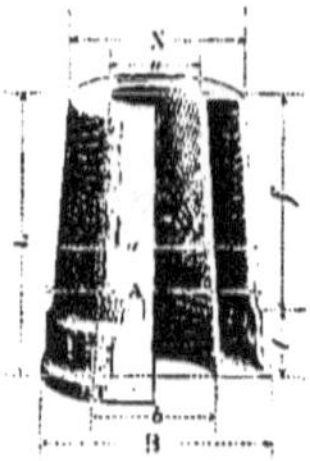

DESCRIPTION.

n—Inside diameter at nose.
b— " " " butt.
L—Length over all.
B—Outside diameter at butt.
A— " " " cooler bearing.
a—Small " beyond cooler bearing
N—Outside " at nose.
l—Length of cooler bearing.
f— " beyond cooler bearing.

5½ INCH TUYERES.

No.	*n*	*b*	*L*	*B*	*A*	*a*	*N*	*l*	*f*	*Wt.*	*Cypher.*
24	5½	8	13	14¾	13⅛	12½	10⅝	3	10	105	Admiral
77	5½	7¼	15½	12⅞	12	11¾	10½	3½	12	115	Axle
326	5½	8	11½	13 3/16	12¼	12	10⅝	3	8½	96	Boast
328	5½	8	13	13 3/16	12¼	12	10⅜	3	10	96	Boaston
682	5½	6⅝	13	12⅜	11⅜	11 3/16	10⅛	3½	9½	87	Canal

6 INCH TUYERES.

No.	*n*	*b*	*L*	*B*	*A*	*a*	*N*	*l*	*f*	*Wt.*	*Cypher.*
23	6	8	13	14¾	13⅛	12½	10⅜	3	10	107	Adept
78	6	7¼	15½	12⅞	12	11¾	10½	3½	12	115	Aztec
259	6	8	13	13 3/16	12¼	12	10⅜	3	10	97	Bennet
361	6	6⅝	13	12⅜	11⅜	11 3/16	10⅛	3½	9½	83	Bootel
385	6	7½	10	12⅝	11⅝	11⅜	10⅛	3½	6½	76	Bowline
440	6	6	12	13¼	12½	12⅛	11	3¼	8¾	100	Brindle
566	6	7	15½	13¼	12½	12⅛	11	3¼	12¼	125	Butternut
567	6	7	12	13¼	12½	12⅜	11	3¼	8¾	95	Buttery

6½ INCH TUYERES.

No.	*n*	*b*	*L*	*B*	*A*	*a*	*N*	*l*	*f*	*Wt.*	*Cypher.*
122	6½	8	13	14¾	13⅛	12½	11½	3	10	110	Balloon
337	6½	6⅞	11½	12⅞	12	11¾	10½	3½	8	90	Bochelet

7 INCH TUYERES.

No.	*n*	*b*	*L*	*B*	*A*	*a*	*N*	*l*	*f*	*Wt.*	*Cypher.*
22	7	8	13	14¾	13⅛	12½	11½	3	10	110	Adder
316	7	8	15½	13¾	12½	12⅛	11	3¼	12¼	130	Blossom
372	7	7	15½	13¼	12½	12⅛	11	3¼	12¼	136	Botargo
407	7	8	11¾	13¾	12½	12⅛	11⅛	3¼	8½	97	Breach
433	7	7	12	13¼	12½	12⅛	11	3¼	8¾	101	Brigade

TUYERES AND NOTCH,

Class H

All Weights given are Approximate.

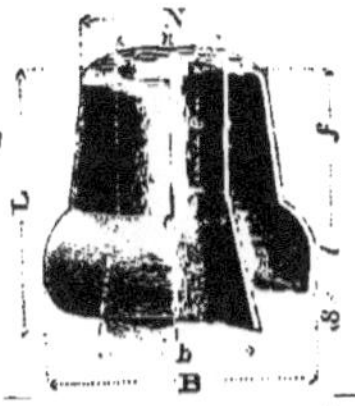

DESCRIPTION.

n—Inside diameter at nose.
b— " " " butt.
L—Length over all.
B—Outside diameter at butt.
A— " " " cooler bearing.
N " " " nose.
S—Length of sleeve.
l—Length of cooler bearing.
f— " beyond cooler bearing.
e— " of nose contraction.
c—Small diameter at nose contraction.

No.	*n*	*b*	*L*	*B*	*A*	*N*	*S*	*l*	*f*	*e*	*c*	*Wt.*	*Cypher.*
7	7	9½	14	15½	13	11½	1¾	5¾	6½	7	7	121	Abnet
8	6	9½	14	15½	13	11½	1¾	5¾	6½	6½	6	116	Abode
9	1⅞	3	5½	8	5½	4⅞		3⅝	1⅞	2¼	1⅞	22	Aboma
74	5	9½	15¼	15½	11⅞	10	1¾	6½	7	6	5	115	Average

TUYERES.

CLASS I

All Weights given are Approximate.

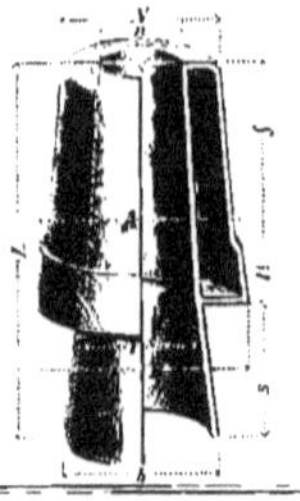

DESCRIPTION.

a—Inside diameter at nose.
b— " " " butt.
L—Length over all.
B—Outside diameter at butt.
I—Inside " " cooler bearing.
A—Outside " " " "
N— " " " nose.
S—Length of sleeve.
l— " " cooler bearing.
f— beyond cooler bearing.

4½ INCH TUYERES.

No.	*a*	*b*	*L*	*B*	*I*	*A*	*N*	*S*	*l*	*f*	*Wt.*	*Cypher.*
250	4½	7	16½	10	5¼	9⅜	8¾	6	3	7½	69	Belone
374	4½	9¼	18	12	7½	11¼	9¼	6	3	9	73	Bottle

5 INCH TUYERES.

No.	*a*	*b*	*L*	*B*	*I*	*A*	*N*	*S*	*l*	*f*	*Wt.*	*Cypher.*
243	5	9	20½	12⅜	6½	11⅜	9	7½	3½	9½	94	Belemnite
425	5	9¼	18	12	8½	11¼	9¼	6	3	9	75	Bribe

5½ INCH TUYERES.

No.	*a*	*b*	*L*	*B*	*I*	*A*	*N*	*S*	*l*	*f*	*Wt.*	*Cypher.*
714	5½	9 3/16	12⅜	13¾	7	12½	9½	1½	4⅝	6	92	Capital

6 INCH TUYERES.

No.	*a*	*b*	*L*	*B*	*I*	*A*	*N*	*S*	*l*	*f*	*Wt.*	*Cypher.*
382	6	7¼	28	11½	7	...	10⅛	6	...	22	100	Bourse
651	6	9	23½	13¼	7½	12½	11¼	11½	3	9	123	Calomel

6½ INCH TUYERES.

No.	*a*	*b*	*L*	*B*	*I*	*A*	*N*	*S*	*l*	*f*	*Wt.*	*Cypher.*

7 INCH TUYERES.

No.	*a*	*b*	*L*	*B*	*I*	*A*	*N*	*S*	*l*	*f*	*Wt.*	*Cypher.*
318	7	9⅛	12¾	13¾	8	12⅜	11⅜	2	3¾	7	93	Blouse

TUYERES.

Class J

All Weights given are Approximate.

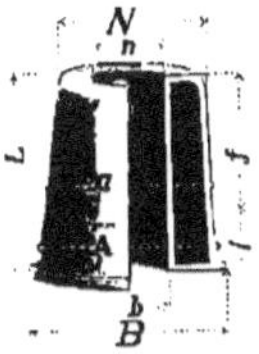

DESCRIPTION.

n—Inside diameter at nose.
b— " " " butt.
L—Length over all.
B—Outside diameter at butt.
A— " " inside of cooler.
a— " " at cooler bearing.
N— " " " nose.
R—Length of collar.
l— " " cooler bearing.
f— " beyond cooler bearing.

4 inch TUYERES

No.	*n*	*b*	*L*	*B*	*A*	*a*	*N*	*R*	*l*	*f*	*Wt.*	*Cypher.*
585	4	5½	7	10	9½	9 3/16	8½	½	2½	4	40	Cabinet

4½ inch TUYERES.

No.	*n*	*b*	*L*	*B*	*A*	*a*	*N*	*R*	*l*	*f*	*Wt.*	*Cypher.*
539	4½	5¼	11	10	9½	9⅜	8¼	½	2½	8	56	Burgee
544	4½	5¾	12	10⅝	9 9/16	...	8	1		11	74	Burgrass

5 inch TUYERES.

No.	*n*	*b*	*L*	*B*	*A*	*a*	*N*	*R*	*l*	*f*	*Wt.*	*Cypher.*
503	5	5½	7	10	9½	9 3/16	8½	½	2½	4	40	Buhl
520	5	6	12	11 13/16	10¾		9¼	⅝		11⅜	77	Bumble
545	5	6	10	11 13/16	10¾		9½	⅝		9⅝	70	Burgrave
657	5	6	12	11¾	10¾		9¼	½		11½	78	Calvary

5½ inch TUYERES.

No.	*n*	*b*	*L*	*B*	*A*	*a*	*N*	*R*	*l*	*f*	*Wt.*	*Cypher.*

6 inch TUYERES.

No.	*n*	*b*	*L*	*B*	*A*	*a*	*N*	*R*	*l*	*f*	*Wt.*	*Cypher.*

BEST, FOX & CO.

BEST. FOX & CO.

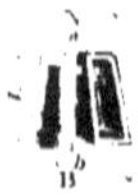

CINDER NOTCHES

CLASS A

All Weights given are Approximate.

DESCRIPTION.

n—Inside diameter at nose.
b— " " " butt.
L—Length over all.
B—Outside diameter at butt.
N— " " " nose.

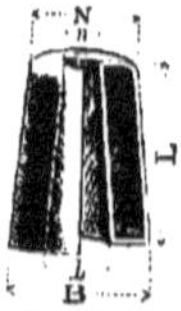

SHORT.

No.	*n*	*b*	*L*	*B*	*N*	*Wt.*	*Cypher.*
150	1½	2½	4¼	5¼	4¼	10	Banquet
190	1½	3	9	7	5⅞	23	Basset
214	2½	3½	6	6½	5½	15	Bay
327	2	3½	7	7	6	25	Boaster
334	3	3½	7	7	6	25	Bobbin
338	3	3¼	5	6¼	5¾	15	Bockey
342	1½	3½	7	7	6	26	Boiarin
374	2	3¼	4½	6¼	5⅞	15	Botanist
410	1¼	3½	7	7	6	24	Bream
417	2	3½	6	6½	5½	18	Breton
478	2½	3	4	7	6¼	15	Brush
480	2½	3	5½	6	5	14	Brute
534	2½	3½	7	7	6	27	Burden
653	1¾	3½	8	6⅞	6¼	28	Caltrap
693	3	3¼	5	6 7/16	5¾	16	Candroy
725	2	3½	8	6⅞	6¼	28	Captive

MEDIUM AND LONG.

No.	*n*	*b*	*L*	*B*	*N*	*Wt.*	*Cypher.*
236	2½	4	10	7⅞	6⅜	40	Bee
319	1¼	6	16	11	8	82	Blower
352	3	5	10	9⅛	7¼	56	Bonbon

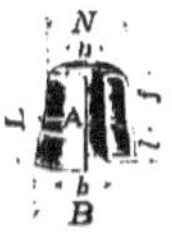

CINDER NOTCHES

CLASS B

All Weights given are Approximate.

DESCRIPTION.

n—Inside diameter at nose.
b— " " " butt.
L—Length over all.
B—Outside diameter at butt.
A— " " " cooler bearing.
N— " " " nose.
l—Length of cooler bearing.
f— " projecting beyond cooler.

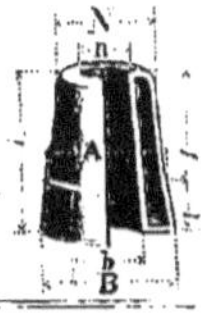

SHORT.

No.	*n*	*b*	*L*	*B*	*A*	*N*	*l*	*f*	*Wt.*	*Cypher.*
324	2	2 9/16	4	5 9/16	4 7/8	4½	2	2	10	Board
336	3	3¾	6	7 1/8	7	6½	3½	2½	23	Bocasine
387	2	3	5	5¾	5	4 3/8	2½	2½	11	Boyar
516	3	3¾	6	7¾	7	6½	3½	2½	24	Bulrush
569	2	3½	5	6	5 5/16	4½	2	3	12	Buttress
574	2½	3¾	6	7¾	7	6½	3½	2½	25	Byard
586	1½	3	5	7	6¼	5 5/8	2	3	16	Cabireau
599	1½	3	5	6	5¼	4½	2	3	12	Cactus
614	2½	3½	6	7 1/8	6	5½	3	3	21	Caisson
623	1½	3	5	7	6½	5 5/8	2	3	16	Calamus
643	2	4	5	7	6½	5 5/8	2	3	18	Caliphate
730	2	3¾	6	7 1/8	7	6½	3½	2½	23	Carafe

MEDIUM.

No.	*n*	*b*	*L*	*B*	*A*	*N*	*l*	*f*	*Wt.*	*Cypher.*

CINDER NOTCHES

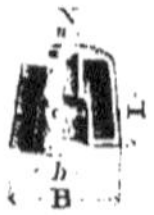

CLASS C

All Weights given are Approximate.

DESCRIPTION.

n—Inside diameter at nose.
b— " " " butt.
L—Length over all.
B—Outside diameter at butt.
N— " " " nose.
C—Small diameter at nose contraction.
e—Length of " "

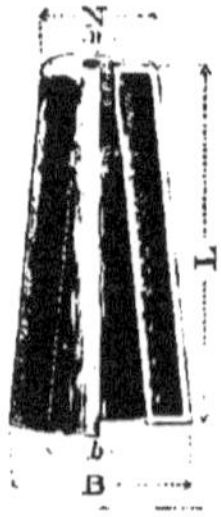

SHORT.

No.	n	b	L	B	N	C	e	Wt.	Cypher.
48	3	3½	7	7	6	2½	2	25	Annual
50	1½	2½	4¼	5¾	4¼	1½	2	10	Antidote
51	1¼	2½	4¼	5¾	4¼	1¼	2	10	Antique
70	1¾	2½	4¼	5¾	4¼	1¼	2	10	Aunt
97	2	2½	4¼	5¾	4¼	2	2	10	Baftas
167	2¼	2½	4¼	5¾	4¼	2	2	10	Baron
192	2	3	4¼	6	5	2	2	12	Bastile
489	3	3¼	5	6¼	5½	2½	1½	13	Buckra
674	2¼	2½	4¼	5¾	4¾	1¼	2	12	Camlet
692	2	2¼	4¼	5¾	4¾	1	2	12	Candock

MEDIUM AND LONG.

No.	n	b	L	B	N	C	e	Wt.	Cypher.
232	2	6	15½	10⅛	8	2	2	80	Bedlem
247	2	6½	20	10¾	8	2	2	102	Belief
261	2½	7½	24	12	8¾	2½	3	145	Bergamot
381	3	4	10	8⅞	6¾	3	3	34	Bouquet
468	2½	6½	20	10¾	8	2½	2	100	Brose
673	3	7½	24	12	8¾	3	3	137	Camisade

CINDER NOTCHES

CLASS D

All Weights given are Approximate.

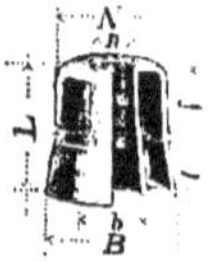

DESCRIPTION.

n—Inside diameter at nose.
b— " " " butt.
L—Length over all.
B—Outside diameter at butt.
A— " " " cooler bearing.
N— " " " nose.
C—Small " " nose contraction.
e—Length of nose contraction.
l— " " cooler bearing.
f— " projecting beyond cooler.

No.	n	b	L	B	A	N	C	c	l	f	Wt.	Cypher.
92	2¼	2½	6	6¼	5⅛	4½	1¾	1¾	3	3	18	Bacon
293	2	3	5	6	5¼	4½	2	2	2	3	12	Bittern
302	1½	2½	4¼	5 9/16	3 13/16	3⅝	1½	1¾	2¾	1½	10	Blea
528	2	2½	5	6	5¼	4½	2	2	2	3	13	Bungalow
575	2	3	5	6¼	5½	4½	2	2	2¼	2¾	14	Byzant
582	2⅝	4	5	7	6¼	5⅝	2¾	2¼	2	3	18	Cabbage
594	1¾	3	5	6	5¼	4½	2	2	2	3	12	Cache
718	2	3⅝	7	6 11/16	4 9/16	4½	2⅛	2⅜	6	1	18	Caponet

TUYERES.

Class A

SHORT.

All Weights given are Approximate.

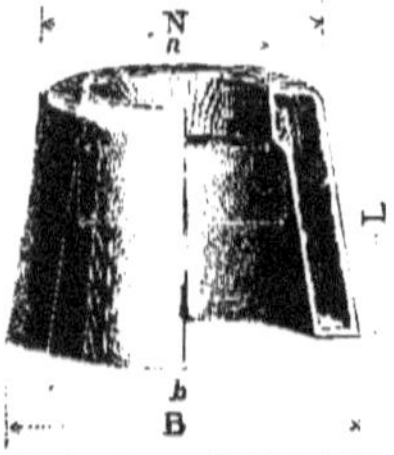

DESCRIPTION.

n—Inside diameter at nose.
c—Small " " " contraction.
e—Length of " "
d—Large " " " "
b—Inside " " butt.
B—Outside " " "
L—Length over all.
N—Outside diameter at nose.

FOR SMALL TUYERES.

No.	*n*	*c*	*e*	*d*	*b*	*B*	*L*	*N*	*Wt.*	*Cypher.*
83	10½	12	3	12⅜	15¼	20	14	16	206	Bablah
112	9⅞	10¾	3	12⅜	15¼	20	14	16	205	Baker
173	10½	12	3	15½	21	26	20	19	385	Barrow
240	10 11/16	11 1/16	3	..	15¼	20	19	14⅝	250	Beginner
406	10½	11¼	3	12⅜	15¼	20	14	16	208	Brasier
461	10⅞	11¼	2½	13½	16¼	20¼	17	17	225	Bronzist
579	9 5/16	9⅝	2½	10¼	12¾	17½	20	14½	237	Caballine

FOR LARGE TUYERES.

No.	*n*	*c*	*e*	*d*	*b*	*B*	*L*	*N*	*Wt.*	*Cypher.*
84	13 7/16	15	3	15½	21	26	20	19	380	Baboon
239	12	12½	2¾	13½	16¼	20¼	17	17	230	Beggar
351	12 9/16	13 9/16	3	14¾	18	22⅝	18	18½	304	Bonasus
470	13¼	14¾	3	15	18	22⅝	18	18½	287	Brougham
482	12	13	3½	13⅝	17½	22	21	17¼	338	Bryony
685	12	13⅛	3⅞	13⅞	16¼	20¼	17	17	238	Cancer
719	12 13/16	13 7/16	2¾	14¾	18	22⅝	18	18½	295	Capote

FOR MEDIUM TUYERES.

No.	*n*	*c*	*e*	*d*	*b*	*B*	*L*	*N*	*Wt.*	*Cypher.*
348	11 3/16	11 13/16	3	15¼	18⅞	23	20	18½	350	Bomb
375	11½	12⅛	3	..	12½	18	15	16	178	Bottom
699	11 3/16	12⅛	3	15¼	18⅞	23	20	18½	351	Cannon

COOLERS

CLASS A.

LONG.

All Weights given are Approximate.

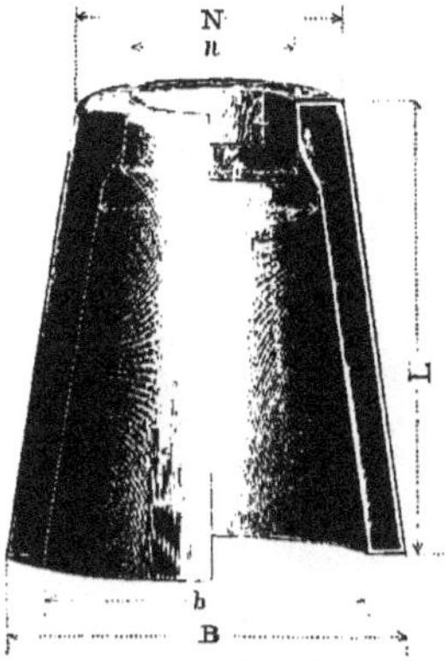

DESCRIPTION.

n—Inside diameter at nose.
c—Small " " " contraction.
e—Length of nose contraction.
d—Large diameter at nose contraction.
b—Inside diameter at butt.
B—Outside " " "
L—Length over all.
N—Outside diameter at nose.

FOR SMALL TUYERES.

No.	*n*	*c*	*e*	*d*	*b*	*B*	*L*	*N*	*Wt.*	*Cypher.*
32	10 5/8	11 1/4	2 3/4	12 3/4	20	24 1/2	26	16	410	Anvil
145	10 1/2	11 1/16	3	13 1/8	18	22 1/4	22	16 1/2	350	Bank
158	9	10 5/8	4 1/2	15 1/4	19	23 1/2	22	18 1/2	390	Barbecue
193	10 3/4	11 3/4	3	15 1/2	21 1/2	26 1/4	26 1/2	19	496	Bastion
322	10 5/8	11 5/8	3	11 7/8	19	23 1/2	35 1/2	16	549	Blush
354	10 1/8	11	2 7/8	12 3/4	20	24 1/2	26	16	418	Bonfire
393	10 3/8	10 13/16	3	13 1/8	18	22 1/4	22	16 1/2	331	Braid
431	9 13/16	10 3/4	3 1/2	13 1/8	17 1/2	21 3/4	22	16	316	Bridoom
463	10 13/16	12 1/8	2 1/4	12 3/4	20	24 1/2	26	16	403	Brook
512	10 1/8	10 3/4	2 3/4	12 3/4	20	24 1/2	26	16	433	Bullet
529	10 3/4	11 7/8	3 3/8	15 1/2	21 1/2	26 1/4	26 1/2	19	491	Bunker
621	10 1/2	12	3	15 1/4	19	23 1/2	22	18 1/2	380	Calamine
662	10	11	3	11 5/8	13 3/8	19	27	15	348	Calyptra
706	10 7/8	11 13/16	2 7/8	15 1/4	19	23 1/2	22	18 1/2	383	Canticle

FOR MEDIUM TUYERES.

No.	*n*	*c*	*e*	*d*	*b*	*B*	*L*	*N*	*Wt*	*Cypher.*
34	11 1/8	12 1/8	3	13 1/8	18	22 1/4	22	16 1/2	340	Apostate
65	11 7/8	12 1/2	3	15 1/2	22 3/8	27 1/4	30	19	535	Asp
102	11 9/16	12 3/16	3	15 1/2	21 1/2	26 1/4	26 1/2	19	490	Bagnet
125	11 3/16	12 1/8	3	15 1/2	21 1/2	26 1/4	26 1/2	19	500	Balsam
191	11	12	6	15 1/4	19	23 1/2	22	18 1/2	350	Bassoon
205	11 3/16	12 1/8	3	12 3/4	20	24 1/2	26	16	420	Baulk
233	11 9/16	12 3/16	3	15 1/2	22 3/8	27 1/4	30	19	515	Bench
273	11 7/8	12 1/2	3	15 1/2	21 1/2	26 1/4	26 1/2	19	490	Bidder
330	11 5/8	12 3/8	3 1/4	12 3/4	20	24 1/2	26	16	415	Boatswain
365	11 3/16	12 1/16	3	13 1/8	18	22 1/4	22	16 1/2	343	Border
394	11 3/16	12 1/8	3	15 1/2	22 3/8	27 1/4	30	19	525	Brake
397	11 1/16	11 7/8	3 3/8	15 1/2	21 1/2	26 1/4	26 1/2	19	520	Brancher
419	11 13/16	12 7/8	3 3/8	15	19	23 1/2	22	18 1/2	361	Bretzel
435	11 7/8	13	3 3/8	15 1/2	21 1/2	26 1/4	26 1/2	19	459	Brigantine
443	11 3/16	11 13/16	3	13 1/8	18	22 1/4	22	16 1/2	340	Bristle
448	11 5/8	12 1/2	3 1/8	13 1/8	18	22 1/4	22	16 1/2	343	Broacher
467	11 5/8	13	3 1/2	15 1/2	21 1/2	26 1/4	26 1/2	19	463	Brookweed
488	11 3/16	12 3/8	3 1/8	12 3/4	19 1/2	24	24	16	339	Buckler
518	11 3/8	12 1/8	3	15 1/4	19	23 1/2	22	18 1/2	380	Bultow
556	11 3/16	12	3 1/4	15 1/4	19	23 1/2	22	18 1/2	380	Bursar
568	11 7/16	12 9/16	3 1/2	...	17 1/2	21 3/4	24	16	360	Buttock
681	11 9/16	12 1/2	3 1/2	13 1/4	19	23 1/2	30	16 1/2	441	Canakin

COOLERS

Class A

LONG.

All Weights given are Approximate.

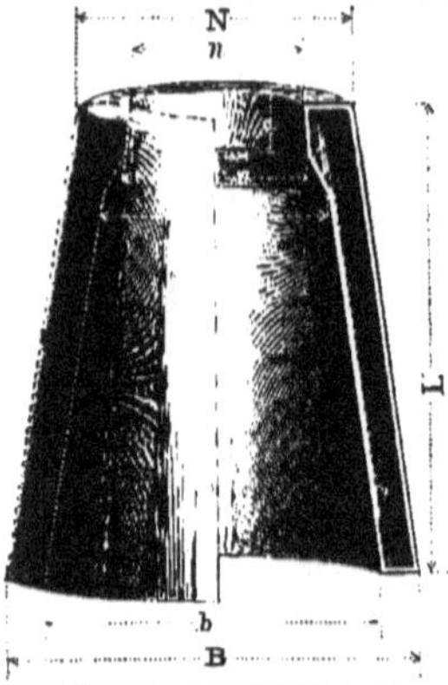

DESCRIPTION.

n—Inside diameter at nose.
c—Small " " " contraction.
e—Length of nose contraction.
d—Large diameter at nose contraction.
b—Inside diameter at butt.
B—Outside " " "
L—Length over all.
N—Outside diameter at nose.

FOR LARGE TUYERES.

No.	*n*	*c*	*e*	*d*	*b*	*B*	*L*	*N*	*Wt.*	*Cypher*
55	12 1/2	14 9/16	6	15 1/4	19	23 1/2	22	18 1/2	340	Apple
56	13	13 1/2	3	15 1/2	22 3/8	27 1/4	30	19	530	Apricot
164	12 9/16	13 5/16	3	15 1/2	22 3/8	27 1/4	30	19	531	Barley
284	12 13/16	13 13/16	2 3/4	15 1/2	21 1/2	26 1/4	26 1/2	19	470	Biped
291	12 9/16	13 5/16	3	15 1/2	21 1/2	26 1/4	26 1/2	19	490	Bistort
315	12 9/16	13 5/16	3	15 1/2	20 3/4	25 3/4	24	19	436	Bloomer
366	12 1/4	13	3	15 1/4	19	23 1/2	22	18 1/2	371	Boreas
380	12 13/16	13 7/16	3	13 5/8	19	24 5/8	26	18	420	Bounty
395	12	13	3 3/8	15 1/2	21 1/2	26 1/4	26 1/2	19	495	Bramble
426	12	13	3 3/8	15 1/2	22 3/8	27 1/4	30	19	553	Brick
473	12	13	3 1/2	13 1/4	19	23 1/2	30	16 3/4	445	Brucina
502	12 3/4	14 1/8	4 1/2	15 1/2	21 1/2	26 1/4	26 1/2	19	493	Bugloss
591	12	13	3 1/2	13 3/8	19 5/8	24 5/8	32	17 1/4	538	Caburn
610	15 5/8	17 5/8	6	18	25	34	30	24 3/4	755	Cahier
612	12 9/16	13 5/16	3	15 3/4	24	30	26 1/2	20 1/4	523	Caique

COOLERS.

CLASS B

All Weights given are Approximate

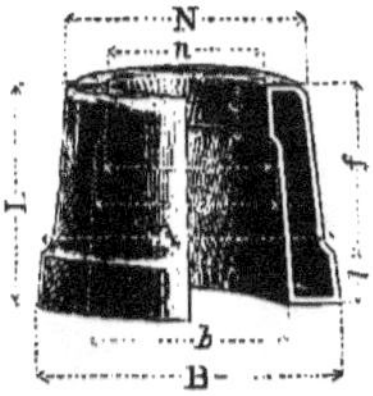

DESCRIPTION.

n—Inside diameter at nose.
c—Small " " contraction.
e—Length of " "
d—Large " "
p—Inside " butt.
B—Outside " "
L—Length over all.
A—Outside diameter at large bearing.
N— " " nose.
l—Length of outside bearing.
f— " projecting beyond large bearing.

FOR SMALL TUYERES.

No.	n	c	e	d	b	B	L	A	N	l	f	Wt.	Cypher.
258	9 11/16	10 1/2	3	11	12 3/4	18	12 1/2	17	14 1/2	3	9 1/2	150	Bengal
399	10 3/8	11 5/16	2 3/4	11 3/4	12 3/8	18	15	17	16	3	12	194	Brander

FOR MEDIUM TUYERES.

No.	n	c	e	d	b	B	L	A	N	l	f	Wt.	Cypher.
310	11 7/16	12 7/16	3	13 5/8	16 1/8	21 1/4	17 3/4	19 3/4	16 3/4	3	14 3/4	245	Bloater
476	11 1/2	11 3/4	3	...	12 3/8	18	15	17	16	3	12	195	Brunette
511	11 1/2	12 1/8	3	...	12 1/2	18	15	17	16	3	12	195	Bullary
530	11 1/4	12	3	12 1/4	13 3/8	19 1/2	18	17 7/8	16	3	15	215	Buntline

FOR LARGE TUYERES.

No.	n	c	e	d	b	B	L	A	N	l	f	Wt.	Cypher.
383	12 3/8	13 1/4	3 1/4	14 1/4	17 1/2	23 1/4	17 3/4	21 1/2	17 3/8	3 1/2	14 1/4	272	Bovate
436	12 13/16	13 9/16	3 1/4	...	15 7/8	21 1/4	15 1/4	19 7/8	17	3	12 1/4	224	Brill

COOLERS.

CLASS F

All Weights given are Approximate.

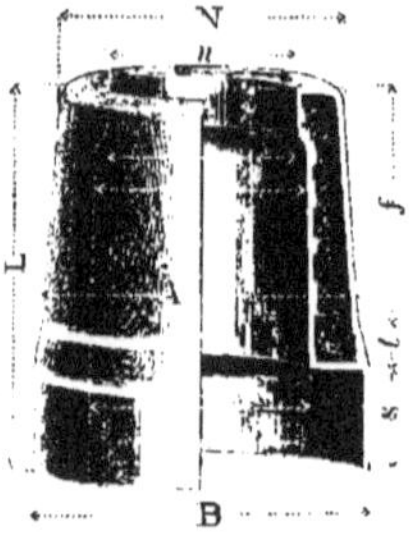

DESCRIPTION.

a—Inside diameter at nose.
c—Small " " " contraction.
e—Length of " "
d—Large " " " "
b—Inside " " butt.
B—Outside " " "
L—Length over all.
A—Outside diameter at large bearing.
N— " " " nose.
O— " " of sleeve.
S—Length of sleeve.
l— " " outside bearing.
f— " projecting beyond large bearing.

FOR SMALL TUYERES.

No.	*a*	*c*	*e*	*d*	*b*	*B*	*L*	*A*	*N*	*O*	*S*	*l*	*f*	*Wt.*	*Cypher.*
79	10 1/4	11 1/8	2 1/2	12 1/2	14 1/4	20	20	19 3/8	17	20	6 1/2	2 1/2	11	230	Baal

FOR MEDIUM TUYERES.

No.	*a*	*c*	*e*	*d*	*b*	*B*	*L*	*A*	*N*	*O*	*S*	*l*	*f*	*Wt*	*Cypher.*
53	11 7/16	12 3/8	2 1/2	12 5/8	14 1/4	20	22 1/2	19 1/2	16 1/2	20	6 1/2	2 1/2	13 1/2	280	Ape
215	11 5/8	12 1/2	3 1/8	13 1/8	17 1/2	23	22	22 3/4	16 1/2	23	2	3	17	320	Beacon

FOR LARGE TUYERES.

No.	*a*	*c*	*e*	*d*	*b*	*B*	*L*	*A*	*N*	*O*	*S*	*l*	*f*	*Wt.*	*Cypher.*

NOTCH COOLERS.

CLASS C.

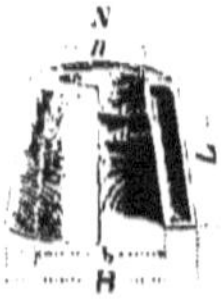

All Weights given are Approximate.

DESCRIPTION.

n—Inside diameter at nose.
c—Small " " " contraction.
e—Length of nose contraction.
d—Large diameter at nose contraction.
b—Inside diameter at butt.
B—Outside " " "
L—Length over all.
N—Outside diameter at nose.

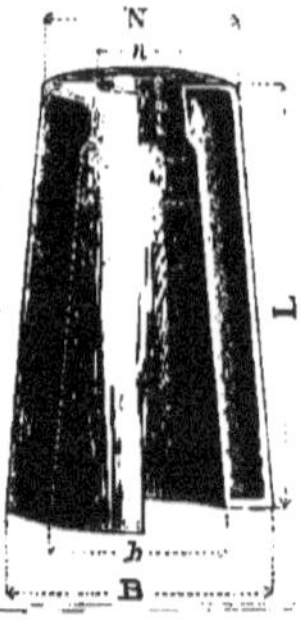

SHORT AND MEDIUM.

No.	n	c	e	d	b	B	L	N	Wt.	Cypher.
69	4	...	...	...	5 5/8	10 5/8	4 5/8	9	35	Auger
427	4 3/4	5 3/4	3	...	6 3/8	12	6	10	45	Brickbat
475	5	5 7/8	2 1/2	...	7 1/2	12	12	9	74	Brume
479	5 1/8	5 13/16	2 1/2	6 1/4	7 3/4	10 3/4	8 1/4	8 7/8	53	Brusher
500	5 1/4	6 1/8	2 7/8	6 3/8	7 1/2	12	9	9 7/8	60	Buggy
559	4 7/8	5 3/4	2 1/2	6 1/8	7 1/2	12	9	9 7/8	60	Bushel
589	4 3/4	5 7/8	3	...	6 3/16	12 3/4	4	11 1/4	43	Caboose
687	5 1/16	5 13/16	2	6 1/2	7 1/2	11 7/16	7	9 5/8	43	Canderos
694	5 3/4	6 3/8	4 1/2		6 5/8	12	6	10	43	Cane

LONG.

No.	n	c	e	d	b	B	L	N	Wt.	Cypher.
191	6 7/16	7 3/8	3	8	12	17	30	12	295	Bat
197	4 7/8	5 3/8	2 1/4	8	11 1/2	16 1/2	27	12	270	Batlet
198	5 9/16	6 1/8	2 1/2	8	11	16	24	12	230	Batman
254	5 1/4	6 3/16	3	7 1/2	10 3/4	15 3/8	25	10 1/2	192	Bencher
290	4 7/8	5 5/8	2 1/4	8	11	16	24	12	233	Bison
309	4 7/8	5 3/8	2 1/4	8	12	17	30	12	308	Blister
367	4 13/16	5 1/2	2 3/4	7 1/2	10 3/4	15 3/8	25	10 1/2	200	Borough
464	5 3/16	6 3/8	3	8	12	17	30	12	287	Brooklet
477	6 7/16	7 1/8	3	8	11	16	24	12	234	Brunion
503	6 5/8	7 1/8	3	8	11	16	24	12	235	Bulb
546	4 7/8	5 7/8	2 3/4	9 7/8	14	19	20	13	450	Burin
592	5 3/16	6 3/8	3	8	11	16	24	12	235	Cacoa
702	5 9/16	6 1/8	2 1/2	8	11 1/2	16 1/2	27	12	249	Canonist

NOTCH COOLERS.

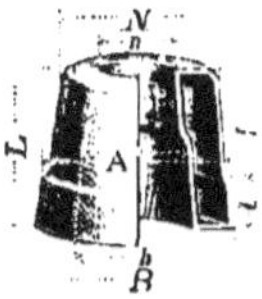

CLASS D.

All Weights given are Approximate.

DESCRIPTION.

n—Inside diameter at nose.
c—Small " " " contraction.
e—Length of nose contraction.
d—Large diameter at nose contraction.
b—Inside diameter at butt.
B—Outside " " "
L—Length over all.
A—Outside diameter at large bearing.
N—Outside diameter at nose.
l—Length of outside bearing.
f— " projecting beyond large bearing.

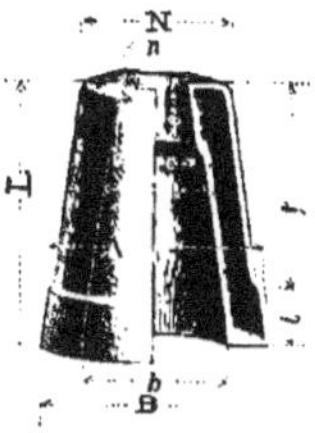

SHORT.

No.	*n*	*c*	*e*	*d*	*b*	*B*	*L*	*A*	*N*	*l*	*f*	*Wt.*	*Cypher.*
249	4½	5¾	3½	...	6⅞	11⅜	9	11	9¾	3	6	60	Bell
294	5 5/16	6	2	6½	7½	11	7	10	9	3	4	45	Blackball
323	4 13/16	5 9/16	2½	5⅞	6¼	11⅛	6	10 9/16	10	3⅛	2⅞	44	Bluster
347	5	5¾	2	6½	7½	11	7	10	9	3	4	46	Boltonite
379	5⅜	5¾	1	6	9	14¼	11	13	10¼	4	7	93	Boundary
384	6⅛	6⅝	3⅛	...	7	11	9	10	9½	3	6	52	Bowlder
459	5¼	6⅜	3	6⅝	7	11	9	10	9½	3	6	57	Brond
613	6⅛	7¼	3		8¼	12⅛	9	11⅛	10¼	3	6	63	Caird

NOTCH COOLERS.

CLASS D

All Weights given are Approximate.

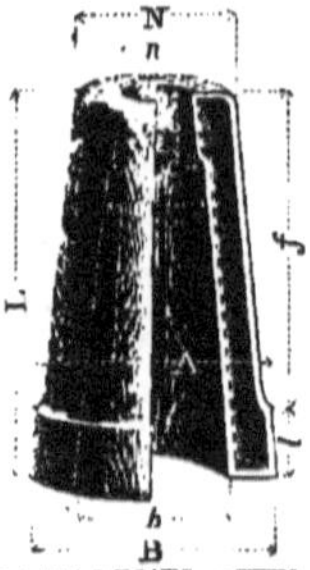

DESCRIPTION.

n — Inside diameter at nose.
r — Small " " nose contraction.
e — Length of " "
d — Large " " "
b — Inside " " butt.
B — Outside " " "
L — Length over all.
A — Outside diameter at large bearing.
N — " " " nose.
l — Length of outside bearing.
f — " projecting beyond large bearing.

NOTCH COOLERS, CLASS D LONG.

No.	*n*	*r*	*e*	*d*	*b*	*B*	*L*	*A*	*N*	*l*	*f*	*Wt.*	*Cypher.*
231	4¾	5 13/16	3⅛	7⅛	9	13¾	22	13¾	11	4	18	169	Beech
238	5⅛	6⅜	3½	...	9	13¾	32	12½	10½	7	25	240	Beetle
362	4⅞	5 9/16	2	6¼	9½	15¼	25	13¾	10	4	21	191	Booth
472	4⅞	5 9/16	2	5¾	9½	15¼	30	13¾	9½	4	26	207	Browse
527	4¾	5 9/16	2	6½	9	13½	24	12¾	10¼	4	20	170	Bundle
553	6	6¼	2½	7⅝	9	13¼	19	12½	10½	3½	15½	144	Burrel
555	6⅛	6⅝	3	7⅛	9	13¾	22	13¼	11	4	18	173	Burrow
558	6 1/16	6 9/16	3	...	9	13½	24	12¾	10¼	4	20	171	Busby

BOSH BOXES

CLASS A

FRONHEISERS'S PATENT.

Sept. 22, 1891.

All Weights given are Approximate.

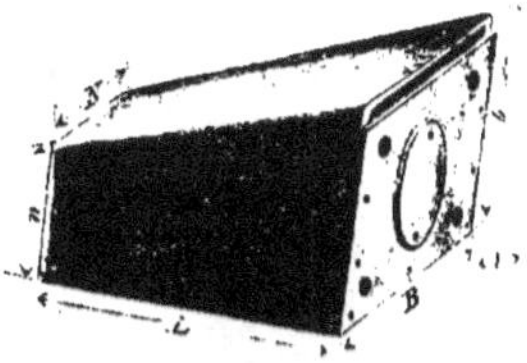

ESCRIPTION.

n—Height at nose.
N—Width " "
b—Height " butt.
B—Width " "
L—Length " base.
l—Batter of bosh wall.

BOSH BOXES, CLASS A.

No.	*n* x *N*	*b* x *B*	*L*	*l*	*Wt.*	*Cypher.*
38	10 x 15	15 x 20	22	3	168	Alpaca
221	10 x 13	14¼ x 16¼	18½	2¾	137	Bearer
222	14 x 14	17 x 17	16	...	150	Beast
266	11½ x 16¼	15 x 20	16	3	135	Beryl
267	12 x 14	14¼ x 16⅜	12	3	103	Beseiger
268	14½ x 14½	17 x 17	13½	...	127	Betuline
281	10 x 16	17 x 21	30	3½	228	Binder
373	9 x 10	11 x 12	10	1¾	76	Botch
396	10½ x 10½	15 x 13	18	2¼	104	Branch
432	10 x 10	15 x 13	21	2¼	109	Brief
509	9 x 10	11 x 12	16	2½	79	Bulchin
690	12¼ x 14	14½ x 16¼	12		82	Canditeer

BEST, FOX & CO.

BOSH BOXES.

CLASS B

FRONHEISER'S PATENT.

Sept. 22, 1891.

All Weights given are Approximate.

DESCRIPTION.

n—Short height at nose.
N—Width at nose.
h—Long height at nose.
b—Short " " butt.
B—Width at butt.
H—Long height at butt.
L—Length at base.
l—Batter of bosh wall.

BOSH BOXES, CLASS B.

No.	n x N	h	b x B	H	L	l	Wt.	Cypher.
704	10 x 15	16	15 x 20	22	22	3	174	Cantar

BOSH BOXES.
CLASS C
FRONHEISER'S PATENT.
Sept. 22, 1891.
All Weights given are Approximate.

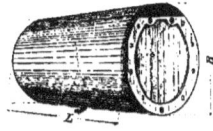

DESCRIPTION.

N—Diameter at nose.

B—Diameter at butt.

L—Length.

BOSH BOXES, CLASS C.

No.	N	B	L	Wt.	Cypher.
57	17	22	22	192	Apron
389	14	18	18	123	Bracelet
428	8¾	12	24	88	Bricole
515	12	16½	27	142	Bullion
540	13	16½	21	123	Burgeois

BEST, FOX & CO.

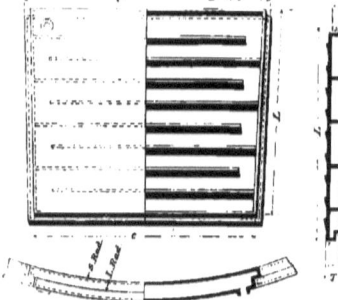

HEARTH AND BOSH JACKETS.

HUNT'S PATENT.

May 19, 1891.

All Weights g ven are
Approximate.

DESCRIPTION.

S Rad—Short radius.

L " —Long

C—Long chord.

c—Short

L.—Length.

T—Thickness.

HEARTH JACKET.

No.	S. Rad.	L. Rad.	C	c	L	T	Wt.	Cypher.
58	4 ft. 4 in.	4 ft. 4 in.	3 ft. 9 in.	3 ft. 6 in.	40	2¼	222	Arch

BOSH JACKET.

No.	S. Rad.	L. Rad.	C	c	L	T	Wt.	Cypher.
286	5 ft. 3 in.	5 ft. 6½ in.	2 ft. 8¾ in.	2 ft. 7¼ in.	2 ft. 1½ in.	2½	253	Birrus
287	5 ft. 6½ in.	5 ft. 9½ in.	2 ft. 8 in.	2 ft. 6½ in.	do	do	279	Biscotin
288	5 ft. 9½ in.	6 ft. ½ in.	2 ft. 7¾ in.	2 ft. 6 in.	do	do	300	Biscuit
289	6 ft. ¾ in.	6 ft. 3½ in.	2 ft. 6½ in.	2 ft. 5¾ in.	do	do	322	Bishop

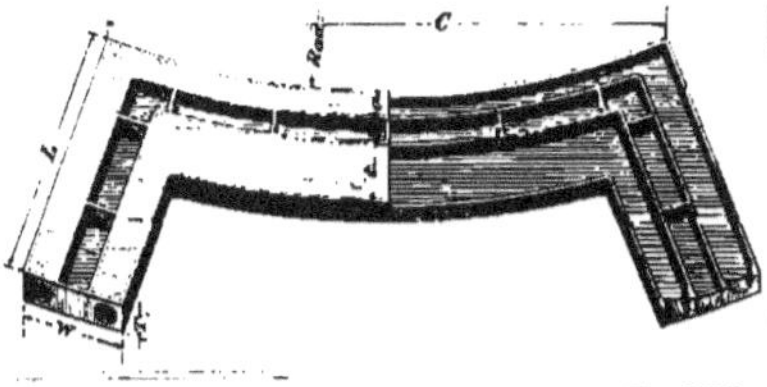

BOSH PLATES.

Class A

KENNEDY'S PATENT.

Feb. 25, 1888.

All Weights given are Approximate.

DESCRIPTION.

Rad—Radius of plate.
C—Chord.
L—Length of arm.
W—Width of arm.
T—Thickness.
a—Width of inner water course
b—Width of space between courses.
c—Width of outer water course.

KENNEDY'S PATENT.

No.	Rad.	C	L	W	T	a	b	c	Wt.	Cypher.
26	6 ft. 2 in.	4 ft. 8½ in.	27	8½	2¼	3½	2	6	300	Adz
27	6 ft. 9 in.	5 ft. 1 in.	29	8½	2¼	3½	2	6	327	Affix
28	7 ft. 3½ in.	5 ft. 6 in.	31½	8½	2¼	3½	2	6	400	Agate
153	6 ft. 9 in.	5 ft. 2 in.	27	8½	2¼	3½	2	6	327	Babtist
154	7 ft. 3½ in.	5 ft. 6 in.	27	8½	2¼	3½	2	6	347	Bar
274	5 ft. 11 in.	4 ft. 5 in.	25½	8½	2¼	3½	2	6	305	Bifer
275	6 ft. 4½ in.	4 ft. 8½ in.	25½	8½	2¼	3½	2	6	335	Biffin
276	6 ft. 10 in.	5 ft. 1 in.	25½	8½	2¼	3½	2	6	332	Bigamist
277	7 ft. 2 in.	5 ft. 4½ in.	25½	8½	2¼	3½	2	6	352	Bigot
278	7 ft. 7½ in.	5 ft. 8½ in.	25½	8½	2¼	3½	2	6	376	Bijou
279	8 ft. 1 in.	6 ft. 1 in.	25½	8½	2¼	3½	2	6	388	Bilalo
363	5 ft. 11 in.	4 ft. 0 in.	27	8½	2¼	3½	2	6	289	Boracite
400	5 ft. 10½ in.	2 ft. 0 in.	27	8½	2¼	3½	2¼	5¾	140	Brandrith
401	5 ft. 10½ in.	4 ft. 0 in.	27	8½	2¼	3½	2¼	5¾	275	Braulin
402	6 ft. 4 in.	4 ft. 8 in.	27	8½	2¼	3½	2¼	5¾	268	Brash
403	6 ft. 9½ in.	5 ft. 0 in.	27	8½	2¼	3½	2¼	5¾	274	Brassart
404	7 ft. 3 in.	5 ft. 5 in.	27	8½	2¼	3½	2¼	5¾	287	Bray
405	7 ft. 8½ in.	5 ft. 7 in.	27	8½	2¼	3½	2¼	5¾	314	Brayer
420	6 ft. 1 in.	4 ft. 6 in.	30	8½	2¼	3½	2¼	6¼	272	Brevet
421	5 ft. 8¾ in.	5 ft. 0 in.	30	8½	2¼	3½	2¼	6¼	294	Brevier
422	7 ft. 3½ in.	5 ft. 5½ in.	30	8½	2¼	3½	2¼	6¼	316	Breviped
423	7 ft. 10¼ in.	5 ft. 10½ in.	30	8½	2¼	3½	2¼	6¼	334	Brewer
462	5 ft. 10½ in.	2 ft. 6 in.	27	8½	2¼	3½	2½	6	177	Brooch
483	5 ft. 1½ in.	3 ft. 9½ in.	22	8½	2¼	3½	2¼	5¾	230	Bubble
484	5 ft. 7½ in.	4 ft. 2 in.	22	8½	2¼	3½	2¼	5¾	257	Buccan
485	6 ft. 1½ in.	4 ft. 6 in.	25	8½	2¼	3½	2¼	5¾	275	Buccaneer
486	6 ft. 7½ in.	4 ft. 11 in.	28	8½	2¼	3½	2¼	5¾	313	Bucket
721	7 ft. 8½ in.	5 ft. 0 in.	20	8½	2¼	3½	2	6	249	Capsicum

BEST, FOX & CO.

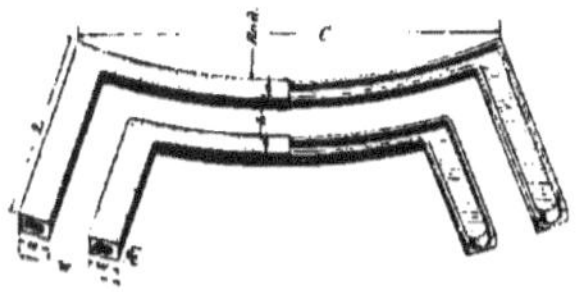

BOSH PLATES.

Class B

All Weights given are Approximate.

DESCRIPTION.

Rad—Radius of plate.
C—Chord.
L—Length of arm.
w—Width of each arm.
W—Width of two arms and space.
T—Thickness.
a—Width of water courses
b—Width of space between courses.

BOSH PLATES, CLASS B.

No.	*Rad.*	*C*	*L*	*w*	*W*	*T*	*a*	*b*	*Wt.*	*Cypher.*
521	7 ft. 0 in.	5 ft. 2 in.	22½	3½	12	2¼	3½	5	112	Bumboat
521A	7 ft. 8½ in.	4 ft. 4½ in.	14	3½	12	2¼	3½	5	84	
522	6 ft. 7 in.	4 ft. 11 in.	22½	3½	12	2¼	3½	5	110	Bumkin
522A	7 ft. 3½ in.	4 ft. 1¼ in.	14	3½	12	2¼	3½	5	83	
523	6 ft. 2¼ in.	4 ft. 7 in.	22½	3½	12	2¼	3½	5	110	Bummer
523A	6 ft. 10¾ in.	3 ft. 9¼ in.	14	3½	12	2¼	3½	5	77	
524	5 ft. 9¼ in.	4 ft. 3 in.	22½	3½	12	2¼	3½	5	106	Bump
524A	6 ft. 5½ in.	3 ft. 5½ in.	14	3½	12	2¼	3½	5	73	
525	5 ft. 4½ in.	3 ft. 4 in.	22½	3½	12	2¼	3½	5	91	Bumper
525A	6 ft. 1 in.	2 ft. 4¾ in.	14	3½	12	2¼	3½	5	57	
526	5 ft. 4½ in.	1 ft. 6 in	22½	3½		2¼	3½		64	Bunch

BEST, FOX & CO.

BOSH PLATES.

CLASS C

POLLOCK'S PATENT.

April 21, 1891.

All Weights given are Approximate.

DESCRIPTION.

Rad—Radius of plate.
C—Chord.
L—Length of arm.
B—Width of plate.
W—Width of arm.
T—Thickness.
a—Width of inner water course.
b—Width of outer water course.
c—Length of arm outside of water courses.

BOSH PLATES, CLASS C.

No.	Rad.	C	L	B	W	T	a	b	c	Wt.	Cypher.
151	5 ft. 9 in.	2 ft. 10 in.	18	13	12	3	5½	7½	5	179	Brodekin
152	6 ft. 4½ in.	4 ft. 8½ in.	18	13	12	3	5½	7½	5	279	Brogan
153	7 ft. 0 in.	5 ft. 2 in.	18	13	12	3	5½	7½	5	321	Broiler
154	7 ft. 9 in.	5 ft. 9½ in.	18	13	12	3	5½	7½	5	340	Broker
155	8 ft. 5 in.	6 ft. 3½ in.	18	13	12	3	5½	7½	5	375	Broma
156	9 ft. 0 in.	6 ft. 8½ in.	18	13	12	3	5½	7½	5	370	Bromate
157	9 ft. 7 in.	7 ft. 2 in.	18	13	12	3	5½	7½	5	435	Bromide
158	10 ft. 1½ in.	7 ft. 7 in.	18	13	12	3	5½	7½	5	450	Bromuret
625	5 ft. 10½ in.	4 ft. 3 in.	18	13	12	3	5½	7½	5	240	Calangay
626	5 ft. 3 in.	3 ft. 9 in.	18	13	12	3	5½	7½	5	212	Calash
627	5 ft. 3 in.	2 ft. 4 in.	18	13	12	3	5½	7½	5	146	Calcar

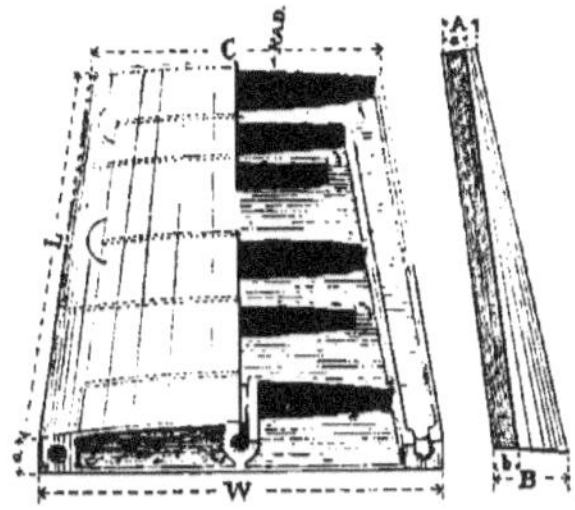

BOSH PLATES.

Class D

SCOTT'S PATENT.

May 19, 1891.

All Weights given are Approximate.

DESCRIPTION.

Rad—Radius of plate.
C—Chord.
L—Length.
a—Short height at nose.
A—Long height at nose.
b—Short height at butt.
B—Long height at butt.
W—Width outside.

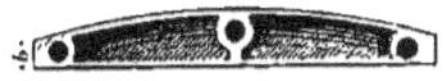

BOSH PLATES CLASS D.

No.	*Rad.*	*C*	*L*	*a*	*A*	*b*	*B*	*W*	*Wt.*	*Cypher.*
496	5 ft. 11 in.	1 ft. 4 3/8 in	31	2 1/4	3	2 1/4	4 1/4	27	222	Buffer
497	6 ft. 5 in.	1 ft. 6 1/4 in.	31	2 1/4	3 1/4	2 1/4	4 1/2	28 1/2	244	Buffeter
498	6 ft. 10 in.	1 ft. 8 in.	31	2 1/4	3 3/8	2 1/4	4 7/8	30 3/8	257	Buffin
499	7 ft. 3 1/2 in.	1 ft. 10 in	31	2 1/4	3 1/2	2 1/4	5 1/4	32 1/4	287	Buffoon
587	6 ft. 8 1/2 in.	1 ft. 6 in.	21	1 7/8	3	2 1/4	4	22 5/8	135	Cablet
588	7 ft. 10 1/4 in.	1 ft. 6 1/2 in.	21	1 7/8	3	2 1/4	4	22 5/8	142	Cabob
644	7 ft. 9 1/2 in.	2 ft. 0 in.	25	2 1/4	3 3/4	2 1/4	5 1/4	32 1/4	230	Caliver
645	7 ft. 2 in.	1 ft. 9 1/4 in.	27	2 1/4	3 1/2	2 1/4	4 7/8	30 3/8	221	Calker
648	6 ft. 7 in.	1 ft. 7 in.	29	2 1/4	3 1/4	2 1/4	4 1/2	28 1/2	217	Calliope
661	5 ft. 9 in.	1 ft. 7 in.	27	2 1/4	3 1/4	2 1/4	4 3/4	29	198	Calyon
663	5 ft. 4 1/2 in.	1 ft. 11 in.	18	2 1/4	3 3/4	2 1/4	4 3/4	29 1/2	153	Camaieu
666	5 ft. 4 1/2 in.	1 ft. 11 in.	22 1/2	2 1/4	3 3/4	2 1/4	5	30 5/8	196	Cambist
672	5 ft. 4 1/2 in.	1 ft. 11 in.	12	2 1/4	3 3/4	2 1/4	4 1/2	27 3/8	109	Camion
684	9 ft. 2 in.	3 ft. 5/8 in.	21	1 3/4	3 1/8	2	4	43 3/4	268	Canaster
703	6 ft. 9 1/2 in.	1 ft. 7 in.	22 1/2	2 1/4	3 7/16	2 1/4	4 3/4	27 3/4	168	Canopy
711	5 ft. 4 1/2 in.	1 ft. 11 in.	21	2 1/4	3 3/4	2 1/4	5	30 5/8	185	Canyon
712	6 ft. 6 in.	1 ft. 11 in.	18	2 1/4	3 3/4	2 1/2	4 3/4	28 1/4	156	Capelan
713	6 ft. 9 1/2 in.	1 ft. 7 in.	22 1/2	2 1/4	3 1/2	2 1/4	4 3/4	27 3/4	165	Capias
727	6 ft. 1 1/2 in.	1 ft. 4 7/8 in.	13 1/2	2 1/4	3 1/2	2 1/4	4	20	81	Capture

BEST, FOX & CO.

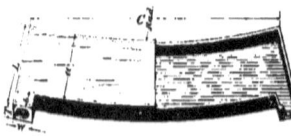

BOSH PLATES

CLASS E

All Weights given are Approximate.

DESCRIPTION.

$Rad.$—Radius of plate.
C—Chord.
L—Length of arm.
W—Width of arm.
T—Thickness.
a—Width of water course.
b—Length of arm outside of water course.

BOSH PLATES CLASS E.

No.	Rad.	C	L	W	T	a	b	Wt.	Cypher.
563	7 ft. 1 in.	3 ft. 4 in.	13	3	$2\frac{7}{8}$	11	2	158	Buster
564	7 ft. 9 in.	3 ft. 8½ in.	13	3	$2\frac{7}{8}$	11	2	173	Butcher
565	8 ft. 5 in.	4 ft. ... in.	13	3	$2\frac{7}{8}$	11	2	182	Butler
628	5 ft. 6 in.	1 ft. 8 in	13	3	$2\frac{1}{4}$	11	2	83	Calcimine
629	5 ft. 9 in.	3 ft. 10¼ in.	13	3	$2\frac{1}{4}$	11	2	154	Calculator
630	6 ft. 1 in.	4 ft. 1¼ in.	13	3	$2\frac{1}{4}$	11	2	160	Calculus
631	6 ft. 7 in.	4 ft. 6 in.	13	3	$2\frac{1}{4}$	11	2	185	Caldron
632	7 ft. 1½ in	4 ft. 11 in.	13	3	$2\frac{1}{4}$	11	2	199	Calender
633	7 ft. 7½ in	5 ft. 3½ in	13	3	$2\frac{1}{4}$	11	2	220	Calendula
634	9 ft. 2 in	4 ft. 2 in.	13	3	$2\frac{1}{8}$	11	2	182	Calenture
635	9 ft. 8 in	4 ft. 5 in.	13	3	$2\frac{5}{8}$	11	2	195	Calf
656	6 ft. 1½ in	2 ft. 6½ in.	12	...	$3\frac{1}{2}$	12	...	121	Calumet
667	4 ft. 7½ in.	1 ft. 9 in.	18	$3\frac{1}{4}$	$2\frac{1}{4}$	14	4	130	Cambric
671	7 ft. 6 in.	2 ft. 11 in.	18	$3\frac{1}{4}$	$2\frac{1}{4}$	16	2	175	Camera
696	4 ft. 7½ in.	2 ft. 9 in	18	$3\frac{1}{4}$	$2\frac{1}{4}$	14	4	163	Cannister
708	7 ft. 6 in.	2 ft. 11 in	40	6	$2\frac{1}{4}$	16	24	265	Canton
709	7 ft. 6 in.	2 ft. 11 in.	31	6	$2\frac{1}{4}$	16	15	224	Canvas
710	9 ft. 2 in.	4 ft. 2 in.	27	6	$2\frac{1}{8}$	11	16	241	Canvasser

BEST, FOX & CO.

BOSH PLATES

CLASS F.

All Weights given are Approximate.

DESCRIPTION.

Rad.—Radius of plate.
C—Chord.
L—Length of arm.
W—Width of arm.
T—Thickness.
a—Width of inner water course.
b—Width of outer water course.
c—Length of arm outside of water course.

BOSH PLATES. CLASS F.

No.	Rad.	C	L	W	T	a	b	c	Wt.	Cypher.
493	5 ft. 10½ in.	2 ft. 5 in.	27	6½	2¼	11½	11½	4	255	Budger
494	5 ft. 10½ in.	4 ft. 0 in.	27	6½	2¼	11½	11½	4	400	Budlet
541	6 ft. 6½ in.	2 ft. 5 in.	33	6½	2¼	11½	11½	10	280	Burgher
542	6 ft. 6½ in.	4 ft. 0 in.	33	6½	2¼	11½	11½	10	420	Burglar
616	5 ft. 10½ in.	2 ft. 3⅜ in.	27	6½	2¼	11½	11½	4	211	Cajeput
619	5 ft. 0 in.	1 ft. 4 in.	27	6½	2¼	11¼	11¼	4½	153	Calade
641	5 ft. 10½ in.	3 ft. 8½ in.	27	6½	2¼	11½	11½	4	341	Calipee

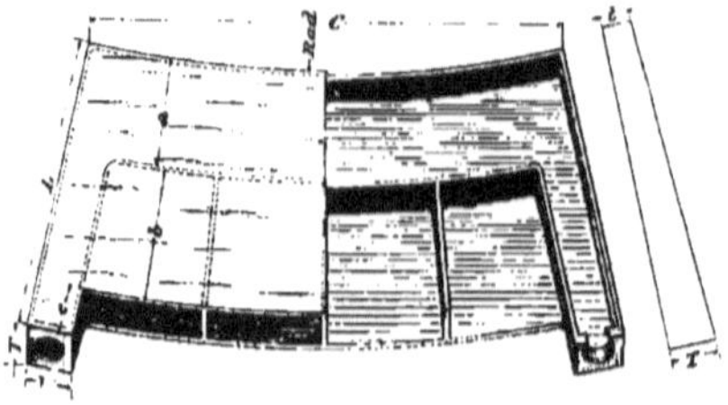

BOSH PLATES

CLASS G.

GAYLEY'S PATENT.

Nov. 24, 1891.

DESCRIPTION.

Rad—Radius of plate.
C—Chord.
L—Length of arm.
W—Width.
t—Thickness at nose.
T—Thickness at butt.
a—Width of inner water course.
b—Width of outer water course.
c—Length of arm outside of water course.

BOSH PLATES, CLASS G.

No.	*Rad.*	*C*	*L*	*W*	*t*	*T*	*a*	*b*	*c*	*Wt.*	*Cypher.*
495	6 ft. 6 in.	2 ft. 10 in.	27	2⅞	2½	4	10½	12½	4	265	Buffalo
531	7 ft. 7½ in.	3 ft. 4¼ in.	27	2⅞	2½	4	10½	12½	4	332	Bunyon
532	8 ft. 1½ in.	3 ft. 7⅛ in.	27	2⅞	2½	4	10½	12½	4	340	Buoy
571	7 ft. 1½ in.	2 ft. 11 in.	27	2⅞	2½	4	10½	12½	4	303	Buyer
572	9 ft. 1½ in.	4 ft. 2½ in.	27	2⅞	2½	4	10½	12½	4	383	Buzzard
577	4 ft. 8 in.	2 ft. 1⅛ in.	22	3	2½	4	10½	7	4	183	Cabalist
578	5 ft. 0 in.	2 ft. 3¼ in.	17½	3	2½	4	10½	2½	4½	133	Caballer
601	5 ft. 8¼ in.	2 ft. 3 in.	25½	3	2½	4¼	10½	10½	4⅛	215	Caddy
602	2 ft. 5 in.	2 ft. 4 in.	12	2½	2½	3	6⅝	5⅜	...	125	Cadet
603	2 ft. 5 in.	2 ft. 6 in.	12	2½	2½	3	6⅝	5⅜		125	Cadillac
604	3 ft. 6 in.	2 ft. 7 in.	12	2½	2½	3	6⅝	5⅜		105	Cadmia
605	3 ft. 6 in.	2 ft. 8 in.	12	2½	2½	3	6⅝	5⅜	...	119	Caduceus
608	5 ft. 7½ in.	2 ft. 5 in.	27	2⅞	2½	4	10½	12½	4	246	Cagit
617	6 ft. 4½ in.	2 ft. 6¼ in.	30	2⅞	2¼	4	13½	12½	4	282	Cajoler
668	4 ft. 10 in.	2 ft. 3⅝ in.	18	2⅞	3	4	10½	5½	2	172	Camel
669	5 ft. 4 in.	2 ft. 6½ in.	18	2⅞	3	4	10½	5½	2	179	Cameleopard
670	5 ft. 11 in.	2 ft. 11 in.	18	2⅞	3	4	10½	5½	2	200	Cameo
679	6 ft. 0 in.	2 ft. 1 in.	27	2⅞	2½	4	10½	12½	4	238	Camphene
729	6 ft. 4½ in.	2 ft. 6¼ in.	26	2⅞	2¼	4	13½	12½	...	285	Caracal

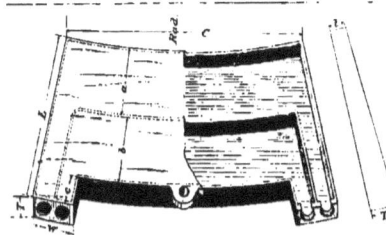

BOSH PLATES

CLASS H.

GAYLEY'S PATENT.

May 24, 1891.

DESCRIPTION.

Rad.,--Radius of plate.
C—Chord.
L—Length of arm.
W—Width of arm.
T—Thickness.
a—Width of inner water course.
b—Width of outer water course.
c—Length of arm outside of water course.

BOSH PLATES, CLASS H.

No.	Rad.	C	L	W	t	T	a	b	c	Wt.	Cypher.
543	7 ft. 0 in.	3 ft. 0 in.	27	6½	2½	4	19½	12½	4	353	Burgonet

86   BEST, FOX & CO.

BEST, FOX & CO.

BEST, FOX & CO.

VALVE SEATS.

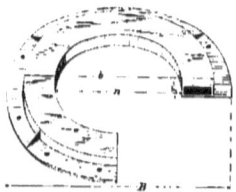
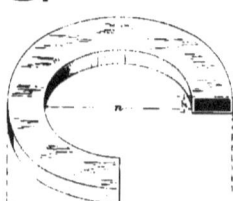

DESCRIPTION.

a—Inside diameter.
b—Outside diameter water space.
B—Outside diameter over all.
T—Thickness.

VALVE SEATS.

CLASS A.						CLASS B.				
No.	*a*	*b*	*B*	*T*	*Wt.*	*Cypher.*	*No.*	*a*	*B*	*T*	*Wt.*	*Cypher.*
39	30	40½	47	2½	326	Alter	137	30	47	2½	345	Bandoleer
81	24	36⅜	43	2¼	335	Babe	199	26	43	2½	329	Batter
93	26	37	43	2½	285	Bacule	487	24	49⅜	3	592	Buckeye
300	24	44	50½	3⅜	606	Blanket						
680	15	21	36	2⅞	235	Camphor						

VALVE SEATS.

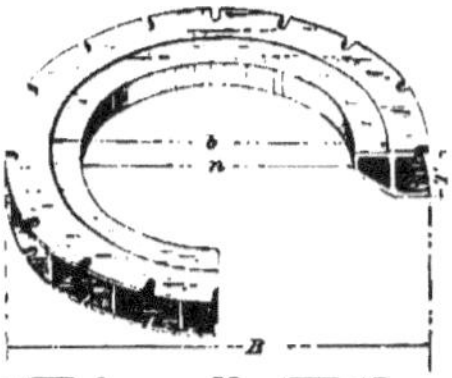

Berg's Patent.

DESCRIPTION.

n—Inside diameter.

b—Outside diameter of water space.

B—Outside diameter over all.

T—Thickness.

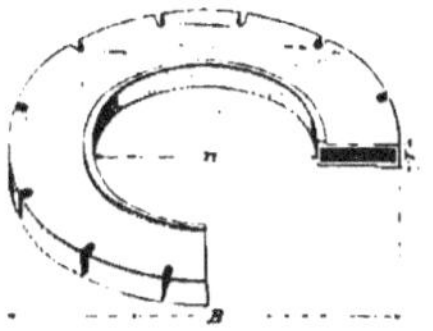

VALVE SEATS.

CLASS C.

No.	*n*	*b*	*B*	*T*	*Wt.*	*Cypher.*
66	26	33¼	40½	4¼	495	Atlas
200	30	37½	44½	4¼	485	Battle
228	30	36	42	5½	430	Beck
229	24	29½	37½	5½	382	Becket
329	18	25	32½	4¼	350	Boatman
437	24	33	40	4	460	Brilliant
492	24	31½	38¼	4¼	400	Budge
580	24	32½	40	4⅝	492	Cabaret
618	30	35½	43	4¼	483	Calabash
620	22	31½	36	4⅛	403	Calamar
624	24	32	40	4⅜	441	Calandra
720	28	33¼	41	4¼	387	Caprifole
724	30	37½	44½	4½	456	Captain

CLASS D.

No.	*n*	*B*	*T*	*Wt.*	*Cypher.*
490	22	39	3	304	Buckskin

BEST. FOX & CO.

VALVE SEATS.

DESCRIPTION.

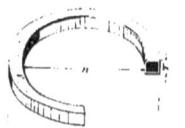

n —Inside diameter.
b —Outside diameter of water space.
B —Outside diameter over all.
T —Thickness.

VALVE SEATS.

CLASS E.						CLASS F.					
No.	*n*	*B*	*T*	*Wt.*	*Cypher.*	No.	*n*	*b*	*B*	*T*	*Wt.*	*Cypher.*
388	24	30	3	154	Boyuna	112	18¾	24¼	27½	2⅝	112	Breccia
438	36	42	3	216	Brimmer	414	37	44	47½	3½	269	Brehou

VALVE SEATS.

DESCRIPTION.

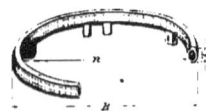

u—Inside diameter.
b—Outside diameter of water space.
B—Outside diameter over all.
T—Thickness.

VALVE SEATS.

CLASS G.

No.	u	B	T	Wt.	Cypher.
418	22	27	$2\frac{1}{2}$	85	Brettice
424	24	28	$2\frac{1}{2}$	100	Brewis
597	30	$34\frac{1}{8}$	$2\frac{3}{8}$	82	Cachunde

VALVES.

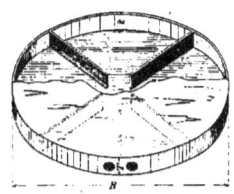

DESCRIPTION.

B—Outside diameter.

T—Thickness large end.

t—Thickness small end.

VALVES.

CLASS A.

No.	B	T	t	Wt.	Cypher.
413	20¼	3½	3	135	Breeder
415	38¾	4⅜	4	502	Brennage
533	23	3¼	2⅞	165	Burbot

BEST, FOX & CO.

VALVES.

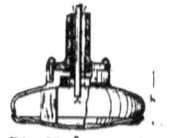

DESCRIPTION.

B—Outside diameter.

T—Thickness large end.

t—Thickness small end.

VALVES.

CLASS B.

No.	B	T	t	Wt.	Cypher.
705	24½	9		292	Canteen

Several cooling devices are numbered but not illustrated, as will be seen by referring to numerical index.

Special cooling devices made to order.

BEST, FOX & CO.

BEST, FOX & CO.

KENNEDY'S PATENT BOSH PLATE.

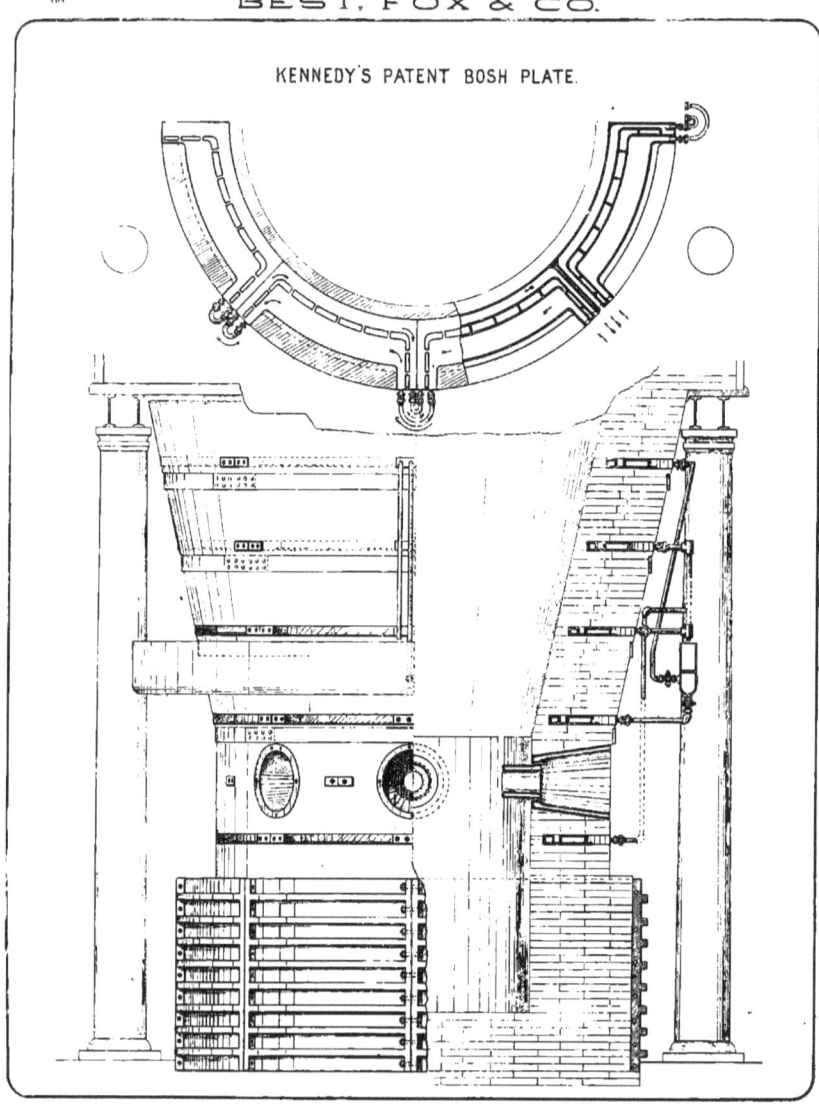

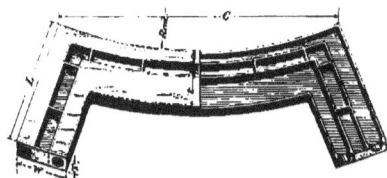

KENNEDY'S
PATENT
BOSH-PLATE.

Owing to iron pipe in old style of Bosh-plate corroding and choking up, a pipe made of copper was bent and cast in iron Bosh-plate with satisfactory results. When furnace was blown out metal was entirely gone and copper pipe found hanging down inside of furnace, proving this or its equivalent was the proper material to make Bosh-plates of, and from this experiment the above style of plate was designed.

The advantages obtained are : No corrosion, wide water-ways giving effective cooling, and with long arms at ends of plate. Tilting of plate is avoided. The double water way gives opportunity of using the outside course in case the inner one is destroyed, and with this hold the lines intact. Plates can be made with single or triple water ways, also with arm on one end only.

This was the first Bosh-plate made of climax bronze in 1886 and was put in

The Lucy Furnaces, Pittsburg, Pa.,   2 Furnaces.

EdgarThomson "   Bessemer, "   8   "

Isabella   "   Pittsburg, "   2   "

Joliet Steel Co., Joliet, Ills.,   2   "

Maryland Steel Co., Sparrows Point, Md., 4   "

Monongahela Furnaces, McKeesport, Pa., 2   "

Palmer Ship Building Co., Jarrow, Eng.

Bristol Iron & Steel Co., Bristol, Tenn.

BEST, FOX & CO.

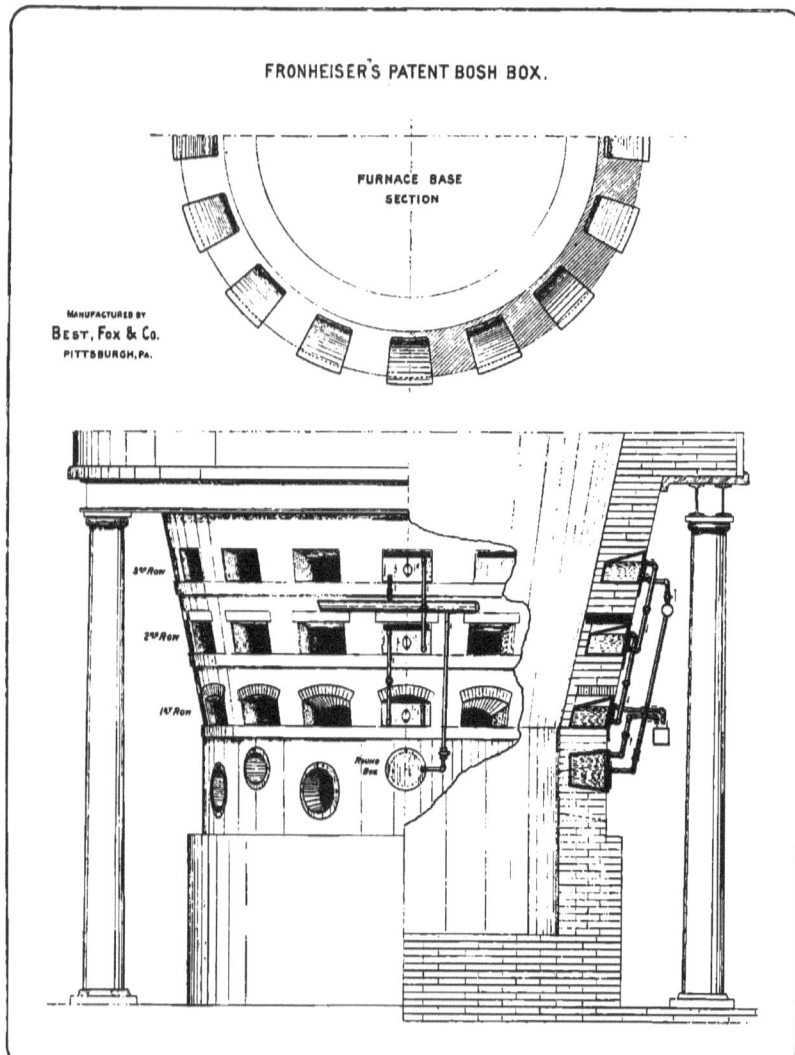

FRONHEISER'S PATENT BOSH BOX.

FURNACE BASE
SECTION

MANUFACTURED BY
BEST, FOX & CO.
PITTSBURGH, PA.

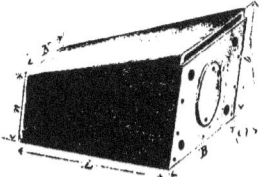

FRONHEISER'S
PATENT B.OSH-BOX.

Advantages of Cooling Bosh by Use of Patented Bosh Boxes.

1. Positive and easy detection of leaks, as the water is not under pressure but overflows, and the back of the box being open at the top, STEAM AND GAS WILL DEVELOP at this point in case of leak.

2. EASY REMOVAL WHEN NECESSARY, as the box is made tapering on sides and top for this purpose. Round boxes tapered same as Tuyeres, or square boxes with arch top are also made for this purpose. (See page 44.)

3. ECONOMY in the USE of WATER, as the capacity of a 1½ inch pipe is sufficient to supply a tier of six (6) or eight (8) boxes, the water overflows from upper box to one below, and this in turn to next, until bottom is reached.

4. ACTUAL EXPERIENCE has proven that original bosh lines are held intact by the use of these boxes. A continuous blast of FOUR YEARS, with a production exceeding 300,000 tons, have been made, with no serious slipping or irregular working, and a low fuel consumption no greater the FOURTH YEAR than the FIRST ; the blast being brought to a close by the inwall of the furnace, giving away to ft. above the bosh, the hearth and bosh being but a few inches larger than when the furnace was first blown in.

5. The saving in fuel for one year will pay for a set of boxes, and their use makes the bosh practically indestructible. Owing to the large amount of water they contain, they cannot be destroyed by a stoppage of water of more than three times the length of time that would destroy any other device in use, allowing ample time to correct the trouble. If for any reason the furnace has to be relined, the boxes can be reset and used time after time.

6. By means of a hand hole plate, which can readily be removed, the inside of box can be reached and thoroughly cleaned.

7. The LARGE VOLUME of WATER has a COOLING EFFECT not obtained by the water circulating through pipe or small space. Any portion of the bosh can be cooled more or less at will.

8. The thickness of bosh walls can be materially reduced by the use of these boxes. Several 18 ft. furnaces have reduced their walls from 27 in. to 21 in., thereby making a material reduction in the original cost of brick and bronze work, and an INCREASED OUTPUT, owing to a foot large diameter in the hearth and bosh without shortening the life of the furnace.

9. The actual cost of a set of bronze bosh boxes is but a trifle over the cost of IRON PLATES or PIPES, allowance for scrap taken into consideration, not considering the increased life of bronze over iron.

Yours truly,

JOHNSTOWN, PA.   J. J. FRONHEISER.

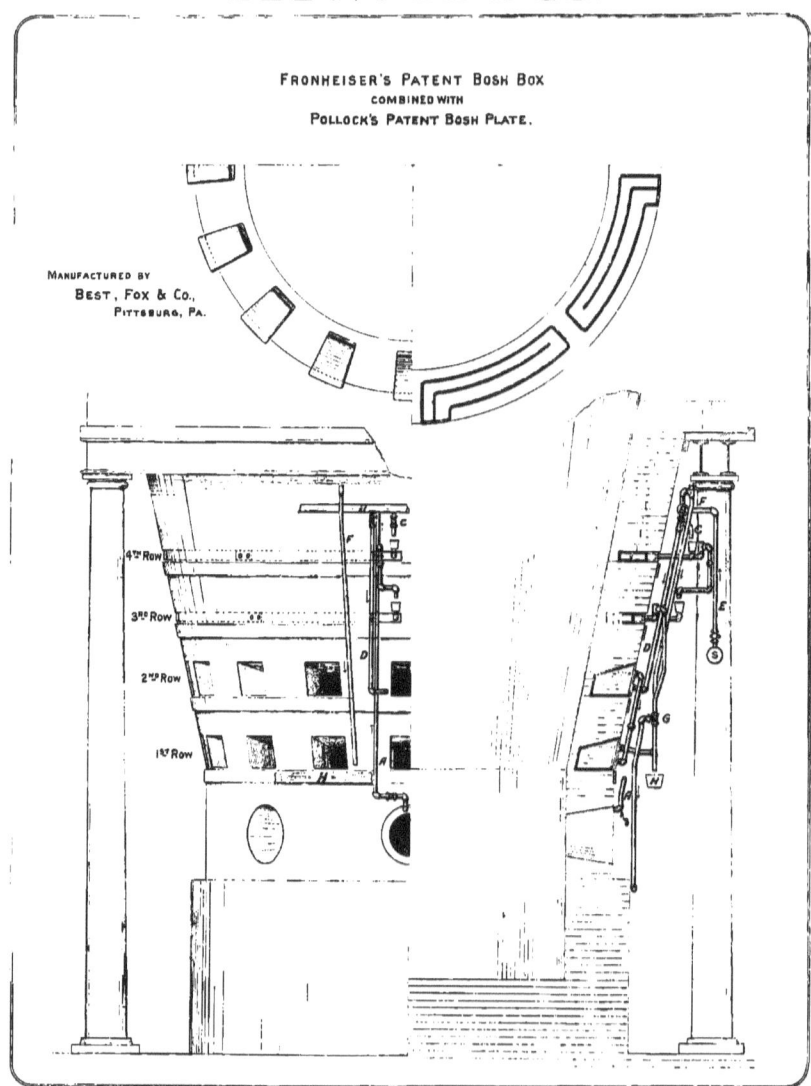

FRONHEISER'S PATENT BOSH BOX
COMBINED WITH
POLLOCK'S PATENT BOSH PLATE.

MANUFACTURED BY
BEST, FOX & CO.,
PITTSBURG, PA.

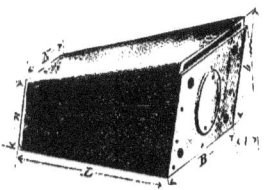

EFFECTIVE BOSH COOLING

OBTAINED BY USING

Waste Water from Tuyere Coolers.

On the opposite side is shown a combination of Bosh Box and Plate Cooling with water NOT under pressure.

Particular attention is called to the system of piping shown, which admits of complete Bosh Cooling (with either Fronheiser Box or Pollock's Plate or both,) without requiring additional water; thereby SAVING STEAM, PUMPS AND PIPING. Where water is scarce this system is of special advantage.

The supply is obtained by utilizing discharge water from Tuyere Coolers. The temperature of the water is but slightly increased after having passed through the Cooler.

The Piping system, as illustrated, is as follows:

A is the discharge pipe from Tuyere Cooler and is connected with circular supply pipe B which is located near the mantel or above Plates or Boxes that are to be fed from it. A cock is placed on the discharge next to Cooler, so as to prevent water from coming back when Cooler requires replacing. If a Three-way Cock is used at this point and connected as shown in Figure F 35, page 96, the volume and temperature of the water can be obtained in an instant. Elevating the discharge from Cooler to circular pipe B will create additional back pressure on the Cooler, but if the bottom of the tank is ten feet higher than the mantel, this back pressure will not be a detriment to the Cooler, as ample circulation is secured. Circular pipe B therefore acts as a receiver for the discharge from Coolers, and at the same time a "head" is obtained for feeding the Cooling devices beneath it. Openings C and D are tapped into pipe B and are used for supply to the Plates and Boxes as shown. The overflow from the first Plate or Box drops into the next beneath it, which in turn overflows and acts as a feed to the one beneath it. The water then overflows into trough H; or by using Three-way Cock G, this waste water, after having done DOUBLE DUTY, can be used for the third time, to spray the hearth jacket as shown.

In case of an accident causing the loss of several Tuyere Coolers at once, and thus greatly reducing the supply to B, sufficient WATER IS OBTAINED through pipe E (which is connected to main circular supply pipe S) by opening cock on this line until the Coolers are replaced.

If the furnace should be working cold, assistance can be given by choking down cocks on feed pipes C and D and allowing water to remain at boiling point in Boxes or Plates.

The question may be asked: Does not this choking down increase back pressure on Coolers to such an extent that there is danger of burning them? Such would be the result if provision for removing this excess pressure from circular pipe B was not provided for, through overflow pipe F, which conveys the excess water from B to waste trough H.

AMPLE PROVISION therefore is provided for all emergencies; making the entire system as reliable and safe as though the supply was obtained from tank pressure direct.

This system of piping has been in satisfactory use for years at several furnaces in various sections of the country.

We have experienced men to do this work and guarantee satisfaction in every particular.

BEST, FOX & CO.

POLLOCK'S PATENT BOSH PLATE.

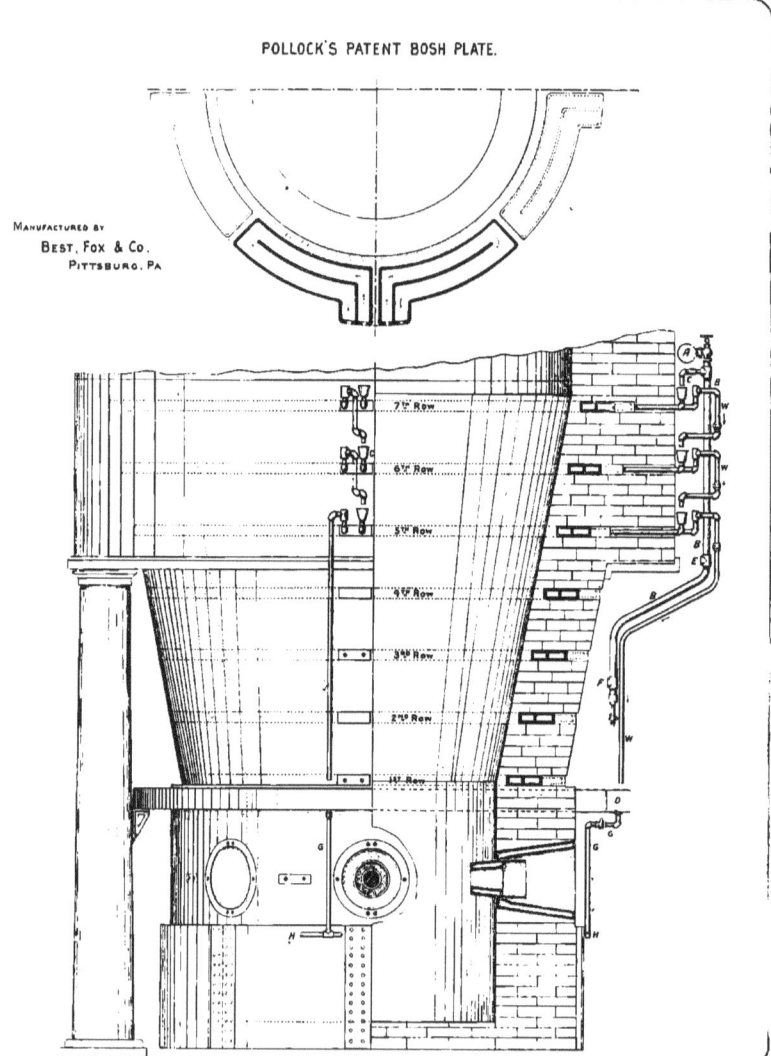

Manufactured by
BEST, FOX & CO.
PITTSBURG, PA

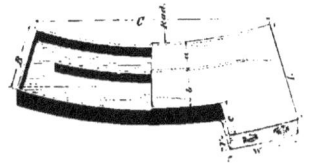

POLLOCK'S PATENT

BOSH PLATE.

My Bosh Plate is a hollow bronze casting with inlet and outlet openings on one end. A partition, as shown, divides the water space, contracting the inner course so as to produce rapid circulation where most needed. The principal advantage derived in connection with my plate is, the method of feeding the water to, and taking it from the plate, with practically no pressure on same, insuring *positively* no water getting into furnace even if the plate so connected should leak. *My patent covers this method of feeding any plate.*

This I accomplish as follows: Water is taken from circular supply pipe A and in place of connecting up solid with plate, the water is allowed to drip into funnel C, elevated above inlet opening 12 inches, as shown. Discharge from plate is carried up 8 inches to tee, open on top, and side opening W is used to convey water to next plate below, and in this manner three or more plates can be supplied from one supply opening, and all without being under pressure.

If any plate should leak it is at once detected by steam and gas coming out of funnel or top of tee, owing to pressure of blast in furnace. To wash out the plate, pressure hose is forced into the funnel and the rapid circulation carries off all sediment. To facilitate piping from circular supply pipe A, a pipe B, with valve next to A is carried down, from which the three upper rows are supplied from first opening, 4th and 3d rows are supplied, from opening E, and 2 lower rows from opening F, with cock on bottom to wash out each drop pipe B.

Water in waste through D can be further used to spray jacket through pipes G and H.

Perfect cooling with least amount of water and the impossibility of any water to get into the furnace is positively obtained with the use of my plate and connections.

Yours truly,

YOUNGSTOWN, O.

T. M. POLLOCK.

BEST, FOX & CO.

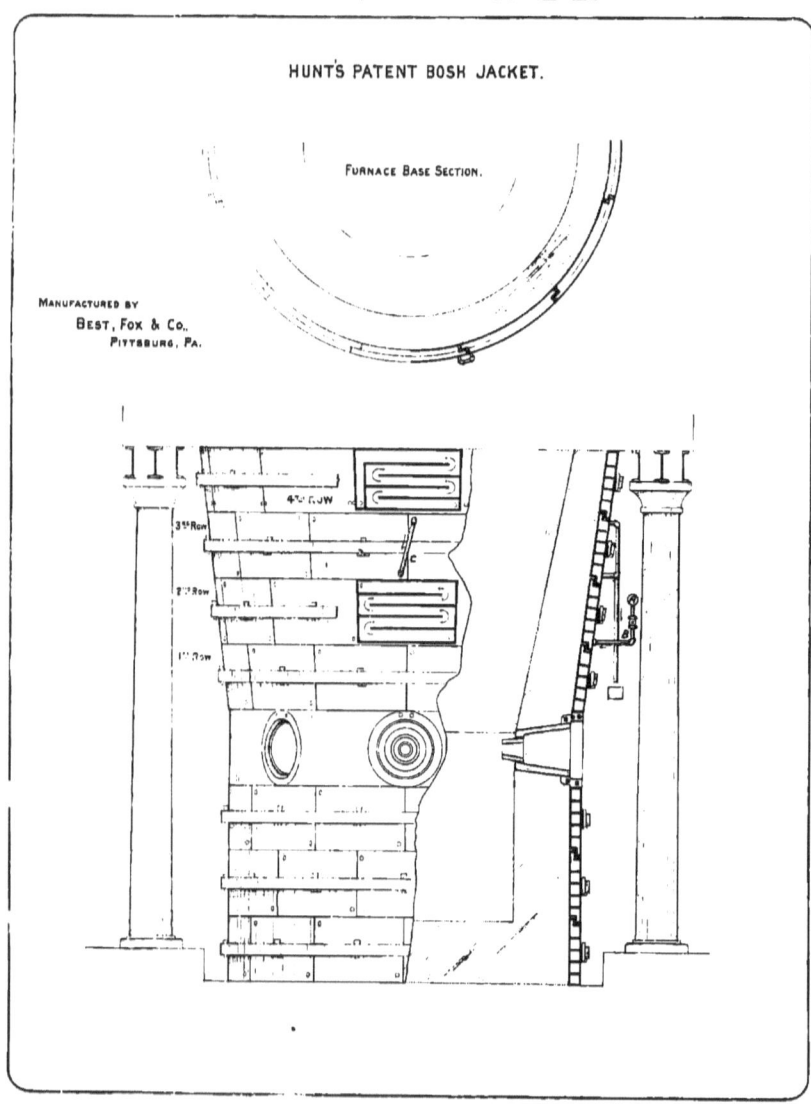

HUNT'S PATENT BOSH JACKET.

FURNACE BASE SECTION.

MANUFACTURED BY
BEST, FOX & Co.,
PITTSBURG, PA.

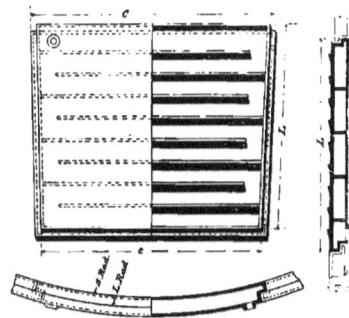

HUNT'S PATENT BOSH PLATE.

The accompanying illustration shows my improved design of cooling plate applicable to both bosh and crucible, although more particularly intended for boshes of furnaces, for effectually protecting and cooling the same. One of the principal objections to building *circular plates* in the brick work of the bosh, at regular distances apart vertically, is, that the spaces between these plates, not being subjected to or protected by the cooling influences, are *gradually cut away*, owing to intense heat, *forming ledges* or projections into the furnace. These irregular surfaces or series of scaffolds *prevent* the regular and uniform descent of the stock, and thereby cause irregular working of the furnace with increased consumption of fuel. Bosh walls cut away sooner or later, and any device is objectionable which prevents their wearing away uniformly. My device admits of the building in of the *minimum* amount of *brick work* inside of plates, and the inner wall is gradually and *uniformly* worn away until further wearing or widening of this portion of the furnace is prevented by the cooling effects of these plates. In fact, the plates can be so arranged as to *preserve any given angle* or lines desired.

One of the most effectual outside cooling devices heretofore known is a steel jacket, which, being double riveted, forms a water-tight shell around the bosh and is cooled by a system of sprays, with a water trough at the bottom for collecting the water which flows over its surface. This device is ordinarily ½ to ¾-in. thick and its cooling is dependent upon the amount of water from the sprays, which flow by gravity down its exterior. Hence it cannot be effectually cooled, as steam is formed by the water coming in contact with the hot plate, which prevents a close contact of cold water with it. *All the difficulties* above mentioned *are avoided* with the use of my plate, which is ordinarily constructed, as shown, in sections of rows 1, 2 and 3, in which water enters at lower right hand corner and passing through the tortuous passages as indicated leaves the plate at outlet in upper left hand corner. Sections shown in row 4 have inlet and outlet at bottom to avoid making connections behind mantel.

The entire jacket can be placed on the outside of the brick work of the furnace when completed, or the plates can be erected and firmly banded and keyed and the masonry built inside of same, which latter form is preferred. The object of the interlocking projections top, bottom and sides is to make the *jacket* practically *continuous throughout*, horizontally and vertically, and as strong as a ½ in. to ¾ in. steel jacket. By a luting of fire clay and asbestos, placed on the face of these projections, a *positive* gas and water tight jacket is secured. By constructing the bands which surround the plates of such circumference as to engage the lugs, the keys (which are shown in half section,) may be readily removed and one or more plates can be quickly removed and replaced, should occasion require, and that without affecting the remaining support afforded by any band. Thus no portion of the entire bosh is weakened except the point where the plates are taken out. That this arrangement admits of the *renewal* of a destroyed plate and the replacing of a new one, in a *very short time*, is apparent: and I know of no other outside cooling device which will admit of this.

Water connections for these plates can be connected singly or in series of any number, as desired. The two bottom rows that are subjected to the greatest heat can be supplied with separate feeds and discharges if necessary. Lugs, as constructed on the inside of plates for the purpose of intercepting and holding the kish, or graphitic coating mixed with slag, which is deposited on the walls, after the brick work has been worn away, and the furnace can be run on this lining. This device is also particularly adapted to the many copper and lead -melting furnaces which require perfect water cooling plates.

Yours respectfully,

M. R. HUNT.

Ashland, Wis.

BEST, FOX & CO.

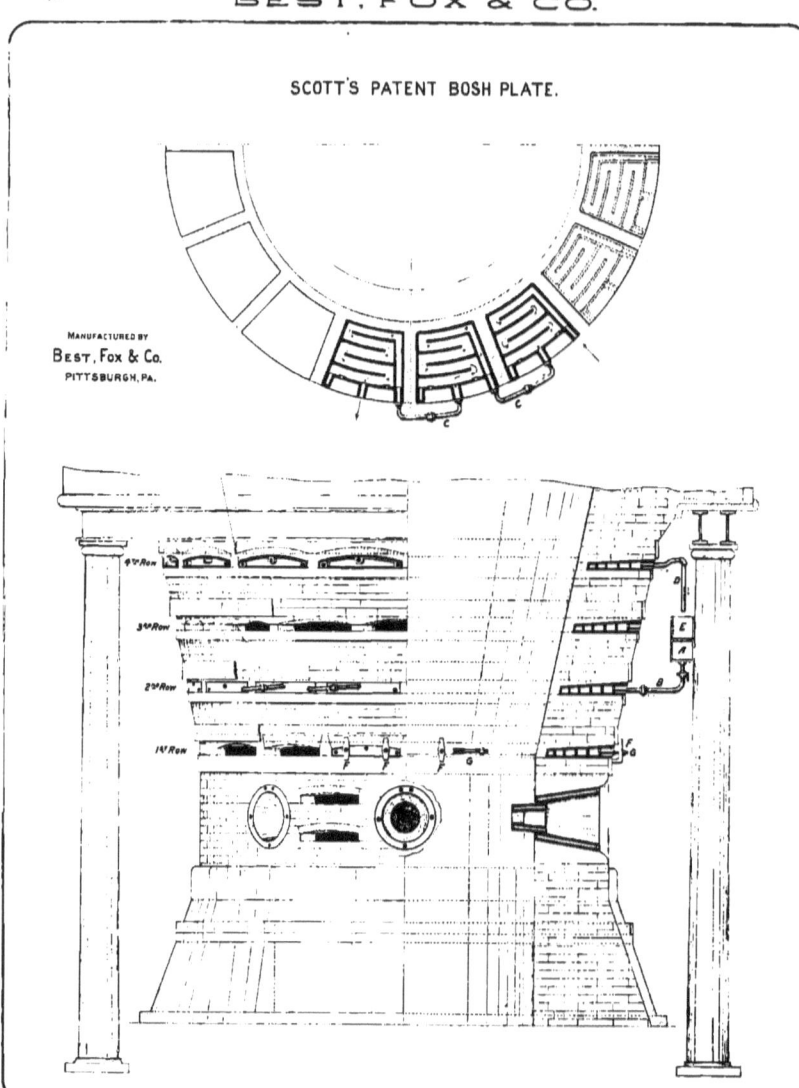

SCOTT'S PATENT BOSH PLATE.

Manufactured by
Best, Fox & Co.
PITTSBURGH, PA.

SCOTT'S PATENT BOSH PLATE.

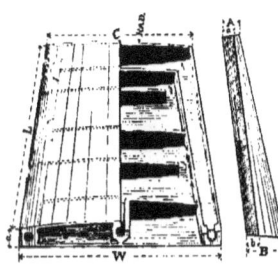

THE principal objection offered to bronze plates as made heretofore has been their **cracking or breaking** at point where arms connect with main body of plate, and owing to their size and **difficulty to remove** a plate when necessary. I overcome both objections by making plate smaller with no arms and **constructed tapering** so as to allow ready removal when necessary. This is accomplished by setting clamp bar "F" against furnace, attaching bolt "G" to plate and by turning same, plate is loosened, and readily removed. No more time is required to **change a plate** than that consumed in **changing a Tuyere.** By this means practically no time is lost, no bronze is destroyed and original lines held intact by insertion of new plate. Furnace working irregular, also irregular in product owing to water getting in same, is entirely avoided by removing leaky plate readily **without detriment** to masonry of furnace. Thorough circulation is produced by means of webs as shown. Two, three or four plates can be connected together without detriment to plate serving purpose intended. I prefer using arched plate with brick-work as shown in rows 1 and 4, as weight of bosh is not resting directly on plate. Brick-work, however, can be arranged as shown in row 3, and where objection is offered to arch plate, flat top plate as shown in row 2 can be used and also readily removed, owing to its taper on top and sides. Recesses for receiving plate should be somewhat larger than plate and intervening space lined with clay. Setting plates in this manner admits furnace to **expand and contract freely** without crushing plate and causing them to leak. For the purpose of strengthening bosh, I place bands so as to encircle arches and below bosh plates as shown.

Yours respectfully,

JAMES SCOTT.

Superintendent Lucy Furnaces,

PITTSBURG, PA.

BEST, FOX & CO.

GAYLEY PATENT BOSH PLATE.

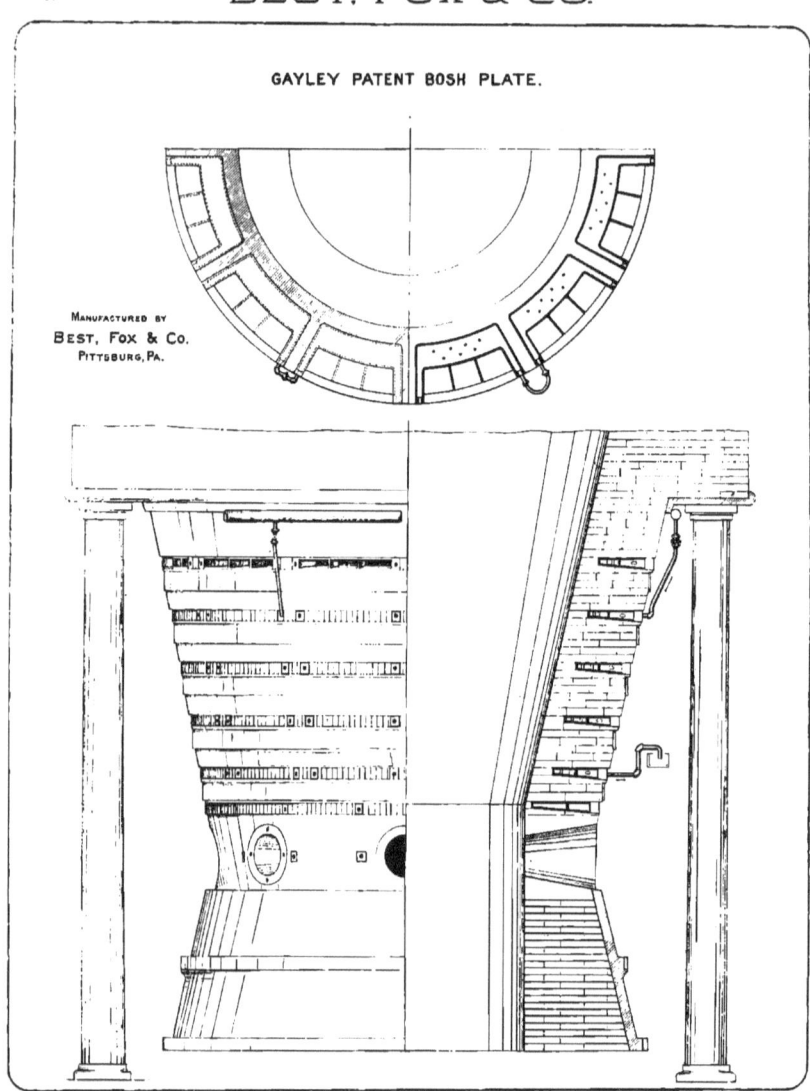

Manufactured by
BEST, FOX & CO.
PITTSBURG, PA.

GAYLEY'S PATENT BOSH PLATE.

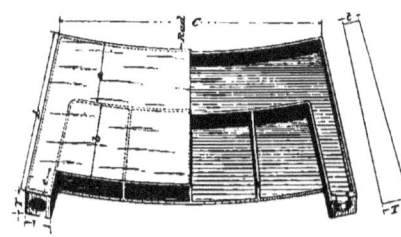

This bronze plate is wedge shaped, and has a plain surfaced top and bottom. (The latter is a special feature of the patent.) There is but one water course. The water is admitted through one arm to the cooling chamber, passes through, and is discharged at the other arm. This uninterrupted passage prevents the deposit of sediment.

The studs in the water course and the webs outside, resist any crushing by the brick work; long experience has shown, however, that there is practically no crushing force, as the brick courses above plate retain their position when the plate is removed as rigidly as if arched. The webs are provided with openings for the insertion of a withdrawing hook. The plates can be withdrawn as readily as a tuyere, and a new one one inserted. If the plate is found to have been "drilled" by iron, it can be plugged and reinserted. The water space being ten inches wide, provides a large body of water at the hottest part of the furnace, and prevents the walls from cutting back. This space is of such capacity that it produces eight times the cooling effect obtained from a plate with two iron coils 1¼ inches in diameter.

In building these plates in the bosh wall, put in a clay packing ⅝ inch thick around plate, and a strip of wood one inch thick along ends of plate. This will char and allow for expansion. As the arms are short, bricks on edge can be placed in between if desired, to give a better finish to exterior brick work. This plate does not require bricks of special shape, and only one band is required for each row of plates. These plates possess a great advantage in that they may be of any size without interfering in any way with the construction.

Practical results obtained by the use of these plates demonstrate that:

The removable plates cause no loss of Bronze metal.

They will preserve in perfect shape the interior of the furnace.

The fuel consumption does not increase as the furnace gets older.

The insertion of these plates in the bosh wall of an old furnace will increase its output ten per cent. This change can be made in twenty-four hours.

The bosh walls are so thoroughly protected that they will continue in perfect shape for a product of 400,000 to half a million tons in a single blast.

They will enable the furnace to produce more iron, and of a better quality, and on a lower fuel consumption, than by the addition of any other appliance requiring an outlay several times greater.

Yours truly,

EDGAR THOMSON WORKS,
BRADDOCK, PA.

JAMES GAYLEY.

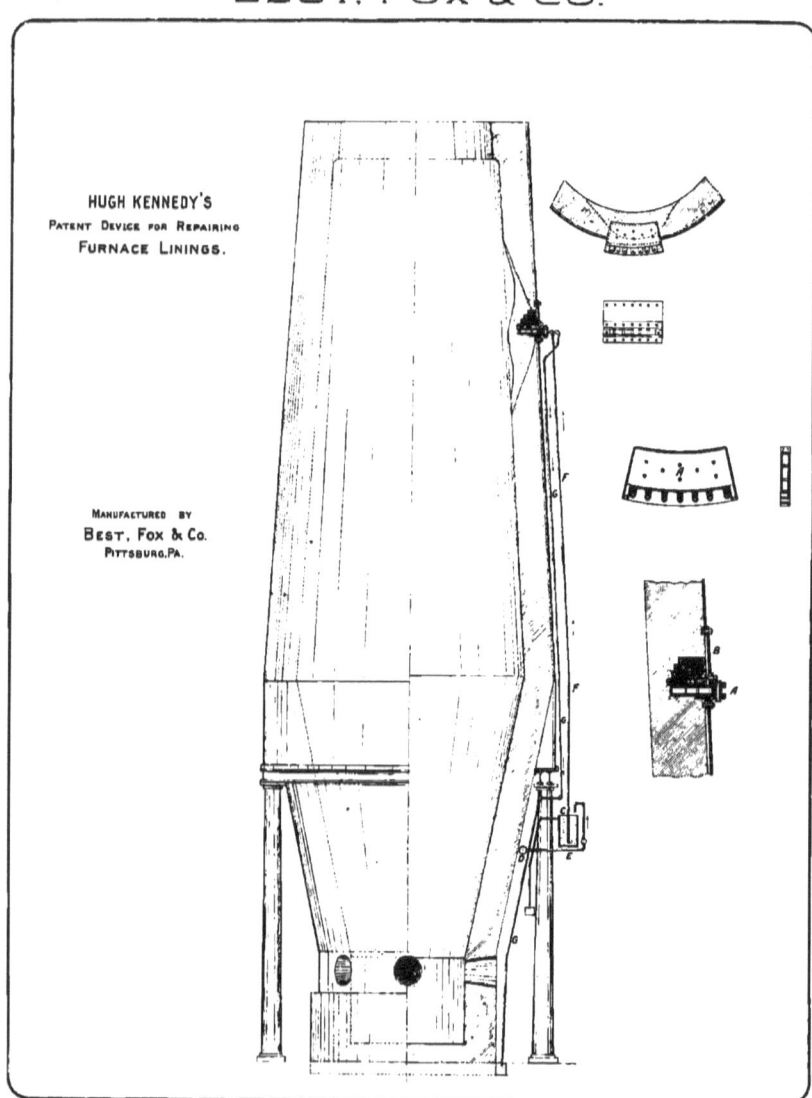

HUGH KENNEDY'S
PATENT DEVICE FOR REPAIRING
FURNACE LININGS.

MANUFACTURED BY
BEST, FOX & CO.
PITTSBURG, PA.

HUGH KENNEDY'S DEVICE FOR REPAIRING FURNACE LININGS.

On opposite page, a thin place, where the lining is worn through, is shown. When the point of danger is discovered, the blast is stopped and the spot cooled by a stream of water thrown against it. A piece of the shell, of sufficient size to expose the thin part of the lining, is then cut out and angle iron riveted or bolted to the inside of the shell at the lower edge of the cut, and another piece of angle iron on the outside. On the horizontal flanges of the angle iron a special plate is placed. The plate is held firmly by bolts passing through plate, outside angle iron referred to, and angle iron attached to sheet B.

On the top of this plate, on the inside, brick work is placed as shown. This being an obstruction in the path of the descending stock, it will deflect same away from the plate and prevent the stock from rubbing against the thin part of the lining below the plate ; and also deflect the ascending stream of air out into the furnace and cause it to find a new channel. This causes a layer or pocket of partly melted stock, furnace dust, etc., to form below and under cover of the plate, against the thin portion of the wall, which protects the plate from the heat and in that way further insures its safety.

This device has been used on two occasions at the Isabella Furnaces, Pittsburgh ; in one instance having made 16,000 tons of iron thereafter, and in the other instance 30,000 tons. The time required to do the entire work did not exceed twenty-four hours.

The method of furnishing this plate with water to insure perfect safety is shown by reference to the cut.

Tank C, placed near the mantel and fed from main supply pipe D, and is provided with overflow to main waste trough around furnace.

From tank C the water is drawn up to the plate through pipe F, on the syphon principle. The waste from the plate is carried down through pipe G below tank C and emptied at bottom of furnace. The moment the plate develops the slightest leak, air is admitted into same and the water immediately falls back to its original level, thereby insuring positively that no water will get into the furnace.

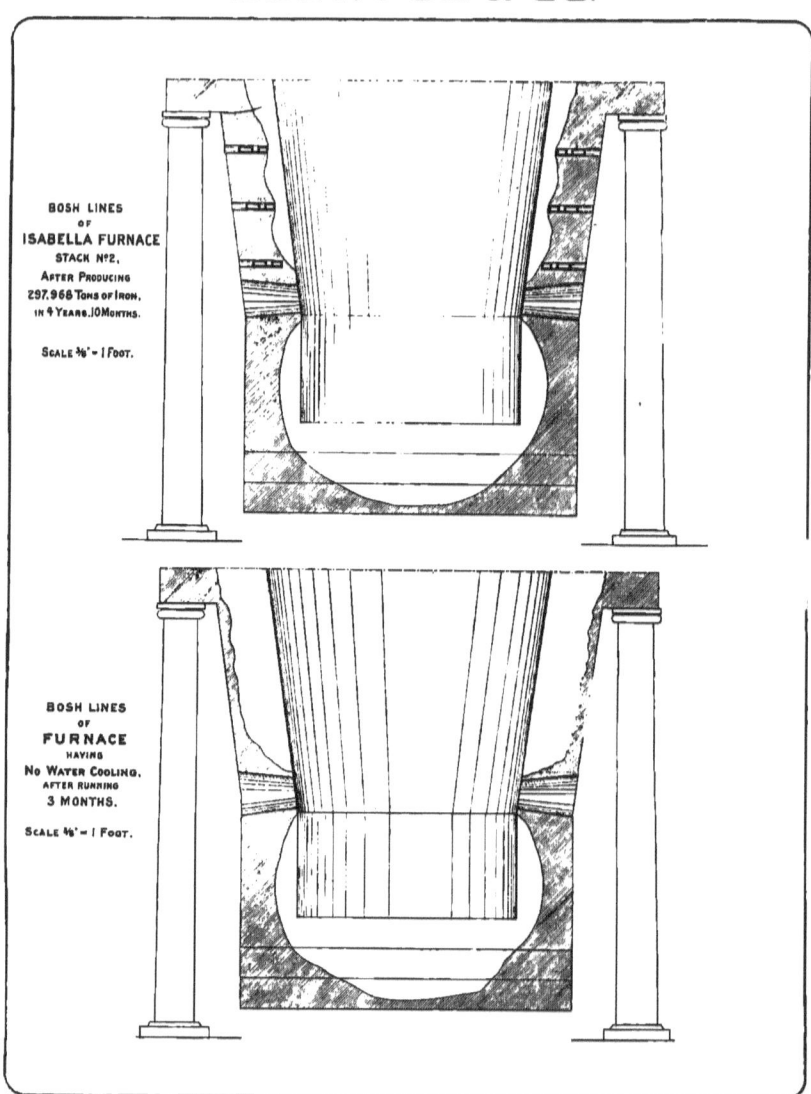

BOSH LINES
of
ISABELLA FURNACE
STACK N⁰2,
After Producing
297.968 Tons of Iron,
in 4 Years. 10 Months.

Scale ⅜" = 1 Foot.

BOSH LINES
of
FURNACE
having
No Water Cooling,
after running
3 MONTHS.

Scale ⅜" = 1 Foot.

BOSH COOLING vs. NO BOSH COOLING.

On the opposite page the ADVANTAGES of BRONZE BOSH COOLING, as compared with NO COOLING, is clearly set forth.

We recommend BRONZE bosh cooling, instead of Pipe or Iron plates, for the same reasons that BRONZE tuyeres are superior to iron ; i. e.:

IRON COOLING is

INEFFECTUAL,

EXPENSIVE,

NOT REMOVABLE,

CORRODES and CHOKES up.

The object of all Bosh Cooling is to hold the Original Lines Intact as nearly as possible. This can only be done with the use of Climax Bronze Cooling devices.

The following advantages are thereby obtained :

1. Long and satisfactory run.
2. Large and regular product.
3. No slipping.
4. Low fuel consumption and cheap iron.

Where no bosh cooling is used the brick work is soon cut out, as shown in lower cut on opposite page. This enlarged space must be filled with fuel, with an actual decrease in product.

We know of instances where 27 inch bosh walls were cut in 30 days to 4½ inch, and one instance where this occurred with iron plates, owing to faulty spacing.

We do not claim that any of the bosh cooling devices made by us will accomplish wonders as to quality, quantity and cost of output, without No. 1 fire clay and brick well laid in connection with same.

Harbison & Walker's " Benizet" were used in Isabella Bosh.

The large output on Isabella Furnace Bosh, as shown (this was from May 27th, '86 to April 2d, '91), is nothing unusual, as several furnaces at Edgar Thompson Steel Works have made outputs of over 500,000 tons on a single bosh lining, and still left the BRONZE plates in GOOD CONDITION for use in relining again.

The average life of a bronze plate is from three to five blows, which brings the cost of same (taking value of scrap into consideration,) cheaper by 50 per cent, as compared with iron.

BEST, FOX & CO.

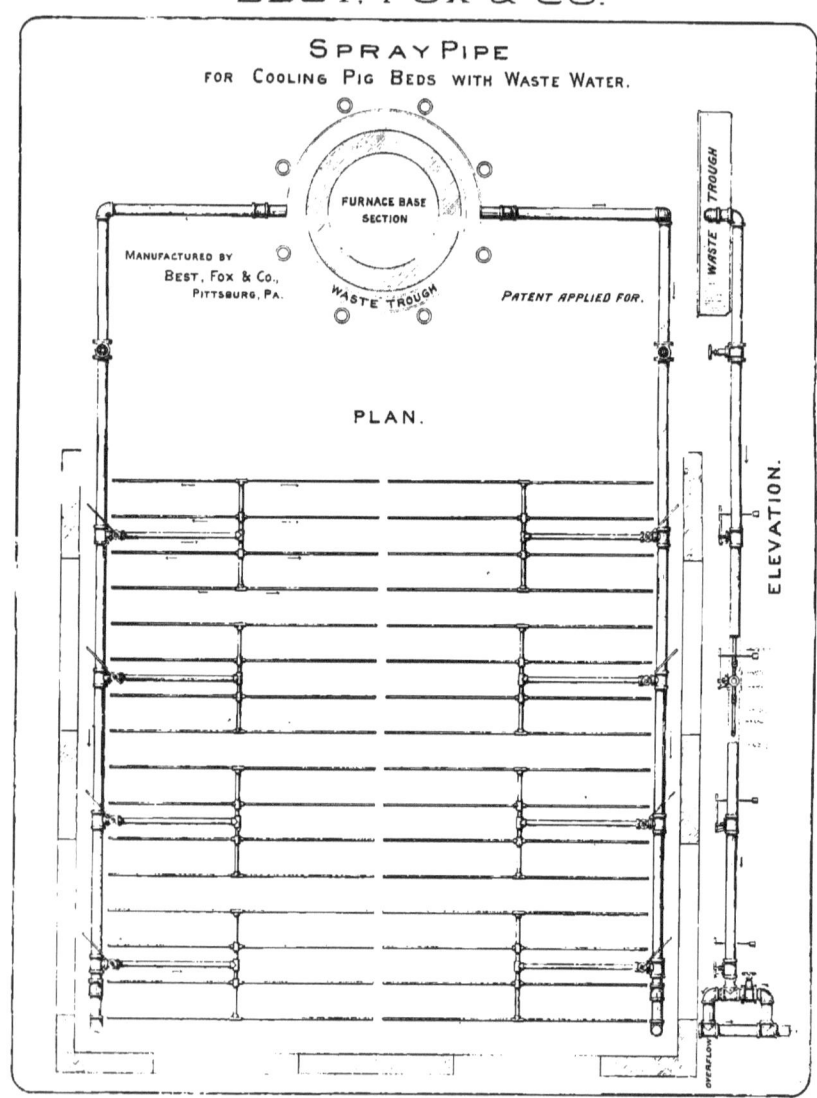

SPRAY PIPE

FOR COOLING PIG BEDS WITH WASTE WATER.

FURNACE BASE
SECTION

MANUFACTURED BY
BEST, FOX & CO.,
PITTSBURG, PA.

WASTE TROUGH

PATENT APPLIED FOR.

PLAN.

WASTE TROUGH

ELEVATION.

BIG BED SPRINKLING SYSTEM.

PATENTED.

On opposite side we show a piping system for cooling the pig beds of blast furnaces, by making use of the discharge water from the trough.

A large water feed is run down the sides of the cast house, supported from the roof trusses, as shown. From this main, which is generally 6 inches, 3-inch branches are run, with a lever valve to control each section. From each 3-inch pipe a series of spray pipes again branch off, and are placed directly over the pig beds.

When any section of the beds is required to be cooled a hook or weight, that is attached to the lever of the table is removed, and the valve is so constructed that the pressure will at once raise the lever, open the valve and allow the water to pass along to the section that is to be sprayed. Replacing the hook or weight at once shuts off this section.

To insure the 6-inch main supply always being full of water, and giving the required pressure, an overflow is provided as shown, and is so arranged as to prevent overflow at waste trough of furnace. When the furnace is banked, and the water not required at the pig beds, the waste can be run direct to sewer by opening a valve in connection with the overflow arrangement.

If at any time repairs are needed in connection with this piping system, valve near waste trough can be closed, and any part of the system repaired or taken down while the furnace is running.

This system insures a heavy shower of water without any labor or expense connected with same, and does away with the wasting and wearing out of hose, and requires no power to elevate water for this purpose.

Plans, specifications, and estimates on application.

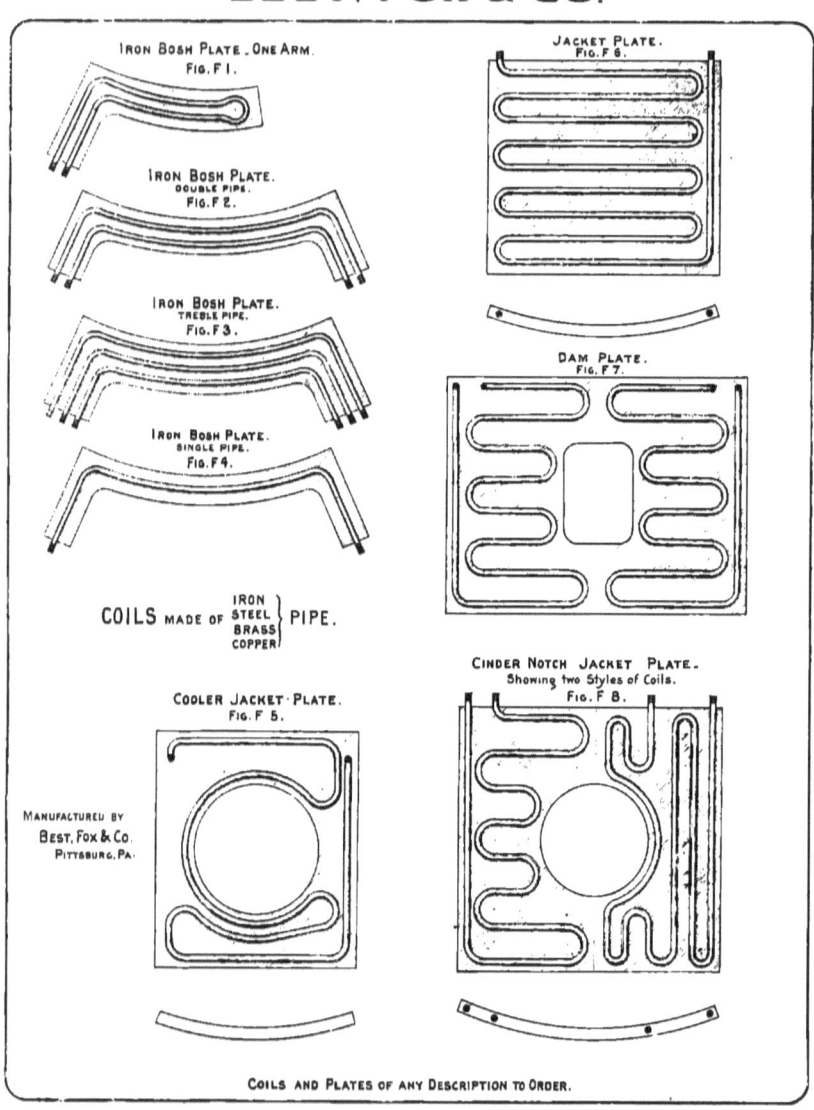

IRON BOSH PLATE. ONE ARM.
FIG. F I.

IRON BOSH PLATE.
DOUBLE PIPE.
FIG. F 2.

IRON BOSH PLATE.
TREBLE PIPE.
FIG. F 3.

IRON BOSH PLATE.
SINGLE PIPE.
FIG. F 4.

COILS MADE OF $\left.\begin{array}{l}\text{IRON}\\\text{STEEL}\\\text{BRASS}\\\text{COPPER}\end{array}\right\}$ PIPE.

COOLER JACKET PLATE.
FIG. F 5.

MANUFACTURED BY
BEST, FOX & CO.
PITTSBURG, PA.

JACKET PLATE.
FIG. F 6.

DAM PLATE.
FIG. F 7.

CINDER NOTCH JACKET PLATE.
Showing two Styles of Coils.
FIG. F 8.

COILS AND PLATES OF ANY DESCRIPTION TO ORDER.

COMBINATION OF
N° 50 BRONZE CINDER NOTCH &
N° 197 BRONZE CINDER COOLER.

FIG. F 9.

COMBINATION OF
N° 50 BRONZE CINDER NOTCH
AND IRON CINDER COOLER.

FIG. F II.

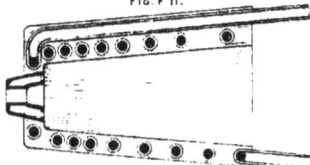

COMBINATION OF N°92 BRONZE CINDER NOTCH.
N°323 BRONZE INTERMEDIATE COOLER,
N° 145 BRONZE CINDER COOLER.

FIG. F 10.

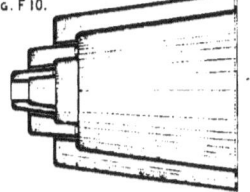

COMBINATION OF N°92 BRONZE CINDER NOTCH.
N°323 BRONZE INTERMEDIATE COOLER.
AND IRON CINDER COOLER.

FIG. F 12.

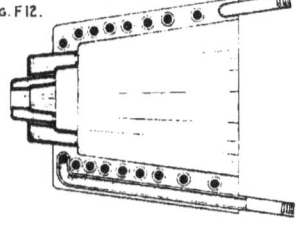

IRON TUYERE WITH COILED PIPE.

FIG. F 13.

IRON COOLER WITH COILED PIPE.

FIG. F 14.

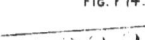

BOSH JACKET COILS.

FIG. F 15.

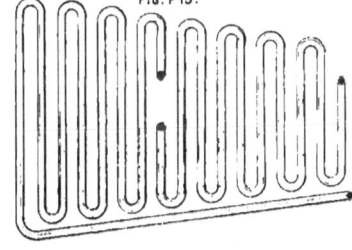

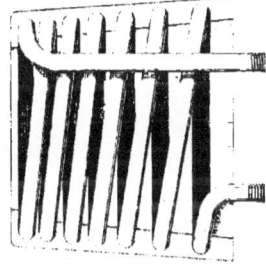

MANUFACTURED BY

BEST, FOX & CO.
PITTSBURG, PA

TUYERE AND COOLER COILS OF ANY DIMENSION FURNISHED WITH OR WITHOUT METAL ATTACHED.

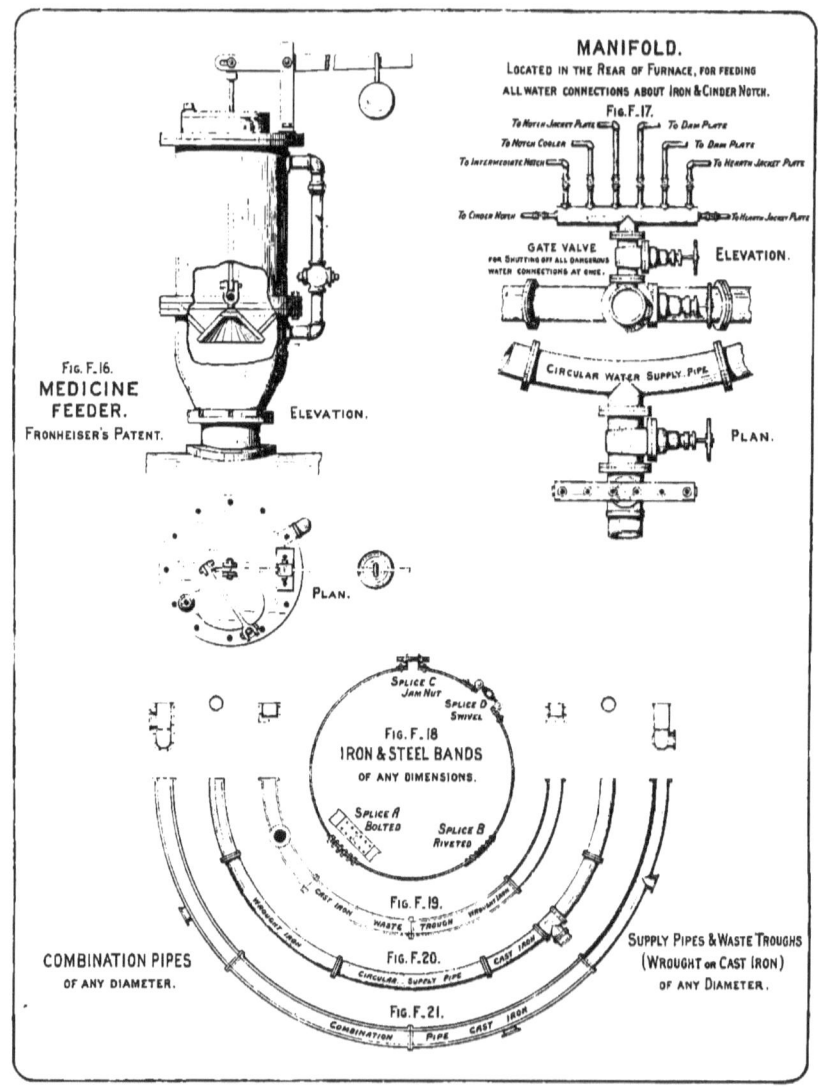

MANIFOLD.
LOCATED IN THE REAR OF FURNACE, FOR FEEDING
ALL WATER CONNECTIONS ABOUT IRON & CINDER NOTCH.

FIG. F. 17.

To Notch Jacket Plate — To Dam Plate
To Notch Cooler — To Dam Plate
To Intermediate Notch — To Hearth Jacket Plate
To Cinder Notch — To Hearth Jacket Plate

GATE VALVE
FOR SHUTTING OFF ALL DANGEROUS
WATER CONNECTIONS AT ONCE.

ELEVATION.

CIRCULAR WATER SUPPLY PIPE

PLAN.

FIG. F. 16.
MEDICINE
FEEDER.
FRONHEISER'S PATENT.

ELEVATION.

PLAN.

SPLICE C
JAM NUT
SPLICE D
SWIVEL

FIG. F. 18
IRON & STEEL BANDS
OF ANY DIMENSIONS.

SPLICE A
BOLTED
SPLICE B
RIVETED

CAST IRON

FIG. F. 19.
WASTE TROUGH   WROUGHT IRON

COMBINATION PIPES
OF ANY DIAMETER.

FIG. F. 20.
CAST IRON
CIRCULAR SUPPLY PIPE

SUPPLY PIPES & WASTE TROUGHS
(WROUGHT OR CAST IRON)
OF ANY DIAMETER.

FIG. F. 21.
COMBINATION PIPE   CAST IRON

MANIFOLD CONNECTION, Fig. F. 17.

In case of *Explosions or Breakouts* at tapping hole or cinder notch it is very desirable to have the cocks controlling water to notch and dam plate connections away from place of danger and at a point that can be reached safely.

By the use of a manifold located at the rear of the furnace all these connections can be shut off at once by closing the valve directly under the manifold or any single connection by closing cock directly above same.

By referring to illustration on opposite page the advantage of this connection will be understood.

MEDICINE FEEDER FOR BLAST FURNACES, Fig. F 16.

(FRONHEISER'S PATENT.)

Feeder is secured to Bustle Pipe immediately over openings leading to tuyeres. Feeder is charged by removing slide on top by simply unloosing a thumb nut. Adjustment for feeding is obtained by moving weight on lever, and by means of operating cock on bypass, the full blast pressure can be brought on top of material and forced through valve at any required speed.

This apparatus is used for **introducing solid materials**, fuel or fluxes into a blast furnace, through the tuyeres, without throwing off the blast, and having these bodies introduced into the hearth of the furnace just at the point where their effects are required to **promptly clean out** any accumulations of excessive lime, metal, etc., without affecting the quality or grade of metal produced, or interfering with the continuous operation of the furnace.

It often happens that when a blast furnace is hanging or scaffolded, too cold, or when the metal and slag from some other cause are **too thick to run from the furnace**, it becomes necessary to put sand, common salt, fluor spar, or other chemicals or fuels of different kinds into the hearth of the furnace. Under the present customary arrangements, the blow pipes are either taken down entirely and the material introduced through the tuyeres, or a cap on the end of the blow-pipe is removed and the pipe is filled with the material, so that it will be carried into the hearth after the blast is turned on.

All of these manipulations, however, **necessitate throwing the blast** off from the furnace before the material can be introduced, and this has the disadvantage that just as soon as the blast pressure is removed, cinder and metal are apt, in some part of the furnace, to run back into the tuyeres, causing not only hard work to remove the same, but in addition, great loss of time. By putting the sand, etc., into the furnace at the tunnel heads with the ore, etc., you are not only obliged to **wait from 12 to 24 hours** or more till it reaches the tuyeres, but it likewise has the disadvantage of rendering the slag more acid in composition, producing pig iron higher in content of sulphur and combined carbon of a much lower grade, during the entire time that it is at work. By this apparatus material can be fed into the blast furnace through the tuyeres continuously, if desired, without stopping the blast.

BEST, FOX & CO.

It likewise sometimes happens with the most carefully handled and skillfully managed blast furnaces that the materials in the upper part will **stick and slip;** during the hanging the fuel around the tuyeres will all be consumed, and the blast air not coming in contact with incandescent fuel, to convert it into a reducing gas (C. O.) acts as in the Bessemer converter; namely, it will oxidize the carbon in the accumulated metal, and the results are that when the **mass drops into the hearth** we have the metal chiefly in the form of wrought iron, a difficult fusible mass of iron, free from or very low in content of carbon, which accumulates around the tuyeres, and by the ordinary way can be removed only by slow, tiresome and costly operation, and can be done only while the blast is off the furnace, during which time the inside is becoming colder, and the trouble still more augmented.

One of the common methods of treatment of troubles of this kind is to try to melt out the accumulations around and in the tuyere, by means of a petroleum blow pipe. While this method is in many cases effective, it can be applied only to one or two tuyeres at a time; will cover only a small area of the tuyere space at the same time, and while the heat generated in many cases is intense enough to melt the mass of decarbonized iron and slag, yet they will remain in the molten condition only long enough to drop out of the hot zone of the blow-pipe flame, from whence it must again be removed by means of a chipping bar and sledge.

With this apparatus, in troubles of this kind, it becomes only necessary to drill a hole through the mass, so that the blast air can enter the inside of the hearth; then feed a mixture of fine charcoal, braze and common salt or sand through the tuyeres. The solid carbon of the charcoal will recarbonize the decarbonized iron, and render it much more fusible. The salt or sand will enter into chemical combination with the infusible slag, and **make it as fusible** as can be desired, so that by this method the trouble can be **easily overcome.**

Then again, we find this apparatus to be very effective in every day work in making foundry or high grade metal from sulphurous coke or selicious ores. It is well known that the more sulphur the coke contains, and the higher in content of selicia the ore is, the greater will be the quantity of limestone necessary to use with them, and the more basic must be the slag. It is likewise well known that by continuing to run a blast furnace on a very basic slag for some time, the **hearth will soon fill up** with this difficult fusible mass. The common practice in cases of this kind, is to turn the furnace off on a sharp scouring slag and metal for a few turns. With this apparatus a **furnace can be kept on a basic slag** by filling through the tuyeres enough of dry sand, immediately after each cast, and when the hearth is empty, to scour out all of this limy accumulation. The sand enters the furnace at a point where it does not affect the grade of the metal produced, and by this means a **furnace can be kept running** for a long time on a very limy slag, without filling up the hearth, particularly if the limestone of the charge be broken up into small pieces before it is charged into the top of the furnace with the ore, etc.

We find that the best results are always obtained by increasing the fineness of the lumps of limestone charged into the tunnel head, with the quantity of that material it becomes necessary to use.

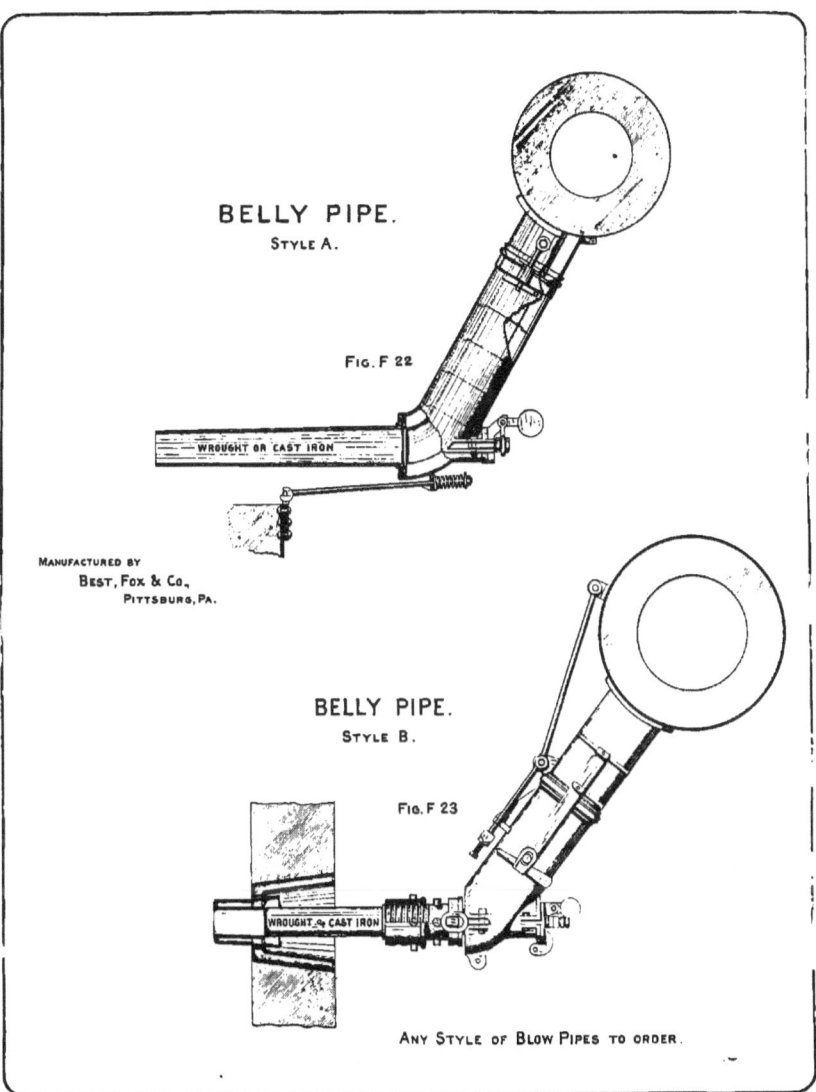

BELLY PIPE.
STYLE A.

FIG. F 22

WROUGHT OR CAST IRON

MANUFACTURED BY
BEST, FOX & Co.,
PITTSBURG, PA.

BELLY PIPE.
STYLE B.

FIG. F 23

WROUGHT OR CAST IRON

ANY STYLE OF BLOW PIPES TO ORDER.

BEST, FOX & CO.

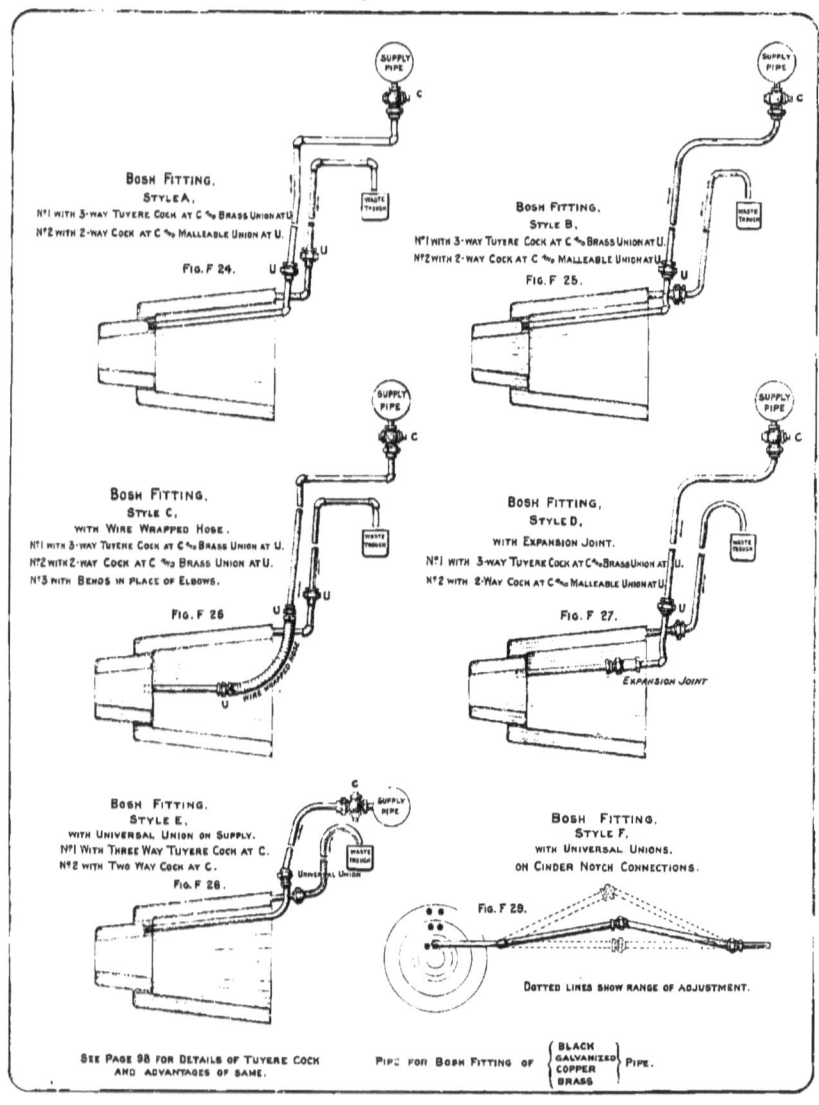

BOSH FITTING,
STYLE A,
Nº1 WITH 3-WAY TUYERE COCK AT C ⁰⁄₀ BRASS UNION AT U.
Nº2 WITH 2-WAY COCK AT C ⁰⁄₀ MALLEABLE UNION AT U.
FIG. F 24.

BOSH FITTING,
STYLE B,
Nº1 WITH 3-WAY TUYERE COCK AT C ⁰⁄₀ BRASS UNION AT U.
Nº2 WITH 2-WAY COCK AT C ⁰⁄₀ MALLEABLE UNION AT U.
FIG. F 25.

BOSH FITTING,
STYLE C,
WITH WIRE WRAPPED HOSE.
Nº1 WITH 3-WAY TUYERE COCK AT C ⁰⁄₀ BRASS UNION AT U.
Nº2 WITH 2-WAY COCK AT C ⁰⁄₀ BRASS UNION AT U.
Nº3 WITH BENDS IN PLACE OF ELBOWS.
FIG. F 26.

BOSH FITTING,
STYLE D,
WITH EXPANSION JOINT.
Nº1 WITH 3-WAY TUYERE COCK AT C ⁰⁄₀ BRASS UNION AT U.
Nº2 WITH 2-WAY COCK AT C ⁰⁄₀ MALLEABLE UNION AT U.
FIG. F 27.

BOSH FITTING,
STYLE E,
WITH UNIVERSAL UNION ON SUPPLY.
Nº1 WITH THREE WAY TUYERE COCK AT C.
Nº2 WITH TWO WAY COCK AT C.
FIG. F 28.

BOSH FITTING,
STYLE F,
WITH UNIVERSAL UNIONS.
ON CINDER NOTCH CONNECTIONS.

FIG. F 29.

DOTTED LINES SHOW RANGE OF ADJUSTMENT.

SEE PAGE 98 FOR DETAILS OF TUYERE COCK AND ADVANTAGES OF SAME.

PIPE FOR BOSH FITTING OF { BLACK GALVANIZED COPPER BRASS } PIPE.

BOSH FITTING.

By referring to pages 94 and 96, various ways of fitting Bosh Cooling devices are shown that we hope may be of benefit to our present customers and also to those in prospect. This portion of the work about the Bosh is considered by many as of no importance. "Anything will do and any one can do it," seems to be the common practice, and what is the result?

More cooling devices are lost in a single blast than would pay for piping the Bosh first-class a number of times, to say nothing of the loss sustained through numerous stoppages of furnace, inferior iron from the same cause, possibly an explosion or two, and all because of a clumsily fitted and consequently "sloppy" looking Bosh.

Copper or brass pipes make the best and most durable work, and necessarily the most expensive, (first cost only considered), but cheapest in the end.

The advantages of Three-way Tuyere Cocks are set forth clearly on page 99.

Brass Unions should be used on all connections, as iron corrodes in a short time, requiring Unions to be broken when necessary to take them apart.

Figure F 24, No. 2, shows the least expensive connection, namely: Two-way Cock at C and Malleable Unions at U, using Elbows at all quarter turns. No. 1, with Tuyere Cock and Brass Unions is frequently used.

Figure F 25, is the same in every particular as F 24, except that pipe is bent at all quarter turns possible, thereby reducing friction to the minimum. This is the style of fitting mostly used.

Figure F 26, shows the advantage of having Wire-wrapped Hose on the Tuyere supply, allowing ready adjustment of connection with the Tuyere.

Figure F 27, shows an Expansion Joint on the Tuyere supply, making it possible to move the Tuyere back into Cooler when desired.

Figure F 28, shows Brass Universal Union connections to Tuyere and Cooler, and is the LATEST, BEST and NEATEST device for connecting pipes not coming true. This Union is being generally adopted.

Figure F 29, shows the great advantage of the Universal Union on Cinder Notch connections. If pipe is cut so as to couple up, as shown in full lines, a Notch not setting in precisely the same position as one removed, can be coupled up without "profanity" or loss of time, as the range of adjustment clearly indicates.

We make all Tuyere Cocks and Valves extra heavy to stand the rough usage they are subjected to in blast furnace practice.

BEST, FOX & CO.

BOSH FITTING.

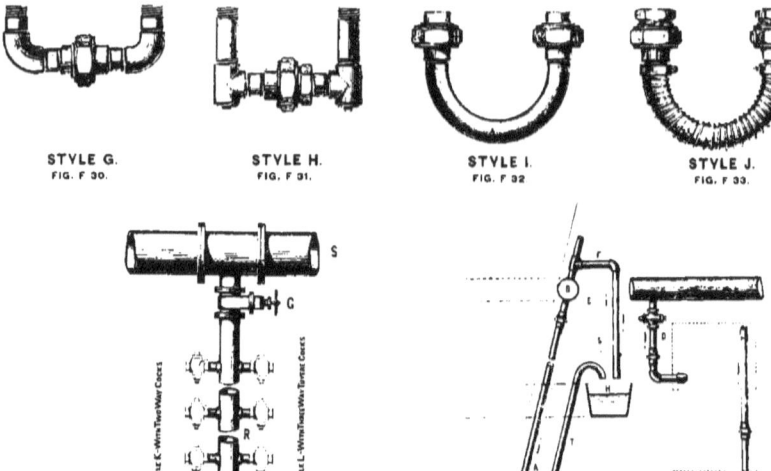

STYLE G.
FIG. F 30.

STYLE H.
FIG. F 31.

STYLE I.
FIG. F 32

STYLE J.
FIG. F 33.

STYLE K.
FIG. F 34.

See page 90 for Manifold on top of Combination Pipe, also page 120, Catalogue A, for Bosh Fitted, style K.

STYLE L.
FIG. F 35.

See pages 70 and 72, showing Bosh Fitted, style L, and full description on page 73.

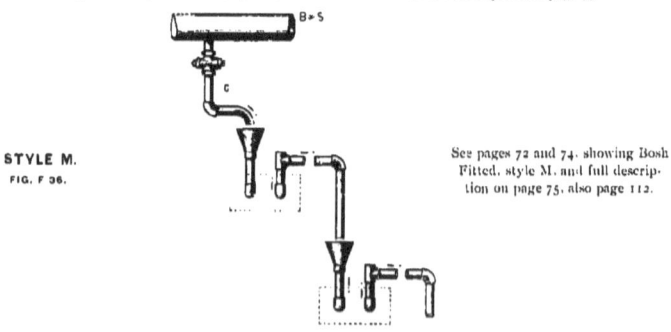

STYLE M.
FIG. F 36.

See pages 72 and 74, showing Bosh Fitted, style M, and full description on page 75, also page 112.

BOSH FITTING.

Figure F 30, shows the method of coupling two Bosh Plates together with Elbows.

Figure F 31, is for the same purpose as Figure 30, having Tees in place of Elbows. By removing plugs a wire can be inserted through the Tee, and if an iron plate is used, obstructions can thus be removed.

Figure F 32, shows two plates coupled together by means of two Unions and bent pipe. This reduces friction to the lowest possible point, and makes the best and neatest job and is mostly used.

Figure F 33, is the same as Figure 32, except Wire-wrapped Hose is used in place of bent pipe. This wire on hose prevents buckling, which would choke off the water and destroy the hose in a short time.

Figure F 34, shows Manifold or Multiple system of Bosh Fitting. This arrangement is the neatest of all Bosh Piping, as it reduces the number of pipes, as compared with each supply being taken independently from the Supply Pipe S. Four or five Tees (according to the number of drops required) with large outlets are placed in the Main Circular Supply S. Next to each Tee, a Valve G, is placed to shut off the entire connection should occasion require. On the Drop Pipe R, openings are used to supply Plates or Boxes, making connections to same short and compact. From Manifold H, the top connections are used for the lower rows of Plates ; end and bottom connections for Tuyeres, Coolers, Notch and Notch Cooler, Spray, &c. By means of Cock D, any sediment in the Manifold can be blown out. The Cocks for controlling water are close and easy of access. Additional openings on Manifolds are made as ordered.

Figure F 35, shows the system of piping for open Boxes, with water not under pressure, and also of utilizing waste water from the Coolers for this purpose. By referring to pages 72 and 73, a clear description is given of the working of this latter arrangement. See also page 114.

Figure F 36, shows how open Plates are supplied from Main Supply Pipe S direct, or from Auxiliary Supply Pipe B, same as shown in Figure F 35, and described on pages 74, 75 and 112.

Quotations and plans furnished for any style of Bosh Fitting erected complete, or will furnish the material only and instructions for erecting when so desired,

BRASS COCKS.

TWO-WAY.
FIG. F 37.

TWO-WAY, with Coupling.
FIG. F 38.

THREE-WAY.
FIG. F 39.

TUYERE COCK, New Style.
Without Coupling.
FIG. F 40.

TUYERE COCK, Old Style.
With Coupling for Iron or Lead Pipe.
FIG. F 41.

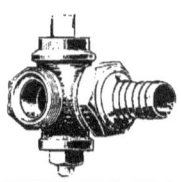

TUYERE COCK, Old Style.
With Coupling for Hose.
FIG. F 42.

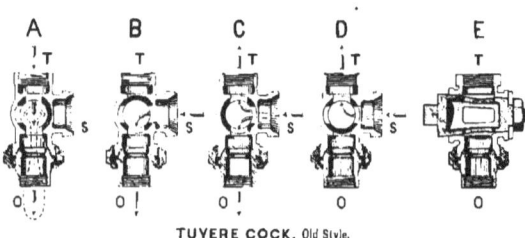

TUYERE COCK, Old Style.
Section.
FIG. F 43.

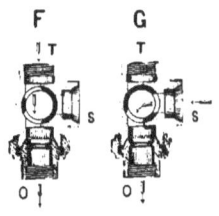

TUYERE COCK, New Style.
Section.
FIG. F 44.

See page 99 for description.

Save your Tuyeres, Coolers and Bosh Plates by Removing Dirt and Sediment Lodged in them.

This is accomplished not merely by having Bosh fitted with Three-way Tuyere Cocks, but by using them often with steam or water from pressure pump forcing through them.

A quarter of a turn of cock-key, allowing it to remain in this position for a few moments, then turn back to original position, is all that is required to keep castings clean.

EXPLANATION:—Referring to cuts on opposite page, note position of cock-body. The inlet to it is on top or T; outlet to Tuyeres, &c. at O; thread to receive blow out at side S.

The dotted lines in Figure A show the relative position of the Wrench to the Key.

With the key in position as shown in Figure A, water is fed through openings T and O. A quarter turn of the key to the right brings openings in position as shown in B, opening high pressure for cleaning out Tuyere through S and O, as indicated by arrows, the communication to the main supply being shut off at same time. The key in this position shuts the water off the Tuyere entirely if pressure connection is not made at S or side opening.

Another quarter turn of key admits blowing out Tuyere through S and O, and main supply through S and T, as shown in Figure C. The cock should not be used in this position.

Another quarter turn brings key in position shown in Figure D, brings blow-out into main supply through S and T, which is desirable in case pipe is choked above cock. In the meantime, however, water is shut off Tuyere.

Another quarter turn brings the key to original position, as shown in Figure A. Position of key is invariably as shown in either A and B. Ground joint coupling at O for connection to Tuyere can be used at S and blow-off connected at O, if so desired, for convenience in piping or blowing off.

Figure E shows section of Cock looking at same from side on S. Ample opening is provided in the key, so full area of pipe is obtained through it.

Figure F and G show sections of our new style Tuyere Cock, which must always be open or closed, as a stop on the key prevents further movement of same. With this cock, there is no danger of shutting Tuyere water off without knowing it instantly. Blowing into main supply through S and T with this style cock *is not* possible.

UNIONS.

MALLEABLE UNION.
FIG. F 45.

KEYSTONE UNION, (Section.)
Composition Seat.
FIG. F 46.

UNION ELBOW.
Female.
FIG. F 47.

UNION TEE.
Female.
FIG. F 48.

BRASS UNION, (Stand.)
FIG F 49.

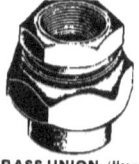 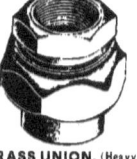

BRASS UNION, (Heavy.)
For Iron Pipe.
FIG. F 50.

BRASS UNION, (Heavy.)
Section.
FIG. F 51.

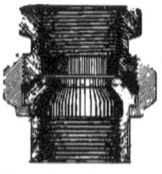 

BRASS UNION, (Heavy.)
For Iron Pipe and Hose.
FIG. F 52.

PARTS OF HEAVY BRASS UNION.
Male Half.   Female Half or Nut and Swivel.
FIG F 53.   FIG. F 54.

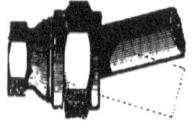 

UNIVERSAL UNION.
(Heavy.)
FIG. F 55.

EYE SIGHT.
FIG. F 56.

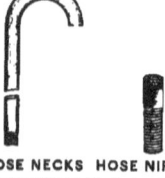

FUNNELS FOR BOSH AND STOVES.
Round.   Flat Back.
FIG. F 57.   FIG. F 58.

GOOSE NECKS
For Bosh and Stoves.
FIG. F 59.

HOSE NIPPLES
For Bosh and Stoves.
FIG. F 60.

CLIPS
For Bosh and Stoves.
FIG. F 61.

BELL CYLINDERS

of any diameter to operate with steam is located on furnace platform. Connection is made to beam at F. Cylinder swings on Trunnion G.

OPERATION:—Steam enters Four-way Cock at A, passes through Pipe B and Passage C, forcing piston to bottom as shown, which closes the bell. Steam on lower side of piston has in the mean time been forced through Pipe D and escaped through opposite side of cock and out of E opening. To lower the Bell, Cock Key is reversed. This Four-way Cock is gland packed, provided with brass key, and will not stick or leak.

FOUR-WAY COCKS.

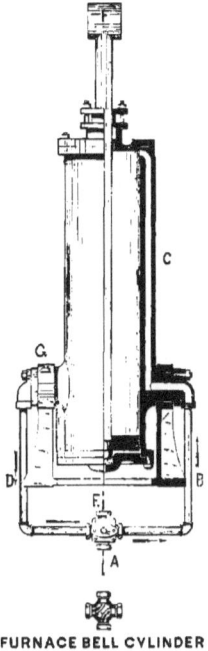

FURNACE BELL CYLINDER
FIG. F 62.

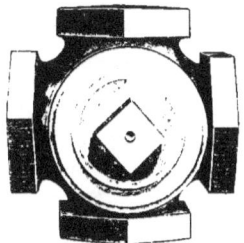

REGULAR.
Screwed or Flanged.
FIG. F 63.

WITH PACKED GLAND.
Screwed or Flanged.
FIG. F 64.

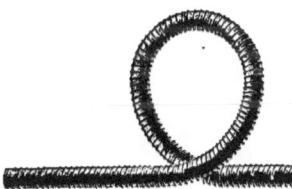

WIRE WRAPPED HOSE.
FIG. F 65.

WIRE ROPE—ALL SIZES.
FIG. F 66.

BLOWING ENGINE BEARINGS.

BOTTOM BRASS.	TOP BRASS.	SIDE BRASS.	STRAP BRASS.
FIG. F 67.	FIG. F 68.	FIG. F 69.	FIG. F 70.

CINDER CAR BRASS.
FIG. F 71.

CAR BRASS.
FIG. F 72.

FOR REPAIRING TUYERES, ETC.
Countersunk Plug Brass.   Copper Rod.
FIG. F 73.   All Sizes.
                         FIG. F 74.

STEEL HEARTH JACKETS.
ALL SIZES AND STYLES.

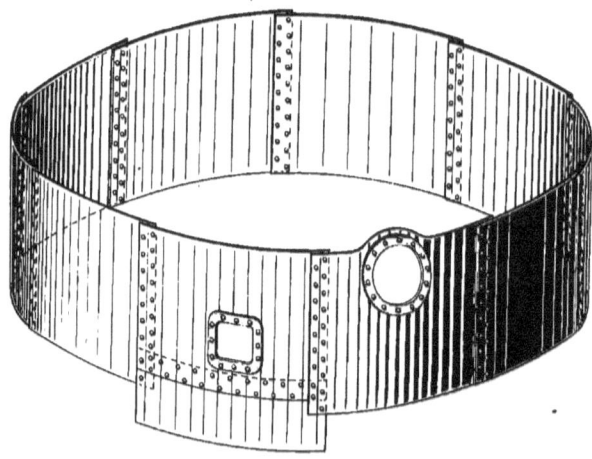

FIG. F 75.

HOT BLAST VALVES.

(With Berg's Patent Seat, Made of Climax Bronze.)

FIG. F 76.

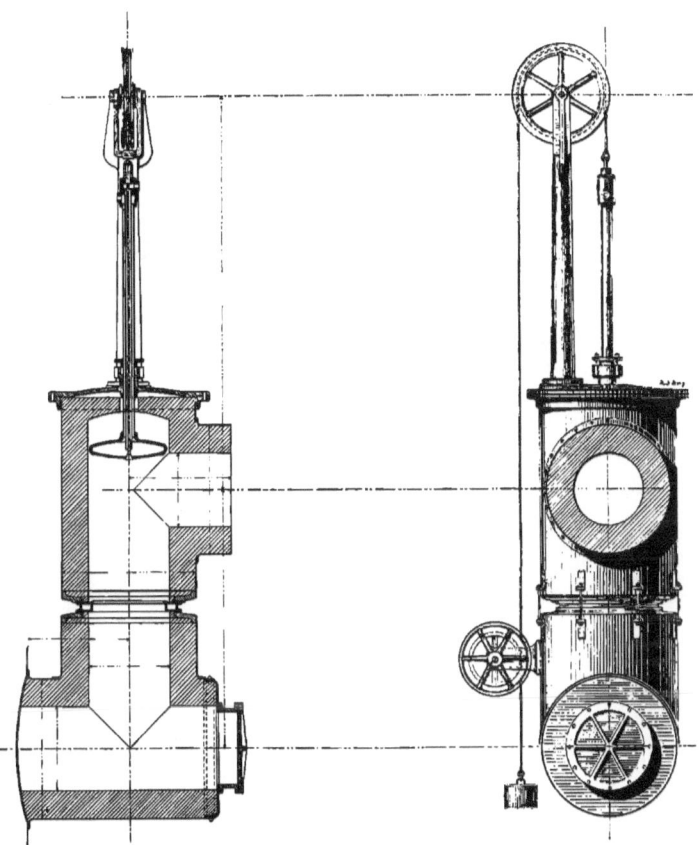

All styles and sizes made to order.

CHIMNEY VALVES.
ALL STYLES AND SIZES.
FIG. F 77.

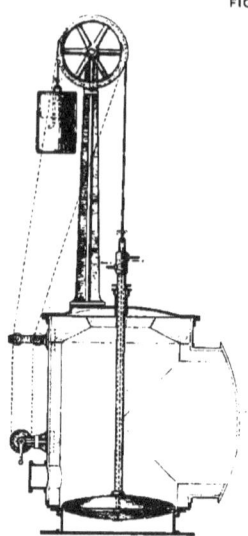

COLD BLAST VALVES.
FIG. F 78.

AIR RELIEF VALVE.
FIG. F 79.

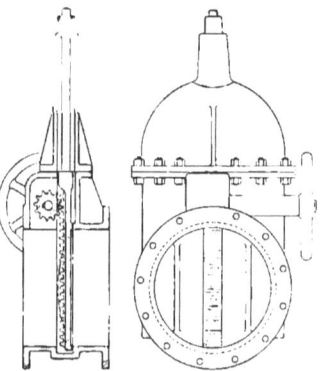

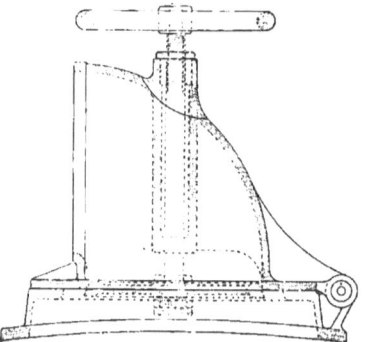

GAS BURNERS FOR STOVES AND BOILERS.

Patented by J. J. Spearman and Hugh Kennedy.

STOVE BURNER.

FIG. F 90.

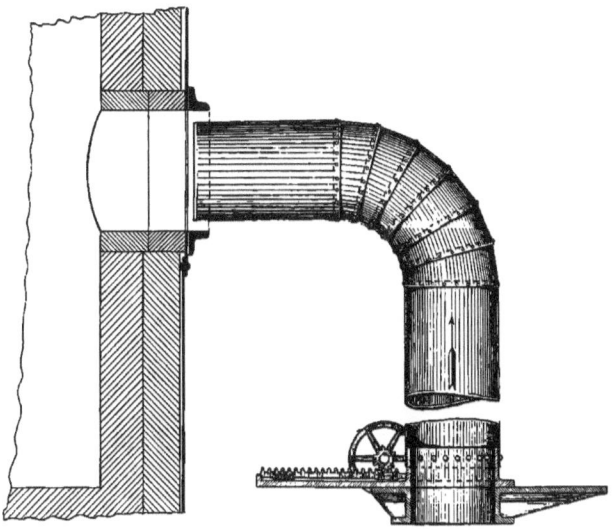

BOILER BURNER.

FIG. F 91.

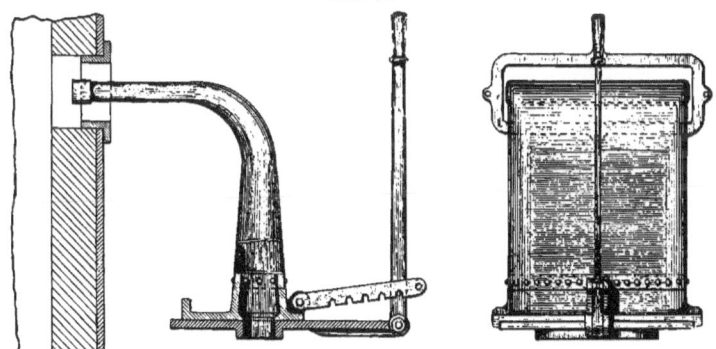

THE EDGAR THOMSON STEEL WORKS AND BLAST FURNACES.

THE EDGAR THOMSON BLAST FURNACES FROM THE SOUTH.

The Edgar Thomson Steel Works and Blast Furnaces

AT BESSEMER, PA.

CARNEGIE STEEL COMPANY, LIMITED,

PITTSBURG, PA.

On the opposite side a view of the above well-known works is given. The capacity of the nine Furnaces shown (and two Lucy Furnaces owned by the same Company) is 1,200,000 tons per annum.

Furnace **A**--65 ft. x 15 ft., with four Siemens-Cowper-Cochran Stoves, 65 ft. x 15 ft. each.

"   **B**--80 ft. x 18 ft. } with ten Siemens-Cowper-Cochran Stoves, eight of
"   **C**--80 ft. x 20 ft. } same 75 ft. x 20 ft., and two 75 ft. x 21 ft.

D--80 ft. x 21 ft. } with six Siemens-Cowper-Cochran Stoves, 78 ft. x 21 ft. each,
E--80 ft. x 21 ft. } and one Whitwell Stove 78 ft. x 20 ft.

F--90 ft. x 22 ft. }
                       } with seven Siemens-Cowper-Cochran Stoves, 78 ft. x 21 ft. each.
G--90 ft. x 22 ft. }

"   **H**--90 ft. x 22 ft. }
                         } with seven Cowper Stoves, 79 ft. x 21 ft. each.
"   **I**--90 ft. x 22 ft. }

All the above furnaces are equipped with "Gayley's" Removable Bronze Bosh Plates. Furnace A running on Spiegel has eleven rows of which six rows are above the mantel.

Owing to the thorough bosh protection, several of these furnaces have produced 500,000 tons in one blast of a uniform quality and remarkable low fuel consumption.

These Bosh Plates are removable, which assures the bosh being kept in perfect shape. See pages 80 and 81.

The two Lucy Furnaces at Pittsburg, Pa., each 85 ft. x 20 ft., with eight Stoves of the Whitwell & Cowper type are equipped with "Scott's" Removable Bronze Bosh Plates. See pages 78 and 79.

THE MARYLAND STEEL CO.'S FURNACES, SPARROWS POINT, MD.

THE MARYLAND STEEL CO.'S FURNACE BASE B.

MARYLAND STEEL COMPANY.

SPARROWS POINT, MD.

On the opposite side a view of the above Company's Blast Furnaces is given, 4 in number, which were built from 1889 to 1891.

Each furnace is 85 feet high, 22 feet bosh diameter.   11 feet 6 in. hearth diameter.

Stove equipment consists of 16 in. Witherows' improved Whitwell type.

Blast is furnished by 4 Double Vertical condensing beam engines, built by the Southwark Foundry & Machine Co., Philadelphia, Pa., from designs furnished by Pennsylvania Steel Co., Steelton, Pa.

Steam Power is furnished by 32 Babcock & Wilcox Boilers, approximating 8000 H. P.

Average Temperature of blast, 1300 degrees.

Average Pressure, approximate, $8\frac{1}{2}$ lbs.

ANNUAL CAPACITY, 400,000 TONS.

The four furnaces were equipped, originally, with Kennedy's Patent Bosh Plate, made of Climax Bronze. When relining A Bosh "Gayley's" removable Bronze plate was used, and in relining B Bosh "Scott's" removable plate was used.   See lower cut on opposite page.

The B System of Bosh fitting is used.

For description of Gayley's Patent Bosh Plate see pages 80 and 81.

For description of Scott's Patent Bosh Plate see pages 78 and 79.

GRACE FURNACE NO. 2. BRIER HILL IRON AND COAL CO., YOUNGSTOWN, OHIO.

GRACE FURNACE, No. 2,

OF THE

BRIER HILL IRON & COAL COMPANY.

YOUNGSTOWN, OHIO.

On the opposite side a general view of the above furnace is given. This furnace was completed June 1st, 1891, and was put in blast six days later. Its dimensions are: 77 feet high, 18 feet 9 in. diameter of bosh, 10 feet well, 13 feet 6 in. at stock line.

Stove equipment consists of 4--19 feet 6 in. by 65 feet Massicks & Crooke's Stoves, built by McClure & Amsler, Pittsburg, Pa.

Blast is furnished by two Robinson-Rea engines, 36 in. by 54 in. by 84 in., and one Wm. Tod & Co. engine, 42 in. by 48 in. by 84 in.

Steam power is furnished by 14 Two-flue Boilers, 50 in. by 30 feet each. Six 6 inch Tuyeres are used.

Total output from June 7th, 1891, to April 1st, 1893, 22 months, 143,340 Tons. Largest month's output, 7890 Tons. Largest day's output, 282½ Tons.

Ran on Bessemer from Aug. 26, 1892, to Jan'y 31, 1893, without a cast of No. 3 Iron and Coke under 2000 lbs. 790 Casts in all, and an average output for this time of 240 Tons per day.

Average Temperature, 1200 degrees, and a very uniform pressure of 7 to 8 lbs. on 2800 cubic feet blast.

Furnace at this date is apparently in as good shape as the day it was blown in, and is doing as good work now as any time during blast. As yet have not lost a single cooling plate.

R. C. STEESE, Supt.

Youngstown, Ohio, April 1, 1893.

This furnace is equipped with **"Pollock's" Bronze Bosh Plates.**

SEE NEXT PAGE.

BEST, FOX & CO.

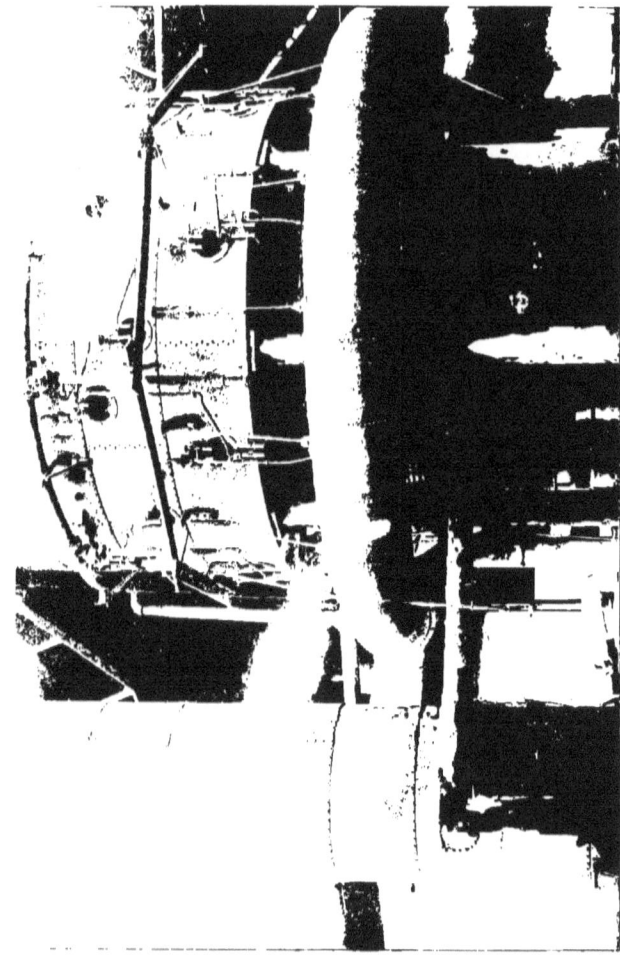

BOSH OF GRACE FURNACE NO. 2. BRIER HILL IRON AND COAL CO., YOUNGSTOWN, OHIO.

GRACE FURNACE, No. 2,

OF THE

BRIER HILL IRON AND COAL COMPANY,

YOUNGSTOWN, OHIO.

On the opposite page a view of the lower part of this Furnace is given. Eight rows of Pollock's Patent Bosh Plates made of Climax Bronze are used to protect the bosh walls, three rows of which are placed above the mantel as shown. This gives effectual cooling to the greatest bosh diameter, and insures no cutting above mantel which is so often the case where cooling plates come no higher than the mantel.

The K. & M. style of fitting is used on this bosh. See cut. An 8 in. wrot. iron circular coil with eight 8x4 Flanged Tees is placed about 18 in. above topmost row of plates. Next to each of these Tees a 4 in. Gate Valve is placed so as to control each large drop feed independent of the main circular pipe. 1¼ in. holes are tapped directly into the circular pipe to feed the three upper rows, which is accomplished by the water dropping into open funnel on supply inlet of top row, and over-flowing to row below, and this in turn overflowing into third row, then wasting into trough.

The rows below mantel obtain their supply from 1¼ in. pipes tapped into 4 in. drops which feed into open funnels and overflowing into lower rows similar to connections above mantel, except waste from lowest plate is connected to spray pipe, and by means of Three-way Tuyere Cock is carried to the bottom of furnace direct when sprinkling is not desired.

Plates are cleaned thoroughly by forcing heavy hose connected with boiler feed pumps into the open funnels which stirs up all sediment, and which is carried off through waste pipe.

Tuyeres, Coolers, Notch and Notch Coolers are supplied from a separate circular pipe inside of columns, the bustle pipe hiding the same from view.

No plate has been lost from the time furnace went into blast to the time of this writing, Nov. 1, 1894, or forty-one months.

Full description of **Pollock's Patent Plate** is given on pages 74, 75, 76 and 77.

BEST FOX & CO.

BASE OF ONE OF THE CAMBRIA IRON CO.'S FURNACES, JOHNSTOWN, PA.

CAMBRIA IRON COMPANY,

JOHNSTOWN, PA.

This Company has six Furnaces, four of which were originally built in 1853-54.

Nos. 1 and 2, each 76 ft. x 16 ft., were rebuilt in 1883.

Nos. 2 and 3, each 76 ft. x 16 ft., were rebuilt in 1886.

No. 5, 76 ft. x 19 ft. was built in 1876.

No. 6, 76 ft. x 19 ft. was built in 1879.

Twenty Whitwell Stoves are used in connection with same. Annual capacity 350,000 tons.

All these furnaces are equipped with "Fronheiser's Patent Bosh Boxes," removable, and with water not under pressure, and this cooling device has been in use for fifteen years, giving entire satisfaction.

Until the year 1887, the bosh walls were made 27 in. thick and boxes 22 in. long used with same. Owing to the excellent condition of boshes being preserved by the boxes, (furnaces having given out above same), it was decided to reduce the walls to 22 in. This thickness of wall has been in use seven years, giving satisfactory results. Owing to the thinner walls, increased diameter of bosh and hearth has been obtained with corresponding increase of product, and at the same time a decrease in the cost of material and labor entering into the construction of the bosh.

The base of furnace shown on opposite side is one of four, having cast iron jacket at bottom and steel riveted jacket around bosh. The remaining two furnaces use no steel jacket, bands only being used above tuyeres. The L system of Bosh fitting is used.

Very few boxes are lost as the hand-hole plate in the back of boxes gives access to the inside of box for thorough cleaning.

For full description of **Fronheiser's Bosh Box,** see pages 70, 71, 72 and 73.

BEST, FOX & CO.

BOSH COOLING PLATES OR BOXES

MADE OF CLIMAX BRONZE HAVE BEEN

Furnished by us to the following Furnaces:

ANDREWS BROS. CO.,	Hazleton, Ohio.
ATLANTIC IRON AND STEEL CO.,	New Castle, Pa.
BELLAIRE NAIL WORKS,	Bellaire, Ohio.
BRIER HILL IRON AND COAL CO.,	Brier Hill, Ohio.
BRISTOL IRON AND STEEL CO.,	Bristol, Va.
BUFFALO FURNACE CO.,	Buffalo, N. Y.
CARBON IRON AND STEEL CO.,	Parryville, Pa.
CAMBRIA IRON CO.,	Johnstown, Pa. 6 Furnaces.
CARNEGIE STEEL CO.,	Bessemer, Pa. 9 "
CARNEGIE STEEL CO.,	Pittsburg, Pa. 2 "
CARRIE FURNACE CO.,	Rankin, Pa. 2 "
CHARLOTTE FURNACE CO.,	Scottdale, Pa.
CHERRY VALLEY IRON WORKS,	Leetonia, Ohio.
CLEVELAND ROLLING MILL CO.,	Cleveland, Ohio. 3 Furnaces.
CLINTON IRON AND STEEL CO.,	Pittsburgh, Pa.
COLEBROOK FURNACE,	Lebanon, Pa.
COOK, D. S.,	Glen Wilton, Va.
CORNWALL IRON CO.,	Cornwall, Pa. 2 Furnaces.
GIRARD IRON CO.,	Girard, Ohio.
GRAHAM FURNACE CO.,	Graham, Va.
HAINSWORTH STEEL CO.,	Allegheny, Pa.
ILLINOIS STEEL CO.,	Joliet, Ills. 2 Furnaces.
IRIQUOIS FURNACE CO.,	South Chicago, Ills.
ISABELLA FURNACE CO.,	Etna, Pa. 3 Furnaces.
ISABELLA FURNACE CO.,	Wyebrook, Pa.
JEFFERSON IRON WORKS,	Steubenville, Ohio.
JUNCTION IRON CO.,	Mingo Junction, Ohio.
KING, GILBERT & WARNER CO.,	Columbus, Ohio.
KING, GILBERT & WARNER CO.,	Moxahala, Ohio.
MARYLAND STEEL CO.,	Sparrows Point, Md. 4 Furnaces.
MAHONING VALLEY IRON CO.,	Youngstown, Ohio.
MONONGAHELA FURNACE CO.,	McKeesport, Pa. 2 Furnaces.
NORTH CORNWALL FURNACE.,	North Cornwall, Pa.

FURNACES USING BRONZE BOSH COOLING DEVICES
CONTINUED.

PALMER SHIP BUILDING CO., .	Jarrow, England.
PENNA. STEEL CO.,	Steelton, Pa. 4 Furnaces.
PIERCE, KELLY & Co.,	Sharpsville, Pa.
POUGHKEEPSIE IRON CO.,	Poughkeepsie. N. Y.
POTTSTOWN IRON CO.,	Pottstown, Pa.
PULASKI IRON CO., .	Pulaski, Va.
RADFORD-CRANE IRON CO.,	Radford, Va.
READING IRON CO.,	Temple, Pa.
ROANE IRON CO.,	Rockwood, Tenn.
ROSENA FURNACE CO.,	New Castle. Pa.
SALEM IRON CO., . .	Leetonia, Ohio.
SHENANGO VALLEY STEEL CO.,	New Castle, Pa.
SHARON IRON CO.,	Sharon, Pa.
SHOENBERGER & CO.,	Pittsburg. Pa. 2 Furnaces.
SPATHITE IRON CO.,	Florence, Ala.
STICKNEY IRON CO .	Baltimore, Md.
THOMAS FURNACE CO.,	Niles, Ohio.
THROPP, JOS E.,	Everett. Pa.
UNION ROLLING MILL CO .	Cleveland, Ohio.
VIRGINIA IRON AND R. W. CO.,	Goshen, Va.
WARWICK IRON CO.,	Pottstown. Pa.
YOUNGSTOWN STEEL CO.,	Youngstown, Ohio.

Plans in Detail with Specifications and Estimates

submitted for any style of Bosh-Cooling. **Satisfaction Guaranteed.**

Reverse the book and see pages 122, 123, 124 for Furnaces and Boshes fitted by us.

We will not attempt to enumerate the furnaces using our **Climax Bronze Tuyeres, Coolers, Notches, Valves, Seats, etc.,** but will only say that we have over eight hundred patterns to satisfy the demand coming from all parts of the world.

WE KEEP	⎞ 500 Tuyeres,
IN STOCK	⎟ 200 Notches,
CONSTANTLY	⎨ 40 Coolers and Notch Coolers,
	⎠ Assortment of Plates, Boxes and Seats.

PROMPT SHIPMENT THEREBY ASSURED.

BEST, FOX & CO.

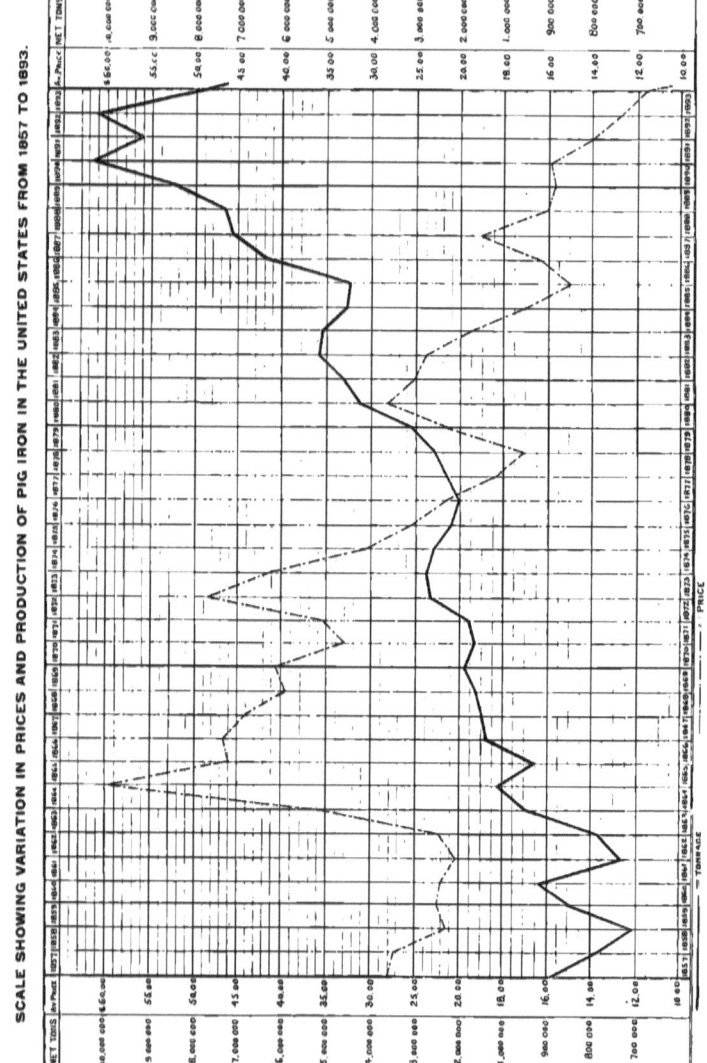

SCALE SHOWING VARIATION IN PRICES AND PRODUCTION OF PIG IRON IN THE UNITED STATES FROM 1857 TO 1893.

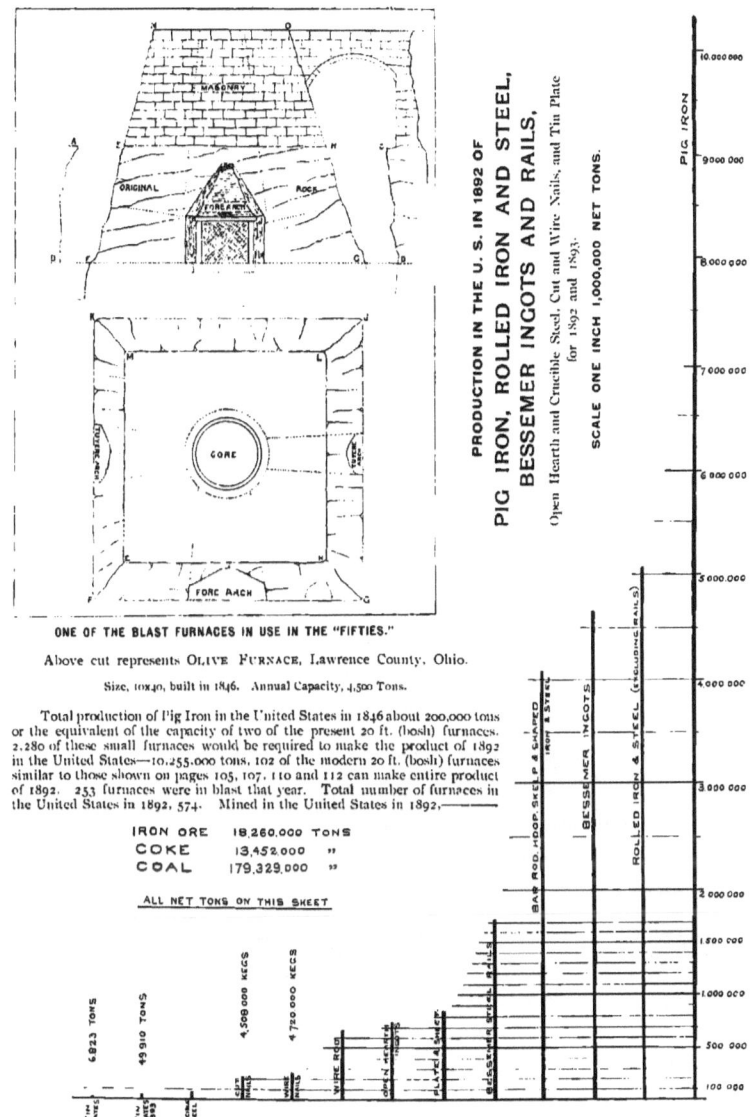

PIG IRON, ROLLED IRON AND STEEL, BESSEMER INGOTS AND RAILS,

PRODUCTION IN THE U. S. IN 1892 OF

Open Hearth and Crucible Steel, Cut and Wire Nails, and Tin Plate for 1892 and 1893.

SCALE ONE INCH 1,000,000 NET TONS.

ONE OF THE BLAST FURNACES IN USE IN THE "FIFTIES."

Above cut represents OLIVE FURNACE, Lawrence County, Ohio.

Size, 10x40, built in 1846. Annual Capacity, 4,500 Tons.

Total production of Pig Iron in the United States in 1846 about 200,000 tons or the equivalent of the capacity of two of the present 20 ft. (bosh) furnaces. 2,280 of these small furnaces would be required to make the product of 1892 in the United States—10,255,000 tons, 102 of the modern 20 ft. (bosh) furnaces similar to those shown on pages 105, 107, 110 and 112 can make entire product of 1892. 253 furnaces were in blast that year. Total number of furnaces in the United States in 1892, 574. Mined in the United States in 1892,———

IRON ORE	18,260,000 TONS
COKE	13,452,000 "
COAL	179,329,000 "

ALL NET TONS ON THIS SHEET

BEST, FOX & CO.

TUYERE WITH PIPE INSIDE.   **REDUCING NOZZLES.**

We make Reducing Nozzles to suit Tuyeres of any size of Climax Bronze.

NOTE.

FIRST. All Tuyeres, Coolers, Bosh Plates and Boxes should always have their discharge on top in every instance. No air can possibly remain in them if this is observed.

SECOND. It is not material at what point Supply is connected to the Tuyere; it is important, however, that this Supply should be connected into the opening having plug with projecting square which has pipe inside for the purpose of conveying Feed Water to nose. (See sketch.) This pipe is found in all Tuyeres and Coolers 12 in. long and over.

THIRD. Tuyeres and Coolers burned at the nose, or outside as large as 2 in. square we can often repair and make practically as good as new. Furnace men can repair small holes in bronze castings at the Furnace with annealed Copper Rod that can be threaded and screwed into said holes, and in addition to the tapping, this Copper can be piened to assist in making the casting tight. This Copper Rod we can furnish of any size, also Taps and Dies to cut threads. We also carry in stock Brass Counter Sunk Plugs that are often used for closing drill holes in bronze castings.

FOURTH. How to detect leaky Tuyeres. The metal joint between the Tuyere and Cooler will if there is any leak in the Tuyere, or at the nose of the Cooler, draw the moisture to the heel or butt of the Tuyere; moisture only indicates a slight leak; blue trickling water means that leaky casting should be promptly removed. The old way of detecting leaky Tuyeres was at casting time, to draw the gas through the stoves, insert rod in Tuyeres, and the leaky one could be detected by the moisture on the rod.

FIFTH. How to detect leaky Plates with water under pressure. If the leak is a serious one, both gas and steam will show with the discharge water. If the leak is slight, slack the water supply to Plates under suspicion, turn discharge pipe down below level of these Plates, hold lighted lamp at discharge water, and if any Plate in the group leaks, it will develop by gas igniting; if this does not occur, it can be depended upon that no Plate in said group leaks; (it being understood that blast is meantime constantly on the Furnace). To detect which Plate in the group leaks, make temporary connections to one Plate at a time by means of emergency hose and coupling connections, that each furnace should have two or three of. In case no spare Plates are on hand, the leaky one can remain in the Furnace without fear of damage as long as discharge pipe is kept below the level of leaky Plate, and the water pressure no greater than the blast pressure.

How to prevent frequent loss of Tuyeres by drilling. Remove Tuyere in question; ram clay in the opening the Tuyere came out of; then shove Tuyere into same, but do not blow through it for an hour, and the molten steam will then have found a new current.

How to force the blast across the Hearth when required in emergencies. Plug a Tuyere solid with good furnace clay, drive a tapered wooden plug through same, of the size wanted, and you have a reduced Tuyere that will last several hours before the clay is gone.

N. B.—We are at the service of our friends for such information as we can and will cheerfully give. Don't hesitate to ask.

WE MAKE

WATER AND AIR COOLED DEVICES

OF ANY CONSTRUCTION OF

CLIMAX BRONZE

FOR

SILVER,
COPPER,
GLASS,
STEEL
AND IRON

SMELTING FURNACES.

CORRESPONDENCE SOLICITED.

FOR————

PIPE,

FITTINGS,

VALVES,

AND SPECIALTIES OF ANY DESCRIPTION

REQUIRED TO CONVEY

STEAM, WATER, GAS, OIL, AIR, ETC., ETC.

REVERSE THE BOOK.

A
B
C
D
E
F
G
H
I
J
K
L
M
N
O
P
Q
R
S
T
U
V
W
X
Y

54,000 Square Feet, or 1¼ Acres Floor Space.

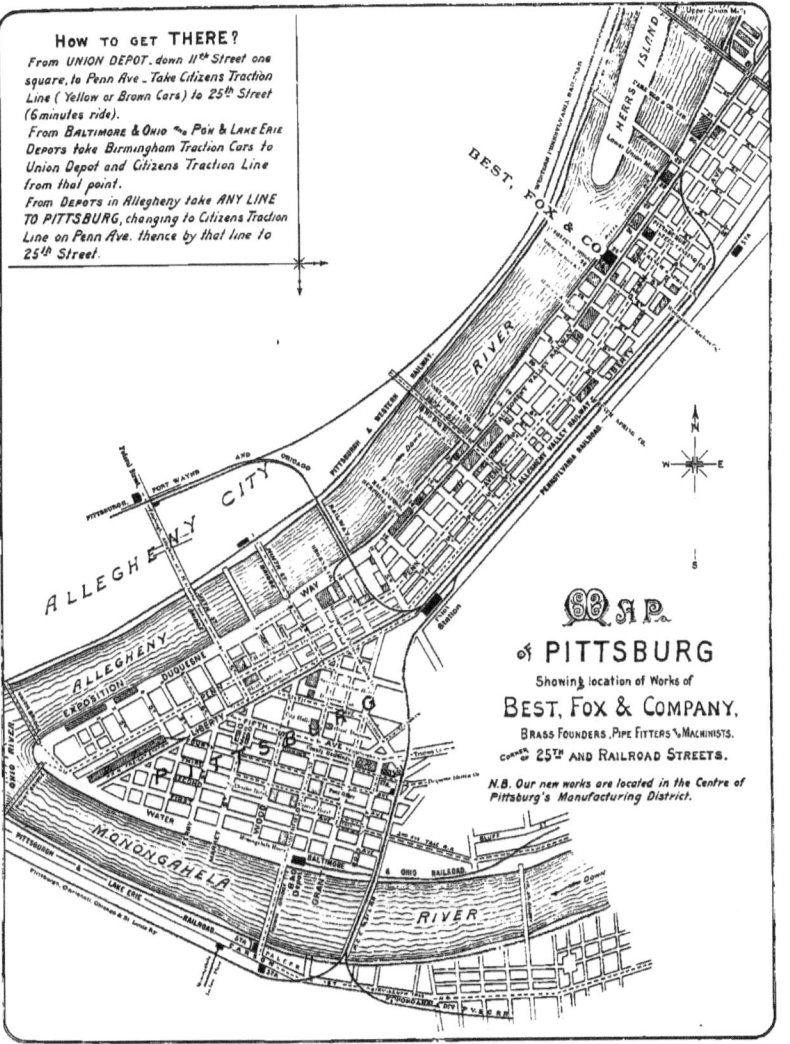

How to get THERE?

From *UNION DEPOT*, down 11th Street one square, to Penn Ave. Take Citizens Traction Line (Yellow or Brown Cars) to 25th Street (6 minutes ride).

From BALTIMORE & OHIO and PAN & LAKE ERIE Depots take Birmingham Traction Cars to Union Depot and Citizens Traction Line from that point.

From DEPOTS in Allegheny take ANY LINE TO PITTSBURG, changing to Citizens Traction Line on Penn Ave. thence by that line to 25th Street.

MAP

of PITTSBURG

Showing location of Works of

BEST, FOX & COMPANY,

BRASS FOUNDERS, PIPE FITTERS & MACHINISTS.

CORNER OF 25TH AND RAILROAD STREETS.

N.B. Our new works are located in the Centre of Pittsburg's Manufacturing District.

A B C D E F G H I J K L M N O P Q R S T U V W X Y

TRADE MARK.

CABLE ADDRESS *"BESTFOX"* PITTSBURGH.

LONG - - - *TELEPHONE*
DISTANCE *PITTSBURGH.*

DIRECT COMMUNICATION TO ALL POINTS.

TELEPHONE AND TELEGRAPH MESSAGES

RECEIVE PROMPT ATTENTION AT

ALL HOURS, DAY AND NIGHT.

PRESS OF J. B. SAVAGE
CLEVELAND, O.

ESTABLISHED 1884.

GEORGE BEST. DANIEL FOX. WM. H. H. SHEETS.

BEST, FOX & CO.,

BRASS FOUNDERS, IRON PIPE FITTERS
AND
MACHINISTS.

• • • • •

SOLE MANUFACTURERS OF

CLIMAX BRONZE,

ALSO

VALVES AND FITTINGS.

• • • • •

DEALERS IN

PIPE, FITTINGS AND SUPPLIES

FOR ALL PURPOSES.

Pipe from $\frac{1}{8}$ to 24 Inch Diameter Bent to Order.
Heavy Pipe Work a Specialty.
Erected in All Parts of the World.

———

OFFICE AND WORKS.

TWENTY-FIFTH & RAILROAD STS. & ALLEGHENY RIVER,
PITTSBURGH. PA., U. S. A.

———

CATALOGUE F. 1894.

ESTABLISHED 1884.

ANNOUNCEMENT.

FIRST CATALOGUE. IT IS WITH PLEASURE that we present our first Illustrated Catalogue to our friends, and hope it will prove to be of value to them.

The illustrations show the principal articles we manufacture and handle. We invite enquiries for anything in the pipe fitting, machine or brass foundry line that may be wanted and is not shown.

TEN YEARS OLD. Ten years ago we began business in a small shop. Reliable work and prompt delivery have increased our business to such an extent as to require the large buildings shown in which to execute our work.

NEW SHOPS. Our new fitting and machine shop, and brass and bronze foundries, are among the largest and best equipped in the country. We make bronze castings weigh-

CAPACITY. ing from 1 oz. to 12,000 lbs., of any character, and lead the world in Bronze Cooling Specialties for Blast Furnaces.

LARGE PIPE BENDING. Our equipment for making valves and fittings from 48 inches down is complete, and our power appliances for bending wrought and steel pipes are not equalled anywhere.

We have experienced fitters to erect pipe work in all parts of the world.

PLANS. Plans and specifications submitted for any work in our line.

With sidings from Pennsylvania R. R. system directly in front of our

SHIPPING FACILITIES. property, and from the Baltimore & Ohio immediately in the rear, (and property also abutting on the Allegheny river) we have unsurpassed shipping facilities.

We will use the same diligence and zeal that achieved our past success to retain and increase our business in the future.

We thank our many friends for past favors, and shall endeavor to merit future orders from old and new customers by prompt and careful attention to all business entrusted to us.

Sincerely,

BEST. FOX & CO.

Pittsburgh, Pa., October 1st, 1894.

INDEX.

PAGE.

A
B
C
D
E
F
G
H
I
J
K
L
M
N
O
P
Q
R
S
T
U
V
W
X
Y

BEST, FOX & CO.

INDEX.—Continued.

D
E
F
G
H
I
J
K
L
M
N
O
P
Q
R
S
T
U
V
W
X
Y

BEST, FOX & CO.

INDEX.—CONTINUED.

M
N
O
P
Q
R
S
T
U
V
W
X
Y

INDEX.--Continued.

STEEL OR WROUGHT IRON PIPE.

BLACK OR GALVANIZED.

From ⅜ inch to 15 inch diameter inside.

See dimensions, page 3.

See table, page 107.

FIG. I.

SPIRAL WELD PIPE.

From 6 inch to 24 inch diameter.

See table, page 108.

FIG. 2.

SPIRAL RIVETTED PIPE.

BLACK OR GALVANIZED.

From 6 inch to 24 inch diameter.

Plain, Flanged or Bowl ends.

See table, page 108.

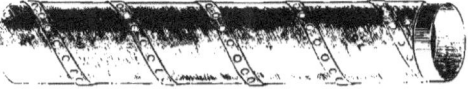

FIG. 3.

CAST IRON BOWL PIPE.

FOR WATER AND GAS.

From 2 in. to 60 in. diameter.

See table, page 109.

FIG. 4.

CAST IRON FLANGED PIPE.

FOR STEAM AND WATER.

From 3 inch to 48 inch diameter.

See table, page 110.

FIG. 5.

LIGHT CAST IRON SOIL PIPE.

From 2 inch to 12 inch diameter.

See table, page 111.

FIG. 6.

WOOD WATER PIPE.

From 1¾ inch to 16 inch diameter.

For Mines, Tanneries, Acid Works, etc.

See table, page 111.

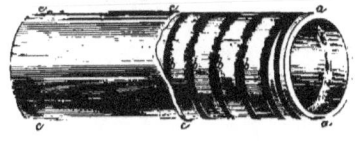

FIG. 7.

Descriptive circular of any of the above pipes on application.

STEEL OR WROUGHT IRON BOILER TUBES OR O. D. PIPE.

From 1 inch to 30 inches diameter.
See dimensions, page 4.
See table, page 112.

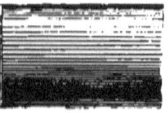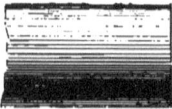

FIG. 8.

LAP WELD CASING.

From 2 inches to 9⅝ inches diameter.
See table, page 111.

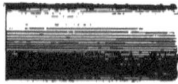

FIG. 9.

EXTRA HEAVY PIPE.

From ⅛ inches to 8 inches diameter.
See dimensions, page 5.
See table, page 113.

FIG. 10.

DOUBLE EXTRA HEAVY PIPE.

From ¼ inch to 8 inches diameter.
See dimensions, page 6.
See table, page 113.

FIG. 11.

RIVETTED PIPE.
HEAVY AND LIGHT.
BLACK OR GALVANIZED.

From 8 inches to 60 inches diameter
For any pressure.

FIG. 12.

SEAMLESS BRASS AND COPPER PIPE.
HEAVY AND LIGHT.

From ⅛ inch to 8 inches diameter.
See table, page 114.

FIG. 13.

LEAD PIPE.
HEAVY AND LIGHT.

From ⅜ inch to 2 inches diameter.
See table, page 114.

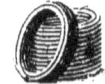

FIG. 14.

BEST, FOX & CO.

STANDARD SIZES STEEL AND WROUGHT IRON PIPE.

Butt Weld 1¼ inch and below.   Lap Weld 1½ and above.

See Table. **page 107.**

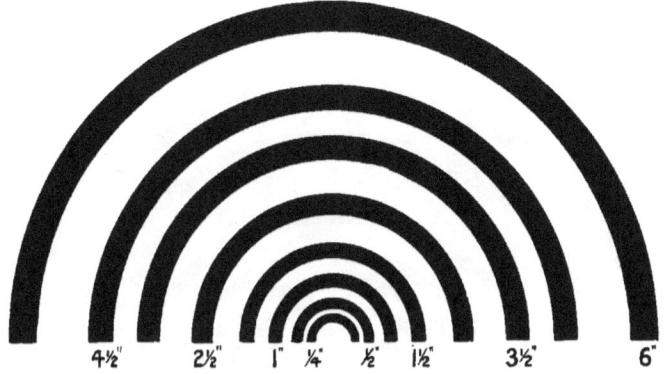

4½"   2½"   1" ¼" ½" 1½"   3½"   6"

5"   3"   1¼" ⅜" ⅛" ¾"   2"   4"   7"

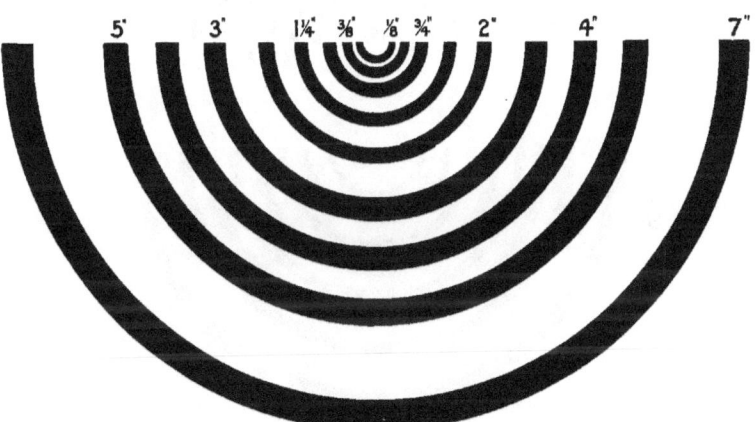

FIG. 15.

We keep in stock all sizes to 15 in. inside diameter, and **Cut, Thread, Bend and Fit** any size to order.

No pipe threaded above 15 in. internal or 16 in. external diameter.

BEST, FOX & CO.

STANDARD SIZES O. D. PIPE OR LAP WELD BOILER TUBES.

MADE OF CHARCOAL IRON OR SOFT STEEL

See page 112.

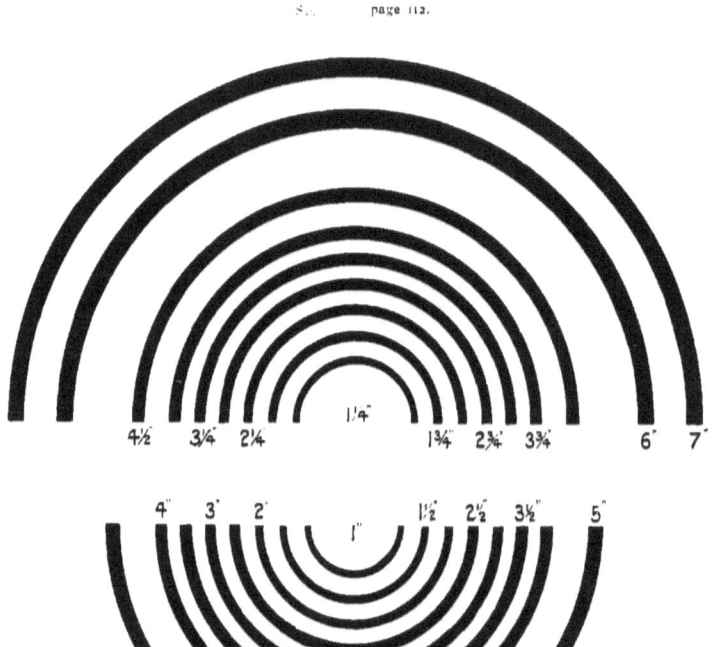

FIG. 16.

BEST, FOX & CO.

STANDARD SIZES EXTRA HEAVY PIPE.

See Table. page 113.

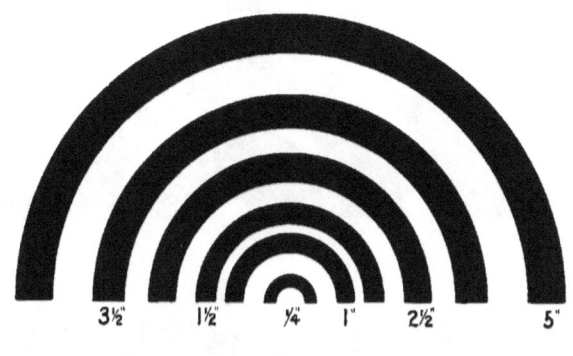

FIG. 17.

All the above **sizes** and to 8 in. kept **in stock**, and Cut. Threaded and Bent to order.

NOTE - External diameters remain the same as standard pipe, and internal diameter is decreased to obtain additional thickness.

BEST, FOX & CO.

STANDARD SIZES DOUBLE EXTRA HEAVY PIPE.
See Table, page 113.

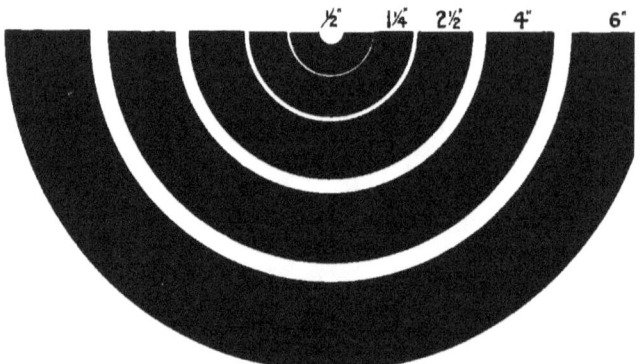

¾"   1½"   3"   5"

½"   1¼"   2½"   4"   6"

FIG. 19.

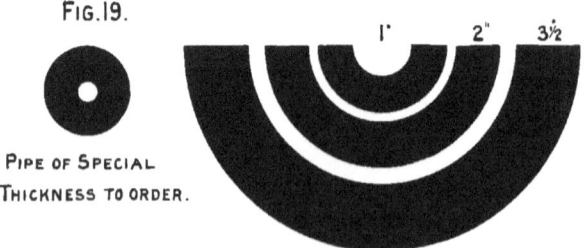

1"   2"   3½"

PIPE OF SPECIAL
THICKNESS TO ORDER.

FIG. 18.
Any of the above sizes and to 8 in., Cut, Threaded and Bent to order.
NOTE.—External diameters remain the same is standard pipe, internal diameter is decreased to obtain additional thickness.

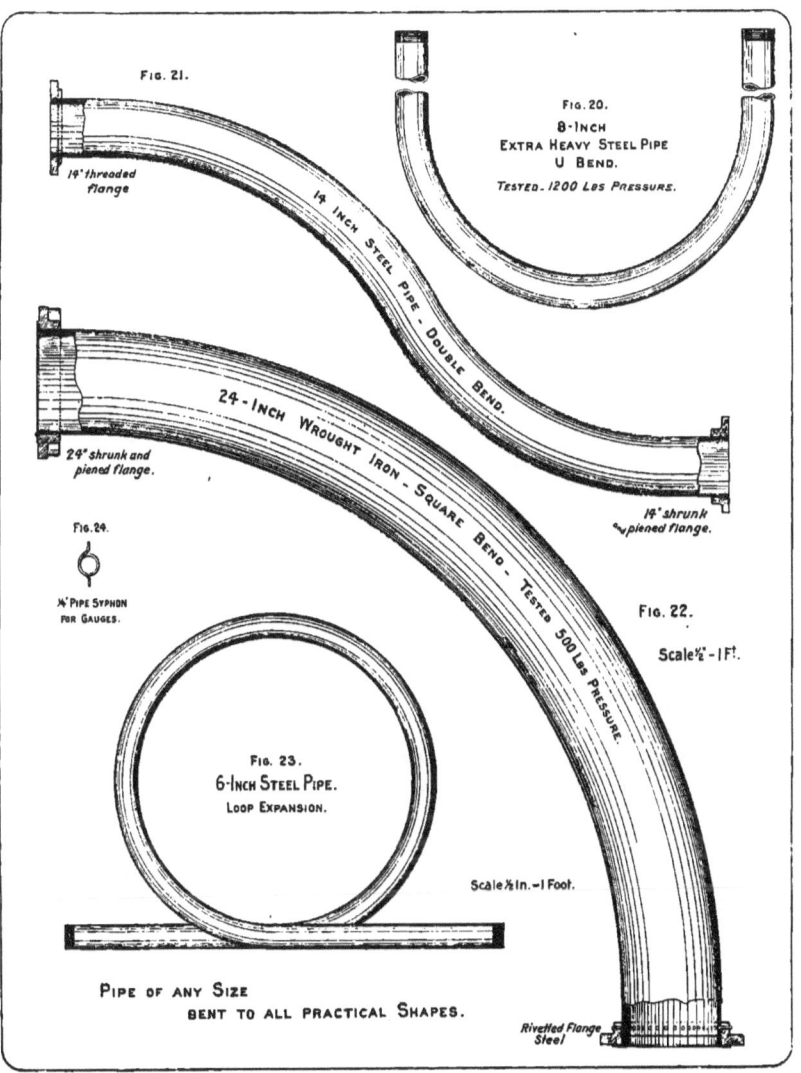

FIG. 21.

14" threaded
flange

FIG. 20.

8-INCH
EXTRA HEAVY STEEL PIPE
U BEND.

TESTED. 1200 LBS PRESSURE.

14 INCH STEEL PIPE - DOUBLE BEND.

24 - INCH WROUGHT IRON - SQUARE BEND - TESTED 500 LBS PRESSURE.

24" shrunk and
piened flange.

14" shrunk
and piened flange.

FIG. 24.

¾" PIPE SYPHON
FOR GAUGES.

FIG. 22.

Scale ½" - 1 Ft.

FIG. 23.

6-INCH STEEL PIPE.

LOOP EXPANSION.

Scale ½ In. - 1 Foot.

PIPE OF ANY SIZE
BENT TO ALL PRACTICAL SHAPES.

Rivetted Flange
Steel

SEE TABLE *PAGE 104* FOR SMALLEST RADIUS.

BEST. FOX & CO.

WROUGHT AND MALLEABLE FITTINGS FOR IRON PIPE.

BLACK OR GALVANIZED, RIGHT OR LEFT HAND THREADS.

FIG. 25.

CLOSE NIPPLE.

FIG. 26.

SHOULDER NIPPLE.

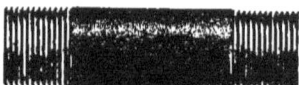

FIG. 27.

LONG NIPPLE.

FIG. 28.

LONG SCREW NIPPLE.

FIG 29

LONG SCREW, WITH RUNNING SOCKET.

FIG. 30.

SOCKET OR COUPLING.

FIG 31

SOCKET, RIGHT AND LEFT.

FEMALE HALF
OR NUT AND SWIVEL

FIG 32

MALLEABLE UNION.

COMPOSITION SEAT.   SECTION.

FIG. 33.

KEYSTONE UNION.

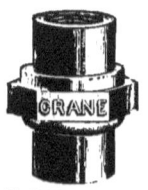

COMPOSITION GASKET.   SECTION.

FIG. 34.

CRANE UNION.

BEST, FOX & CO.

MALLEABLE FITTINGS—PLAIN.

BLACK OR GALVANIZED.

FIG 35.
ELBOW.

FIG 36·
TEE.

FIG 37.
CROSS.

FIG. 38.
CAP.

FIG. 39.
SIDE OUTLET ELBOW.

FIG. 40.
SIDE OUTLET TEE.

FIG. 41.
REDUCER.

FIG. 42.
PLUG.

FIG 43.
DROP ELBOW.

FIG. 44.
DROP TEE.

FIG. 45.
BUSHING.

FIG. 46.
LOCKNUT.

FIG. 47.
EXTENSION PIECE.

FIG. 48
WASTE NUT.

FIG. 49.
RETURN BEND.
OPEN.

FIG. 50.
RETURN BEND.
CLOSE.

Full stock of **Reducing Fittings**, also Male and Female Drop Elbows, etc., etc.

BEST, FOX & CO.

MALLEABLE FITTINGS—BEADED.

BLACK OR GALVANIZED.

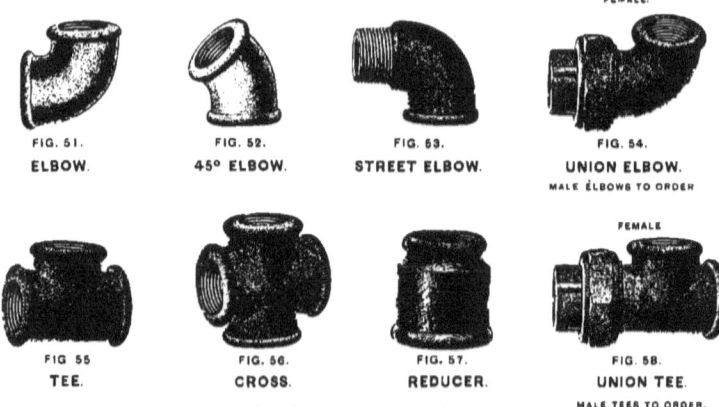

FEMALE.

FIG. 51.	FIG. 52.	FIG. 53.	FIG. 54.
ELBOW.	**45° ELBOW.**	**STREET ELBOW.**	**UNION ELBOW.**

MALE ELBOWS TO ORDER

FEMALE

FIG 55	FIG. 56.	FIG. 57.	FIG. 58.
TEE.	**CROSS.**	**REDUCER.**	**UNION TEE.**

Full stock of **Heavy Reducing Fittings.**

MALE TEES TO ORDER.

MALLEABLE RAILING FITTINGS.

SIZES ¾ INCH TO 2 INCH INCLUSIVE.

FIG 59.	FIG 60.	FIG. 61.	FIG. 62
ELBOW.	**TEE.**	**CROSS**	**ORNAMENT.**

FIG. 63.	FIG. 64.	FIG. 65.	FIG. 66.
SIDE OUTLET ELBOW.	**SIDE OUTLET TEE.**	**SIDE OUTLET CROSS.**	**C. I. RAILING FLANGE.**

Brass Railing Fittings to order.   Fittings tapped left hand when so ordered.

Railings cut and fitted complete.

RAILINGS MADE OF IRON OR BRASS PIPE.

PLAIN OR NICKEL PLATED.

Suitable for enclosing Engines, Wheel Pits, Belts, Machinery, Offices, &c.

FIG. 67.

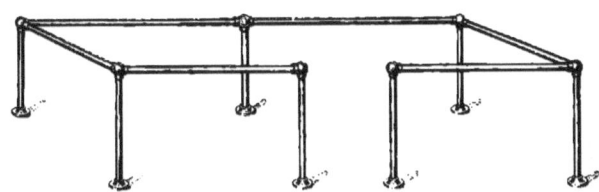

FIG. 68.

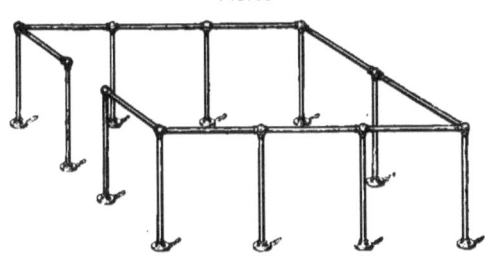

FIG. 69.

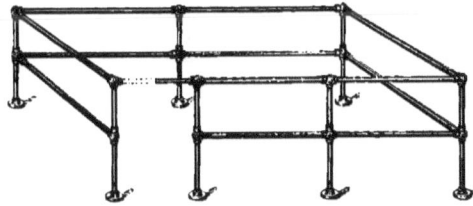

BEST, FOX & CO.

CAST IRON FITTINGS.

FIG. 70.
ELBOW.

FIG. 71.
REDUCING ELBOW.

FIG. 72.
45° ELBOW.

FIG. 73.
SIDE OUTLET ELBOW.

FIG. 74.
TEE.

FIG. 75.
TEE REDUCING ON OUTLET.

FIG. 76.
TEE REDUCING ON RUN.

FIG. 77.
SIDE OUTLET TEE.

FIG. 78.
TEE REDUCING ON END.

FIG. 79
TEE REDUCING ON END AND OUTLET.

FIG 80.
CROSS REDUCING ON SIDE OPENINGS.

FIG 81
CROSS REDUCING ON END AND SIDE OPENINGS.

FIG. 82.
CROSS.

FIG. 83
RETURN BEND OPEN.

FIG. 84
RETURN BEND CLOSE.

FIG 85
OPEN RETURN BEND WITH BACK OUTLET.

To read TEES correctly, always take measurements of run first, then outlet: 2 ——— 1, reads, 2×1×1½.

For Dimensions see **Table, page 103.**

CAST IRON FITTINGS.

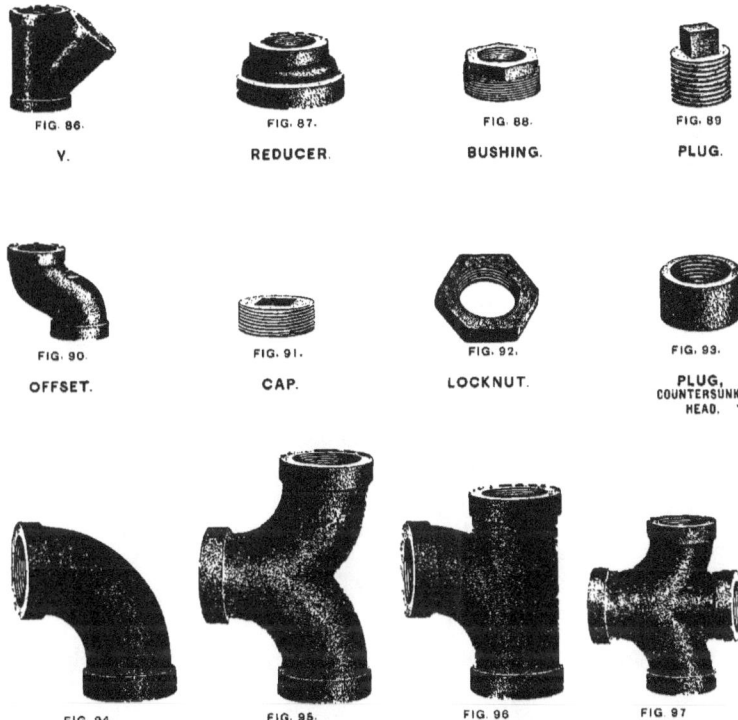

FIG. 86.

V.

FIG. 87.

REDUCER.

FIG. 88.

BUSHING.

FIG. 89

PLUG.

FIG. 90.

OFFSET.

FIG. 91.

CAP.

FIG. 92.

LOCKNUT.

FIG. 93.

**PLUG,
COUNTERSUNK
HEAD.**

FIG 94.

**LONG SWEEP
ELBOW.**

FIG. 95.

**LONG SWEEP
DOUBLE ELBOW.**

FIG. 96

**LONG SWEEP
TEE.**

FIG 97

**LONG SWEEP
CROSS.**

Long Sweep Elbows and Tees with Base, to order.

For Dimensions. See **Table, page 103.**

BEST, FOX & CO.

CAST IRON FITTINGS.

BRANCH TEES OR MANIFOLDS.   **HOOK PLATES.**

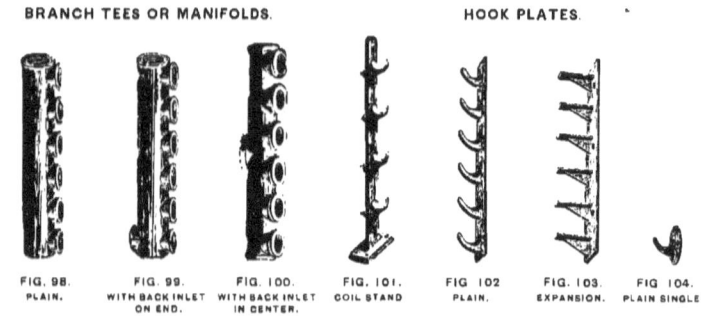

| FIG. 98.
PLAIN. | FIG. 99.
WITH BACK INLET
ON END. | FIG. 100.
WITH BACK INLET
IN CENTER. | FIG. 101.
COIL STAND | FIG 102
PLAIN. | FIG. 103.
EXPANSION. | FIG 104.
PLAIN SINGLE |

For dimensions see Table, **page 103.**

LONG RADIUS FLANGED FITTINGS TO ORDER.

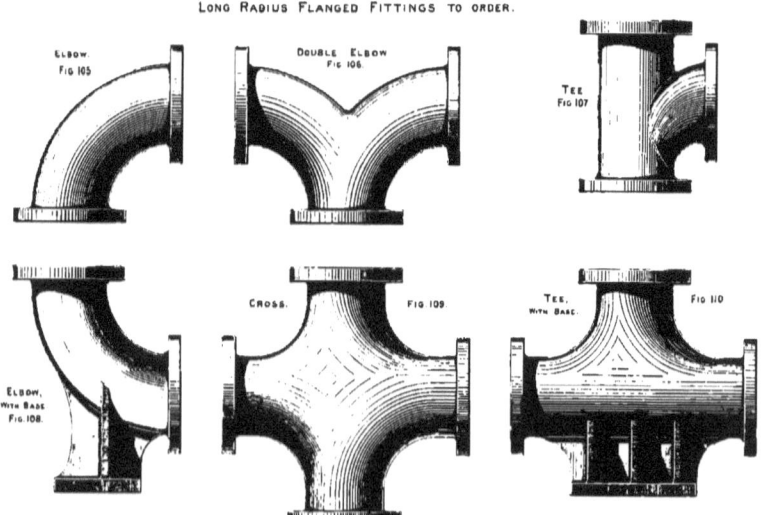

ELBOW.
FIG 105

DOUBLE ELBOW
FIG 106.

TEE
FIG 107

ELBOW,
WITH BASE
FIG. 108.

CROSS.   FIG 109

TEE,
WITH BASE.   FIG 110

For dimensions see Table, **page 104.**

FLANGES.

MADE OF
CAST IRON, CAST STEEL.   TO 30 IN. INTERNAL DIAMETER.   MADE OF
WROUGHT IRON, ROLLED STEEL, OR BRASS.

FIG 111.
FLANGED UNION.

FIG. 112.
**HYDRAULIC
FLANGED UNION.**

FIG 113.
RAISED HOLE FLANGE.

FIG. 114.
PLAIN FLANGE.

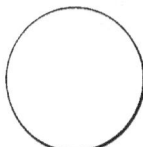

FIG. 115.
BLIND FLANGE.

FIG. 116.
CURVED FLANGE.

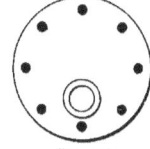

FIG. 117.
ECCENTRIC FLANGE.
FOR FULL DRAINING.

FIG. 118
SADDLE.
STEEL, MALLEABLE OR CAST IRON,
DOUBLE OR SINGLE STRAP.

FIG 119
FLANGES.
MALE AND FEMALE

FIG 120
HEAVY FLANGE.
SHRUNK AND BEADED (for Steam.)

FIG 121
LIGHT FLANGE.
SHRUNK AND BEADED (for Exhaust.)

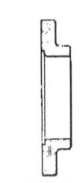

FIG 122
COPPER PIPE FLANGE.

FIG 123
**STEEL OR WROT.
FLANGE.**
FOR RIVETTING

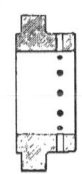

FIG 124
**CAST IRON OR
CAST STEEL FLANGE.**
FOR RIVETTING

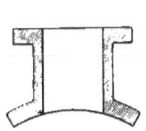

FIG 125
**CAST IRON OR
CAST STEEL NECK.**

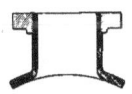

FIG 126
STEEL OR WROT. NECK,
WITH SCREWED FLANGE.

For Sizes and Dimensions see **Table, pages 100 and 101.**

FLANGED FITTINGS.

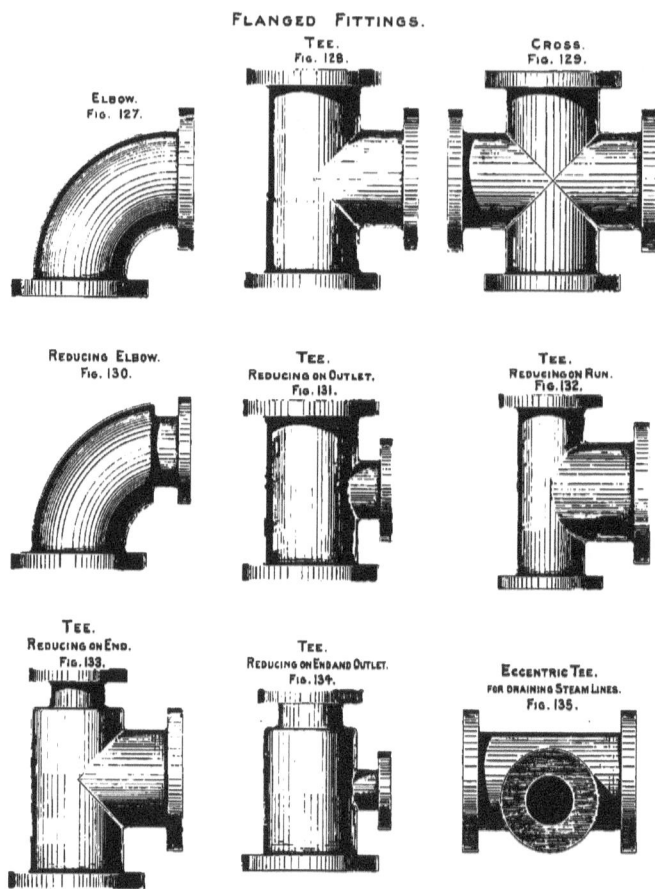

ELBOW.
FIG. 127.

TEE.
FIG. 128.

CROSS.
FIG. 129.

REDUCING ELBOW.
FIG. 130.

TEE.
REDUCING ON OUTLET.
FIG. 131.

TEE.
REDUCING ON RUN.
FIG. 132.

TEE.
REDUCING ON END.
FIG. 133.

TEE.
REDUCING ON END AND OUTLET.
FIG. 134.

ECCENTRIC TEE.
FOR DRAINING STEAM LINES.
FIG. 135.

Side Outlets on any of above and Recessed Joints to order.

For sizes and dimensions see **Table, pages 102 and 105.**

FLANGED FITTINGS.

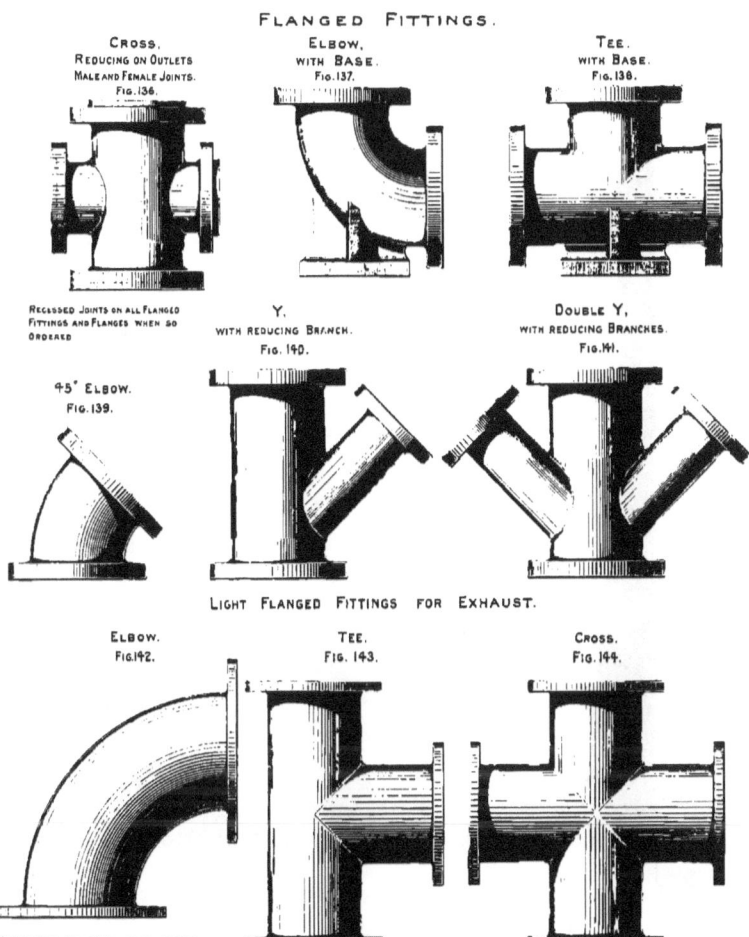

CROSS.
REDUCING ON OUTLETS
MALE AND FEMALE JOINTS.
FIG. 136.

ELBOW,
WITH BASE.
FIG. 137.

TEE.
WITH BASE.
FIG. 138.

RECESSED JOINTS ON ALL FLANGED
FITTINGS AND FLANGES WHEN SO
ORDERED

Y,
WITH REDUCING BRANCH.
FIG. 140.

DOUBLE Y,
WITH REDUCING BRANCHES.
FIG. 141.

45° ELBOW.
FIG. 139.

LIGHT FLANGED FITTINGS FOR EXHAUST.

ELBOW.
FIG. 142.

TEE.
FIG. 143.

CROSS.
FIG. 144.

LIGHT REDUCING FITTINGS TO ORDER.

Side Outlets on any of above and Recessed Joints to order.

For sizes and dimensions see Table **pages 102 and 105.**

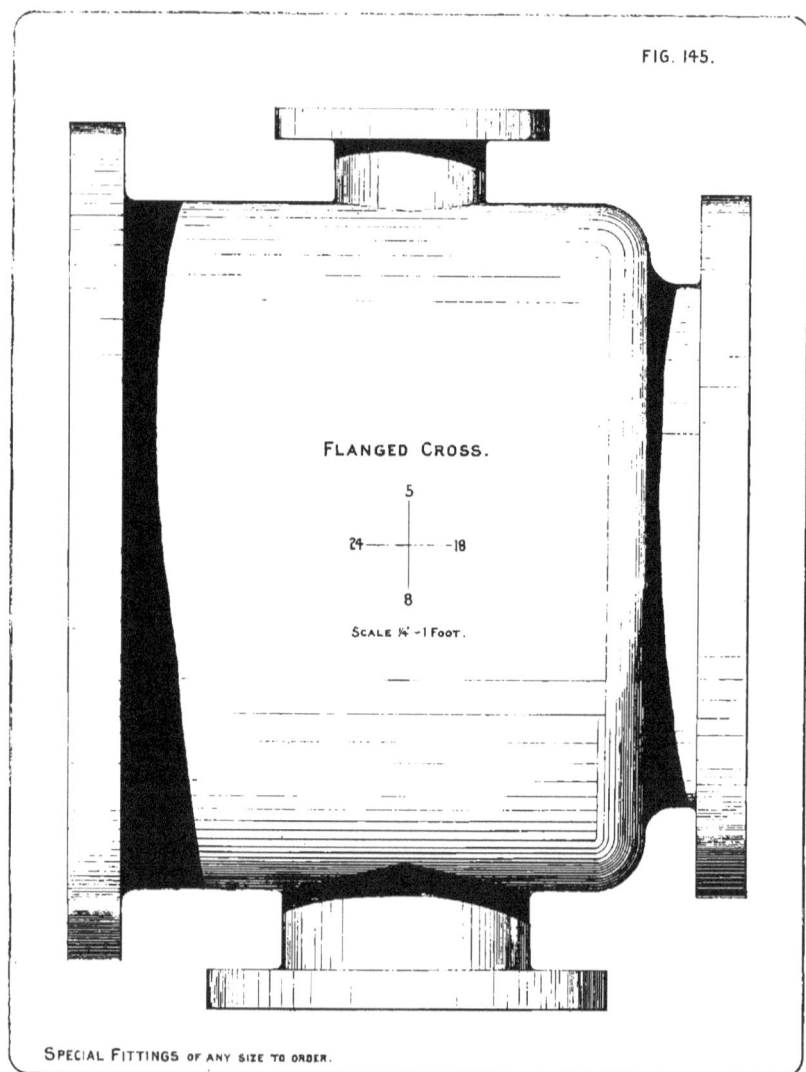

FIG. 145.

FLANGED CROSS.

24 —— 18
5
8

SCALE ¼" -1 FOOT.

SPECIAL FITTINGS OF ANY SIZE TO ORDER.

HEAVY CAST IRON STEAM PIPE FLANGE,

For 16 Inch Outside Diameter Threaded Pipe,

Guaranteed Tight at 300 Lbs. Pressure.

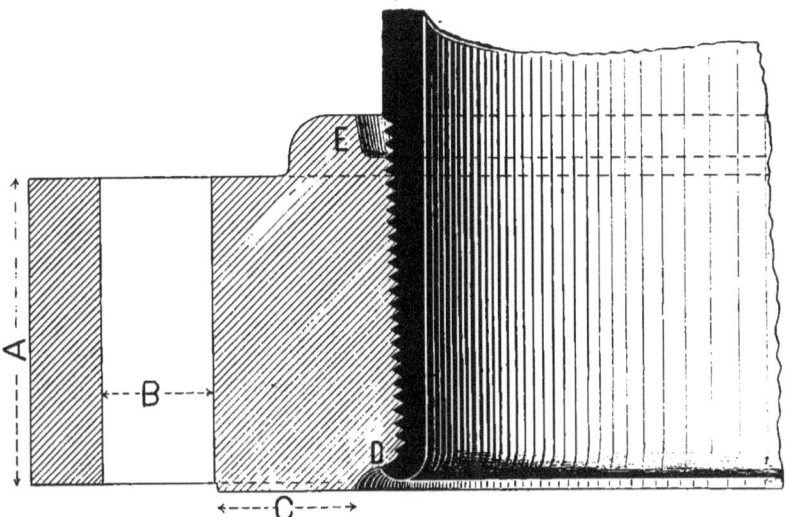

FIG. 146.

NOTE THE SPECIAL ADVANTAGES OF THIS FLANGE:

A—Thickness, giving strength and depth of thread.

B—Large size and number of bolts. (See table pages 100 and 101.)

C—Projection to receive gasket inside of bolt holes. This allows a greater pressure to bear on same than if gasket was distributed over entire face of flange.

D—End of pipe turned and pieued into groove on face of flange and then caulked. The flange is made tight by this means **entirely independent** of thread.

E—Groove or pocket on back of flange to receive copper strip for caulking if ever required.

All size Steam Flanges are made in same proportion to the above of
CAST IRON or STEEL, WROUGHT IRON or ROLLED STEEL.

BEST, FOX & CO.

THE PERFECT JOINT

ROLLED STEEL FLANGE AND STEEL PIPE.

Welded Together by ELECTRICITY.

No Threads,	No Piening.	GUARANTEED	500 lbs. Pressure using Standard Pipe.
No Rivets,	No Caulking.	ABSOLUTELY	1000 " Ex. Heavy "
	No Leaking.	TIGHT AT	2000 Dbl. Ex. "

TIGHT AS LONG AS THE PIPE LASTS.

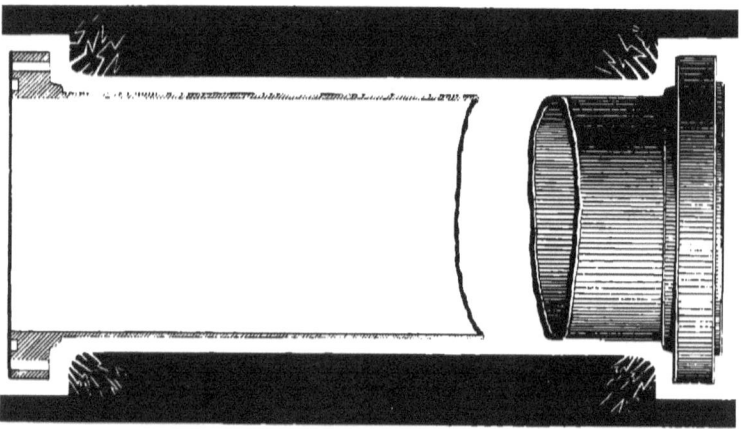

FIG. 147.

Engineers, Superintendents and Managers of High Pressure Steam Plants for Traction and Electric Light Purposes, Steel Mills, Blast Furnaces, Water Works, Paper and Pulp Mills, Sugar Refineries, Steamships, etc., have always felt the need of a **better method** of connecting large steam and hydraulic pipes and flanges together than threading, riveting or piening. This **difficulty is overcome** by welding these pieces together, thereby securing a joint that can be **depended upon absolutely.**

Rolled Steel Flanges Welded to Pipe of any size from 1 to 24 Inches Diameter.

BOWL FITTINGS FOR CAST IRON PIPE.

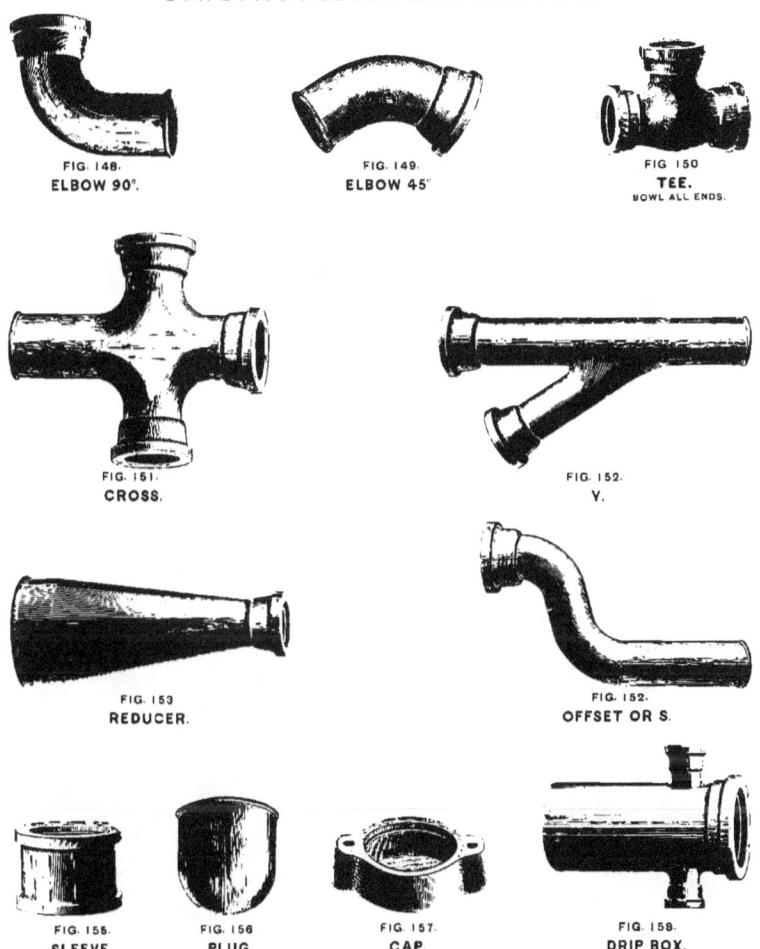

FIG. 148.
ELBOW 90°.

FIG. 149.
ELBOW 45"

FIG 150
TEE.
BOWL ALL ENDS.

FIG. 151.
CROSS.

FIG. 152.
Y.

FIG. 153
REDUCER.

FIG. 152.
OFFSET OR S.

FIG. 155.
SLEEVE.

FIG. 156
PLUG.

FIG. 157.
CAP.

FIG. 158.
DRIP BOX.

For Sizes and Weights, see Table, page 106.

AMMONIA FITTINGS, VALVES, ETC.

FIG. 159.   FIG. 160.   FIG. 161.   FIG. 162.   FIG. 163.
ELBOW.   TEE.   CROSS.   COUPLINGS.   RETURN BENDS.

FIG. 164.   FIG. 165.   FIG 166
FLANGED UNIONS.   STRAINERS.   BRANCH TEE HEADER.

FIG. 167.   FIG. 168.   FIG 169.
GLOBE AND ANGLE   CHECK VALVES.   AUTOMATIC GAUGE.
VALVES.

 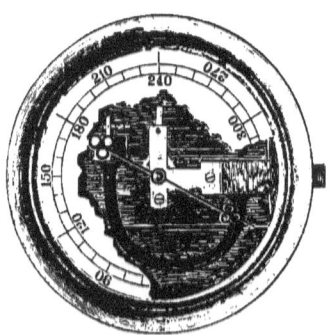

FIG. 170.   FIG. 171
AMMONIA COCK.   AMMONIA GAUGE.
ASBESTOS PACKED.

IRON BODY. **ANGLE VALVES.** BRASS MOUNTED.

FIG. 172.
SCREWED.
FINISHED BRASS TOP

FIG. 173.
CLIMAX HEAVY.
ARCH TOP SCREWED

FIG. 174.
CLIMAX HEAVY.
ARCH TOP FLANGED

GLOBE VALVES.

FIG. 175.
SCREWED.
FINISHED BRASS TOP

FIG. 176.
CLIMAX HEAVY.
ARCH TOP SCREWED

FIG. 177.
CLIMAX HEAVY.
ARCH TOP FLANGED

CHECK VALVES.

   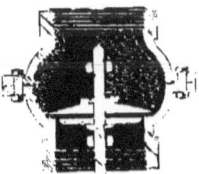

FIG. 178.
GLOBE SCREWED

FIG. 179.
CLIMAX HEAVY, GLOBE FLANGED

FIG. 180.
ANGLE SCREWED

FIG. 181.
VERTICAL SCREWED.
(IN SECTION.)

For Sizes and Dimensions see Table pages 102 and 103.

BEST, FOX & CO.

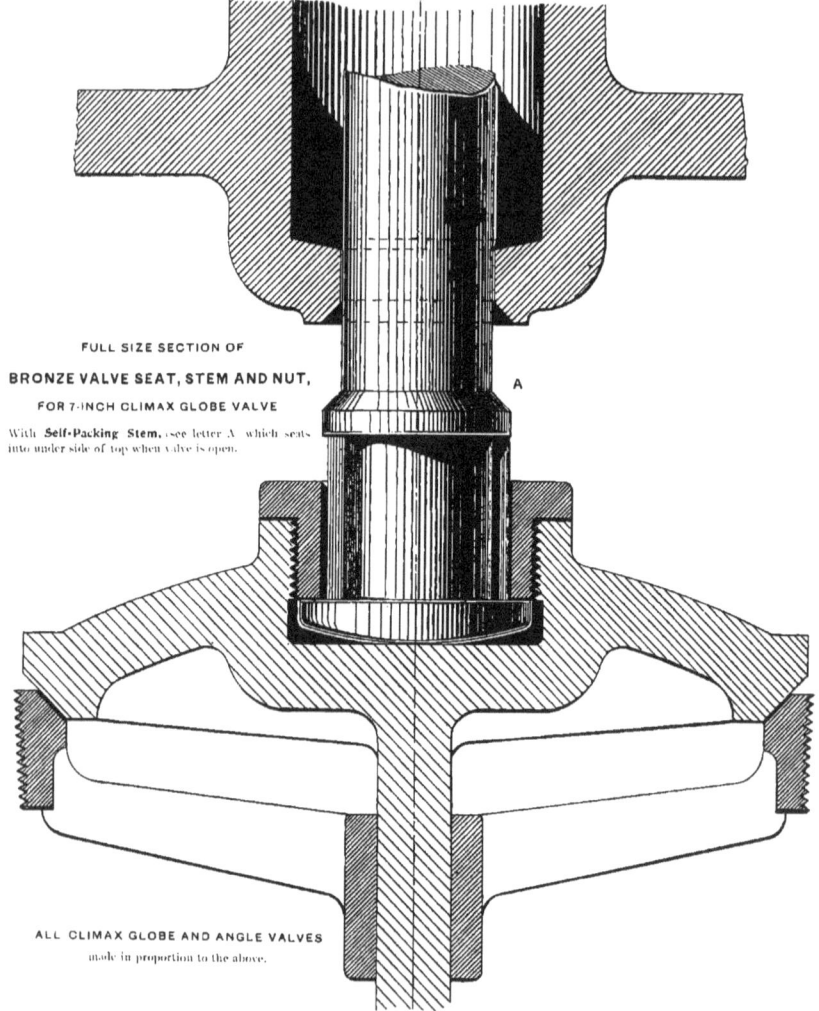

FULL SIZE SECTION OF

BRONZE VALVE SEAT, STEM AND NUT,

FOR 7-INCH CLIMAX GLOBE VALVE

With **Self-Packing Stem,** see letter A which seats into under side of top when valve is open.

A

ALL CLIMAX GLOBE AND ANGLE VALVES

made in proportion to the above.

FIG. 182.

IRON BODY. **SAFETY VALVES.** BRASS MOUNTED.

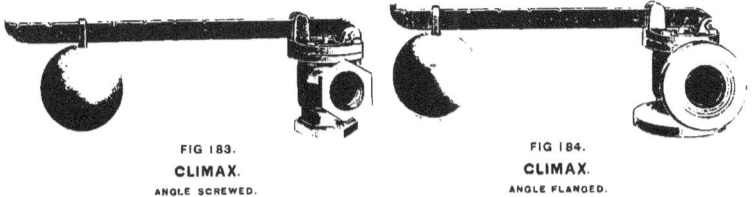

FIG 183.
CLIMAX.
ANGLE SCREWED.

FIG 184.
CLIMAX.
ANGLE FLANGED.

Three Way Climax Safety Valves to order.

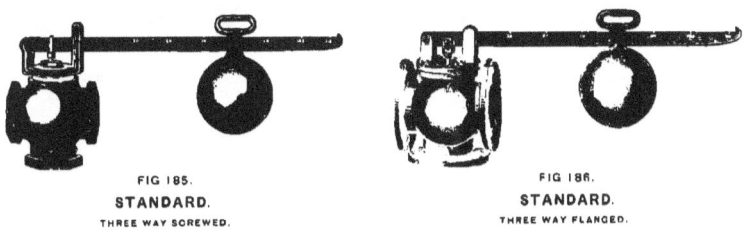

FIG 185.
STANDARD.
THREE WAY SCREWED.

FIG 186.
STANDARD.
THREE WAY FLANGED.

Steam to Engines, etc., can be taken from these Safety Valves.

SWINGING CHECK VALVES.

VALVES IN SAME ALL BRASS OR LEATHER FACE.

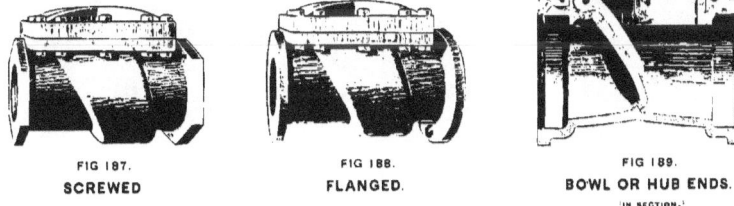

FIG 187.
SCREWED

FIG 188.
FLANGED.

FIG 189.
BOWL OR HUB ENDS.
IN SECTION.

For Sizes and Dimensions see Table pages 102 **and** 103.

BEST, FOX & CO.

IRON BODY. **JENKINS STEAM VALVES.** BRASS MOUNTED.

FIG. 190.
GLOBE VALVE SCREWED.
BRASS TOP FINISHED.

FIG. 191.
GLOBE VALVE SCREWED.
ARCH TOP.

FIG. 192.
GLOBE VALVE FLANGED.
ARCH TOP.

IRON BODY. **ASBESTOS STEAM VALVES.** BRASS MOUNTED.

FIG. 193.
ANGLE SCREWED.
BRASS TOP FINISHED.

FIG. 194.
ANGLE SCREWED.
ARCH TOP.

FIG. 195.
FLANGED.
ARCH TOP.

Discs or Rings for Renewing Jenkins and Asbestos Valves of all sizes in stock.

IRON BODY. **CLIMAX GATE VALVES.** BRASS MOUNTED OR ALL IRON.

HEAVY FOR STEAM, WATER AND GAS.

FIG. 196.
SCREWED.

FIG. 197.
FLANGED.

FIG. 198.
BOWL OR HUB ENDS.

LIGHT GATE VALVES.

FOR EXHAUST.

FIG. 199.
SCREWED.

FIG. 200.
FLANGED.

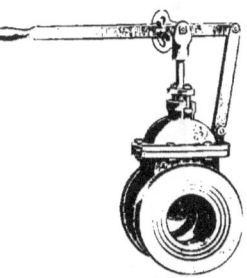

FIG. 201.
SCREWED OR FLANGED.
QUICK OPENING.

FIG. 202.
BUTTERFLY VALVE.
SCREWED OR FLANGED.

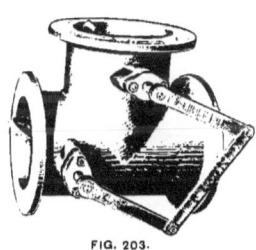

FIG. 203.
DOUBLE BUTTERFLY VALVE.
FLANGED.

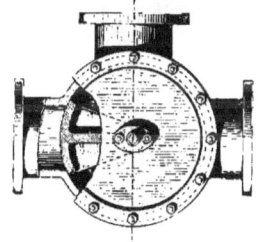

FIG. 204.
TRANSFER VALVE.
FLANGED

For Sizes and Dimensions see Table, pages 102, 103 and 104.

BEST, FOX & CO.

DOUBLE DISC GATE VALVES

WITH

REMOVABLE BRONZE SEATS.

Heavy—Guaranteed tight at 200 lbs. Pressure.
Ex. Heavy –   ''   ''   '' 600   ''   ''
Hydraulic—   '' 1000   ''   or over.

CLIMAX.	BESTS PATENT DUPLEX.
INSIDE SCREW.	OUTSIDE SCREW AND YOKE, SELF PACKING STEM
STRAIGHT FACE	With removable and interchangeable Bronze seats.
	Tested to 600 lbs. Pressure.

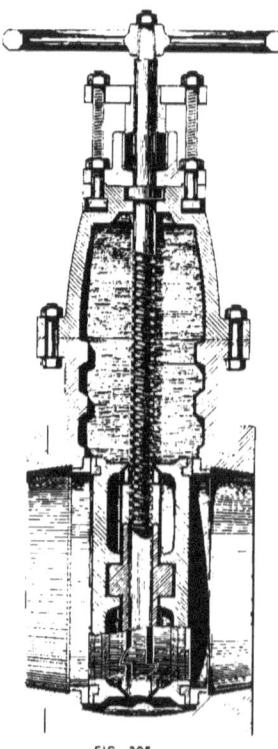

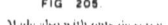

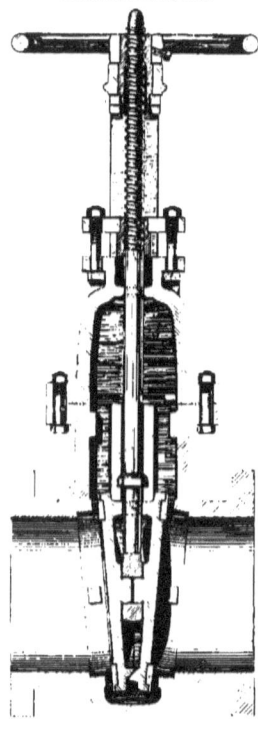

FIG. 205.

Made also with outside screw.

FIG. 206.

Made also with inside screw,

For sizes and dimensions see Table **page 102.**

BEST, FOX & CO.

FIG 205, on opposite side, illustrates a section of our

Climax Double Disc Gate Valve,
WITH · · · · ·
Removable Bronze Seats,

Iron Body, Brass Mounted, made in sizes from 2½ to 24 inches inclusive, either screwed, flanged or bowl ends.

The construction of this valve is such that the eccentrics on center ring or wedge bear on back of discs close to the **outer edge** of same. This insures a tight valve, as there can be no springing of discs, as is the case when wedging takes place from the centre only. This valve will **not stick**, but **works freely** at all times and **in any position.**

FIG. 206, on opposite side, illustrates a section of

Best's Patent Duplex Wedge Gate Valve,
WITH · · · · · ·
Removable Bronze Seats,

Iron Body, Brass Mounted, made in sizes from 2½ to 24 inches inclusive, either screwed, flanged or bowl ends.

This valve is similar to Fig. 205, except wedge disc is made in two parts, and admits of adjustment not obtained with single disc valve, and the strength of discs is not impaired by making same in two pieces. Bronze or steel spindles are made as desired; valves are also made with or without by-pass, using cock, gate or globe valves in by-pass connection. Valves made with or without outside screw.

SINGLE DISC, EXTRA HEAVY GATE VALVE

WITH

Removable Bronze Seats (that are interchangeable)
Self-Packing Stem – Outside Screw and Yoke.
Ribbed Body or Plain, with or without by-pass.
Tested to 600 lbs. pressure.

SECTION
" BEST'S PATENT " EXTRA HEAVY.
OUTSIDE SCREW AND YOKE.
BY-PASS ON BOTTOM OR SIDE.

"BEST'S PATENT" EXTRA HEAVY.
WITH BY-PASS ON BOTTOM AND 3-WAY
COCK IN BY-PASS.

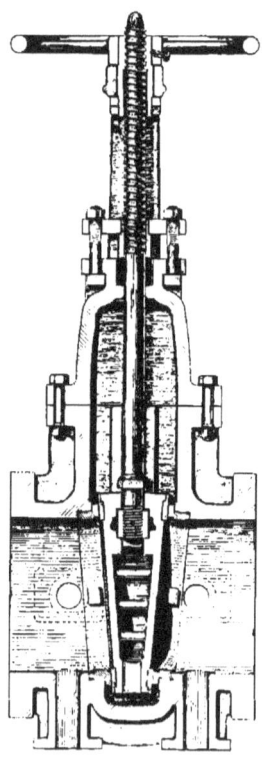

FIG. 207.

FIG. 208.
Made also with inside screw.

For sizes and dimensions see Table **page 102.**

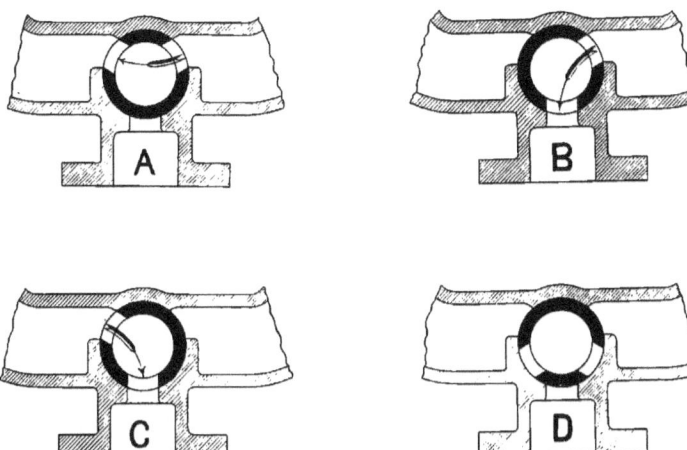

FIG. 209.

TESTED to 600 lbs. Pressure.

On the opposite side we show section and outside elevation of

BEST'S PATENT EXTRA HEAVY WEDGE GATE VALVE

with Renewable Bronze Seats, (that are interchangeable) **Self-Packing Stem,** outside screw and yoke made with or without by-pass. (Note also Fig. 206.)

To meet the large demand for a tight and reliable Gate Valve suitable for Extra Heavy Steam Pressure we have made a special line of patterns from 2½ to 24 inches, having seats that are *readily* removed when necessary, and others inserted in their place and valve be as tight as originally. Disc is faced with bronze, stem made of bronze (or steel, if desired) and gland lined with bronze.

—NOTE

The draining feature combined with our by-pass: Three-way cock with brass plug and packing gland is used for this purpose and warranted to work free and easy at all times and not leak.

With key in position as shown in A—Steam is passed to either side of disc.

B—Water is drained from right side of disc.

C—Water is drained from left side of disc.

D—By-pass and drains closed.

By-pass has only 2 joints where branches connect to body of valve. Gate or Globe can be used in place of cock if so desired and draining feature is not required. By-pass connection made on bottom or side.

BEST, FOX & CO.

IRON BODY. **CHAPMAN GATE VALVES.** BRASS MOUNTED

FIG. 210.
SCREWED.

FIG. 211.
FLANGED.
WITH INDICATOR.

FIG. 212.
ARCH TOP.
FOR HEAVY PRESSURE.

FIG. 213.
SCREWED.
FOR EXTRA HEAVY PRESSURE.

FIG. 214.
FLANGED.
FOR EXTRA HEAVY PRESSURE.

IRON BODY. **KENNEDY GATE VALVES.** BRASS MOUNTED.

FIG. 215.
SCREWED.

FIG. 216.
FLANGED.
DESCRIPTIVE CIRCULAR ON APPLICATION.

FIG. 217.
**OWL OR HUB
ENDS.**

FAIRBANKS GATE VALVES.

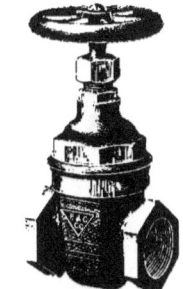

FIG. 218.
ALL BRASS ASBESTOS DISC.
SCREWED OR FLANGED.

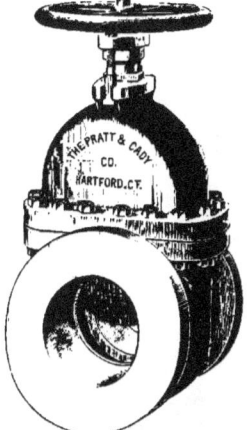

FIG. 219.
IRON BODY ASBESTOS DISC.
SCREWED OR FLANGED.

FIG. 220.
IRON BODY FLANGED.
REMOVABLE BRONZE SEAT ·ARCH TOP.

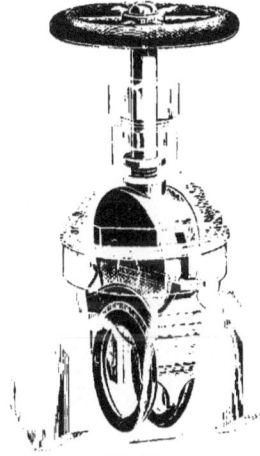

FIG. 221.
IRON BODY SCREWED,
REMOVABLE BRONZE SEAT—SCREWED BONNET.

Descriptive Circular on Application.

IRON COCKS
WITH IRON OR BRASS PLUGS.

FIG. 222.
SCREWED.
SQUARE HEAD.

FIG. 223.
SCREWED.
FLAT HEAD.

FIG. 224.
FLANGED.
SQUARE OR FLAT HEAD

FIG. 225.
THREE-WAY.
SCREWED OR FLANGED.

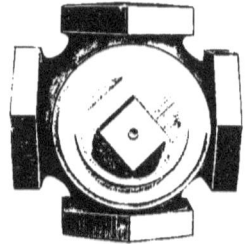

FIG. 226.
FOUR-WAY.
SCREWED OR FLANGED.

FIG. 227.
FOUR-WAY.
(WITH PACKED GLAND.)
SCREWED OR FLANGED.

IRON AND BRASS. ASBESTOS PACKED COCKS. SCREWED AND FLANGED

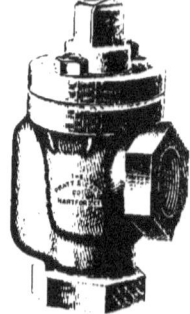

FIG. 228.
ANGLE.

FIG. 229.
TWO-WAY.

FIG. 230.
THREE-WAY.

Descriptive Circular on Application.

MYER'S PATENT BLOW-OFF VALVE.

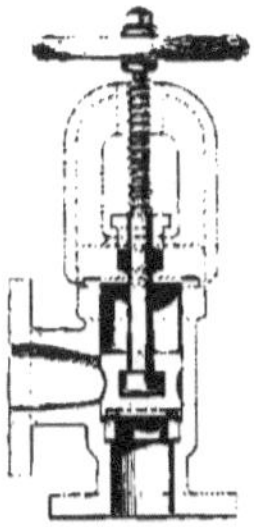

FIG. 233.
BACK PRESSURE VALVE,
SCREWED AND FLANGED.
FOR HORIZONTAL OR VERTICAL LINES.

FIG. 231.
SECTION.

FIG. 232.
FLANGED.

EXPANSION JOINTS.

FIG. 234.
IRON BODY
SCREWED

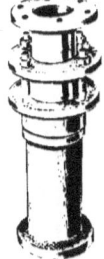

FIG. 235.
IRON BODY.
FLANGED.

FIG. 236.
CORRUGATED COPPER.
SCREWED OR FLANGED.

FIG. 237
COPPER.

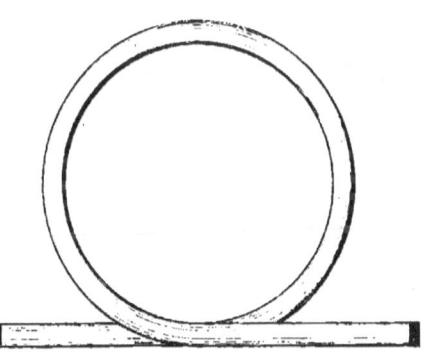

FIG. 238.
IRON PIPE OR LOOP EXPANSION.

For Sizes and Dimensions, see Table page 104

BEST, FOX & CO.

FOOT VALVES AND STRAINERS.

FOOT VALVES.

STRAINERS.

FIG. 239.
SCREWED.

FIG. 240.
FLANGED.

FIG. 241.
GLOBE BODY.
SCREWED OR FLANGED.

FIG. 242.
GATE BODY.
SCREWED OR FLANGED.

For Sizes and Dimensions see Table page 104.

STRAINERS.

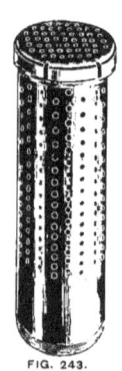

FIG. 243.
WROT. IRON PIPE.
DRILLED.

FIG. 244.
CAST IRON.
SLOTTED.

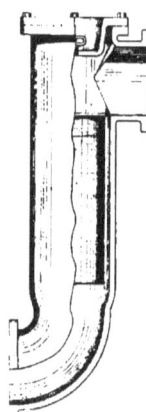

FIG. 245.
PUMP STRAINER.
WITH BASKET.

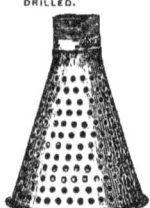

FIG. 246.
WROUGHT IRON.
GALVANIZED.

FIG. 247.
CAST IRON.

FIG. 248.
MALLEABLE IRON.

FIG. 249.
FOR SYPHON PUMPS.

BEST, FOX & CO.

BRASS VALVES.

FIG. 250.

GLOBE VALVE.

FIG. 251.

ANGLE VALVE.

FIG. 252.

CROSS VALVE.

FIG. 253.

CHECK VALVE.

HORIZONTAL.

FIG. 254.

CHECK VALVE.

ANGLE.

FIG. 255.

CHECK VALVE.

VERTICAL.

FIG. 256.

RADIATOR VALVE.

FEMALE.

FIG. 257.

RADIATOR VALVE.

WITH UNION.

FIG. 258.

COKE-OVEN VALVE.

For Dimensions see Table page 103.

BEST, FOX & CO.

POWELL'S STAR RE-GRINDING VALVES.—BRASS.

FIG. 259.
GLOBE VALVE.

FIG. 260.
ANGLE VALVE.

FIG. 261.
CHECK VALVE.

ASBESTOS DISC BRASS VALVES.

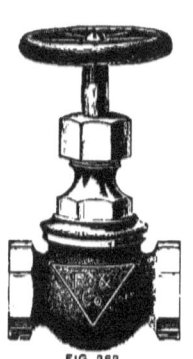

FIG 262.
GLOBE VALVE.

FIG. 263.
ANGLE VALVE.

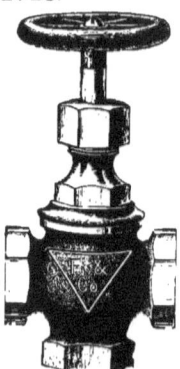

FIG. 264.'
CROSS VALVE

SWINGING CHECK VALVES.—ROTATING DISC.

FIG. 265.
HORIZONTAL OR
VERTICAL.

FIG. 266.
HORIZONTAL.
SECTION

FIG. 267.
ANGLE.

FIG. 268.
ASBESTOS DISC AND
HOLDER COMPLETE.
FOR ALL SIZES

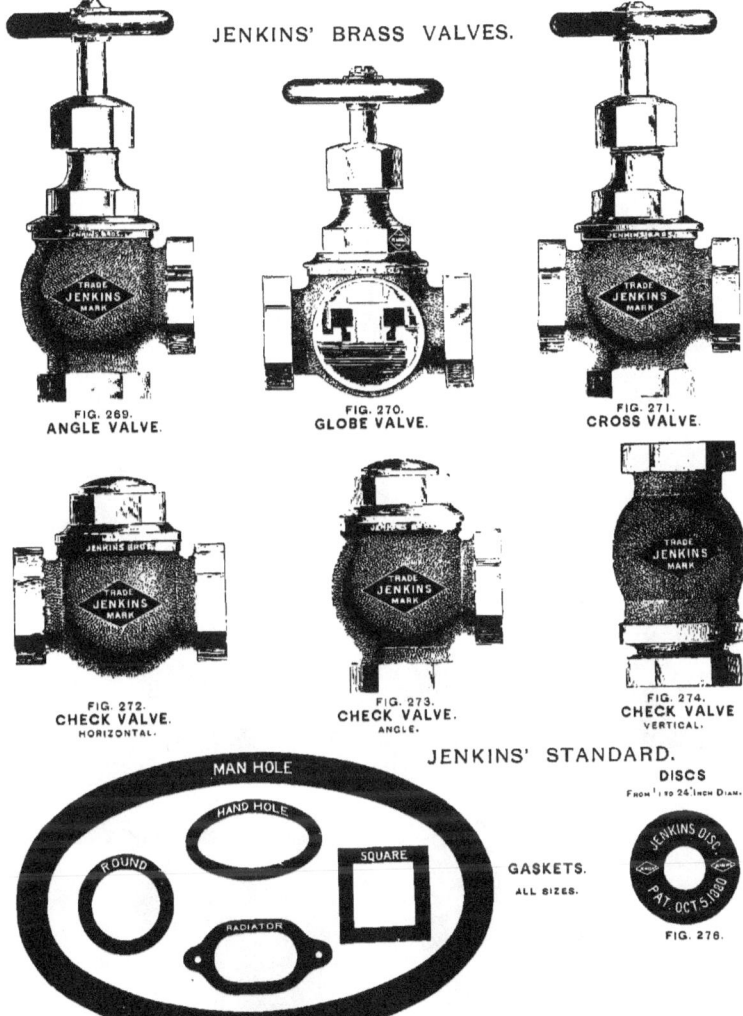

JENKINS' BRASS VALVES.

FIG. 269.
ANGLE VALVE.

FIG. 270.
GLOBE VALVE.

FIG. 271.
CROSS VALVE.

FIG. 272.
CHECK VALVE.
HORIZONTAL.

FIG. 273.
CHECK VALVE.
ANGLE.

FIG. 274.
CHECK VALVE
VERTICAL.

JENKINS' STANDARD.

MAN HOLE

HAND HOLE

ROUND

SQUARE

RADIATOR

GASKETS.
ALL SIZES.

FIG. 275.

DISCS
FROM 1 TO 24 INCH DIAM.

JENKINS DISC.
PAT. OCT 5 1920.

FIG. 276.

BEST, FOX & CO.

BRASS VALVES.

FIG. 277.
GATE VALVE.

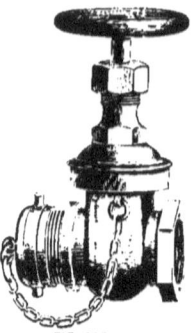

FIG. 278.
GATE VALVE
WITH HOSE CAP.

For Dimensions, see Table page 103.

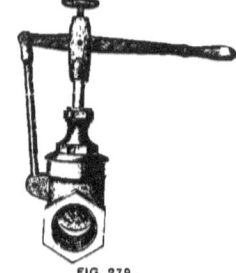

FIG. 279.
GATE VALVE.
QUICK OPENING.

FIG. 280.
HANDY GATE VALVE.
LUNKENHEIMERS.

FIG. 281.
LUNKEN GATE VALVE.
BRASS AND IRON.

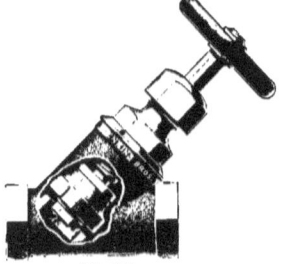

FIG. 282.
Y VALVE.

SECTION.

BRASS SAFETY VALVES.

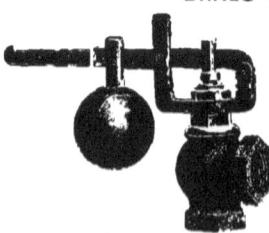

FIG 283.
ANGLE.

FIG. 284
THREE-WAY.

BEST, FOX & CO.

BRASS COCKS.

FIG. 285.
SQUARE HEAD.

FIG. 286.
FLAT HEAD.

FIG. 287.
SQ. AND FLAT HEAD.
FLANGED.

FIG. 288
THREE WAY.

FIG. 289.
FOUR WAY.

FIG 290.
FOUR WAY.
WITH PACKED GLAND.
SCREWED AND FLANGED.

FIG. 291.
COCK, WITH COUPLING.

FIG. 292.
HYDRAULIC COCK.
WITH COUPLING NUTS

FIG. 293
BUTTERFLY VALVE.

FIG. 294.
COCK WRENCHES.
ALL SIZES.

FIG. 295.
BRASS EXPANSION JOINT.

Special Cocks to Order.

BEST, FOX & CO.

TUYERE COCKS AND UNIONS.—GROUND JOINTS.

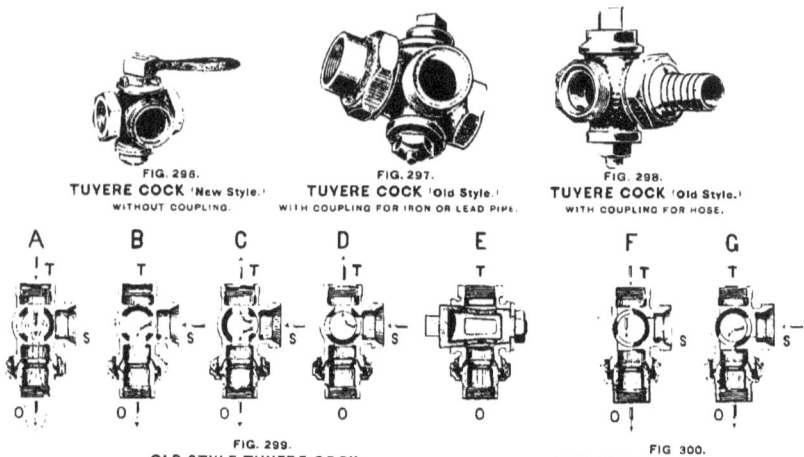

FIG. 296.
TUYERE COCK (New Style.)
WITHOUT COUPLING.

FIG. 297.
TUYERE COCK (Old Style.)
WITH COUPLING FOR IRON OR LEAD PIPE.

FIG. 298.
TUYERE COCK (Old Style.)
WITH COUPLING FOR HOSE.

A   B   C   D   E   F   G

FIG 299.
OLD STYLE TUYERE COCK.
SECTION.

FIG 300.
NEW STYLE TUYERE COCK.
SECTION.

BRASS UNIONS.—GROUND JOINTS.

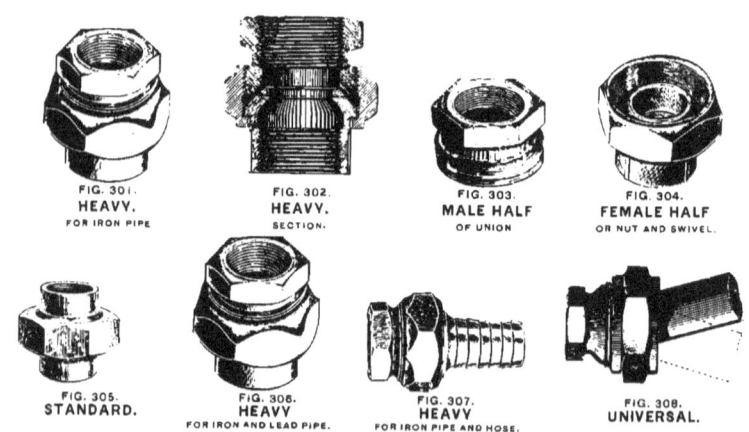

FIG. 301.
HEAVY,
FOR IRON PIPE

FIG. 302.
HEAVY,
SECTION.

FIG. 303.
MALE HALF
OF UNION

FIG. 304.
FEMALE HALF
OR NUT AND SWIVEL.

FIG. 305.
STANDARD.

FIG. 306.
HEAVY
FOR IRON AND LEAD PIPE.

FIG. 307.
HEAVY
FOR IRON PIPE AND HOSE.

FIG. 308.
UNIVERSAL.

STANDARD BRASS FITTINGS.

ROUGH OR FINISHED.

FIG. 309.
90° ELBOW.

FIG. 310.
45° ELBOW.

FIG. 311.
TEE.

FIG 312.
CROSS.

FIG. 313.
REDUCER.

FIG. 314
PLUG.
SQUARE HEAD.

FIG. 315.
PLUG.
COUNTERSUNK HEAD.

FIG. 316.
CAP.

FIG. 317.
LOCKNUT.

FIG. 318.
BUSHING.

FIG. 319.
RETURN BEND.
OPEN.

FIG. 320.
RETURN BEND.
CLOSE.

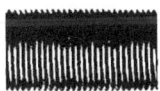

FIG. 321.
CLOSE NIPPLE.

FIG. 322.
SHOULDER NIPPLE.

FIG. 323.
SOCKET OR COUPLING.

FIG 324
SOCKET.
RIGHT AND LEFT.

Reducing and Special Fittings to order.   Copper Plugs to order.

AIR AND CYLINDER COCKS.

FIG. 325.	FIG 326.	FIG. 327	FIG. 328.
TEE HANDLE.	**LEVER HANDLE.**	**DOUBLE THREAD,** MALE.	**DOUBLE THREAD,** FEMALE.

FIG. 329.	FIG. 330.	FIG. 331.	FIG. 332
BIBB NOZZLE. TEE HANDLE.	**BIBB NOZZLE.** LEVER HANDLE.	**CYLINDER COCK.** WITH UNION, TEE HANDLE.	**CYLINDER COCK.** WITH UNION. LEVER HANDLE.

GAUGE COCKS.

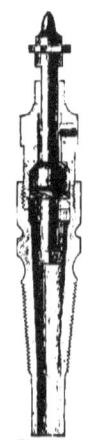

FIG. 333.	FIG. 334.	FIG 335	FIG. 336.
MISSISSIPPI.	**COMPRESSION.**	**COMPRESSION.** REGRINDING.	**REGISTER.**

FIG. 337.
BINGHAM
REGRINDING.

FIG. 338.
BINGHAM REGRINDING WITH LEVER.

Threads Chased to Order.

BEST, FOX & CO.

WATER GAUGES.

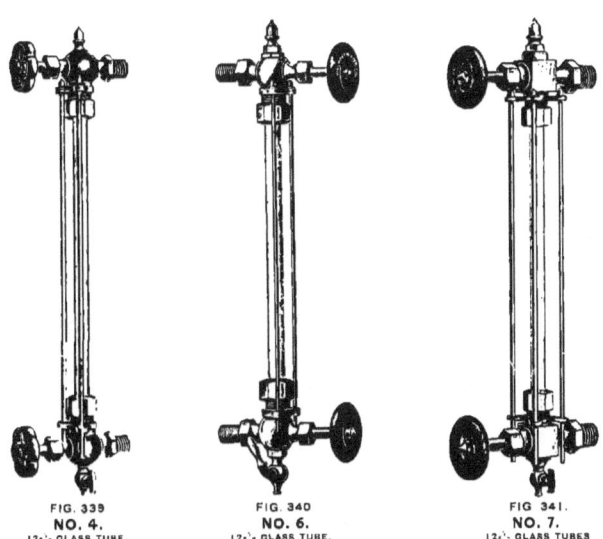

FIG. 339
NO. 4.
12¼" GLASS TUBE.

FIG. 340
NO. 6.
12¼" GLASS TUBE.

FIG 341.
NO. 7.
12¼" GLASS TUBES

Water Gauges with longer and larger tubes furnished from stock.

WHISTLES.

FIG. 342.
PLAIN.

FIG. 343.
WITH VALVE.

FIG. 344.
WHISTLE VALVE.

FIG. 345.
CHIME.

FIG. 346.
CHIME,
IN ONE WHISTLE

BEST, FOX & CO.

WATER GAUGE COLUMNS.

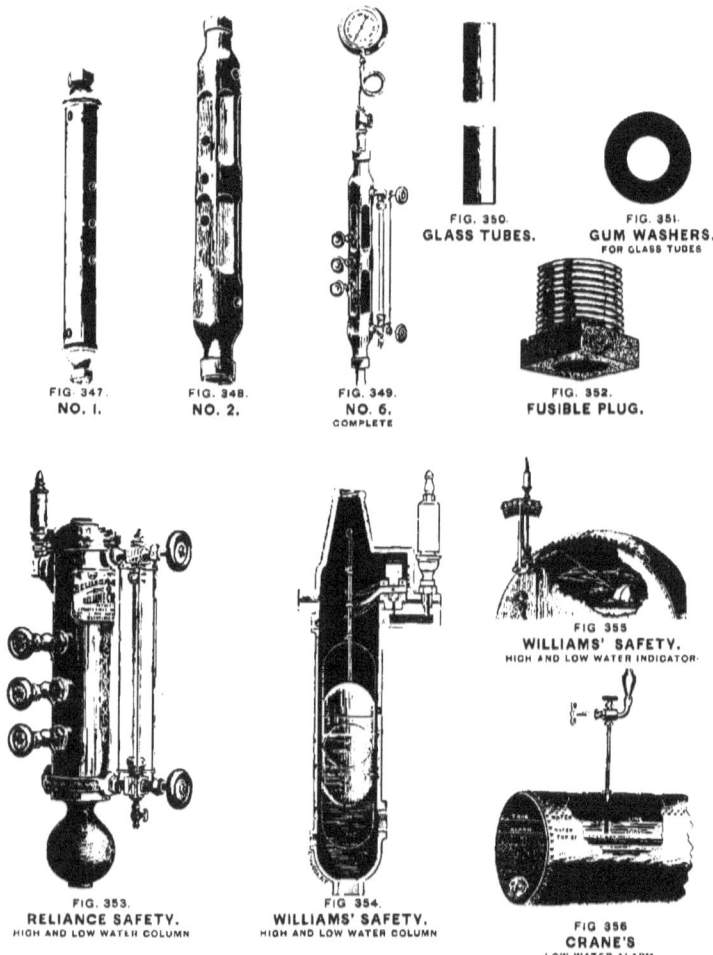

FIG. 347.
NO. I.

FIG. 348.
NO. 2.

FIG. 349.
NO. 6.
COMPLETE

FIG. 350.
GLASS TUBES.

FIG. 351.
GUM WASHERS.
FOR GLASS TUBES

FIG. 352.
FUSIBLE PLUG.

FIG 355
WILLIAMS' SAFETY.
HIGH AND LOW WATER INDICATOR.

FIG. 353.
RELIANCE SAFETY.
HIGH AND LOW WATER COLUMN

FIG 354.
WILLIAMS' SAFETY.
HIGH AND LOW WATER COLUMN

FIG 356
CRANE'S
LOW WATER ALARM.

Descriptive Circular on Application.

BRASS OIL CUPS.

   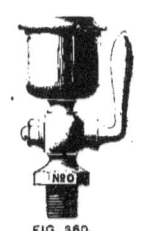

FIG 357.
PLAIN.

FIG. 358.
LOCOMOTIVE.

FIG. 359.
HINGE LID.

FIG. 360.
LEVER HANDLE.

GLASS OIL CUPS.

FIG. 361.
PIONEER.
SLIDE TOP

FIG. 362.
ROYAL.
SIGHT FEED

FIG 363.
CROWN.
INDEX SIGHT FEED.

FIG. 364.
ROD CUP.
FOR CRANK PINS.

   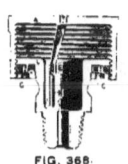

FIG. 365
AJAX.
INDEX.

FIG. 366
RIVAL.
SIGHT FEED.

FIG. 367.
CODY'S
SHAFT CUP.

FIG. 368.
GREASE CUP.

All Sizes of above Cups.

Descriptive Circular on Application

BEST, FOX & CO.

LUBRICATORS.

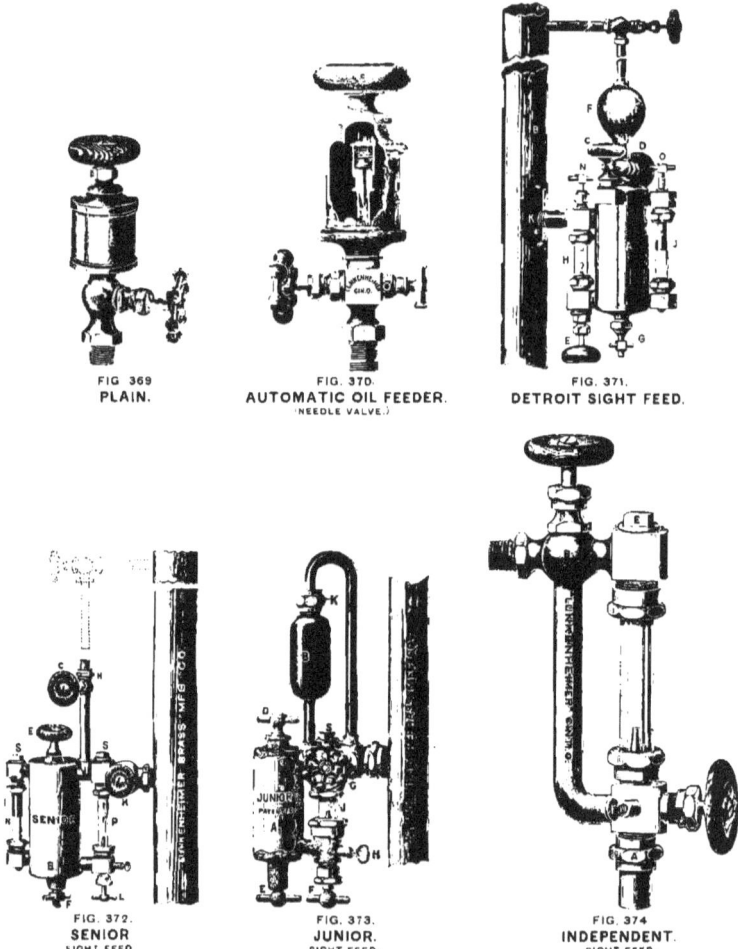

FIG. 369
PLAIN.

FIG. 370.
AUTOMATIC OIL FEEDER.
(NEEDLE VALVE.)

FIG. 371.
DETROIT SIGHT FEED.

FIG. 372.
SENIOR
SIGHT FEED

FIG. 373.
JUNIOR.
SIGHT FEED.

FIG. 374
INDEPENDENT.
SIGHT FEED.

Descriptive Circulars of above on Application.

HOSE CONNECTIONS.

FIG 375.
HOSE COUPLING.

FIG. 376.
NOZZLE.
PLAIN.

FIG 377.
NOZZLE.
WITH COCK.

FIG 378.
HEAVY IRON NOZZLE.
BRASS NUT.

FIG. 379.
HOSE NIPPLE.

FIG 380.
HOSE CLAMP.

FIG 381.
**CALDWELL HOSE
CLAMP.**

FIG. 382.
TUERK HOSE CLAMP.

HEAVY GAS FIXTURE FITTINGS,
FOR FACTORY AND MILL USE.

FIG. 383.
PENDANT COCK.
STRAIGHT.

FIG. 384.
PENDANT COCK.
ELBOW.

FIG. 385.
PENDANT COCK.
SWING.

FIG. 386.
**DOUBLE CENTER
COCK.**

FIG. 387.
**ELBOW BURNER
COCK.**

FIG. 388.
SWING JOINT.
WITH COCK.

FIG. 389.
SWING JOINT.

FIG. 390.
**UNIVERSAL
SWING JOINT.**

Burners and Brackets for above in Stock.

BEST, FOX & CO.

GAS FIXTURES AND BURNERS.

FIG. 391.
IRON BURNER.
BAT WING.

FIG. 392.
IRON BURNER.
FISH TAIL.

FIG. 393.
BRASS PILLAR.
FOR LAVA TIP.

FIG. 394.
MACKLEY BURNER.
FOR NATURAL GAS.

FIG. 395.
JUMBO BURNER.
FOR NATURAL GAS.

FIG. 396.
IRWIN STORM BURNER.
FOR NATURAL GAS.

FIG. 397.
ARGAND BURNER.
AUTOMATIC.

FIG. 398.
EUREKA BURNER.
SELF-LIGHTING.

FIG. 399.
THREE SWING.
STRAIGHT BRACKET.

FIG. 400.
DOUBLE SWING.
STRAIGHT BRACKET UNIVERSAL.

FIG. 401.
DOUBLE SWING.
STRAIGHT BRACKET.

FIG. 402.
SINGLE SWING.
STRAIGHT BRACKET.

FIG. 403.
STRAIGHT BRACKET.
STIFF.

FIG. 404.
C BEND BRACKET.
STIFF.

FIG. 405.
C BEND SINGLE SWING.
BRACKET.

FIG. 406.
S BEND BRACKET.

Iron and Lava Tips in Stock.

BRASS
CAST STEEL **HYDRAULIC FITTINGS AND COCKS** FROM 500 LBS. TO 3000
" IRON LBS. PRESSURE

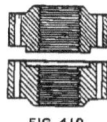

FIG. 410.
FLANGED UNION.

JONES' PATENT HOSE
COUPLING for Steam and
Hydraulic Pressure.

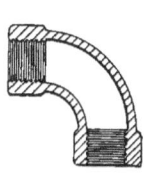

FIG. 407.
ELBOW.

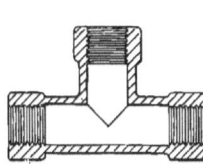

FIG. 408.
TEE.

FIG. 409.
CROSS.

FIG. 414.
FEMALE HALF.

FIG. 415.
MALE HALF.

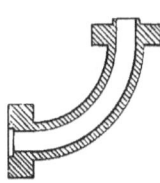

FIG. 411.
FLANGED ELBOW.

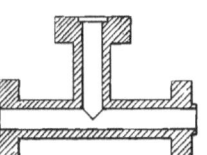

FIG. 412.
FLANGED TEE.

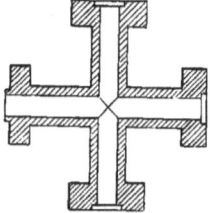

FIG. 413.
FLANGED CROSS.

FIG. 416.
FOLLOWER.

FIG. 417.
HYDRAULIC.
BRASS COCK.

FIG. 418.
HYDRAULIC ASBESTOS COCK.
SCREWED.

FIG. 419.
HYDRAULIC ASBESTOS COCK.
THREE-WAY.

Reducing Hydraulic Fittings to Order.

CLIMAX PATENTED HYDRAULIC VALVE.

Balanced and Full Opening.

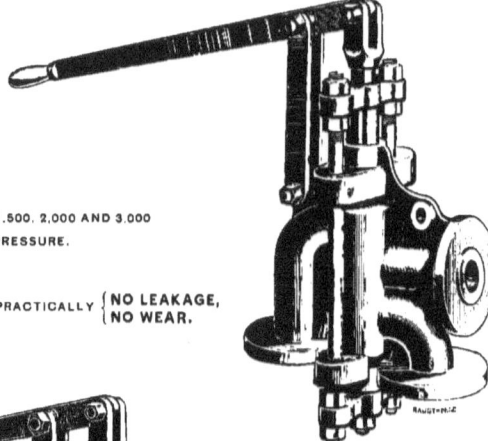

MADE FOR 500, 1,000, 1,500, 2,000 AND 3,000
POUNDS PRESSURE.

NO WASTE,   }   AS THERE IS PRACTICALLY   {NO LEAKAGE,
NO EXPENSE, }   {NO WEAR.

FIG. 420.

THREE WAY.

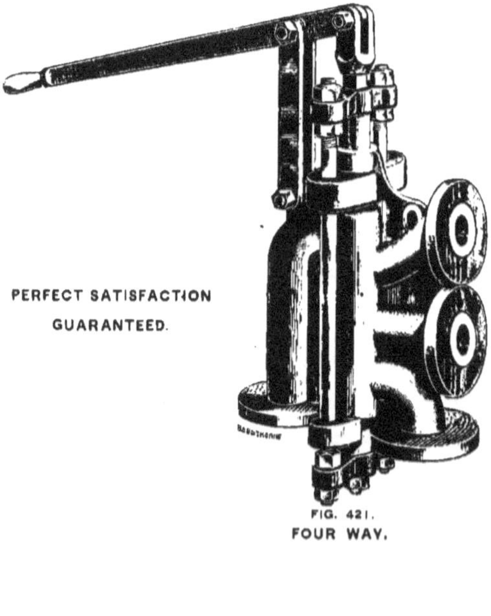

PERFECT SATISFACTION
GUARANTEED.

DETAIL DRAWINGS

FURNISHED ON APPLICATION.

FIG. 421.

FOUR WAY.

HYDRAULIC VALVES.

BRASS.   IRON.

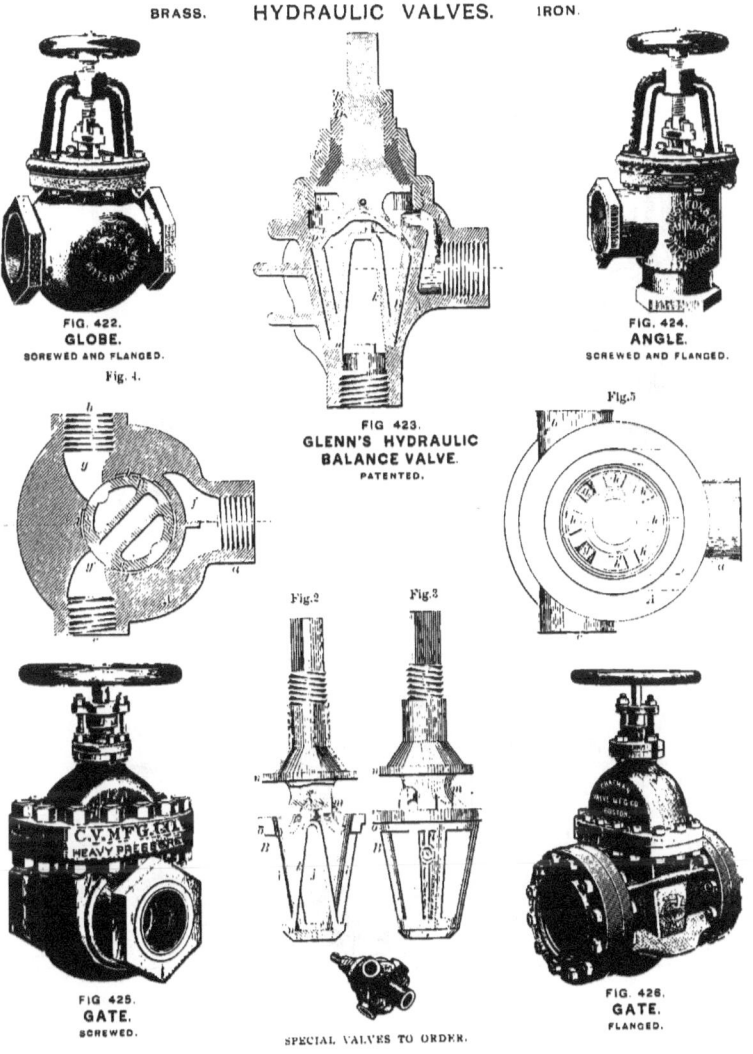

FIG. 422.
GLOBE.
SCREWED AND FLANGED.

Fig. 4.

FIG 423.
**GLENN'S HYDRAULIC
BALANCE VALVE.**
PATENTED.

FIG. 424.
ANGLE.
SCREWED AND FLANGED.

Fig.5

Fig.2   Fig.3

FIG 425.
GATE.
SCREWED.

SPECIAL VALVES TO ORDER.

FIG. 426.
GATE.
FLANGED.

BEST, FOX & CO.

HYDRAULIC VALVES.

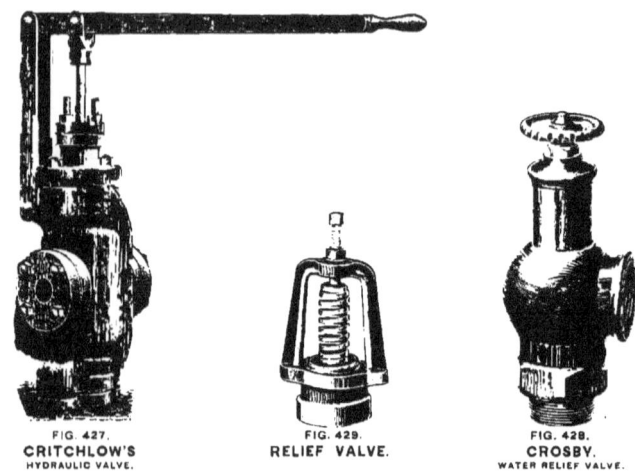

FIG. 427.
CRITCHLOW'S
HYDRAULIC VALVE.

FIG. 429.
RELIEF VALVE.

FIG. 428.
CROSBY.
WATER RELIEF VALVE.

PULPIT.

WITH CRITCHLOW VALVES, ANGLE STOP AND WASTE VALVES.

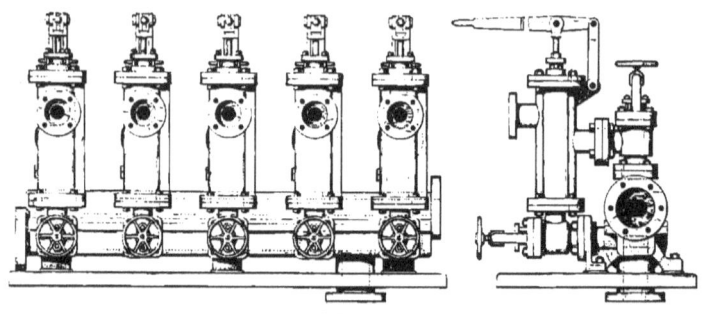

FIG. 430.

Detail Drawings on Application.

GAUGES.

IRON CASE.   BRASS CASE.

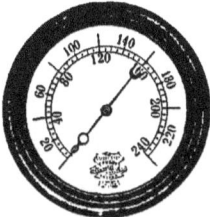

FIG. 431.
STEAM GAUGE.

FIG. 432.
SECTION.

FIG. 433.
VACUUM GAUGE.

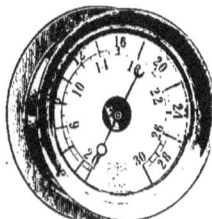

FIG. 434.
BLAST GAUGE.

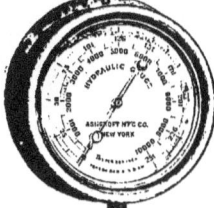

FIG. 435.
HYDRAULIC GAUGE.

FIG. 436.
AMMONIA GAUGE.

FIG. 439.
REVOLUTION INDICATOR.
SQUARE CASE.

FIG. 437.
CLOCK.

FIG. 438.
REVOLUTION INDICATOR.
ROUND CASE.

FIG. 440.
SYPHON FOR STEAM GAUGES.

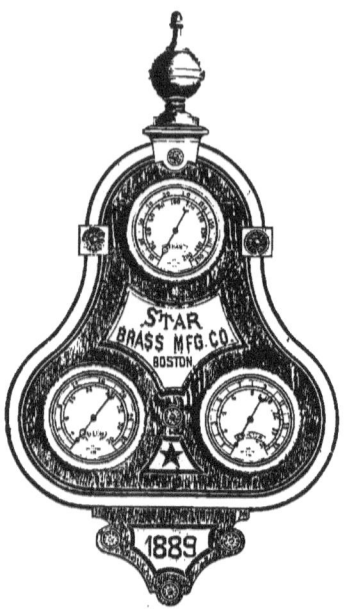

FIG. 441.

**BROWN'S HOT BLAST
PYROMETER.**

PORTABLE.

FIG. 443.

**HOT BLAST
PYROMETER.**

STATIONARY.

FIG. 442.

FRAME FOR GAUGES.

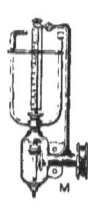

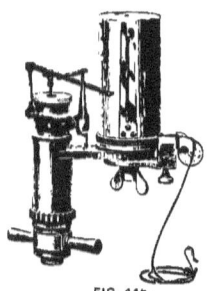

FIG. 444.

REVOLUTION INDICATOR.

FIG. 445.

**THOMPSON
IMPROVED INDICATOR.**

FIG 446.

**TABOR
IMPROVED INDICATOR.**

Descriptive Circulars on application.

SHAW'S MERCURY GAUGES.

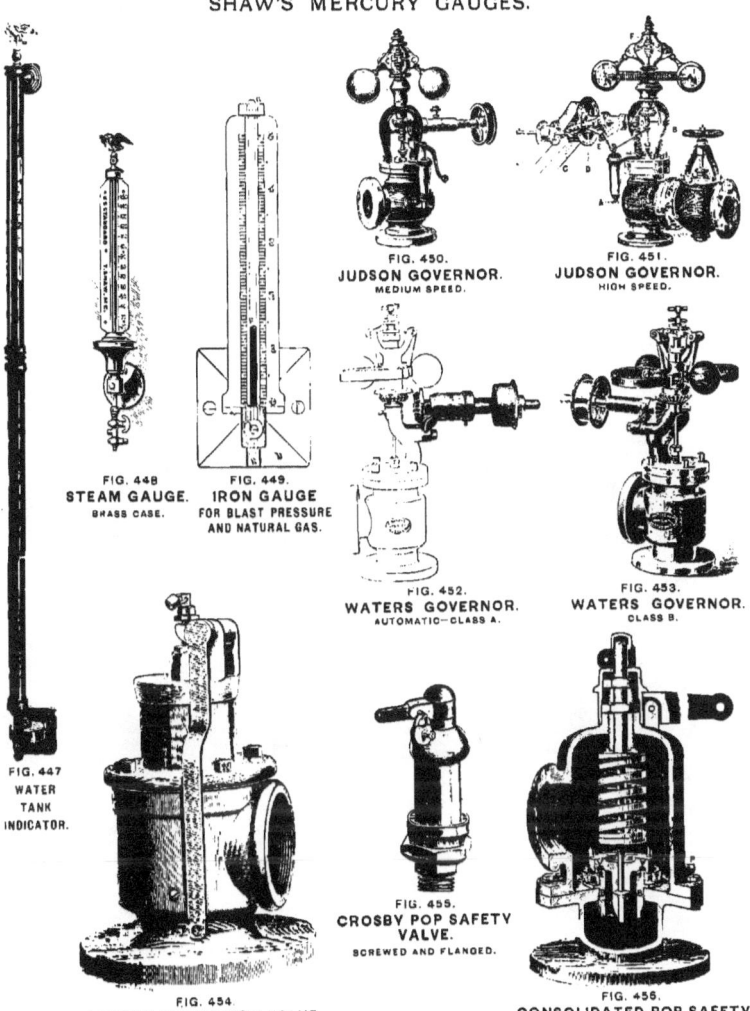

FIG. 450.
JUDSON GOVERNOR.
MEDIUM SPEED.

FIG. 451.
JUDSON GOVERNOR.
HIGH SPEED.

FIG. 448.
STEAM GAUGE.
BRASS CASE.

FIG. 449.
IRON GAUGE
FOR BLAST PRESSURE
AND NATURAL GAS.

FIG. 452.
WATERS GOVERNOR.
AUTOMATIC—CLASS A.

FIG. 453.
WATERS GOVERNOR.
CLASS B.

FIG. 447
WATER
TANK
INDICATOR.

FIG. 455.
**CROSBY POP SAFETY
VALVE.**
SCREWED AND FLANGED.

FIG. 454
ASHTON POP SAFETY VALVE.

FIG. 455.
**CONSOLIDATED POP SAFETY
VALVE.**
SCREWED AND FLANGED.

Governors or Pop Safety Valves of any Make Furnished.

BEST, FOX & CO.

REGULATORS.

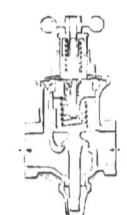

FIG. 457.
CURTIS'
FOR STEAM, WATER AND GAS.
SECTION.

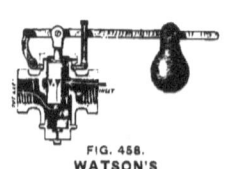

FIG. 458.
WATSON'S
FOR STEAM.

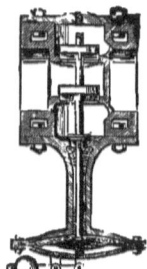

FIG. 459.
EUREKA.
FOR STEAM.

FIG. 460
**FITT'S CHRONOMETER.
AND REGULATOR VALVES.**

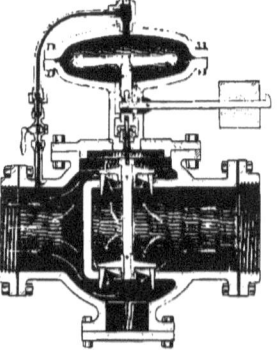

FIG. 461.
CHAPMAN'S
FOR NATURAL GAS.

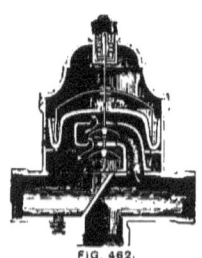

FIG. 462.
STOTT'S LOW PRESSURE
FOR ILLUMINATING AND NATURAL GAS

FIG 463.
PUMP GOVERNOR.
MASONS.

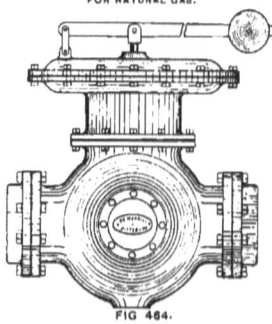

FIG 464.
MERRILL'S
FOR NATURAL GAS.

FIG. 465.
MERRILL'S
(SECTION.) FOR NATURAL GAS.

See also **Page 67.**   Descriptive Circulars on Application.

BEST, FOX & CO.

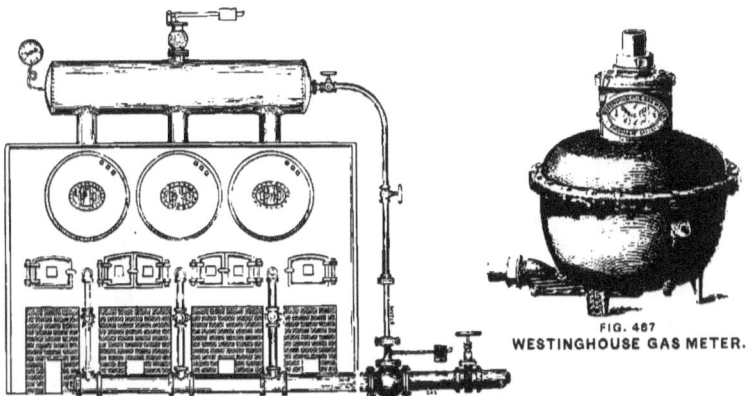

FIG. 466.

FULTON NATURAL GAS REGULATOR FOR STEAM BOILERS.

SHOWING BOILER REGULATOR AND CONNECTIONS.

FIG. 467

WESTINGHOUSE GAS METER.

WATER METERS.

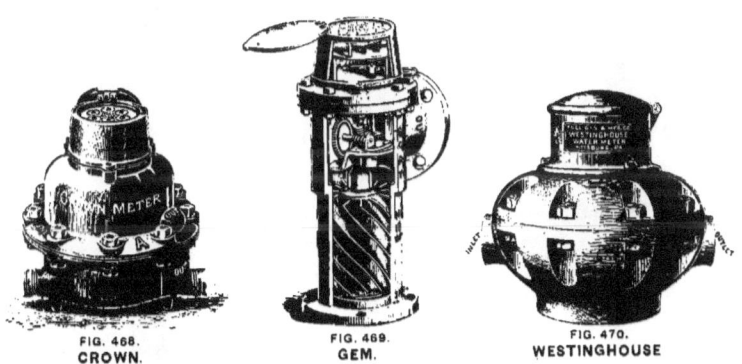

FIG. 468.

CROWN.

FIG. 469.

GEM.

FIG. 470.

WESTINGHOUSE

Descriptive Circulars on Application.

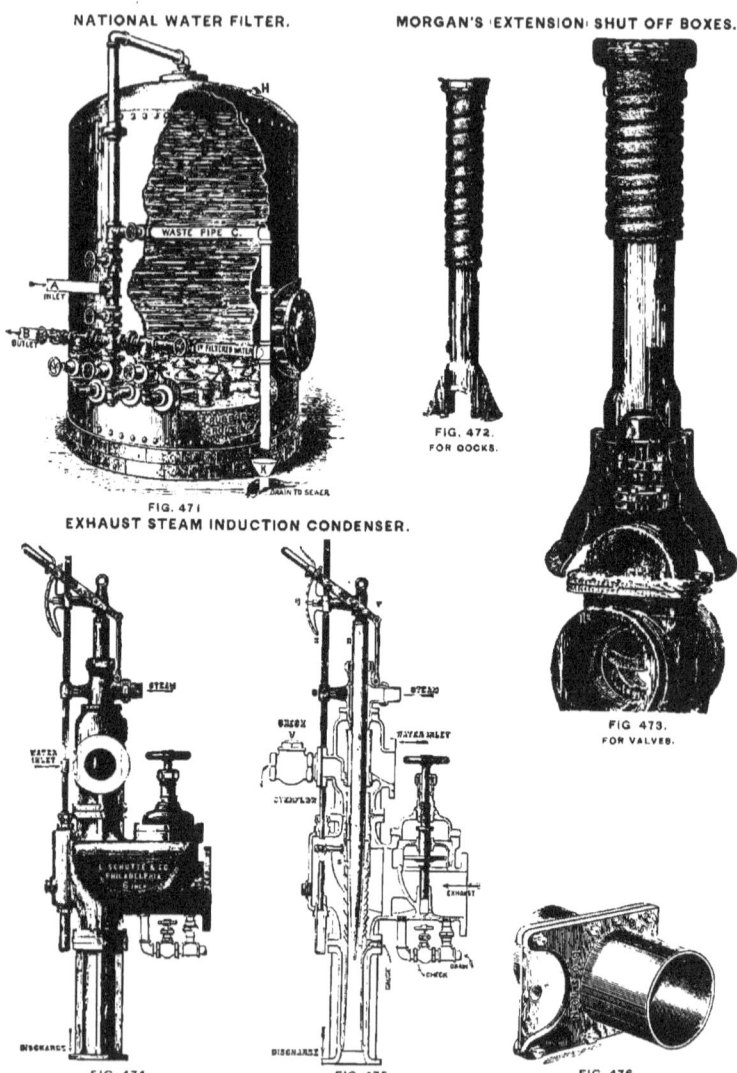

BEST, FOX & CO.

NATIONAL WATER FILTER.

MORGAN'S (EXTENSION) SHUT OFF BOXES.

FIG. 471

FIG. 472.
FOR COCKS.

EXHAUST STEAM INDUCTION CONDENSER.

FIG 473.
FOR VALVES.

FIG 474.
ADJUSTABLE.

FIG. 475.
SECTION.

FIG 476
BLAST GATE.

Descriptive Circulars on Application.

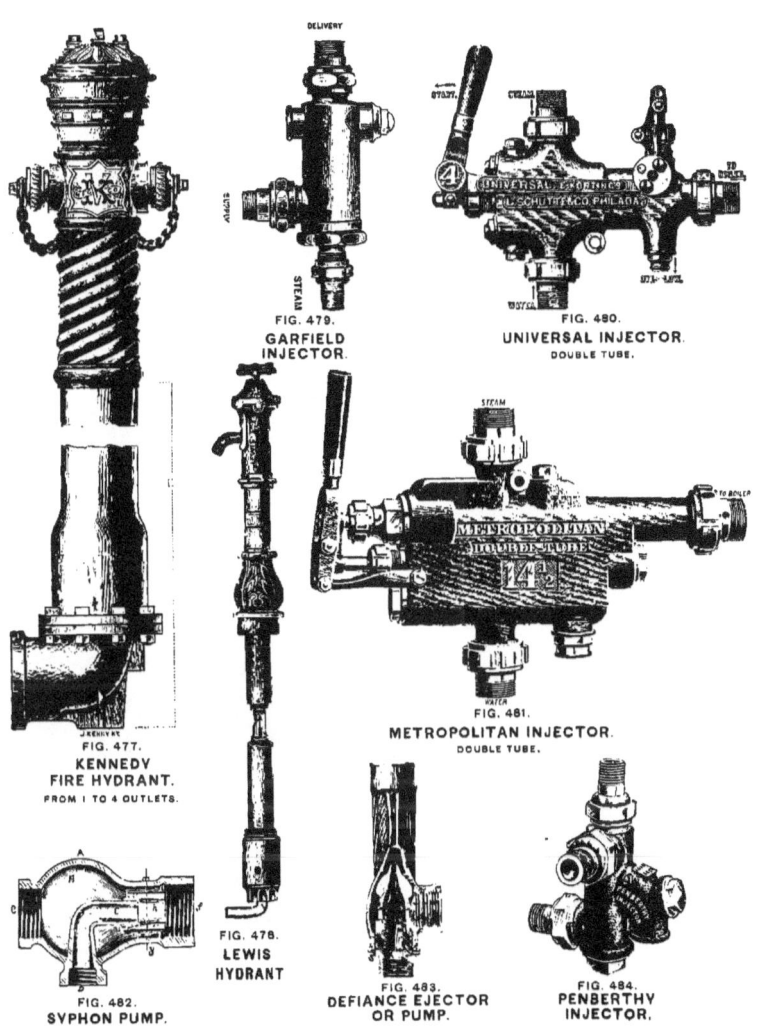

FIG. 479.
GARFIELD INJECTOR.

FIG. 480.
UNIVERSAL INJECTOR.
DOUBLE TUBE.

FIG. 481.
METROPOLITAN INJECTOR.
DOUBLE TUBE.

FIG. 477.
KENNEDY FIRE HYDRANT.
FROM 1 TO 4 OUTLETS.

FIG. 478.
LEWIS HYDRANT

FIG. 482.
SYPHON PUMP.

FIG. 483.
DEFIANCE EJECTOR OR PUMP.

FIG. 484.
PENBERTHY INJECTOR.

Descriptive Circulars on application.

CLIMAX STEAM SEPARATORS.

SCREWED OR FLANGED. For Pipe from 2 In. to 12 In. Diameter.

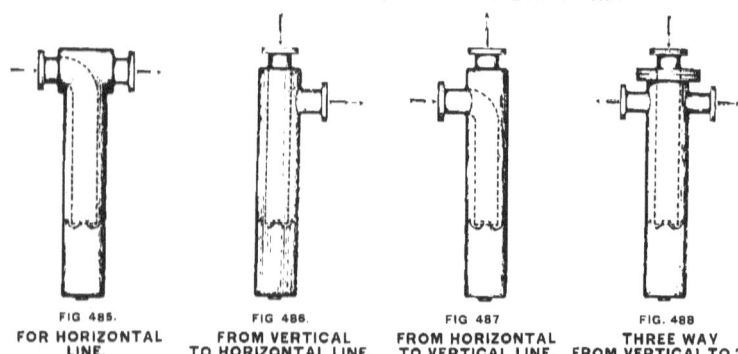

FIG 485.	FIG 486.	FIG 487	FIG. 488
FOR HORIZONTAL LINE.	FROM VERTICAL TO HORIZONTAL LINE.	FROM HORIZONTAL TO VERTICAL LINE.	THREE WAY FROM VERTICAL TO 2 HORIZONTAL LINES.

SPRAY HEATERS.
ALL SIZES.

STEAM RECEIVERS.
ALL SIZES.

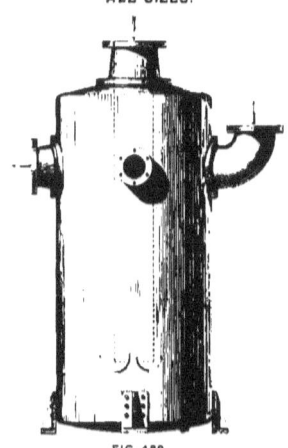

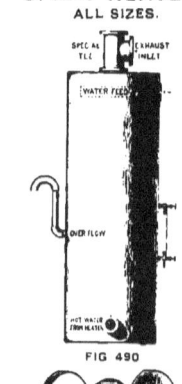

FIG 490

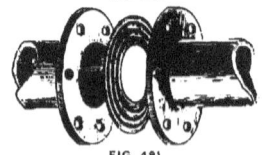

FIG. 491.

CORRUGATED COPPER GASKETS
OF ANY SIZE OR SHAPE.

FIG. 489

BEST, FOX & CO.

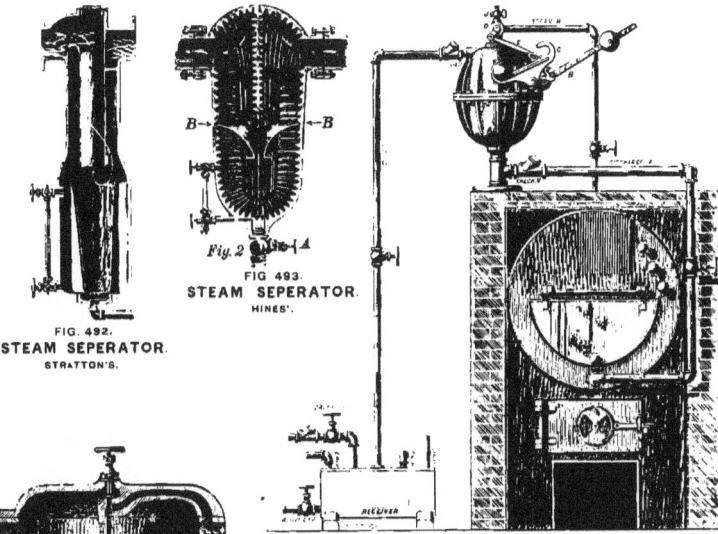

FIG 493.
STEAM SEPERATOR.
HINES'.

FIG. 492.
STEAM SEPERATOR.
STRATTON'S.

FIG 494.
PRATT'S PAT. RETURN STEAM TRAP
FOR RETURNING WATER TO BOILER.

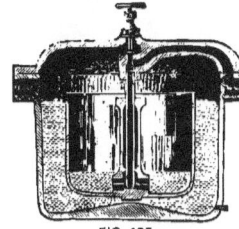

FIG. 495.
IMPROVED STEAM TRAP.
SECTION.

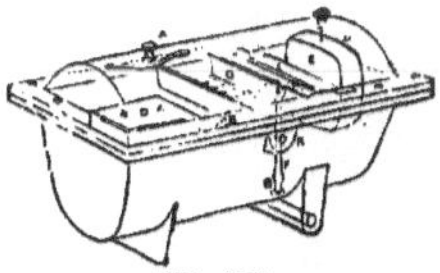

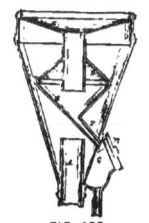

FIG. 496.
CHAPMAN STEAM TRAP
WITH SOAPSTONE FLOAT.

FIG 497.
STANDARD EXPANSION
STEAM TRAP.

FIG 498
CONDENSER HEADS
FOR EXHAUST STEAM.
ANY MAKE.

Descriptive Circulars on Application.

FEED WATER HEATERS.

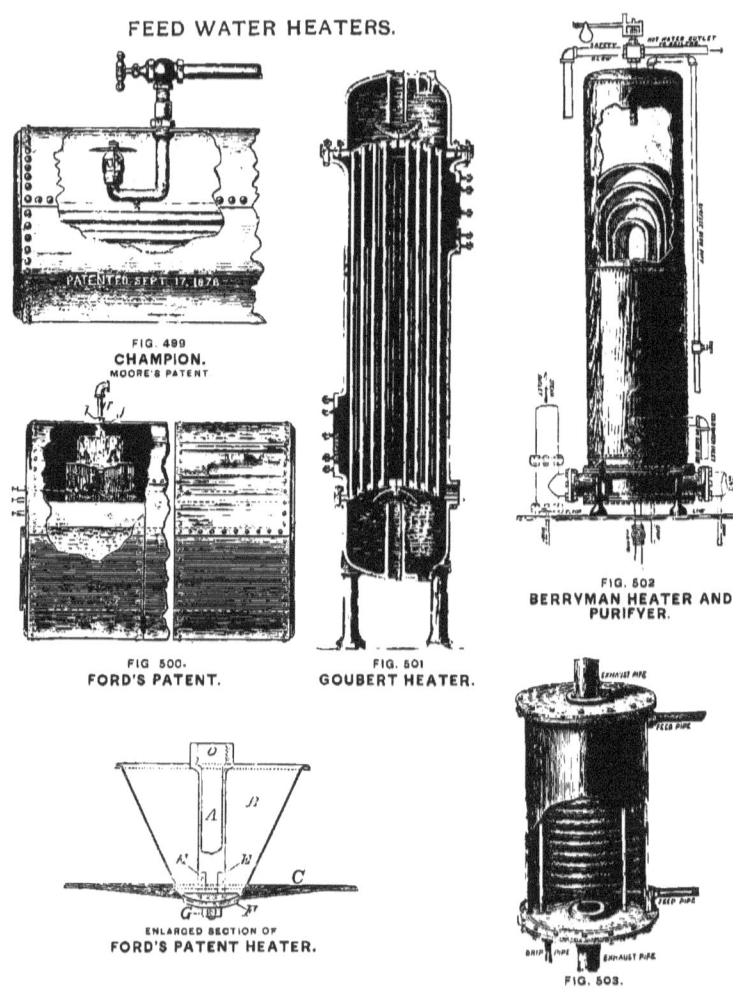

FIG. 499
CHAMPION.
MOORE'S PATENT

FIG. 500.
FORD'S PATENT.

FIG. 501
GOUBERT HEATER.

FIG. 502
BERRYMAN HEATER AND PURIFYER.

ENLARGED SECTION OF
FORD'S PATENT HEATER.

FIG. 503.
NATIONAL FEED WATER HEATER.

Descriptive Circulars on Application.

FIG. 504.

CAST IRON HEATER
WITH IRON PIPE COIL.

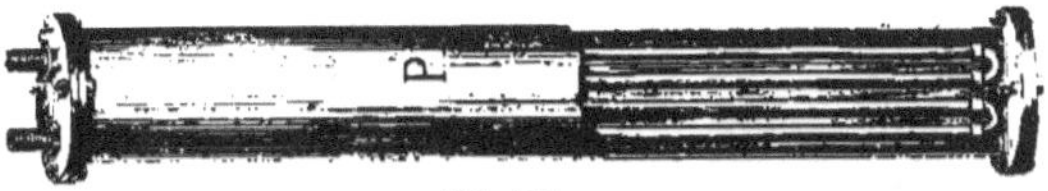

FIG. 505.

FEED WATER HEATER.
WITH RETURN BEND COIL.

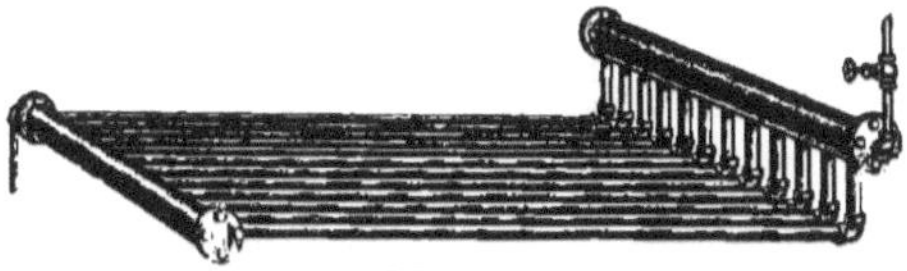

FIG. 507.

HEATER COILS.
IRON, BRASS OR COPPER PIPE.

FIG. 506.

MANIFOLD HEATER
FOR DRYING LUMBER, ETC. WROUGHT IRON HEADERS

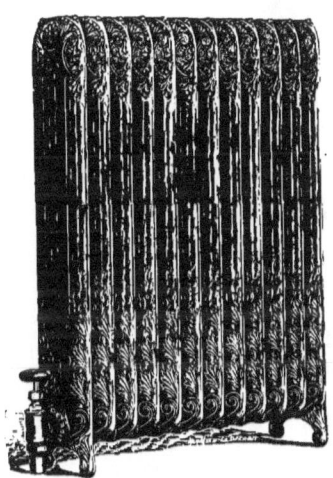

FIG. 508.

WROUGHT IRON
TUBE RADIATOR.

FIG. 509.

CAST IRON RADIATOR.
PERFECTION.

Descriptive Circulars on Application.

BEST, FOX & CO.

FIG. 510.
**BUNDY CIRCULAR
RADIATOR.**

FIG. 511.
**AUTOMATIC
AIR VALVES.**

FIG. 512.
BOX COILS.

FIG. 513.
WALL COILS.
1 - 1¼ - 1½—AND 2 INCH, PIPE,
WITH HEADERS FROM 1¼ TO 8 INCH. DIAM.
See Table, page 103.

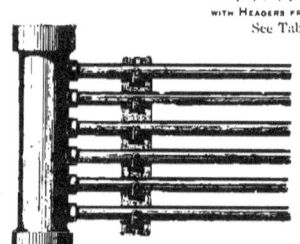

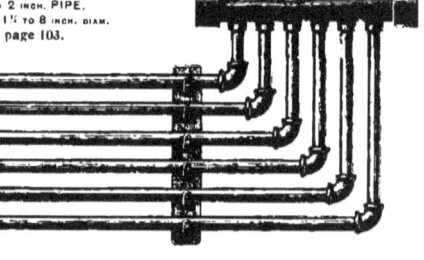

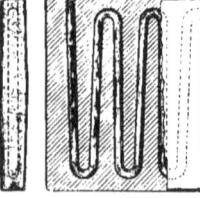

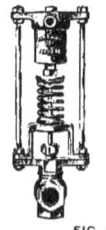

FIG. 514.
STEAM SUPER-HEATER.

FIG. 515.
**SCHUFFS'
STEAM PRESSURE REGULATOR.**

Descriptive Circulars on application.

LOCKE'S DAMPER REGULATORS.

AT LEAST 10 PER CENT. SAVING IN FUEL GUARANTEED.

NO STUFFING BOXES OR PACKING.

NO DIAPHRAGM.

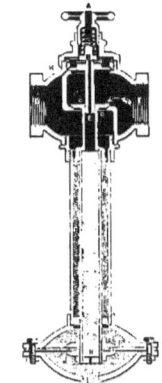

FIG. 517.

LOCKE'S BEATS ALL'

PRESSURE REDUCING VALVE.

FIG. 516.

WARRANTED

TO OPERATE DAMPERS WITH VARIATION OF ¹- LB.

STEAM PRESSURE. AND TO

FULLY CLOSE OR OPEN DAMPER WITH VARIATION OF 1 LB.

SOLD SUBJECT TO 30 DAYS TRIAL.

OVER 4000 OF LOCKE'S DAMPER REGULATORS IN USE.

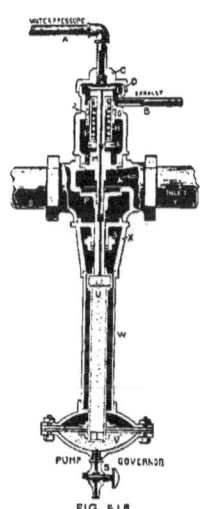

FIG. 518.

LOCKE'S BEATS ALL'

PUMP GOVERNOR.

BEST, FOX & CO.

HEAVY IRON LAMPS. (Brazed)

FOR MILLS AND BLAST FURNACES.

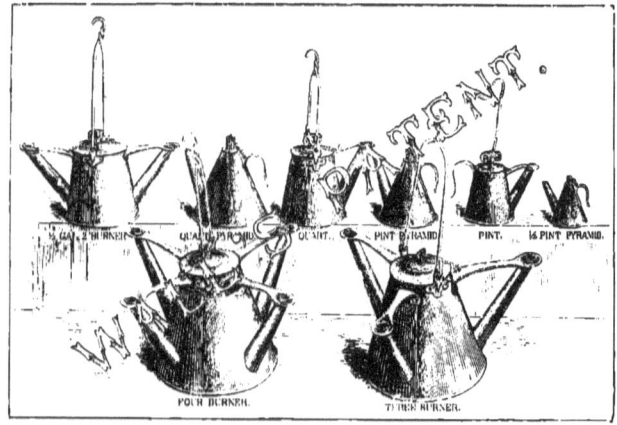

FIG. 519.

BLAKE'S PIPE HANGERS.

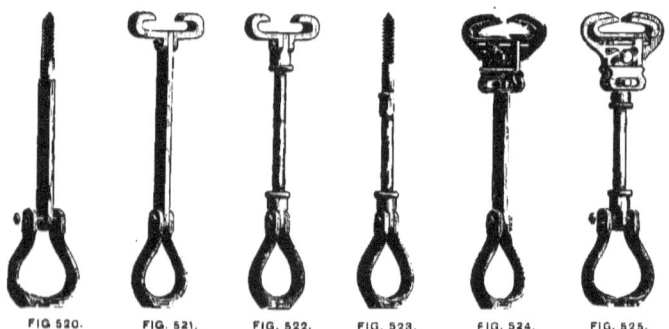

FIG 520.   FIG. 521.   FIG. 522.   FIG. 523.   FIG. 524.   FIG. 525.

Descriptive Circular on Application.

FIG. 526.
PULLEY BLOCKS.
WESTON'S.

FIG 527.
WINDLASS OR CRAB.

TACKLE BLOCKS.

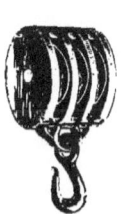

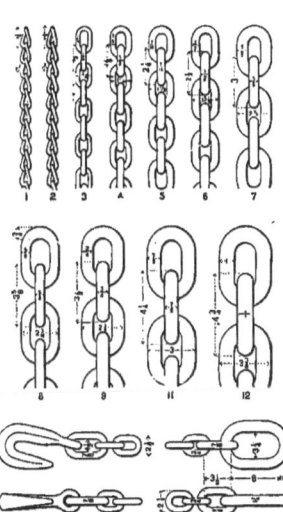

FIG. 528.
SINGLE.

FIG 529.
DOUBLE.

FIG. 530.
TRIPLE.

FIG. 531.
STEEL WIRE ROPE.
ALL SIZES.

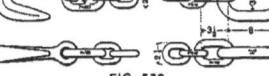

FIG. 532.
TESTED CHAIN.
ALL SIZES.

All Sizes Wire, Manilla and Cotton Rope and Chain.

FIG. 533.
JACK SCREWS.

FIG. 534.
RATCHET JACK.

FIG. 535.
HYDRAULIC JACK.

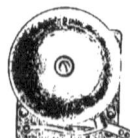

FIG. 536.
TRIP GONG.
FROM 3 IN. TO 18 IN. DIAM.

FIG. 539.
BOILER TUBE CLEANER.
GRIMMS' PATENT.

FIG. 537.
ROLLER TUBE EXPANDER.
HENDERER'S PATENT.

FIG. 540.
NATIONAL TUBE CLEANER.

FIG. 538.
ROLLER TUBE EXPANDER.
COLLINS' PATENT.

FIG. 541.
STEEL WIRE FLUE BRUSH.

All Styles of Flue Cleaners.

SHAFTING—COLD ROLLED OR COLD DRAWN.

FROM 1-4 IN. TO 4 IN.

IRON.   STEEL.

FIG. 542

FIG. 543
PLAIN PULLEY.

FIG. 544.
DOUBLE ARM PULLEY.

FIG. 545.
SPLIT PULLEY.

FIG. 546.
WOOD PULLEY.

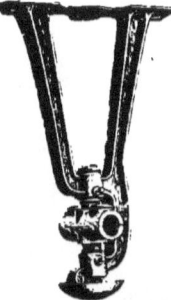

FIG. 547.
ADJUSTABLE HANGER.

FIG. 548.
ADJST. POST HANGER.

FIG. 549.
ADJST. PILLOW BLOCK.

FIG. 550.
FLANGE COUPLINGS.

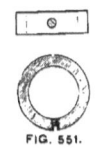

FIG. 551.
LOOSE COLLARS.

MACHINE BOLTS, NUTS, ETC.

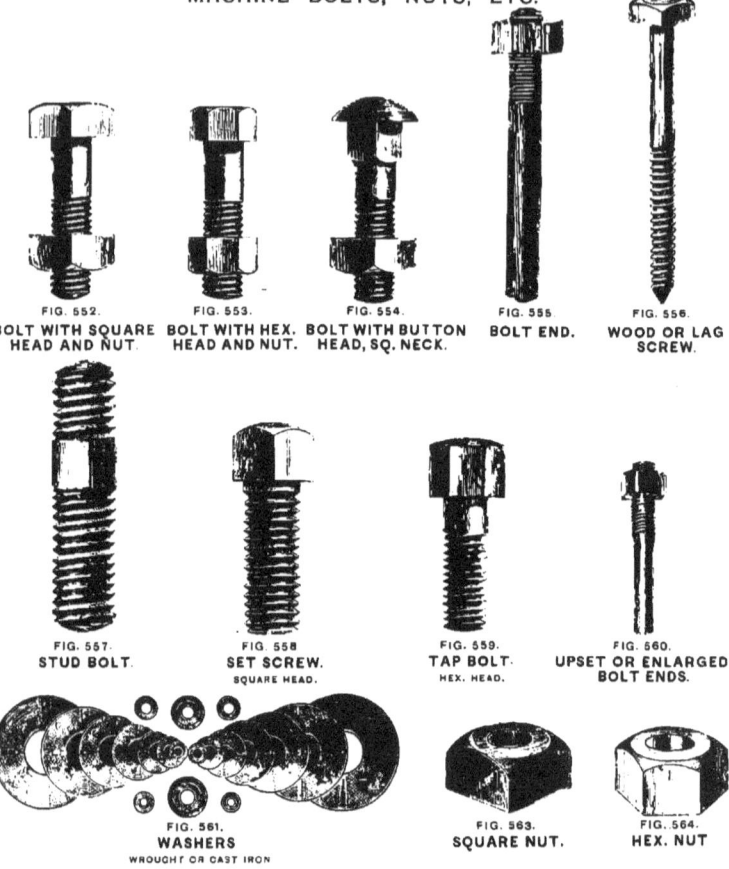

FIG. 552.
BOLT WITH SQUARE
HEAD AND NUT.

FIG. 553.
BOLT WITH HEX.
HEAD AND NUT.

FIG. 554.
BOLT WITH BUTTON
HEAD, SQ. NECK.

FIG. 555
BOLT END.

FIG. 556.
WOOD OR LAG
SCREW.

FIG. 557.
STUD BOLT.

FIG. 558.
SET SCREW.
SQUARE HEAD.

FIG. 559.
TAP BOLT.
HEX. HEAD.

FIG. 560.
UPSET OR ENLARGED
BOLT ENDS.

FIG. 561.
WASHERS
WROUGHT OR CAST IRON

FIG. 563.
SQUARE NUT.

FIG. 564.
HEX. NUT

FIG. 562.
TURN BUCKLES.
DROP FORGED.

FIG. 565.   FIG. 566.   FIG 567.
BOILER AND TANK RIVETS.

TOOLS FOR CUTTING AND FITTING PIPE.

WALWORTH DIE PLATE OR STOCKS.

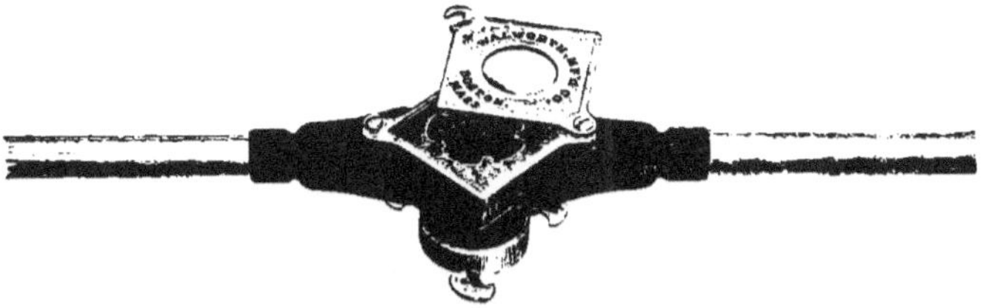

FIG. 568.

No. 1—Cuts from 1/4 to 1 or 1/8 to 1 inch.
No. 2—Cuts from 1 1/4 to 2 or 3/4 to 2 inch.

Separate Dies furnished when so ordered.

MILLER'S REVERSIBLE RATCHET DIE PLATE.

FIG. 569.

No. B—Cuts from 1/4 to 1 inch.
No. C—Cuts from 1 to 1 1/2 inch.
No. D—Cuts from 1 1/4 to 2 inch.
No. E—Cuts from 2 1/2 to 3 inch.

ARMSTRONG'S ADJUSTABLE STOCK AND DIES.

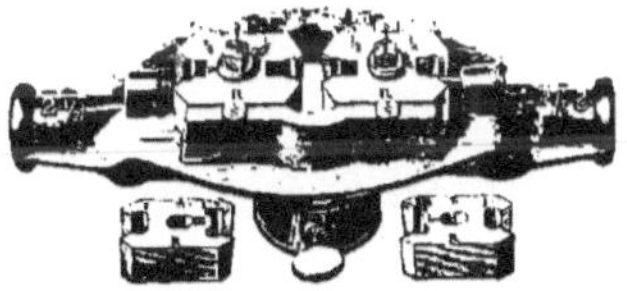

FIG. 570.

No. 1—Cuts from 1/8 to 1/2 inch.
No. 2—Cuts from 1/4 to 1 inch.
No. 3—Cuts from 1 1/4 to 2 inch.
No. 6—Cuts from 2 1/2 to 3 inch.
No. 7—Cuts from 2 1/2 to 4 inch.

BEST, FOX & CO.

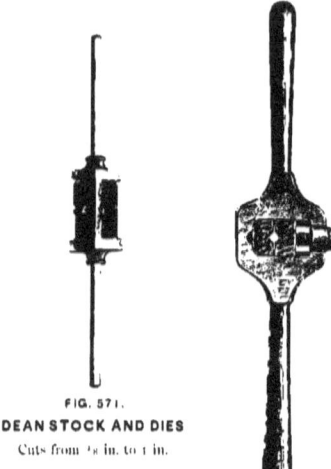

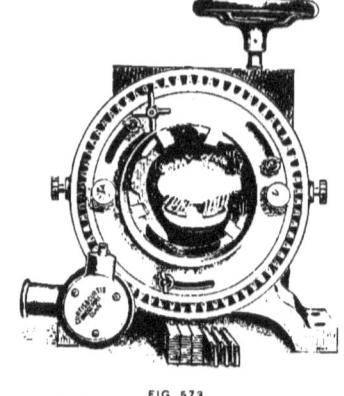

FIG. 571.
DEAN STOCK AND DIES

Cuts from ⅛ in. to 1 in.

FIG. 573.
FORBE'S PATENT DIE STOCKS.
No. 1. Cuts from ½ in. to 2 in.
No. 2. Cuts from 2½ in. to 4 in.
No. 3. Cuts from 4 in. to 6 in.

FIG. 572.
SCREW PLATE AND DIES
FOR BOLTS.
No. A. Cuts from ¼ in. to ½ in.
No. B. Cuts from ⅜ in. to ¾ in.
No. C. Cuts from ½ in. to ⅞ in.
No. D. Cuts from ⅝ in. to 1¼ in.

FIG. 576.
WHEELS FOR CUTTERS
ALL SIZES.

FIG. 574.

STANWOOD PIPE
CUTTER.

No. 1. Cuts from ⅛ in. to 1 in.
No. 2. Cuts from ¾ in. to 2 in.
No. 3. Cuts from 2 in. to 3 in.

FIG. 575.
BARNES 3 WHEEL PIPE
CUTTER.
No. 1. Cuts from ⅛ in. to 1 in.
No. 2. Cuts from ½ in. to 2 in.
No. 3. Cuts from 1½ in. to 3 in.
No. 4. Cuts from 2½ in. to 4 in.
No. 5. Cuts from 4 in. to 6 in.
No. 6. Cuts from 6 in. to 8 in.
No. 7. Cuts from 9 in. to 12 in.

FIG. 577.
PINS FOR CUTTERS.
ALL SIZES.

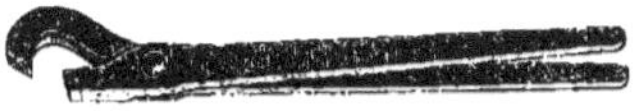

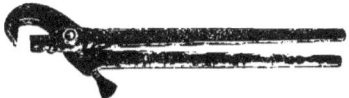

FIG. 578.

COMMON PIPE TONGS.

From ⅛ in. to 8 in. pipe.

FIG. 579.

BROWN'S ADJST. TONGS.

No. 1, ...	takes from ⅛ in. to ¾ in.
No. 1½, ...	takes from ⅜ in. to 1 in.
No. 2, ...	takes from ½ in. to 1¼ in.
No. 3, ...	takes from 1 in. to 2 in.
No. 4, ...	takes from 1½ in. to 3 in.
No. 5, ...	takes from 2½ in. to 4 in.
No. 6, ...	takes from 3 in. to 5 in.
No. 7, ...	takes from 4 in. to 7 in.

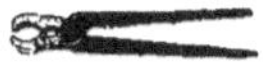

FIG. 580.

PLYERS.

From 8 in. to 14 in. long.

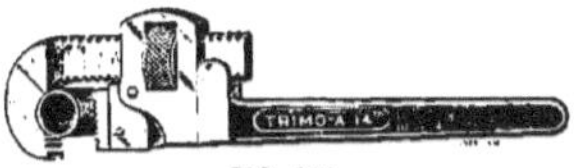

FIG 581.

TRIMO PIPE WRENCH.

No. 6, takes from ⅛ in. wire to ½ in. pipe.
No. 8, takes from ⅛ in. wire to ¾ in. pipe.
No. 10, takes from ⅛ in. wire to 1 in. pipe.
No. 14, takes from ¼ in. wire to 1½ in. pipe.
No. 18, takes from ¼ in. wire to 2 in. pipe.
No. 24, takes from ¼ in. wire to 2½ in. pipe.
No. 36, takes from ½ in. wire to 3½ in. pipe.
No. 42, takes from 1 in. pipe to 5 in. pipe.

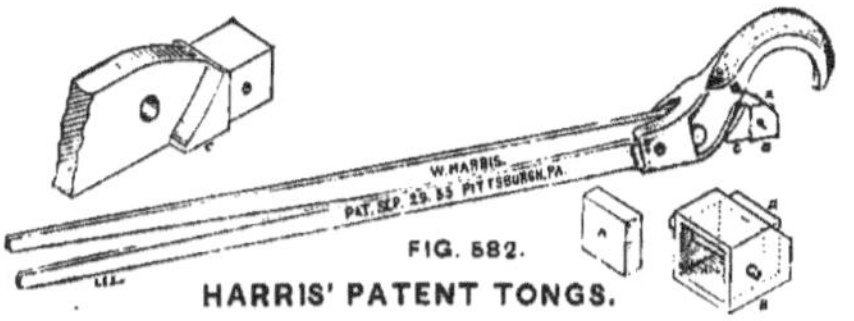

FIG. 582.

HARRIS' PATENT TONGS.

One Tong required for each size of pipe. Steel Handles, Malleable Head, Adjustable Bit, with eight sharp edges.

FIG 583.

ROBBIN'S CHAIN TONGS.

No. 2, .	takes from 1 in. to 2 in. pipe.
No. 3, .	takes from 1½ in. to 4 in. pipe.
No. 4, .	takes from 2 in. to 6 in. pipe.
No. 5, .	takes from 2½ in. to 8 in. pipe.
No. 6, .	takes from 4 in. to 10 in. pipe.
No. 7, .	takes from 4 in. to 16 in. pipe.

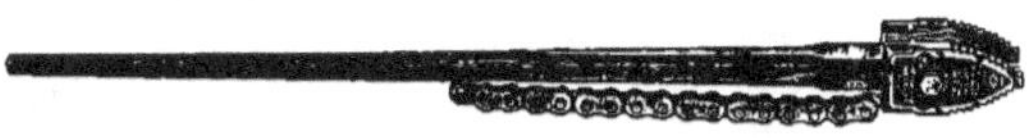

FIG. 584.

BROCK'S PAT. CHAIN TONGS.

No. 0, .	takes from ⅛ in. to ¾ in. pipe.
No. 1, .	takes from ⅛ in. to 1½ in. pipe.
No. 2,	takes from ¼ in. to 2½ in. pipe.
No. 3,	takes from ¼ in. to 4 in. pipe.
No. 4,	takes from 1 in. to 8 in. pipe.
No. 5,	takes from 2 in. to 14 in. pipe.

FIG. 585.
MONKEY WRENCH.
FROM 6 IN. TO 21 IN. LONG.

FIG. 586.
BAXTER S WRENCH.
FROM 4 IN. TO 15 IN. LONG.

FIG. 587.
SMITH'S FRICTION SLEEVE RATCHET.
FROM 10 IN. TO 20 IN. LONG.

FIG. 588.
PACKER BOILER RATCHET.
FROM 10 IN. TO 20 IN. LONG.

FIG. 589.	FIG. 590.	FIG. 591.	FIG. 592.	FIG. 593.	FIG. 594.
PIPE TAP.	**PIPE REAMER.**	**COMBINED TAP, REAMER AND DRILL.**	**PIPE DRILL.**	**TWIST DRILL.**	**COUNTERBORE DRILL.**

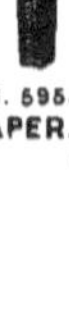

FIG. 595. 　 FIG. 596. 　 FIG. 597.
TAPER.　 PLUG.　 BOTTOMING.
MACHINISTS' TAPS.

FIG. 598.
WRENCH, DROP FORGED.
(ALL SIZES AND STYLES)

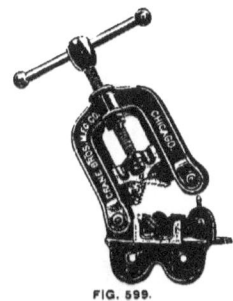

FIG. 599.
PIPE VISE.
MALLEABLE.

FIG. 600.
COMBINATION VISE.
SMITH'S.

FIG. 601.
HAMMERS AND SLEDGES.
MACHINISTS.   COPPER.

FIG. 602.

FIG. 603.
GLASS TUBE CUTTER.

FIG. 604.
COPPER FLOATS.
HEAVY FOR BOILER PRESSURE.
LIGHT FOR TANK PRESSURE.

FIG. 604½.
TANK VALVES.

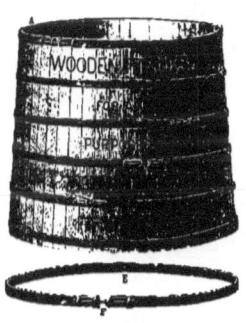

FIG. 605.
WOODEN TANKS.
ANY CAPACITY.

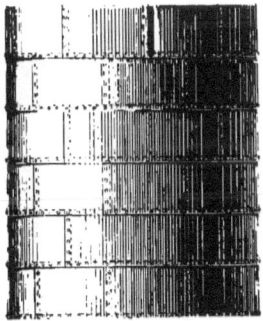

FIG. 606.
IRON TANKS.
ANY CAPACITY.

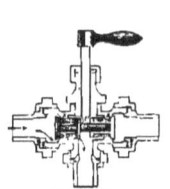

FIG. 607.
LUNKENHEIMER'S AUTOMATIC CYLINDER COCK.

FIG. 608.
TRIUMPH DOUBLE ACTING FORCE PUMP.
SINGLE LEVER.
ALSO MADE WITH DOUBLE LEVER.

Hand pumps furnished of any style.

FIG. 609.
WORKING BARREL.
FOR DEEP WELLS.
From 2 in. to 6 in. in diameter.

FIG. 610.
CLIMAX OIL BURNER.

FIG. 611.
HORIZONTAL CENTRIFUGAL PUMP.

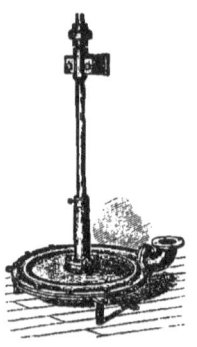

FIG. 612.
VERTICAL CENTRIFUGAL PUMP.

Descriptive circular on application.

BUFFALO DUPLEX STEAM PUMPS.

FIG. 613.
BOILER FEED PUMP.
REGULAR PATTERN.

FIG. 614.
AUTOMATIC FEED PUMP
WITH RECEIVING TANK.

FIG. 615.
LOW SERVICE OR TANK PUMP.

816.
**PUMP AND BOILER
COMBINED.**

Pump Catalogue on Application.

BEST, FOX & CO.

BUFFALO STEAM PUMPS.

FIG. 617.
COMPOUND DUPLEX PUMP.
NON-CONDENSING.

FIG. 619.
IMPROVED SINGLE CYLINDER PUMP.

FIG. 620.
IMPROVED SINGLE CYLINDER.
VACUUM PUMP.

FIG. 618.
UNDERWRITERS' FIRE PUMP.

FIG. 621.
IMPROVED SINGLE CYLINDER.
INDEPENDENT AIR PUMP AND JET CONDENSER.

Pump Catalogue on Application.

BUFFALO DUPLEX STEAM PUMPS.

DUPLEX PUMP

WITH

EXTERNAL

CENTRE PACKED

PLUNGERS.

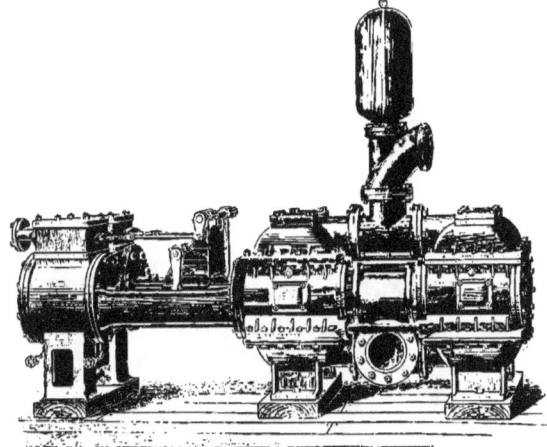

FIG. 622.

DUPLEX PUMP

WITH

EXTERNAL PACKED

PLUNGERS.

OUTSIDE

CONNECTED.

FIG. 623.

Pump Catalogue on Application.

BUFFALO STEAM PUMPS.

FIG. 624.
COMPOUND DUPLEX HYDRAULIC PRESSURE PUMP.

BUFFALO DUPLEX POWER PUMP.
STYLE "B."
WITH INDEPENDENT WATER CYLINDERS.
Size, 6-inch Piston, 10-inch Stroke.

FIG 625.

FIG. 626.
ROTARY FORCE PUMP.

Pump Catalogue on Application.

SNOW DUPLEX STEAM PUMPS.

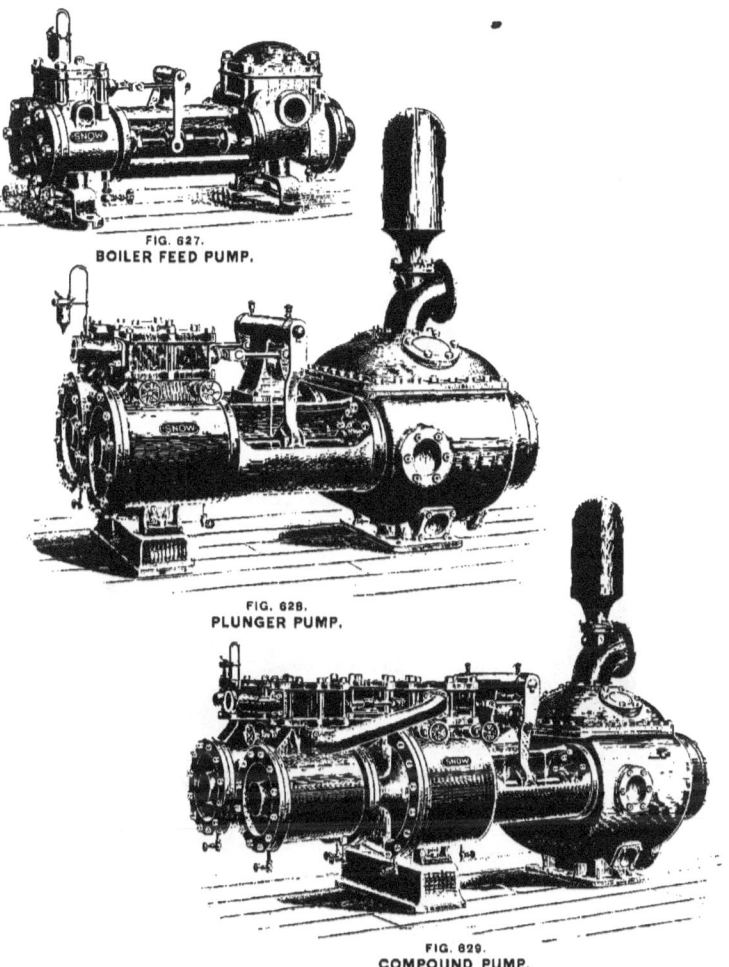

FIG. 627.
BOILER FEED PUMP.

FIG. 628.
PLUNGER PUMP.

FIG. 629.
COMPOUND PUMP.

Pump Catalogue on Application.

BEST, FOX & CO.

SNOW DUPLEX STEAM PUMPS.

FIG. 630.
HYDRAULIC PRESSURE PUMP.

FIG. 631.
MINE PUMP—HIGH PRESSURE.

Pump Catalogue on Application.

BEST, FOX & CO.

HORIZONTAL OR VERTICAL CYLINDERS (60 inch Diameter or less) REBORED

In their permanent position anywhere in the U. S.

ALSO

CORLISS VALVES, LARGE BEARINGS, GEAR AND FLY WHEELS.

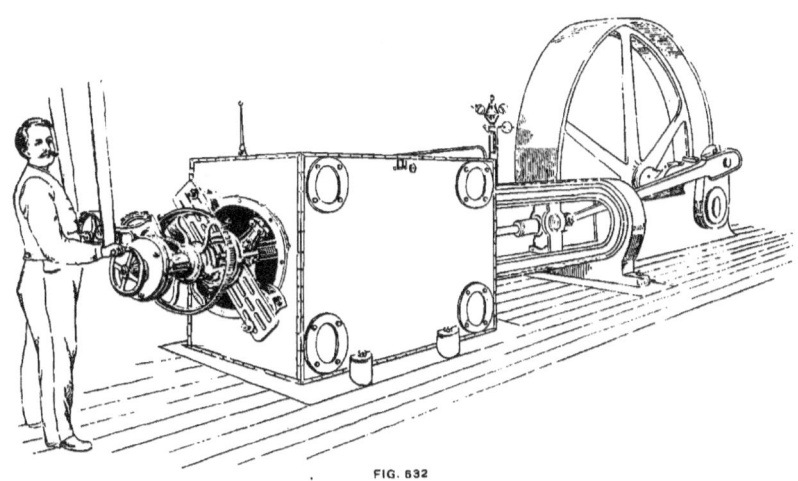

FIG. 632

WE MAKE

PISTON HEADS (Steel or Iron) 60 INCHES DIAM. or less.

PACKING RINGS of CLIMAX BRONZE, BABBITT, Steel or Iron.

PISTON RODS of COLD ROLLED STEEL or PHOSPHOR BRONZE.

STEEL SHAFTS, CRANKS, PITMANS, KEYS, Etc.

CLIMAX BRONZE BEARINGS AND SLIDES.

PITMAN & STRAP BRASSES, Etc., Etc.

REPAIRS

FOR ALL STYLES AND SIZES OF ENGINES.

PUMPS AND SPECIAL MACHINERY AT SHORT NOTICE.

Estimates furnished on Application.

BEST, FOX & CO.

HOSE, PACKING, ETC.

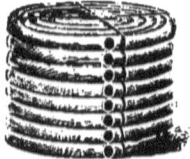

FIG. 633.
RUBBER HOSE.
FROM ¹ IN. TO 4 IN. AND
FROM 2 TO 8 PLY.

FIG. 634.
STEEL WIRE WRAPPED HOSE.

FIG. 635.
RUBBER SUCTION HOSE

FIG. 636.
SHEET PACKING.
FROM 1-64 TO ¹, IN. THICK.

FIG. 637.
FLAX PACKING.

FIG. 638.
JENKINS' PACKING.

FIG. 639.
SQUARE
PISTON PACKING.

FIG. 640.
RUBBER BACK
PISTON PACKING.

FIG. 641.
GARLOCK'S
ELASTIC PACKING.

FIG. 642.
USUDURIAN PACKING.
SELF-VULCANIZING.

FIG. 643.
RUBBER BELTING.
FROM 1 IN. TO 32 IN. WIDE.
FROM 2 TO 8 PLY.

LEATHER BELTING.
FROM 1 IN. TO 48 IN. WIDE.

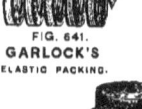

FIG. 644.
PUMP VALVES.
HARD AND SOFT RUBBER OR BRASS.

**BRASS PUMP.
SPRINGS.**
FIG. 645.
STRAIGHT.

FIG. 646.
CONICAL.

Special Packings Furnished.

SECTIONAL COVERINGS FOR STEAM PIPES.

MAGNESIA COVERING.

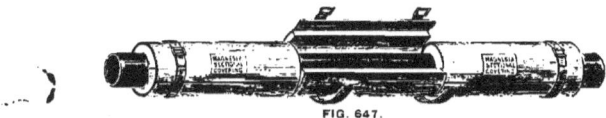

FIG. 647.

FIG. 648.    FIG. 649.    FIG. 650.    FIG 651.    FIG. 652.    FIG. 653.

MAGNESIA OR MAGNABESTOS COVERING FOR FITTINGS.

FIG. 654.

MAGNABESTOS COVERING.

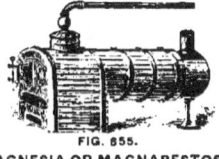

FIG. 855.

MAGNESIA OR MAGNABESTOS.

SECTIONAL BLOCKS AND PLASTIC
COVERING.

FIG. 856.

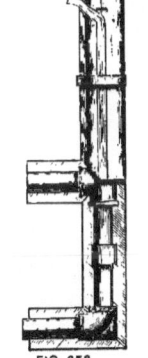

FIG. 857.

FIG. 858.

ABESTOS SECTIONAL COVERING.

ATTACHED TO PIPE.

Mineral Wool, Hair Felt, &c., Furnished as Desired.

BEST, FOX & CO.

CLIMAX BRONZE AND BRASS CASTINGS
From 1-2 oz. to 12,000 lbs. Weight.
ROUGH OR FINISHED.

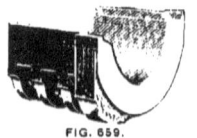

FIG. 659.
ROLL AND ENGINE BEARINGS.

FIG. 660.
STRAP BRASSES.

FIG. 661.
CAR BEARINGS.
WITH OR WITHOUT LEAD LINING.

FIG. 662.
LOCOMOTIVE DRIVING BOX BRASSES.

FIG. 663.
STEP BEARINGS.

FIG. 664.
BUSHINGS.
FOR BLOOMING MILL TABLES.

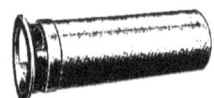

FIG. 665.
PUMP LININGS.
OR BUSHINGS.

FOR ELECTRIC CARS.
PINIONS.   BEARINGS.

FIG. 667.   **FIG. 668.**   **FIG 669.**   **FIG. 670.**
PLAIN.   BEVEL.   PLAIN.   WITH COLLAR.

FIG. 666.
BRONZE PISTON RODS.
ANY DIAMETER OR LENGTH,
WITH OR WITHOUT STEEL CENTRES.

FIG. 671.
TROLLEY SWITCHES.

FIG. 672.
TROLLEY WHEELS.

FIG. 673.
ONE PIECE GEAR WHEEL.
IRON AND STEEL

FIG. 674.
SPLIT GEAR WHEEL.
IRON AND STEEL.

CLIMAX BRONZE AND BRASS CASTINGS.
ROUGH OR FINISHED.

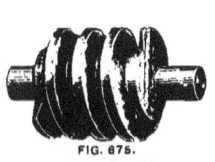

FIG. 675.
WORM WHEEL
CLIMAX BRONZE GRADE.

FIG. 676.
BELLS OF ANY SIZE AND TONE.

FIG. 677.
PACKING RINGS
OF ANY SIZE.
PLAIN OR BABBITTED.

Grade XX Phosphorized
Grade XX
"   X
A

Grade B
"   C
"   D
"   E

FIG. 578.
CLIMAX BABBITT METAL.
ALL GRADES.

FIG. 679.
INGOT
CLIMAX BRONZE.
INGOT BRASS.
ALL GRADES.

FIG. 681.
PHOSPHOR TIN.

FIG. 683.
SHEET LEAD.
ANY THICKNESS.

FIG. 685.
ROUND COPPER ROD.
"   **BRASS**   "
ALL SIZES

FIG. 680.
PIG LEAD.

FIG. 682.
ALUMINUM.

FIG. 684.
SHEET COPPER.
"   **BRASS.**
ANY THICKNESS.

FIG. 686.
SQUARE COPPER ROD.
"   **BRASS**   "
ALL SIZES.

See Table—Page 114.

BEST, FOX & CO.

BLAST FURNACE SPECIALTIES. CLIMAX BRONZE TUYERES.

(800 PATTERNS TO SELECT FROM)

Short—Less than 12 in. long.   Medium—Between 12 and 16 in. long.   Long—Over 16 in. long.

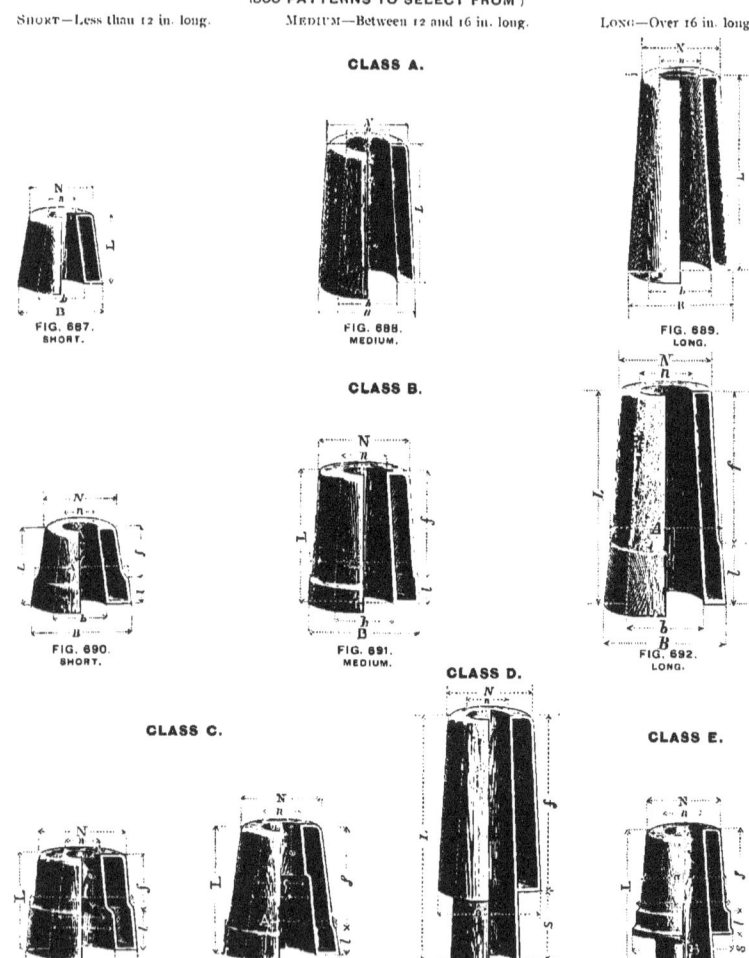

CLASS A.

FIG. 687.
SHORT.

FIG. 688.
MEDIUM.

FIG. 689.
LONG.

CLASS B.

FIG. 690.
SHORT.

FIG. 691.
MEDIUM.

FIG. 692.
LONG.

CLASS C.

CLASS D.

CLASS E.

FIG. 693.
SHORT.

FIG. 694.
MEDIUM.

FIG. 695.
LONG.

FIG. 696.

See Catalogue F for Dimensions of Above.

BEST, FOX & CO.

91

CLIMAX BRONZE TUYERES, NOTCHES AND COOLERS.

(800 PATTERNS TO SELECT FROM.)

SHORT—Less than 12 in. long.   MEDIUM—Between 12 and 16 in. long.   LONG—Over 16 in. long.

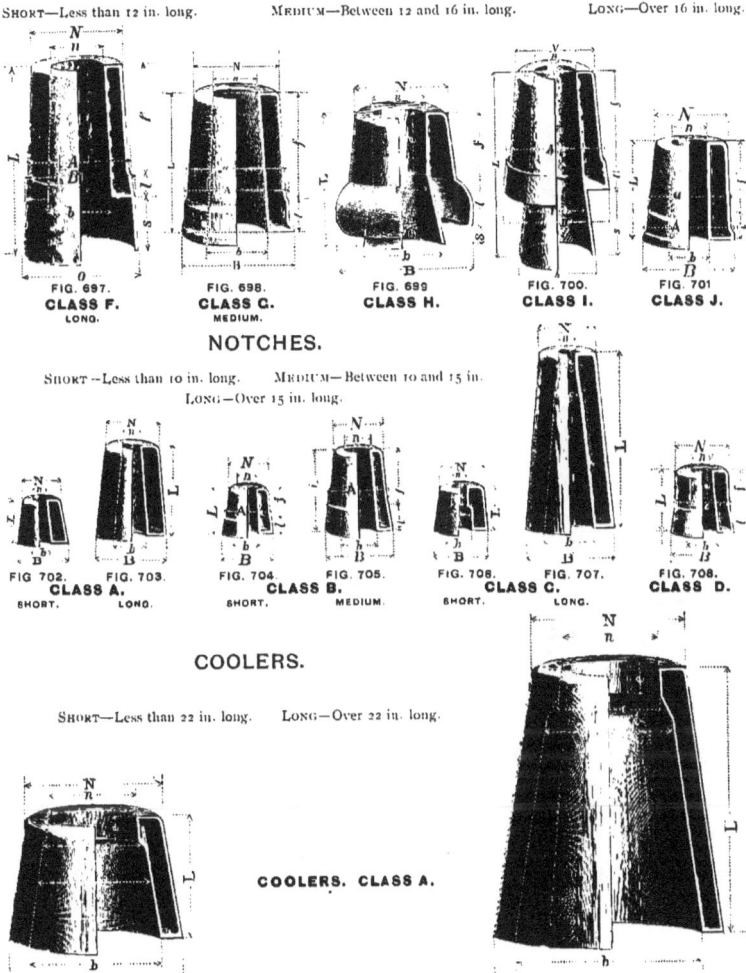

FIG. 697.	FIG. 698.	FIG. 699.	FIG. 700.	FIG. 701
CLASS F.	**CLASS G.**	**CLASS H.**	**CLASS I.**	**CLASS J.**
LONG.	MEDIUM.			

NOTCHES.

SHORT—Less than 10 in. long.   MEDIUM—Between 10 and 15 in.
LONG—Over 15 in. long.

FIG 702.	FIG. 703.	FIG. 704.	FIG. 705.	FIG. 706.	FIG. 707.	FIG. 708.
CLASS A.		**CLASS B.**		**CLASS C.**		**CLASS D.**
SHORT.	LONG.	SHORT.	MEDIUM.	SHORT.	LONG.	

COOLERS.

SHORT—Less than 22 in. long.   LONG—Over 22 in. long.

COOLERS. CLASS A.

FIG. 709.		FIG. 710.
SHORT.	See Catalogue F for Dimensions of Above.	LONG.

BEST. FOX & CO.

CLIMAX BRONZE COOLERS, NOTCH COOLERS, ETC.

Short · Less than 22 in. long.   Long —Over 22 in. long

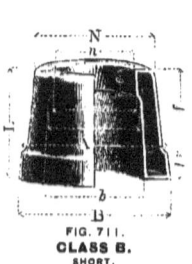

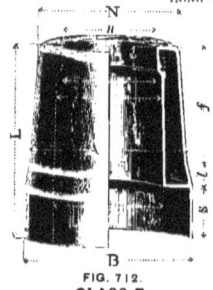

FIG. 711.
CLASS B.
SHORT.

FIG. 712.
CLASS F.
LONG.

NOTCH COOLERS.

Short—Less than 12 in. long.   Medium —Between 12 and 16 in. long   Long · Over 16 in. long

-------- **CLASS C.**   ------- **CLASS D.** --------

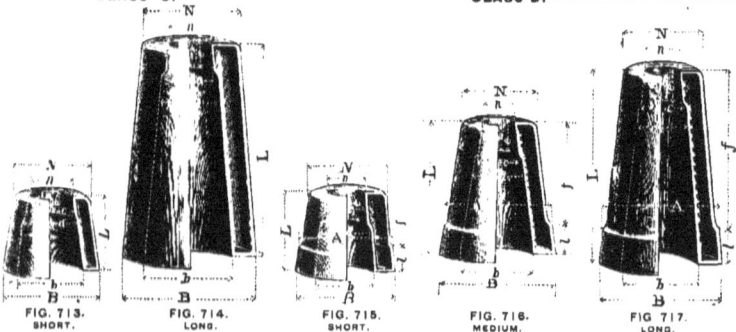

FIG. 713.
SHORT.

FIG. 714.
LONG.

FIG. 715.
SHORT.

FIG. 716.
MEDIUM.

FIG 717.
LONG.

BOSH BOXES. (FRONHEISER'S PATENT.)

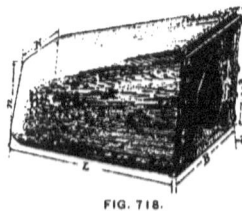

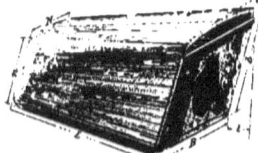

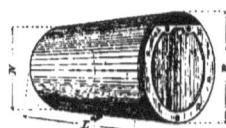

FIG. 718.
CLASS A.

FIG 719
CLASS B.

FIG. 720.
CLASS C.

See Catalogue F for Dimensions of Above.

CLIMAX BRONZE BOSH PLATES, JACKETS, ETC.

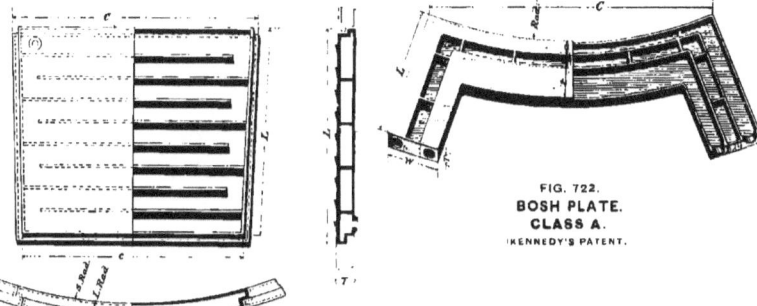

FIG. 722.
BOSH PLATE.
CLASS A.
(KENNEDY'S PATENT.)

FIG. 721.
HUNT'S PATENT BOSH JACKET.

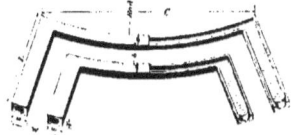

FIG. 723.
BOSH PLATE.
CLASS B.

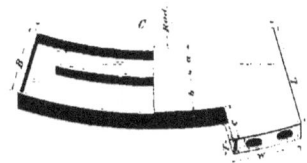

FIG. 724.
BOSH PLATE.
CLASS C.
POLLOCK'S PATENT.

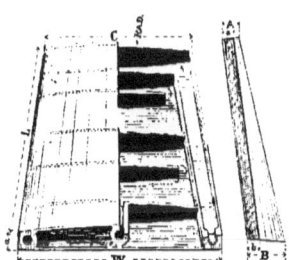

FIG. 725.
BOSH PLATE.
CLASS D.
(SCOTT'S PATENT.)

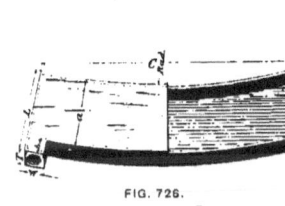

FIG. 726.
BOSH PLATE.
CLASS E.

See Catalogue F for Dimensions of Above.

CLIMAX BRONZE BOSH PLATES, AND VALVE SEATS.

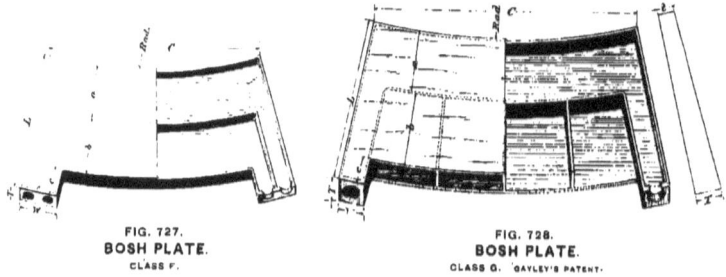

FIG. 727.
BOSH PLATE.
CLASS F.

FIG. 728.
BOSH PLATE.
CLASS G. GAYLEY'S PATENT.

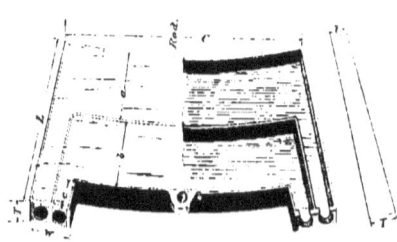

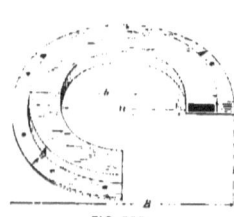

FIG. 729.
BOSH PLATE.
CLASS H. (GAYLEY'S PATENT)

FIG. 730.
VALVE SEAT.
CLASS A.

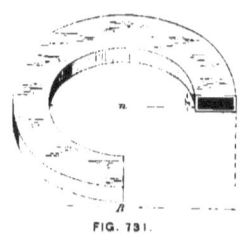

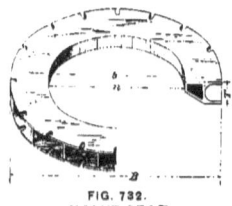

FIG. 731.
VALVE SEAT.
CLASS B.

FIG. 732.
VALVE SEAT.
CLASS C.

See Catalogue F for Dimensions of Above.

CLIMAX BRONZE VALVE SEATS AND VALVES.

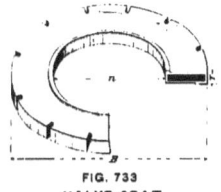

FIG. 733
VALVE SEAT.
CLASS D.

FIG. 734.
VALVE SEAT.
CLASS E.

FIG. 735.
VALVE SEAT.
CLASS F.

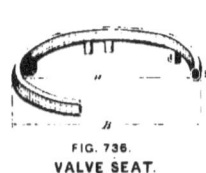

FIG. 736.
VALVE SEAT.
CLASS G.

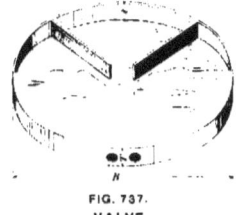

FIG. 737.
VALVE.
CLASS A.

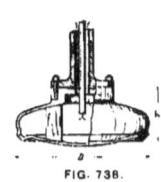

FIG. 738.
VALVE.
CLASS B.

See Catalogue F for Dimensions of above.

WATER AND AIR COOLED DEVICES

OF ANY SHAPE MADE OF

CLIMAX BRONZE,

SILVER, FOR

COPPER,

GLASS,

STEEL

AND IRON

SMELTING FURNACES.

CORRESPONDENCE SOLICITED.

BY-PASS FOR TANKS, HEATER EXHAUST, WATER TO BOILERS, AND STEAM MAINS.

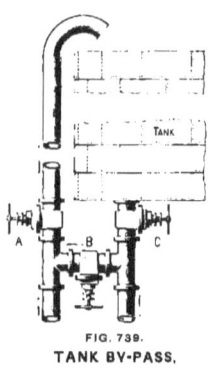

FIG. 739.

TANK BY-PASS.

BALANCED VALVE.

FOR TANKS.
WITH COPPER FLOAT

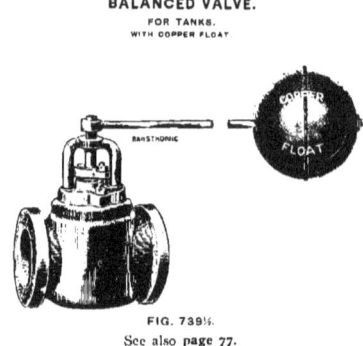

FIG. 739½.

See also page 77.

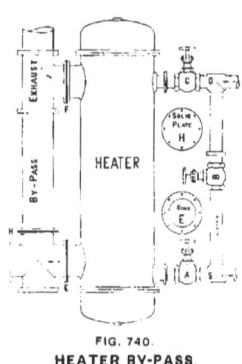

FIG. 740.

HEATER BY-PASS.

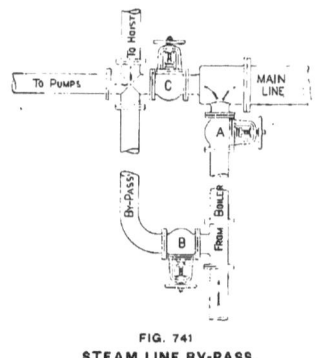

FIG. 741

STEAM LINE BY-PASS.

See Description Next Page

TANK BY-PASS.

Direct pressure from pump to furnace, independent of tank, is obtained, as shown by cut, by closing valves *A* and *C* and opening valve *B*. Tank can then be thoroughly cleaned. By-pass connection need not be placed close to tank. Any convenient point between lines to and from tank will answer for this purpose.

HEATER BY-PASS.

S indicates the cold water supply to the heater. *D*, the hot water line from the heater. If the heater needs repairing, close valves *A* and *C* and open by-pass valve *B*. If exhaust connection is made to heater, as shown on the left of same, it can be by-passed by removing liner or rings *E* and *F* and putting in their places plate *H* and a spare plate same as *H*. Then no exhaust can get into heater.

Put ring *E* where *H* was and steam will pass direct from Cross up through Tee and into atmosphere.

Plates and rings *E*, *F* and *H* are made of bronze ¼ or ⅜ inch thick, so as to prevent rusting and allowing ready removal.

This arrangement saves the expense of three valves and is very neat and compact.

STEAM LINE BY-PASS.

In Blast Furnace practice it is often the case that steam is required only for the pumps and hoist, when the furnace is banked or not blowing, and it is not desirable to have steam in the entire main line. Using the main steam line for this purpose can be avoided by arranging pipe system as shown. Close valves *A* and *C* and steam can be furnished through valve *B*, by only firing one battery of boilers.

BEST, FOX & CO.

WE MANUFACTURE

CLIMAX BRONZE CASTINGS,

Which we claim to be superior to any bronze in use, and guaranteed for the following purposes:

Grade A. For Blast Furnace Tuyeres, Bosh Plates, etc.

Grade B.—For general machine castings, Piston Rods, Cog Wheels, Racks and Pinions, Pump Linings, Bolts, Step Bearings and Hydraulic Work of all kinds, **hard and strong.**

Grade C.—For Heated Rolls, Hydraulic Cranes, Nail Machines, etc., **very tough and hard.**

Grade D.—For Packing Rings, for all purposes **very strong.**

Grade E.—For Bells, Gongs, etc.

Grade F.—For Heavy Bearings for Rolls, Engines, Car Bearings, Locomotive Driving Boxes, Collar Bearings, Heavy Slides, etc. This grade is made **hard and strong,** so as to **resist great pressure,** and is of such a nature as not to cut the journals.

Grade H.—For work subject to acids, chemicals, etc. Designed to take the place of ordinary **acid metal,** being much harder and stronger.

"**Climax Bronze**" of any grade, **in ingots,** in large or small quantities, at a price that enables it to compete with any other Bronze in the market.

PHOSPHORIZED INGOT COPPER.

Made of several grades to suit various purposes. **Guaranteed** to produce **Genuine Phosphor-Bronze Castings,** without additional mixture of metals.

MATERIAL NOT ILLUSTRATED.

Cotton and Hemp Packing,
Sheet Asbestos.
Asbestos Rope Packing,
Plumbago Packing.
Gasket Board.
Soil Pipe Fittings.
Sewer Pipe and Fittings.
Gaskets of any material.
Chain Belting and Shives.

Brass, Copper, Steel and Iron Wire.
Bar and Sheet Iron and Steel.
Bar, Sheet and Spring Steel.
Recording Gauges.
Natural Gas Supplies.
Crucibles and Plumbago.
Phosphorus.
Coal, Ore and Sand Screens.
Thermometers.

BEST, FOX & CO.'S

DIMENSIONS

OF

FITTINGS, VALVES, FLANGES,

STEEL, WROUGHT AND CAST IRON PIPE,

BRASS, COPPER AND LEAD PIPE,

STEEL AND COPPER BENDS,

&c., &c.

For the Convenience of Engineers and Draughtsmen we have embodied in Pamphlet K these tables from Pages 100 to 114.   Furnished on application.

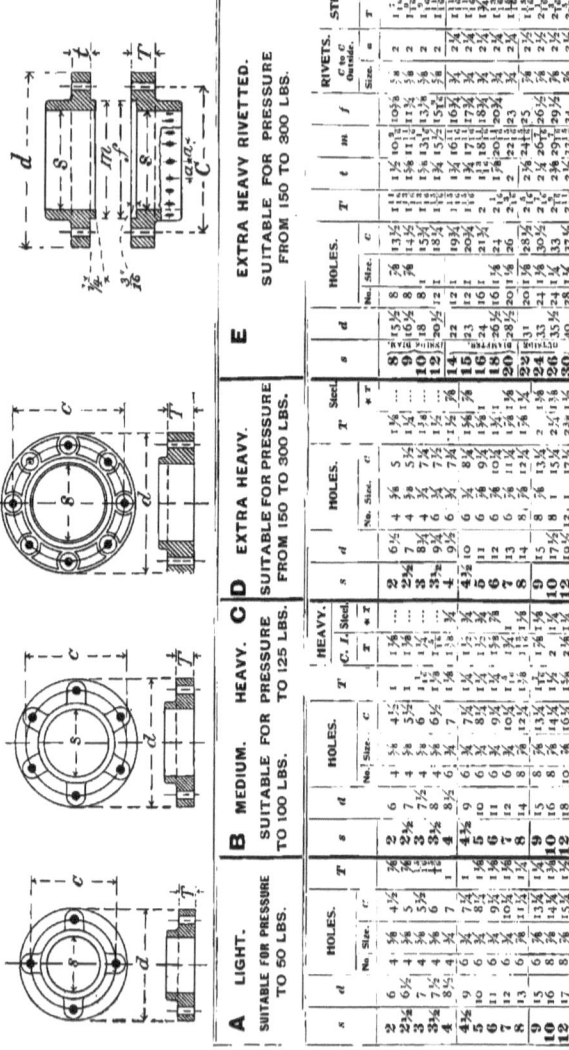

BEST, FOX & COMPANY'S
STANDARD DIMENSIONS
(BASED ON 10 YEARS PRACTICAL EXPERIENCE)
—OF—

CAST IRON AND CAST STEEL FLANGES

FOR THREADED I. D. (INSIDE DIAM.) PIPE.

A LIGHT.
SUITABLE FOR PRESSURE TO 50 LBS.

B MEDIUM.
SUITABLE FOR PRESSURE TO 100 LBS.

HEAVY.
SUITABLE FOR PRESSURE TO 125 LBS.

C **D** EXTRA HEAVY.
SUITABLE FOR PRESSURE FROM 150 TO 300 LBS.

E EXTRA HEAVY RIVETTED.
SUITABLE FOR PRESSURE FROM 150 TO 300 LBS.

CAST IRON AND CAST STEEL HYDRAULIC FLANGES TO ORDER.

ROLLED OR PRESSED STEEL FLANGES TO ORDER.

* STEEL FLANGES (THREADED) ARE NOT **RAISED HOLE.**

See Page........

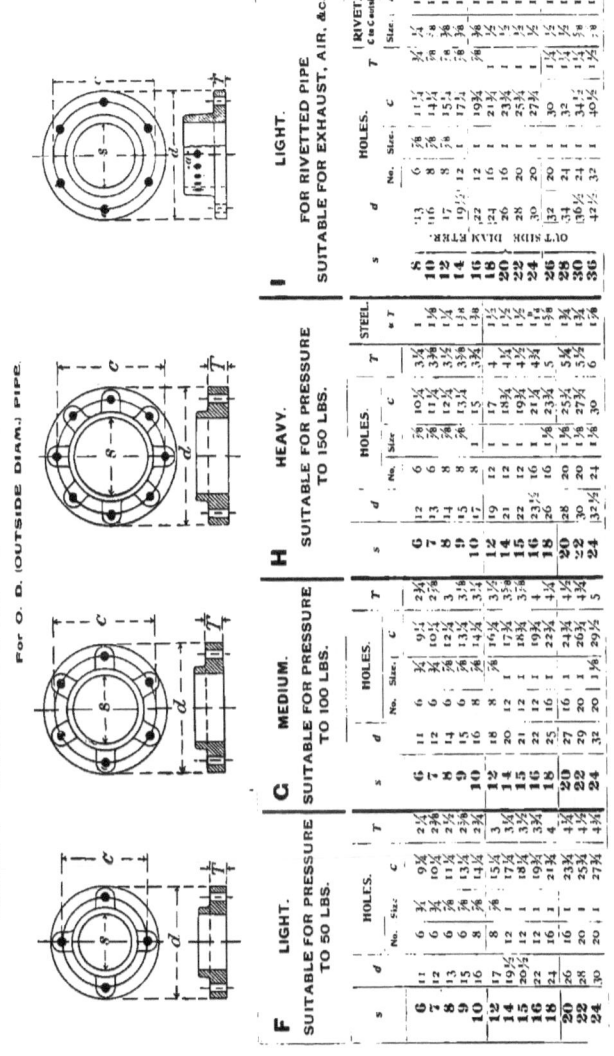

BEST, FOX & COMPANY'S
STANDARD DIMENSIONS
(BASED ON 10 YEARS PRACTICAL EXPERIENCE)
—OF—

CAST IRON AND CAST STEEL FLANGES

For O. D. (OUTSIDE DIAM.) PIPE.

F LIGHT. SUITABLE FOR PRESSURE TO 50 LBS.

C MEDIUM. SUITABLE FOR PRESSURE TO 100 LBS.

H HEAVY. SUITABLE FOR PRESSURE TO 150 LBS.

I LIGHT. FOR RIVETTED PIPE SUITABLE FOR EXHAUST, AIR, &c.

LARGER SIZES TO ORDER.

FLANGES EXPANDED AND PIENED ON PIPE.

* STEEL FLANGES ARE NOT **RAISED HOLE.**

BEST, FOX & COMPANY'S

STANDARD DIMENSIONS OF

FLANGED FITTINGS AND VALVES.

FLANGES.

ELBOWS, TEES, CROSSES.

45° ELBOWS, Ys

CLIMAX ANGLE VALVES & ANGLE CHECK VALVES.

CLIMAX GLOBE VALVES AND GLOBE CHECK VALVES.

CLIMAX GATE VALVES AND GATE STRAINERS.

BEST'S PATENT GATE VALVES. HEAVY AND EXTRA HEAVY.

DRILLING FOR EX. HY.

DIMENSIONS OF EX. HY. FITTINGS ARE LONGER THAN ABOVE.

FITTINGS AND VALVES TO 60 INCH DIAM. TO ORDER.

FOR EXTREME PRESSURES, FITTINGS AND VALVES ARE MADE OF CHARCOAL IRON, STEEL OR BRONZE.

FOR MEASUREMENTS OF REDUCED FITTINGS SEE PAGE 106.

BEST, FOX & COMPANY'S
STANDARD DIMENSIONS OF
SCREWED FITTINGS AND VALVES
FOR MEDIUM AND HEAVY PRESSURES. (NOT EXTRA HEAVY.)

ELBOWS, TEES AND CROSSES.

45° ELBOWS AND Y'S.

LONG RADIUS.

MANIFOLDS AND RETURN BENDS.

CLIMAX ANGLE AND CHECK VALVES

CLIMAX GLOBE AND CHECK VALVES

CLIMAX GATE VALVES AND STRAINERS.

HINGE OR SWING CHECK VALVES.

SCREWED FITTINGS TO 15 IN. INSIDE DIAM. ON HAND.

SCREWED STEEL FITTINGS TO ORDER.

SCREWED BRASS FITTINGS TO ORDER.

SPECIAL VALVES FOR HYDRAULIC PRESSURE MADE OF CHARCOAL IRON OR BRONZE.

EXTRA WIDE RETURN BENDS TO ORDER.

DIMENSIONS OF 2 IN. VALVES AND SMALLER ARE BRASS.

BEST, FOX & COMPANY'S
STANDARD DIMENSIONS
OF
SPECIAL VALVES AND FITTINGS,
ALSO
SMALLEST RADIUS FOR IRON, STEEL AND COPPER BENDS AT WHICH PIPE WILL NOT BUCKLE.

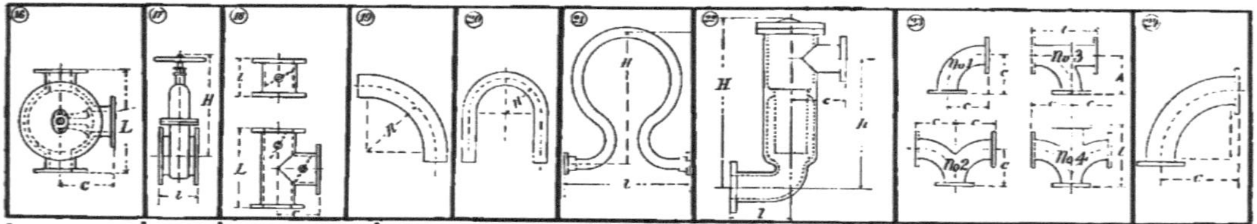

TRANSFER VALVES.			LIGHT GATES for EXHAUST AIR, &c.		BUTTERFLY VALVES. Single & Double.			Flag.
Size.	C	l	l	H	l	C	L	Diam.
4	6½	13	5½	12⅝	4½	6½	13	9
5	7	14	6	15	5¼	7½	15	10
6	7¾	15½	7	18	6	8¾	17½	11¼
7	8½	17	7	19¾	7	10¼	20½	12¼
8	9½	19	7¼	21¼	8	11⅝	23¼	14¼
10	10½	21	7¾	25	9¾	15	30	17½
12	12	24	8	27¾	10¾	17	34	19
14	13½	27	9½	32	12¼	19¼	38½	21¾
16	15	30	11¼	36¼	13¾	21	42	23¾
18	16½	33	12	41	15	23¾	47½	25½
20	18	36	12½	46½	16½	26¼	52½	28
22	19¾	39½	14	51	18½	29¼	58½	30½
24	21	42	15	55	19¼	31½	63	32½

Measurements given in Tables 16, 17 and 18 are for *50 lbs. Pressure.*

Full area of sizes of Pipe given is obtained through Butterfly Valves

BUTTERFLY VALVES for HIGH PRESSURE, SPECIAL.

DIAM. of FLANGES on TRANSFER VALVES and LIGHT GATES same as TABLE 25.

MINIMUM RADIUS OF	SQUARE BENDS. Iron.	SQUARE BENDS. Copper	U BENDS. Iron.	U BENDS. Copper
Size.	R	R	R	R
1"	2"	4	3½	9
1¼	2½	5	4	10
1½	3	5	5	12
2	4	6	6	12
2½	5	6	7	12
3	6½	6	8	15
3½	8	8	10	18
4	10	10	12	20
5	14	15	18	2 ft.
6	18	18	22	2'-6"
7	2'-1"	20	2'-4"	3 ft.
8	2'-8"	2'-6"	3'-6"	3'-4"
10	3'-10"	3'-6"	5'-8"	4'-6"
12	5 ft.	4 ft.	6 ft.	5 ft.
14	6'-2"	4'-6"	7 ft.	6 ft.
16	7'-4"	5 ft.		
18	8'-6"	5 ft.		
20	9'-8"	5'-6"		
22	10'-10"	6 ft.		
24	12 ft.	6 ft.		

COPPER EXPANSION JOINTS.		
Size.	l	H
1	2 ft.	14"
1¼	2'-6"	15
1½	3 ft.	16
2	3 ft.	18
2½	3 ft.	18
3	4 ft.	2 ft.
3½	4'-6"	2'-3"
4	5 ft.	2'-6"
5	6 ft.	3 ft.
6	7 ft.	4 ft.
7	8 ft.	4'-6"
8	10 ft.	5 ft.
10	12 ft.	6 ft.
12	14 ft.	6'-6"
14	16 ft.	7 ft.

PREFER MAKING BENDS (IRON AND COPPER) LONGER RADIUS.

PUMP STRAINERS.				
Size.	C	l	H	h
6	9½	8½	37¼	26½
7	10¾	9	39¾	27¼
8	10¾	9¾	42	29¾
10	12¼	11¼	49½	35½
12	13¼	12½	54	38¼
14	14¾	14	59¾	42
16	17	16	63	44
18	18	17	68½	48¼
20	19	18	72½	51
22	20	19	77½	54
24	22	21	83½	58

LONG RADIUS FLANGED FITTINGS.			
Size.	C	l	a
3	5	10⅛	5
3½	5½	11	5½
4	6¼	12⅜	6⅛
5	7½	14⅝	6⅝
6	8¾	16	7¼
7	10	16¾	6⅝
8	11¼	19¾	7⅞
10	13½	21⅞	8⅜
12	15¼	24⅞	9¾
14	17½		
16	20		
18	23		
20	26		
22	29		
24	32		

EXTRA LONG RADIUS ELBOWS.	
Size.	C
3	6
3½	7
4	8
5	10
6	12
7	14
8	16
10	20
12	2 ft.
14	2'-4"
16	2'-8"
18	3 ft.
20	3'-4"
22	3'-8"
24	4 ft.

LARGER SIZE STRAINERS AND LONG RADIUS FITTINGS TO ORDER.

BEST, FOX & COMPANY'S

STANDARD DIMENSIONS OF

REDUCED FLANGED FITTINGS

For LIGHT, MEDIUM AND HEAVY PRESSURES, (not EX. HY.)

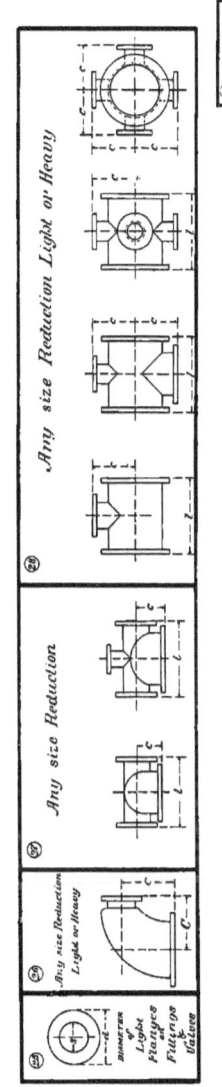

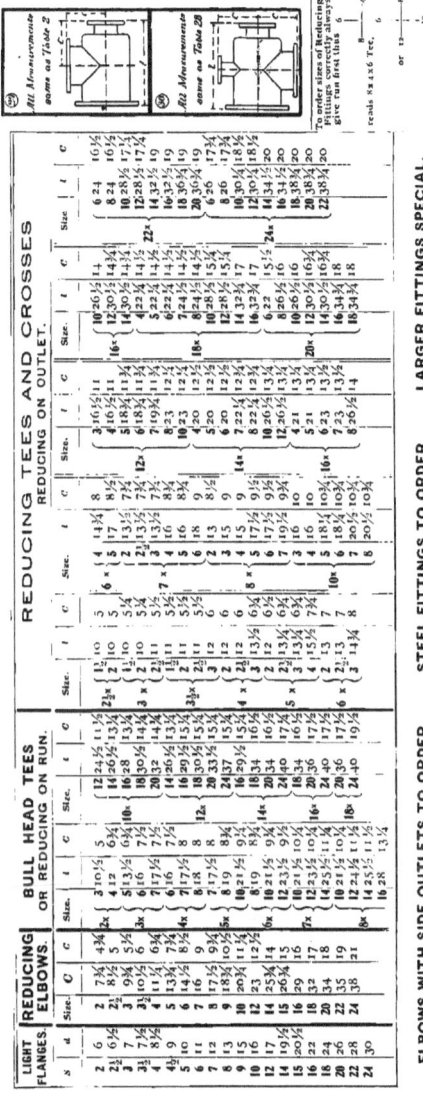

Any size Reduction Light or Heavy

Any size Reduction

Any size Reduction Light or Heavy

REDUCING TEES AND CROSSES
REDUCING ON OUTLET.

BULL HEAD TEES
OR REDUCING ON RUN.

LIGHT FLANGES.	REDUCING ELBOWS.

ELBOWS WITH SIDE OUTLETS TO ORDER.   STEEL FITTINGS TO ORDER.   LARGER FITTINGS SPECIAL.

To order sizes of Reducing Fittings correctly always give run first thus

reads 8 x 2 x 6 Tee,

reads 12 x 8 x 10 x 6 Cross.

BEST, FOX & CO.

APPROXIMATE WEIGHT OF BOWL FITTINGS FOR CAST IRON PIPE.

ELBOWS Size	ELBOWS Weight	45° L's Weight	TEES Weight	CROSSES Size	CROSSES Weight	SLEEVES Weight	PLUGS Weight	REDUCERS Size	REDUCERS Weight	REDUCING TEES, CROSSES Weight	REDUCERS Size	REDUCERS Weight	REDUCING TEES, CROSSES Weight	REDUCING TEES Weight	REDUCING CROSSES Weight
3	34	30	76	3	104	20	5	3X2	35	76	14X6	285	90	545	570
4	48	65	100	4	150	44	8	4X3	42	90	14X8	340	114	575	635
6	110	85	150	6	200	65	12	6X4	95	130	14X10	430	150	630	730
8	145	160	265	8	325	86	26	8X4	116	222	14X12	475	265	650	
10	225	190	390	10	510	140	46	8X6	126	252	16X10	435	265	650	
12	370	290	565	12	700	176	66	10X4	128	292	16X12	475	338	890	1010
14	450	400	700	14	800	208	70	10X6	150	312	20X12	540	388	825	1025
16	535	510	790	16	1025	340	100	10X8	212	330	20X16	690	415	1025	1370
20	900	740	1375	20	1790	500	150	12X4	230	460	24X20	745	525	1115	
24	1400	1425	1875	24	2190	710	185	12X6	230	484	30X24	1300	540	2640	2020
30		2000	3025	30		965	370	12X8	254	492			615		
								12X10	278	510			650		

OFFSETS, Ys, CAPS AND SPECIALS OF ALL SIZES AT SHORT NOTICE.

STEEL OR WROUGHT IRON WELDED STEAM, GAS AND WATER PIPE.

TABLE OF STANDARD DIMENSIONS.

Taper of Threads per inch of Screw, $\frac{1}{32}$ inches from ⅛ to 9 inches, inclusive, and $\frac{1}{24}$ from 10 inches up.

Diameter.			Thickness.	Circumference.		Transverse Areas.			Length of Pipe per Sq. Foot of		Length of Pipe, containing One Cubic Foot.	Nominal Weight per Foot.	Number of Threads per Inch of Screw.	Length of Thread.	Nominal Internal Diam.
Nominal Internal.	Actual External.	Actual Internal.		External.	Internal.	External.	Internal.	Metal.	External Surface.	Internal Surface.					
Inches.	Inches.	Inches.	Inches.	Inches.	Inches.	Sq. Inches.	Sq. Inches.	Sq. Inches.	Feet.	Feet.	Feet.	Lbs.			
⅛	.40	.27	.068	1.27	.84	.13	.057	.071	9.44	14.15	2500.	.24	27	⅜	⅛
¼	.54	.36	.088	1.69	1.14	.23	.104	.125	7.07	10.50	1385.	.42	18	½	¼
⅜	.67	.49	.091	2.12	1.55	.35	.191	.166	5.65	7.67	751.5	.56	"	⅝	⅜
½	.84	.62	.109	2.64	1.95	.55	.304	.249	4.50	6.13	472.4	.84	14	¾	½
¾	1.05	.82	.113	3.39	2.59	.86	.533	.332	3.63	4.63	270.	1.12	"	⅞	¾
1	1.31	1.04	.134	4.13	3.29	1.35	.862	.495	2.90	3.67	166.9	1.67	11½	$\frac{15}{16}$	1
1¼	1.66	1.38	.14	5.21	4.33	2.16	1.496	.668	2.30	2.76	96.25	2.24	"	1	1¼
1½	1.9	1.61	.145	5.97	5.06	2.83	2.038	.797	2.01	2.37	70.65	2.68	"	1$\frac{1}{16}$	1½
2	2.37	2.06	.154	7.46	6.49	4.43	3.356	1.074	1.61	1.84	42.36	3.61	"	1⅛	2
2½	2.87	2.46	.204	9.03	7.75	6.49	4.784	1.708	1.32	1.54	30.11	5.74	8	1$\frac{3}{16}$	2½
3	3.5	3.06	.217	10.99	9.63	9.62	7.388	2.243	1.09	1.24	19.49	7.54	"	1⅜	3
3½	4.	3.54	.226	12.56	11.14	12.56	9.887	2.679	.95	1.07	14.56	9.00	"	"	3½
4	4.5	4.02	.237	14.13	12.64	15.90	12.73	3.174	.84	.94	11.31	10.66	"	1$\frac{7}{16}$	4
4½	5.	4.50	.246	15.70	14.16	19.63	15.961	3.674	.76	.84	9.03	12.34	"	"	4½
5	5.56	5.04	.259	17.47	15.85	24.30	19.99	4.316	.62	.75	7.20	14.50	"	1$\frac{9}{16}$	5
6	6.62	6.06	.28	20.81	19.05	34.47	28.888	5.584	.57	.63	4.98	18.76	"	1⅝	6
7	7.62	7.02	.301	23.95	22.06	45.66	38.738	6.926	.50	.54	3.72	23.27	"	1¾	7
8	8.62	7.98	.322	27.09	25.07	58.42	50.04	8.380	.44	.47	2.88	28.18	"	1⅞	8
9	9.62	8.93	.344	30.23	28.07	72.76	62.73	10.03	.39	.42	2.26	33.70	"	2	9
10	10.75	10.02	.366	33.77	31.47	90.76	78.839	11.924	.35	.38	1.80	40.06	"	2⅛	10
11	12.	11.25	.375	37.79	35.34	113.09	99.402	13.696	.32	.34	1.50	45.	"	2¼	11
12	12.75	11.	.375	40.05	37.7	127.67	113.098	14.579	.30	.32	1.27	48.98	"	2⅜	12
13	14.	13.25	.375	43.98	41.62	153.93	137.887	16.051	.27	.29	1.04	53.92	"	2½	13
14	15.	14.25	.375	47.12	44.76	176.71	159.485	17.23	.25	.27	.90	57.89	"	2½	14
15	16.	15.25	.375	50.26	47.91	201.06	182.655	18.407	.24	.25	.88	62.00	"	2⅝	15
17	18.														
19	20.														
21	22.														
23	24.														

These sizes, as well as all sizes above 12 in. can be made of any thickness required. See Table page 112 for dimensions.

PIPE ABOVE 16 IN. OUTSIDE DIAMETER NOT THREADED.

SPIRAL RIVETTED PIPE, WITH RIVETTED FLANGES, DOUBLE GALVANIZED.

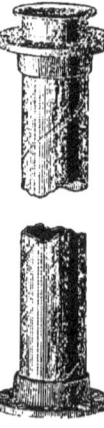

INSIDE DIAMETER IN INCHES.	THICKNESS BIRMINGHAM GAUGE.	NOMINAL WEIGHT PER FOOT.
3	No. 20	2½ lbs.
4	"	3 "
5	"	4 "
6	No. 18	5 "
7	"	6 "
8	"	7 "
9	"	8 "
10	No. 16	11 "
11	"	12 "
12	"	14 "
13	"	15 "
14	No. 14	20 "
15	"	22 "
16	"	24 "
18	"	29 "
20	"	34 "
22	No. 12	40 "
24	"	50 "

Pipe with Crimped Ends, Sleeve or Slip Joints to order. Descriptive Circular of Spiral Riveted Pipe, Connections and Fittings on Application.

SPIRAL WELD PIPE, WITH SLIP FLANGES.

DIAMETER INSIDE.	GRADE.	NOMINAL WEIGHT. Per ft. Lbs.	PROOF STRENGTH. Per Sq. Inch.
6	Standard	6.86	866
	Heavy	8.07	1106
8	Standard	9.12	650
	Heavy	10.78	830
10	Standard	13.74	664
	Heavy	16.73	872
12	Standard	17.11	553
	Heavy	20.71	727
14	Standard	21.07	474
	Heavy	25.27	623
16	Standard	32.03	545
	Heavy	36.69	670
18	Standard	38.85	484
	Heavy	41.96	596
20	Standard	39.49	436
	Heavy	45.57	536
22	Standard	49.67	396
	Heavy	55.95	487
24	Standard	53.39	363
	Heavy	60.28	446

Pipe with Hub and Spigot or Sleeve to order. Descriptive Circular of Spiral Weld Pipe and Connections on Application.

BOWL PIPE.

CAST IRON

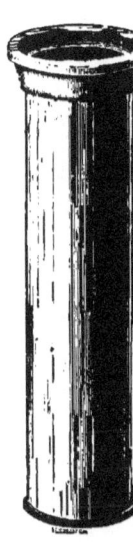

GAS PIPE IN 12 FOOT LENGTHS.

Diameter in Inches.	THICKNESS. Inches.	Approximate Inches.	Approximate Weight Per Foot.
3	.31	5/16	11
4	.33	11/32	15
6	.4	13/32	25
8	.41	7/16	38
10	.44	7/16	50
12	.46	15/32	58
14	.53	17/32	80
16	.56	9/16	103
18	.63	5/8	125
20	.63	5/8	140
24	.72	23/32	185
30	.84	27/32	275
36	.95	15/16	375
48	1.04	1	550

WATER PIPE IN 12 FOOT LENGTHS.

Diameter in Inches.	50 LBS. PER SQUARE INCH. 116 FT. HEAD.			100 LBS. PER SQUARE INCH. 230 FT. HEAD.			130 LBS. PER SQUARE INCH. 300 FT. HEAD.		
	Thickness. Inches.	Approximate Inches.	Approximate Weight Per Foot.	Thickness. Inches.	Approximate Inches.	Approximate Weight Per Foot.	Thickness. Inches.	Approximate Inches.	Approximate Weight Per Foot.
3	.39	3/8	14.5	.407	13/32	15	.419	7/16	17
4	.495	15/32	18.5	.431	7/16	21	.448	15/32	22
6	.438	1/2	30	.484	1/2	33	.505	1/2	34
8	.473	15/32	42	.529	17/32	47	.562	9/16	50
10	.508	1/2	55	.578	19/32	63	.619	5/8	67
12	.543	17/32	71	.627	5/8	82	.677	11/16	88
14	.578	9/16	87	.675	11/16	102	.734	3/4	111
16	.617	5/8	108	.728	3/4	127	.794	13/16	137
18	.648	5/8	127	.773	25/32	152	.848	27/32	166
20	.685	11/16	150	.822	13/16	180	.905	29/32	200
24	.753	3/4	196	.920	15/16	240	1.02	1	265
30	.858	7/8	275	1.067	1 1/16	345	1.19	1 3/16	374
36	.963	31/32	370	1.213	1 7/32	470	1.36	1 3/8	527
48	1.173	1 3/16	607	1.597	1 5/8	777	1.71	1 3/4	880
60	1.411	1 7/16	910	2	2	1,328	2.25	2 1/4	1,500

SPECIAL WEIGHTS TO ORDER.

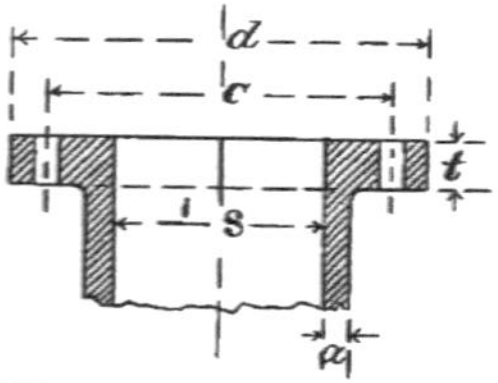

DIMENSIONS OF

CAST IRON FLANGED PIPE,

FOR WATER PRESSURE.

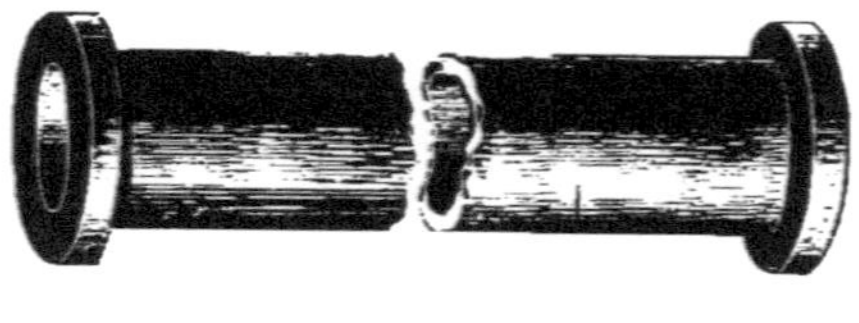

BEST, FOX & CO.

Inside Diam.	Fillet.	Size of Bolts.	No. of Bolts.	P-100 LBS.					P-150 LBS.					P-200 LBS.					P-250 LBS.					P-300 LBS.					Inside Diam.
				a	t	c	d	Wt.	a	t	c	d	Wt.	a	t	c	d	Wt.	a	t	c	d	Wt.	a	t	c	d	Wt.	
4	1/4	5/8	6	1/2	3/4	7	8 1/2	23.4	1/2	3/4	7	8 1/2	23.4	1/2	3/4	7	8 1/2	23.4	1/2	7/8	7	8 1/2	23.6	1/2	15/16	7	8 1/2	23.7	4
4 1/2	1/4	5/8	6	1/2	13/16	7 1/2	9	26.	1/2	13/16	7 1/2	9	26.	1/2	13/16	7 1/2	9	26.	1/2	7/8	7 1/2	9	26.1	1/2	15/16	7 1/2	9	26.2	4 1/2
5	1/4	5/8	6	1/2	13/16	8	10	28.8	1/2	13/16	8	10	28.8	1/2	13/16	8	10	28.8	1/2	15/16	8	10	29.1	1/2	1	8	10	29.3	5
6	1/4	3/4	6	1/2	13/16	9 1/4	11	34.	1/2	13/16	9 1/4	11	34.	1/2	15/16	9 1/4	11	34.3	1/2	1 1/16	9 1/4	11	34.6	1/2	1 3/16	9 1/4	11	34.9	6
7	1/4	3/4	6	9/16	15/16	10 3/8	13	45.1	9/16	15/16	10 3/8	13	45.1	9/16	1 1/16	10 3/8	13	45.6	9/16	1 3/16	10 3/8	13	46.	9/16	1 1/4	10 3/8	13	46.3	7
8	1/4	3/4	8	5/8	1	11 1/2	14	57.3	5/8	1	11 1/2	14	57.3	5/8	1 1/8	11 1/2	14	57.9	5/8	1 1/4	11 1/2	14	58.4	5/8	1 3/8	11 1/2	14	58.9	8
9	1/4	3/4	8	11/16	1	12 5/8	15	69.6	11/16	1	12 5/8	15	69.6	11/16	1 3/16	12 5/8	15	70.3	11/16	1 5/16	12 5/8	15	70.8	11/16	1 7/16	12 5/8	15	71.3	9
10	1/4	3/4	10	3/4	1	13 3/4	16	83.6	3/4	1 1/16	13 3/4	16	83.8	3/4	1 1/4	13 3/4	16	84.6	3/4	1 3/8	13 3/4	16	85.2	3/4	1 1/2	13 3/4	16	85.7	10
11	1/4	3/4	10	3/4	1	14 3/4	17	91.2	3/4	1 1/8	14 3/4	17	91.7	3/4	1 5/16	14 3/4	17	92.6	3/4	1 1/2	14 3/4	17	93.4	13/16	1 5/8	14 7/8	17	96.9	11
12	1/4	7/8	12	3/4	1	16	19	100.2	3/4	1 1/4	16	19	101.7	3/4	1 7/16	16	19	102.8	3/4	1 5/8	16	19	103.9	7/8	1 3/4	16 1/4	19	121.2	12
13	1/4	7/8	12	3/4	1 1/16	17	20	108.8	3/4	1 5/16	17	20	110.5	3/4	1 1/2	17	20	111.7	13/16	1 11/16	17 1/8	20	121.9	1	1 13/16	17 1/2	20	148.8	13
14	1/4	7/8	14	3/4	1 1/8	18	21	116.7	3/4	1 3/8	18	21	118.4	3/4	1 9/16	18	21	119.7	7/8	1 3/4	18 1/4	21	139.5	1 1/16	1 7/8	18 5/8	21	169.7	14
15	1/4	7/8	14	3/4	1 1/8	19	22	124.1	3/4	1 7/16	19	22	126.4	3/4	1 5/8	19	22	127.7	15/16	1 13/16	19 3/8	22	160.	1 1/8	1 15/16	19 3/4	22	191.3	15
16	1/4	7/8	16	3/4	1 3/16	20	23	133.	3/4	1 7/16	20	23	134.	13/16	1 11/16	20 1/8	23	147.	1	1 7/8	20 1/2	23	180.	1 3/16	2	20 7/8	23	214.	16
18	5/16	1	18	13/16	1 3/8	22 1/2	25	164.6	13/16	1 11/16	22 1/2	25	167.7	7/8	1 15/16	22 5/8	26	180.6	1 1/8	2 1/8	23 1/8	26	231.3	1 5/16	2 5/16	23 1/2	26	269.2	18
20	5/16	1	20	7/8	1 7/16	24 5/8	28	195.2	7/8	1 3/4	24 5/8	28	198.5	1	2	24 7/8	28	227.4	1 1/4	2 3/16	25 3/8	28	281.7	1 1/2	2 3/8	25 7/8	29	334.5	20
22	5/16	1	22	7/8	1 1/2	26 5/8	30	213.1	7/8	1 13/16	26 5/8	30	216.7	1 1/8	2 1/8	27 1/8	30	278.6	1 3/8	2 5/16	27 5/8	31	342.6	1 5/8	2 1/2	28 1/8	31	406.	22
24	3/8	1 1/8	24	15/16	1 11/16	29 1/8	32	250.3	15/16	2 1/16	29 1/8	32	254.9	1 3/16	2 5/16	29 5/8	33	325.4	1 1/2	2 9/16	30 1/4	33	406.4	1 13/16	2 13/16	30 7/8	34	468.3	24
26	3/8	1 1/8	26	1	1 3/4	31 1/4	34	288.1	1	2 1/8	31 1/4	34	292.9	1 5/16	2 7/16	31 7/8	35	391.1	1 5/8	2 11/16	32 1/2	36	482.2	1 15/16	2 7/8	33 1/8	36	572.3	26
28	3/8	1 1/8	28	1	1 13/16	33	36	310.1	1 1/16	2 3/16	33 3/8	37	337.5	1 3/8	2 1/2	34	37	433.	1 3/4	2 3/4	34 3/4	38	554.3	2 1/8	3	35 1/2	39	669.3	28
30	1/2	1 1/4	30	1	2	35 3/4	39	338.8	1 1/8	2 7/16	36	39	384.9	1 1/2	2 13/16	36 3/4	40	513.9	1 7/8	3 1/16	37 1/2	41	644.5	2 1/4	3 3/8	38 1/4	42	782.1	30

P-Pressure. *Figures Underlined ____ are greater than obtained by formula.* *Approximate Wt. per ft. in 12 ft. lengths, (Flanges included.)*

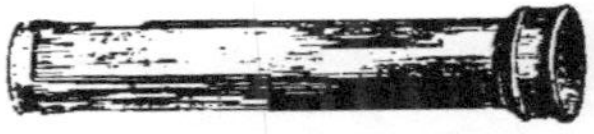

LIGHT CAST IRON SOIL PIPE.

SIZE.	Standard, Wt. Per Foot.	Extra Heavy, Wt. Per Foot.
2	3	5½
3	4½	9½
4	6½	13
5	8½	17
6	10	20
8	18	33½
10	25	45
12	30	54

Special Weights and Sizes to Order.

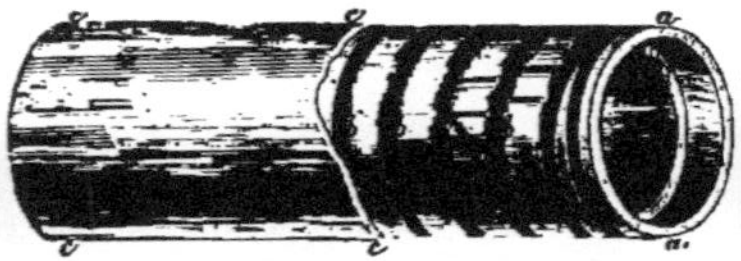

WOOD WATER PIPE STRENGTHENED.

Size Internal.	Size External.	Weight per Foot. Lbs.	Proof Strength, Per Square Inch.
1¼	3½		
1½	3½		
2	4½		
3	6		Grade 1 to stand 160 pounds.
4	7		" 2 " 80 "
5	9		" 3 " 40 "
6	10		
7	9	11	
8	10	13	
10	12	16	
12	14	18	
14	16	20	
16	18	23	

Descriptive Circular on Application.

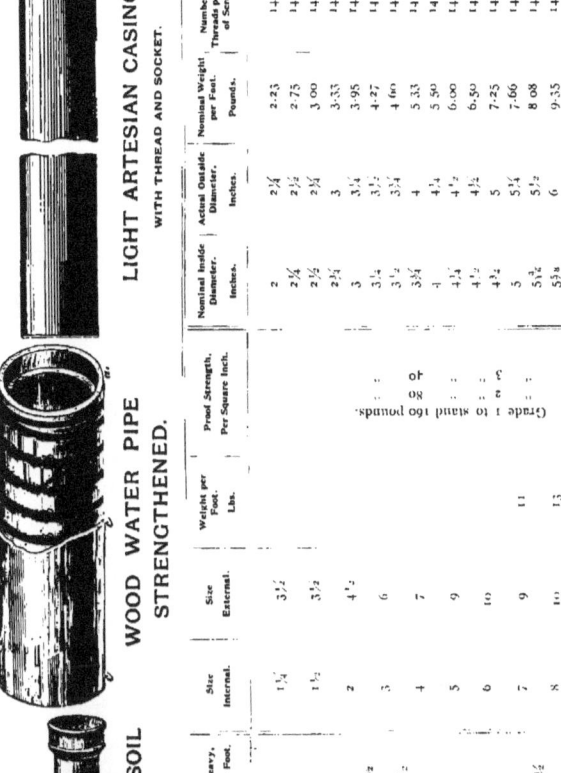

LIGHT ARTESIAN CASING,

WITH THREAD AND SOCKET.

Nominal Inside Diameter. Inches.	Actual Outside Diameter. Inches.	Nominal Weight per Foot. Pounds.	Number of Threads per Inch of Screw.
2	2¼	2·23	14
2¼	2½	2·75	14
2½	2¾	3·00	14
2¾	3	3·33	14
3	3¼	3·95	14
3¼	3½	4·27	14
3½	3¾	4·60	14
3¾	4	5·33	14
4	4¼	5·50	14
4¼	4½	6.00	14
4½	4¾	6.50	14
4¾	5	7·25	14
5	5¼	7·66	14
5 3/16	5½	8·08	14
5⅝	6	9·35	14
6¼	6⅝	10.00	14
6⅝	7	12·45	14
7¼	7⅝	13·50	14
7⅝	8	15·10	11½
8¼	8⅝	16.15	11½
8⅝	9	17·25	11½
9⅝	10	19·00	11½

Special Sizes to Order.

O. D. (Outside Diam.) LAP WELD

STANDARD SIZES AND DIMENSIONS.

PIPE OR BOILER TUBES.

DIMENSIONS NOT GIVEN MADE TO ORDER.

DIAMETER. External. Inches.	DIAMETER. Internal. Inches.	THICKNESS. Standard Inches.	THICKNESS. Nearest Birmingham WIRE GAUGE	CIRCUMFERENCE. External. Inches.	CIRCUMFERENCE. Internal. Inches.	TRANSVERSE AREAS. External. Sq. Inches.	TRANSVERSE AREAS. Internal. Sq. Inches.	LENGTH OF PIPE PER SQ. FT. OF SURFACE. Outside. FEET.	LENGTH OF PIPE PER SQ. FT. OF SURFACE. Inside. FEET.	Nominal Weight Per Foot. Pounds.	External Diameter.
1	0.85	.072	15	3.14	2.68	0.78	0.57	3.81	4.46	.70	1
1¼	1.10	.072	15	3.92	3.47	1.22	0.96	3.05	3.45	.90	1¼
1½	1.33	.083	14	4.71	4.19	1.76	1.39	2.54	2.86	1.24	1½
1¾	1.56	.095	13	5.49	4.90	2.40	1.91	2.18	2.44	1.66	1¾
2	1.80	.095	13	6.28	5.66	3.14	2.55	1.90	2.11	1.91	2
2¼	2.05	.095	13	7.06	6.48	3.97	3.31	1.69	1.85	2.16	2¼
2½	2.28	.109	12	7.85	7.17	4.90	4.09	1.52	1.67	2.75	2½
2¾	2.53	.109	12	8.63	7.95	5.94	5.03	1.39	1.50	3.04	2¾
3	2.78	.109	12	9.42	8.74	7.06	6.08	1.27	1.37	3.33	3
3¼	3.01	.120	11	10.21	9.46	8.29	7.12	1.17	1.26	3.96	3¼
3½	3.26	.120	11	10.99	10.24	9.62	8.35	1.09	1.17	4.28	3½
3¾	3.51	.120	11	11.78	11.03	11.04	9.68	1.01	1.08	4.60	3¾
4	3.74	.134	10	12.56	11.75	12.56	10.99	.95	1.02	5.47	4
4½	4.24	.134	10	14.13	13.32	15.90	14.12	.84	.90	6.17	4¼
5	4.72	.148	9	15.70	14.81	19.63	17.49	.76	.80	7.58	5
6	5.69	.165	8	18.84	17.90	28.27	25.50	.63	.67	10.16	6
7	6.65	.165	8	21.99	20.91	38.48	34.80	.54	.57	11.90	7
8	7.63	.165	8	25.13	23.98	50.26	45.79	.47	.50	13.65	8
9	8.61	.180	7	28.27	27.05	63.61	58.29	.42	.44	16.76	9
10	9.57	.203	6	31.41	30.07	78.54	71.97	.38	.39	21.00	10
11	10.56	.220	5	34.55	33.17	95.03	87.47	.34	.36	25.00	11
12	11.54	.229	4½	37.69	36.26	113.09	103.74	.31	.33	28.50	12
13	12.52	.238	4	40.84	39.34	132.73	123.18	.29	.30	32.06	13
14	13.50	.248	3½	43.98	42.41	153.93	143.18	.27	.28	36.00	14
15	14.48	.259	3	47.12	45.49	176.71	164.71	.25	.26	40.60	15
16	15.45	.270	2½	50.26	48.56	201.06	187.66	.23	.24	45.20	16
17	16.43	.284	2	53.40	51.66	226.98	212.22	.22	.23	49.90	17
18	17.41	.292	1½	56.54	54.71	254.46	238.22	.21	.21	54.81	18
19	18.40	.300	1	59.69	57.80	283.52	265.90	.20	.20	59.47	19
20	19.36	.320	0½	62.83	60.82	314.15	294.37	.19	.19	66.76	20
21	20.32	.340	0	65.97	63.83	346.36	324.31	.18	.18	73.40	21

TUBES TO 30 IN. DIAMETER FURNISHED.

TUBES HEAVIER OR LIGHTER THAN ABOVE MADE TO ORDER.

(X) EXTRA STRONG—STEEL OR WROUGHT-IRON WELDED PIPE.
STANDARD SIZES AND DIMENSIONS. (Dimensions not given Made to Order.)

| DIAMETER | | | THICKNESS | CIRCUMFERENCE | | TRANSVERSE AREAS. | | LENGTH OF PIPE PER FOOT OF | | NOMINAL WT PER FOOT OF LENGTH. | NOMINAL INSIDE DIAM. |
Nominal Inside. Inches.	Actual Inside. Inches.	Actual Outside. Inches	Inches.	Internal. Inches.	External. Inches.	External. Sq. Inches.	Internal. Sq. Inches.	Outside Surface. Feet.	Inside Surface. Feet.		
⅛	.30	.40	.10	.64	1.27	.12	.03	9.43	18.03	.29	⅛
¼	.29	.54	.12	.92	1.69	.22	.06	7.07	12.98	.54	¼
⅜	.42	.67	.12	1.32	2.12	.35	.13	5.65	9.07	.74	⅜
½	.54	.84	.14	1.70	2.63	.55	.23	4.54	7.04	1.09	½
¾	.73	1.05	.15	2.31	3.29	.86	.45	3.63	5.10	1.53	¾
1	.95	1.31	.18	2.98	4.13	1.35	.71	2.90	4.01	2.17	1
1¼	1.27	1.66	.19	3.99	5.21	2.16	1.27	2.30	3.00	3.00	1¼
1½	1.49	1.9	.20	4.69	5.96	2.83	1.75	2.01	2.55	3.63	1½
2	1.93	2.37	.22	6.07	7.46	4.43	2.95	1.66	1.97	5.02	2
2½	2.31	2.87	.28	7.27	9.03	6.49	4.20	1.32	1.64	7.67	2½
3	2.89	3.50	.30	9.08	10.99	9.62	6.56	—	1.32	10.25	3
3½	3.35	4.00	.32	10.54	12.56	12.56	8.85	.95	1.13	12.47	3½
4	3.81	4.50	.34	11.99	14.13	15.90	11.44	.84	1.00	14.97	4
4½	4.25	5.00	.35	13.35	15.71	19.63	14.18	.76	.90	17.60	4½
5	4.81	5.56	.37	15.12	17.47	24.30	18.19	.68	.79	20.54	5
6	5.75	6.62	.43	18.06	20.81	34.47	25.93	.57	.66	28.58	6
7	6.62	7.62	.50	20.81	23.95	45.66	34.47	.50	.58	37.60	7
8	7.50	8.62	.56	23.56	27.10	58.42	44.18	.44	.51	47.85	8

(XX) DOUBLE EXTRA STRONG STEEL OR WROUGHT-IRON WELDED PIPE.

| DIAMETER | | | THICKNESS | CIRCUMFERENCE | | TRANSVERSE AREAS. | | LENGTH OF PIPE PER FOOT OF | | NOMINAL WT PER FOOT OF LENGTH. | NOMINAL INSIDE DIAM. |
Nominal Inside. Inches.	Actual Inside. Inches.	Actual Outside. Inches	Inches.	Internal. Inches.	External. Inches.	External. Sq. Inches.	Internal. Sq. Inches.	Outside Surface. Feet.	Inside Surface. Feet.		
⅜	.23	SAME AS EXTRA HEAVY	.12	.73	SAME AS EXTRA HEAVY	SAME AS EXTRA HEAVY	.04	SAME AS EXTRA HEAVY	15.69	.96	⅜
½	.34		.29	.76			.04		15.66	1.5	½
¾	.42		.31	1.32			.13		9.04	2.3	¾
1	.58		.36	1.84			.27		6.51	3.4	1
1¼	.88		.38	2.78			.61		4.51	5.	1¼
1½	1.08		.40	3.41			.93		3.51	6.45	1½
2	1.49		.44	4.68			1.74		2.56	9.48	2
2½	1.75		.56	5.51			2.41		2.17	13.3	2½
3	2.28		.60	7.17			4.09		1.67	17.7	3
3½	2.71		.64	8.53			5.79		1.4	22	3½
4	3.13		.68	9.85			7.72		1.05	24.7	4
4½	3.56		.72	11.2			9.96		.94	32.45	4½
5	4.06		.75	12.76			12.96		.78	37.1	5
6	5.06		.78	15.89			20.1		.62	50.1	6
7	5.98		.82	18.83			28.16		.55	60.34	7
8	6.88		.87	21.61			37.17			71.52	8

SPECIAL HYDRAULIC PIPE TO ORDER.

LEAD PIPE.

APPROXIMATE WEIGHT PER FOOT, LBS. AND OZ.

Size	Aqueduct	Extra Light	Light	Medium	Strong	Extra Strong	Double Ex. Strong
1/4					.8	.12	
3/8	.8		.6	1.	1.4	1.8	3.8
1/2	.10	.12	.12	1.4	1.12	2.8	4.
5/8	.12	1.4	1.	2.	2.8	3.	5.8
3/4	1.	1.8	1.12	2.4	3.	3.8	
1	1.8	2.	2.	3.4	4.	4.12	5.8
1 1/4	2.	2.8	3.	3.12	4.12	6.	6.12
1 1/2	3.	3.8	4.	5.	6.	7.8	9.
2		4.	5.	7.	8.	9.	10.8

LARGER SIZES TO ORDER.

SHEET LEAD, BRASS AND COPPER.

APPROXIMATE WEIGHT PER SQUARE FOOT.

Thickness	LEAD	BRASS	COPPER
3/64	3	2.	2.1
1/16	4	2.8	3.
5/64	5	3.3	3.7
3/32	6	3.9	4.2
1/8	8	5.5	5.8
3/16	12	7.8	8.3
1/4	16	11.	12.
3/8	24	16.	17.
1/2	32	20.	21.

SPECIAL THICKNESS TO ORDER.

BRASS AND COPPER PIPE. (Seamless Drawn.)

IRON PIPE SIZES.

Iron Pipe Size	Inside Diameter	Outside Diameter	Approximate Weight Per Foot BRASS	COPPER
1/8	.27	13/32	.30	.31
1/4	.36	9/16	.43	.45
3/8	.49	11/16	.38	.61
1/2	.62	13/16	.8	.84
3/4	.82	1 1/16	1.17	1.23
1	1.04	1 5/16	1.67	1.75
1 1/4	1.38	1 5/8	2.42	2.54
1 1/2	1.61	1 7/8	2.92	3.
2	2.06	2 3/8	4.17	4.38
2 1/2	2.46	2 7/8	5.	5.25
3	3.06	3 1/2	8.	8.4
3 1/2	3.5	4	10.	10.5
4	4.	4 1/2	12.	12.6
5	5.	5 9/16	15.9	17.3
6	6.	6 5/8	20.7	22.4
7	7.	7 5/8	26.3	27.8
8	8.	8 5/8	29.9	33.7

SPECIAL LIGHT BRASS AND COPPER PIPE FURNISHED FROM STOCK AS REQUIRED.

EXTRA HEAVY TO ORDER.

We will not attempt to give a list of the Mills, Steel Works, Factories, Electric Light Plants, Etc., fitted complete for STEAM, WATER, GAS, OIL and HYDRAULIC purposes, in all parts of the United States: but only refer to a few

HIGH-PRESSURE POWER PLANTS

for Traction Roads fitted by us.

ALLEGHENY TRACTION CO..	Allegheny. Pa.
CENTRAL TRACTION CO.,	. Pittsburg, Pa.
DUQUESNE TRACTION CO.,	" "
ELECTRIC TRACTION CO.,	Philadelphia, Pa.
Two Power Houses.	
FAIRHAVEN & WESTVILLE R. R. CO., .	New Haven, Conn.
HESTONVILLE, MANTUA & FAIRMOUNT R. R. CO.,	Philadelphia. Pa.
NASSAU ELECTRIC R. R. CO.,	Brooklyn, N. Y.
PHILADELPHIA TRACTION CO..	Philadelphia, Pa.
Three Power Houses.	
PITTSBURGH. ALLEGHENY & MANCHESTER TRACTION CO.,	Allegheny, Pa.
PLEASANT VALLEY PASS. RAILWAY.	" "
WORCESTER TRACTION CO.,	Worcester. Mass.
BROOKLYN CITY ELECTRIC RAILWAY, . . Brooklyn, N. Y.	

Main Steam Lines from 8 inch to 20 inch bent by us for this plant.
"   " Line STEEL FITTINGS machined by us for this plant.

PLANS, SPECIFICATIONS and ESTIMATES submitted for

High and Low Pressure Steam, Exhaust and Condenser Piping

For complete or any part of Power Plants.

We also cut, bend and fit pipe of all sizes to drawings and guarantee correctness of our work.

OVER

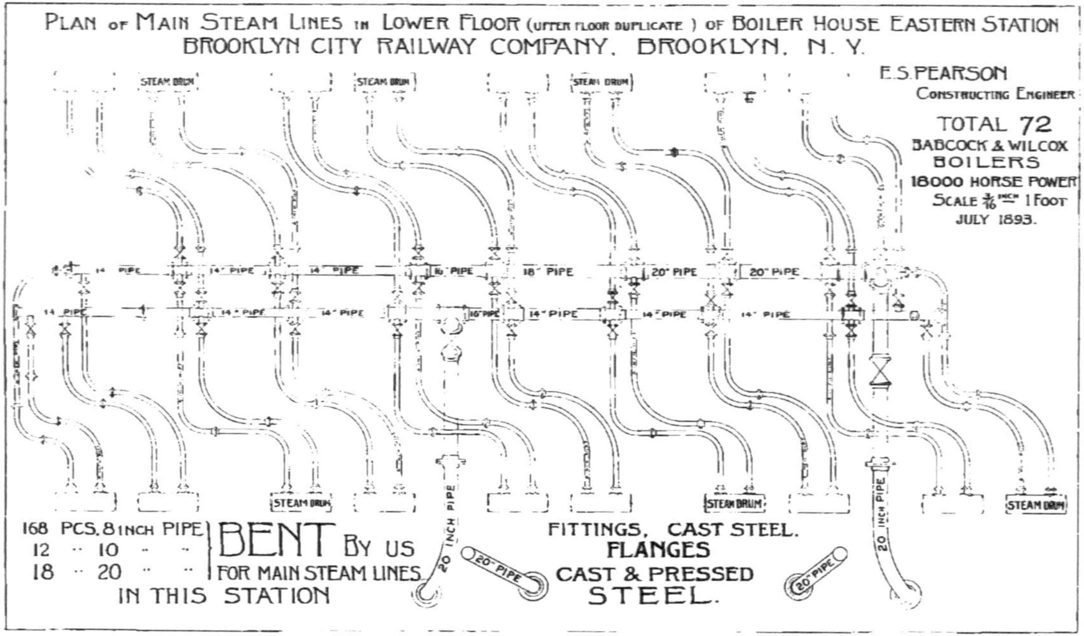

BEST, FOX & CO.

PLAN of MAIN STEAM LINES in LOWER FLOOR (UPPER FLOOR DUPLICATE) of BOILER HOUSE EASTERN STATION

BROOKLYN CITY RAILWAY COMPANY. BROOKLYN, N. Y.

F. S. PEARSON
Constructing Engineer

TOTAL 72
BABCOCK & WILCOX
BOILERS
18000 HORSE POWER
SCALE ⅜ IN. = 1 FOOT
JULY 1893.

STEAM DRUM

20 INCH PIPE

20" PIPE
14" PIPE

STEAM DRUM

20" PIPE
14" PIPE

STEAM DRUM

18" PIPE
14" PIPE

STEAM DRUM

16" PIPE
14" PIPE

20 INCH PIPE

STEAM DRUM

14" PIPE

STEAM DRUM

14" PIPE

FITTINGS, CAST STEEL.
FLANGES
CAST & PRESSED
STEEL.

BENT BY US
FOR MAIN STEAM LINES
IN THIS STATION

168 PCS. 8 INCH PIPE
12 " 10 " "
18 " 20 " "

LARGEST POWER HOUSE IN THE WORLD.

POWER HOUSE
OF THE
BROOKLYN CITY ELECTRIC RAILWAY CO.,

BROOKLYN, N. Y.

On the opposite page a plan of the main steam lines (on one floor) of the largest power house in the world is shown.

By means of the long 8-inch S Bends running from drums to duplicate mains ample provision is made to take up all the expansion and contraction running with main lines and at right angles to same. The 20 inch mains drop to basement by means of bends of peculiar shape, then run under engine room floor and up to respective cylinders with 10 inch bends. By referring to cut at the top of this page the 30° bend in each 8 inch pipe where it connects into main trunk is shown, insuring condensation returning to boilers by gravity.

All fittings and flanges are heavy cast steel, precluding any possibility of breakage ever taking place.

A MODEL BLAST FURNACE PLANT.

MONONGAHELA FURNACES, McKEESPORT, PA.

(DEPARTMENT OF NATIONAL TUBE WORKS.)

Designed by and erected under the supervision of FRANK C. ROBERTS, C. E., Philadelphia, Pa.

ERECTED 1889, 90.

JOHN B. MILES, C. E., Resident Engineer.

On the opposite page a view is given of the

Monongahela Furnaces at McKeesport, Pa.,

Erected in 1889-90 for the National Tube Works Co. The photo was taken from the west side of the Monongahela River.

These furnaces were designed by, and erected under the supervision of, Frank C. Roberts, C. E., of Philadelphia, Pa.

No. 1 was put in blast Dec. 1st, 1890; No. 2 June 1st, 1891.

Dimensions of each furnace: 80 ft. high, 20 ft. diameter of Bosh.

Stove Equipment : 7 Cowper-Kennedy, each 79½ ft. high, 21 ft. diameter.

Blast is furnished by five Reynolds Improved Corliss Engines, made by the E. P. Allis Co., Milwaukee, Wis.: 42 inch Steam Cylinder, 84 inch Air Cylinder, 60 inch stroke.

Boiler equipment consists of 32 Boilers, 54 inch diameter, 30 feet long, two 18 inch flues.

Two Duplex Barr Pumps outside packed plungers, placed in dry well, take water from the river through 16 inch pipe, discharging through 12 inch pipe into reservoir.

Three Duplex Barr Pumps outside packed plungers, in basement of engine house, take water from reservoir through 18 inch pipe, discharging through two 12 inch pipes into two tanks 20 x 18 feet, located between engine and boiler house: also by-passed into two 12 inch lines running to furnaces and stoves.

Two Duplex Barr Pumps outside packed plungers, in basement of engine house, take water from reservoir through the above 18 inch pipe, discharging through two 5 inch lines to heaters and boilers, and by-passed to feed direct.

Six Berryman Heaters, one for each blowing engine and one for pumps are installed in the engine room.

See pages 120 and 121 for Bosh, Steam and Water Piping.

Annual Capacity of both furnaces 180,000 Net Tons.

OVER

BEST, FOX & CO.

SHOWING BOSH FITTING, STYLE K.

MONONGAHELA FURNACE BOSH,

Designed and erected under the supervision of FRANK C. ROBERTS, C. E., PHILADELPHIA, PA.

JOHN B. MILES, C. E.
Resident Engineer.

On the opposite page a view is given of one of the

Monongahela Furnace Boshes

just before going into blast.

Thickness of bosh walls is 31½ inches: protected with five rows of Climax Bronze Bosh Plates (Kennedy's Patent), seven Tuyere Coolers, one Bronze Notch Cooler with Intermediate Cooler and Cinder Notch, and seven 7-inch Tuyeres are used.

Dam Plate made in two parts is used, and a 1½-in. spray pipe is placed on top of rivetted hearth jacket.

Provision is also made to spray furnace lining above mantel.

Main circular supply pipe is 9 inches in diameter. Waste trough 10 x 12 inches.

The I. and K. system of Bosh fitting is used. Six 4-inch Manifolds are connected to circular supply pipe, and 1¼-inch connections taken from same to respective water-cooled devices.

1¼-inch No. 10 Tuyere cocks and brass Unions are used throughout. This style of bosh fitting gives easy access to every stop cock, and makes a neat and symmetrical system of bosh piping. (See cut.)

Steam provided by the thirty-two boilers is conveyed from each battery of two boilers, through 8-inch copper bends into two main lines, beginning with 10 inches and increasing to 14 inches; both connecting into a common 13-inch header in engine room, with 8-inch copper bend to each engine and 6-inch branch line to pumps in basement and dry well.

12-inch exhaust from each engine is brought to its respective heater: and exhaust from three circulating and two boiler feed pumps is connected together and taken into one heater. Exhaust is taken from the six heaters into a trunk line increasing from 12 to 30 inches, thence into atmosphere.

Steam, exhaust and water connections are by-passed, providing for all possible emergencies. Washouts are not only placed on the tanks and reservoir, but all large mains are provided with Washout Valves at lowest points.

For all large steam, exhaust and water lines on the entire plant O. D. (outside diameter) pipe, from 8 to 18 inches, inclusive, is used, with flanges shrunk and piened on.

From 80 to 100 lbs. steam is carried.

The COMPLETE STEAM AND WATER FITTING

has been done by us at the following FURNACE PLANTS :

ASHLAND IRON & STEEL CO.,	Ashland, Wis.
BUFFALO FURNACE CO.,	Buffalo, N. Y.
DECATUR FURNACE CO.,	Decatur, Ala.
De BARDELEBEN COAL AND IRON CO.,	Bessemer, Ala. 2 Furnaces.
DULUTH BLAST FURNACE CO ,	Duluth, Minn.
FORT PAYNE FURNACE CO.,	Fort Payne, Ala.
LADY ENSLEY FURNACE CO.,	Sheffield, Ala.
MONONGAHELA FURNACE CO.,	McKeesport, Pa 2 Furnaces.
NASHVILLE IRON, STEEL, AND CHARCOAL CO , .	Nashville, Tenn 2 Furnaces
OREGON IRON AND STEEL CO ,	Oswego, Oregon.
POWELLS, ROBT. HARE SONS & CO.,	Saxton, Pa.
PULASKI DEVELOPMENT CO.,	Pulaski, Va.
ROSENA FURNACE CO.,	New Castle, Pa.
SALEM FURNACE CO.,	Salem, Va.
SHEFFIELD FURNACE CO.,	Sheffield, Ala.
SHEFFIELD & BIRMINGHAM COAL, IRON & R. W. CO.,	3 Furnaces.
SLOSS IRON AND STEEL CO., .	Birmingham, Ala. 2 Furnaces.
VALENTINE ORE LAND ASSOCIATION,	Bellefont, Pa.
VANDERBILT IRON AND STEEL CO.,	Birmingham, Ala.
WATTS IRON AND STEEL SYNDICATE,	Middlesboro, Ky. 2 Furnaces.
WOODSTOCK IRON CO.,	Anniston, Ala. 2 Furnaces.

PLANS, SPECIFICATIONS and ESTIMATES submitted for STEAM EXHAUST and WATER

PIPING COMPLETE for FURNACE PLANTS.

We have erected complete the water piping for the following

BLAST FURNACE BOSHES:

ÆTNA IRON CO., . . .	Aetna, Tenn.	
ASHLAND IRON AND STEEL CO.,	Ashland, Wis.	
BELLAIRE NAIL WORKS,	Bellaire, O.	(Copper Pipe.)
BRIER HILL IRON AND STEEL CO.,	Brier Hill, O.	
BUFFALO FURNACE CO.,	Buffalo, N. Y.	
CARRIE FURNACE CO.,	Rankin, Pa.	2 Boshes.
CHERRY VALLEY IRON CO., .	Leetonia, O.	
CHICAGO FURNACE CO., .	South Chicago, Ill.	
CLIFTON IRON CO.,	Ironaton, Ala.	
CORNWALL IRON CO.,	Cornwall, Pa.	2 Boshes. (Galvanized Pipe.)
DECATUR FURNACE CO.,	Decatur, Ala.	
DeBARDEBEN COAL AND IRON CO., .	Bessemer, Ala.	2 Boshes.
DULUTH BLAST FURNACE CO.,	Duluth, Minn.	
FORT PAYNE FURNACE CO.,	Fort Payne, Ala.	
GADSDEN-ALABAMA FURNACE CO.,	Gadsden, Ala.	
HAINSWORTH STEEL CO.,	Allegheny, Pa.	
JEFFERSON IRON WORKS,	Steubenville, O.	
JUNCTION IRON CO.,	Mingo Junction, O.	
JUNIATA MINING AND MANUFACTURING CO.,	Newport, Pa.	
KING, GILBERT & WARNER CO.,	Columbus, O.	
KING, GILBERT & WARNER CO.,	Moxahala, O.	
LADY ENSLEY FURNACE CO.,	Sheffield, Ala.	
MINERVA FURNACE CO.,	Milwaukee, Wis.	
MONONGAHELA FURNACE CO.,	McKeesport, Pa.	2 Boshes.
NASHVILLE IRON, STEEL AND CHARCOAL CO.,	Nashville, Tenn.	2 Boshes.
NORTH CORNWALL FURNACE,	North Cornwall, Pa.	(Galvanized Pipe.)
OREGON IRON AND STEEL CO.,	Oswego, Ore.	
POUGHKEEPSIE IRON CO., .	Poughkeepsie, N. Y.	(Copper Pipe.)
POWELLS, ROBT. HARE, SONS & CO.,	Saxton, Pa.	
PULASKI DEVELOPMENT CO.,	Pulaski, Va.	

OVER.

BEST, FOX & CO.

Furnace Bosh Fitting Continued.

RIVERSIDE IRON WORKS.	Wheeling, W. Va.	
ROANOKE IRON CO.,	Roanoke, Va.	
ROBESONIA IRON CO.,	Robesonia, Pa.	
ROME IRON CO.,	Rome, Ga.	
ROSENA FURNACE CO.,	New Castle, Pa.	
SALEM FURNACE CO.,	Salem, Va.	
SALEM IRON CO.,	Leetonia, O.	2 Boshes.
SHEFFIELD FURNACE CO.,	Sheffield, Ala.	
SHEFFIELD AND BIRMINGHAM COAL, IRON & R. W. CO.,	Sheffield, Ala.	3 Boshes.
SHENANGO VALLEY STEEL CO.,	New Castle, Pa.	(Copper Pipe.)
SLOSS IRON AND STEEL CO.,	Birmingham, Ala.	2 Boshes.
UNION ROLLING MILL CO.,	Cleveland, O.	
VALENTINE ORE LAND ASSOCIATION,	Bellefont, Pa.	
VANDERBILT IRON AND STEEL CO.,	Birmingham, Ala.	
VIRGINIA IRON AND R. W. CO.,	Goshen, Va.	
WATTS IRON AND STEEL SYNDICATE,	Middlesboro, Ky.	2 Boshes.
WOODSTOCK IRON CO.,	Anniston, Ala.	2 Boshes.
YORK IRON CO.,	Black River Falls, Wis.	

PLANS, SPECIFICATIONS and ESTIMATES submitted for complete Bosh Fitting of Iron, Galvanized, Brass or Copper Pipe, or we will furnish all pipe cut and bent to exact requirements according to drawings or sketches furnished or to our measurements, with full instructions for erection when customers wish to do their own fitting.

www.ingramcontent.com/pod-product-compliance
Lightning Source LLC
Chambersburg PA
CBHW021045030726
47496CB00006B/1700